"Your price," he repeated.

"Twenty pounds." Lucy struggled to keep the tremor out of her voice.

"Twenty pounds!" Robert's dark eyebrows arched in surprise, putting her very much in mind of the image of the devil.

"Twenty pounds," Lucy forced herself to repeat more firmly.

"Very well, madame." He peeled off several notes and carelessly dropped them on the bedside table. Lucy watched them land with an impotent feeling of frustration. Those few bills meant her brother's life and her freedom, and yet they seemed of little concern to him. The roll of bills didn't even look any smaller.

"Ah, no, my pretty." He followed her glance, but misinterpreted its cause. "Enough is enough. However—" his voice deepened perceptibly "—if you please me sufficiently, I might be inclined to give you a little more...."

Dear Reader,

April brings us another great batch of titles!

Readers of contemporary romance will surely recognize Judith McWilliams. In her first historical, *Suspicion*, she pens a tale of intrigue and danger in which young Lucy Langford must team up with Colonel Robert Standen in order to find a would-be killer.

Popular historical author Elizabeth Lane brings us *MacKenna's Promise*. Meg MacKenna travels to East Africa to get a divorce from her estranged husband, Cameron. But when tragedy strikes, they must band together to save their family and their love.

When ruthless businessman Oliver Keane inherits part of a Barbados plantation, he learns how to love from Alexa Fairfield—a woman he's been raised to despise. *Island Star* is by Kit Gardner, one of the 1992 March Madness authors.

In *The River Sprite* by Kate Kingsley, Serena Caswell is determined to take over as pilot of her father's steamboat. But handsome riverboat gambler—and half owner of the boat—Nathan Trent has other plans.

We hope you enjoy these titles. Next month look for four brand-new releases from your favorite Harlequin Historical authors!

Sincerely,

Tracy Farrell
Senior Editor

Please address questions and book requests to:
Reader Service
U.S.: P.O. Box 1325, Buffalo, NY 14269
Canadian: P.O. Box 1050, Niagara Falls, Ont. L2E 7G7

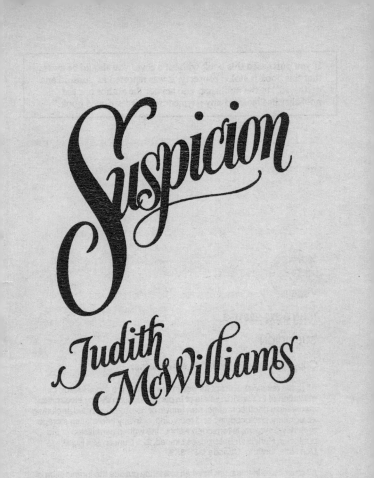

Suspicion

Judith McWilliams

Harlequin Books

TORONTO • NEW YORK • LONDON
AMSTERDAM • PARIS • SYDNEY • HAMBURG
STOCKHOLM • ATHENS • TOKYO • MILAN
MADRID • WARSAW • BUDAPEST • AUCKLAND

ISBN 0-373-28815-8

SUSPICION

JUDITH McWILLIAMS

For years, Judith McWilliams has delighted readers with her entertaining contemporary romances written for the Harlequin Temptation and the Silhouette Romance lines. Now, Judith has written her first historical, *Suspicion*, for the Harlequin Historicals line. The author makes her home in Texas where she is hard at work on her second historical, to be released by Harlequin in 1995.

To my father and mother,
Charles and Dolores Hines,
with much love always

Prologue

Southern France, 1803

"Lucy? Are you there?" The faint words slipped between Ann Danvers's bloodless lips, the loving warmth immediately sucked out of them by the barren room's icy chill.

"I'm here, Mama." Lucy grasped her mother's trembling hand in her own strong, young grip.

"My darling angel..." Ann's voice faltered, and Lucy swallowed the rising sense of fear that coated her mouth with a metallic taste. She focused on her mother's sunken blue eyes, desperately trying to believe that their glazed stare was simply exhaustion caused by her new brother's difficult birth, but in her heart she knew it was more than that. Much more.

"I love you, Mama." Lucy forced the words out past a throat clogged with tears.

"Your baby brother..." Her mother's weary voice faded.

"Is in prime twig. He looks exactly like Papa," Lucy lied stoutly. In truth, she thought her brother looked more like one of the skinned rabbits the village priest had occasionally brought to them during the past, seemingly interminable winter.

"So many years..."

Lucy leaned closer to hear her mother's muffled words. "For so many years your father and I prayed for an heir, and then to have him finally come, here in a farmhouse in the wilds of France..."

"But with a good doctor," Lucy said with a quick, sideways glance at the black-clad old man who was checking the warmth of the water-filled wine bottles that lined her tiny brother's rough cradle.

"Yes, a good doctor." Her mother's head moved almost imperceptibly in agreement. "And an even better man, to risk helping an Englishwoman with Napoleon's secret police everywhere.... Listen to me." Her mother's voice firmed for a second, sounding almost normal, and her emaciated fingers closed around Lucy's wrist with a strength born of desperation. "There isn't much time left."

"Mama, no—" Lucy's voice broke with a strangled sob.

"Don't grieve for me, my darling child. With your father gone, I don't..." She paused, as if gathering her inner resources, and then continued, "Lucy, you must take care of your brother."

"I will. I swear it. Sacred word of a Danvers," Lucy promised. "Marthe will help me."

"Of course I will," Marthe promptly agreed in her heavy French accent. "Why, before I married my Paul—God rest his soul—was I not first nursery maid to the children of the Duc de Daunton? And did he not have seven healthy babes, thanks to my care?"

"Thank you, Marthe." Ann's voice was a faint thread of sound that threatened to break at any moment.

She seemed to make an effort to collect her thoughts and then said, "Lucy, the box." Ann's gaze flickered toward the battered metal box her husband had used to safeguard his precious maps of the Roman ruins he'd come to France to excavate.

"Yes, Mama, what about it?"

"Inside is your father's signet ring, a letter from him claiming the boy as his and a last letter to your grandfather Langford. Both the doctor and the priest have agreed to write letters verifying that the baby is your father's and my son. Put their letters in the box and guard it well." She paused and took several shallow breaths. "You must take the box back to England with you to prove that the boy is your grandfather's heir.... Lucy, this war can't last much longer. Once Napoleon has been defeated, sell the bits and pieces of my jewelry to pay for your passage home."

"I understand, Mama," Lucy said. "We'll take him back just as soon as—"

"No, my precious one. I will not be returning to England with you. I'm going to stay here with your papa."

"Mama..." Lucy closed her eyes against the wave of fear and panic that threatened to engulf her.

"Don't be afraid, Lucy," her mother whispered. "You can do it. Are you not the practical one in our family?"

"The image of Grandpapa Langford..." Lucy repeated the old family joke in a desperate bid to ease her mother's mind.

"Lucy, call the boy Vernon after your father, and Adolphus James after his two grandfathers. And always remember how much your papa and I loved you. Always." The final word came out on a sigh as the blue in Ann's eyes dimmed to slate and their gaze became vacant and unfocused.

Lucy caught her lip between her teeth and bit hard, drawing blood, in a vain attempt to hold back the tears that began to pour down her face. This couldn't be happening, her mind screamed in denial. It simply couldn't!

"*La pauvre petite.* May God have mercy on her soul." Marthe sketched the sign of the cross on her bony chest.

"Oh, Marthe," Lucy gasped. "It isn't fair!"

"*Ah, non.*" Marthe enveloped Lucy in a comforting hug. "The good Lord does not promise fairness. Only the strength to endure. And your mama, she loved your papa so. After he was murdered by those monsters Napoleon calls soldiers, the light went out of her soul. Now she is with him and happy again. Do not begrudge her her happiness."

"Oh, Marthe." Lucy tried to gulp back her tears. "If only I could be sure..."

"There can be no doubt." Marthe's voice held absolute conviction. "I have prayed to the Virgin, and was she not a mother, too? At this moment your mama is being embraced by your papa."

Lucy awkwardly wiped the tears from her cheek with the back of her hand. "And he's probably telling her about a great archeological site that he found in heaven." Lucy tried to smile, but her lips were trembling so badly she couldn't.

"It will be all right, *ma petite,*" Marthe soothed her.

"Marthe?" Lucy grasped the old woman's hand. "I promised Mama that I would take him—Vernon," she corrected, "back to England."

"And so you shall. Are you not a great girl of thirteen years? Just as soon as *Napoleon*—" Marthe spat the word out as if it had a bad taste "—is gone, then you shall take the boy back to where he belongs. Go look upon your brother now while the good doctor and I do what is necessary for your mama."

"Yes." Lucy forced out the word past jaws she held locked together to hold back more tears. Tears wouldn't help her mother now, and her brother needed her.

Slowly, she kissed her mother's cheek one last time and then resolutely turned away, trying to draw comfort from the old woman's beliefs. Marthe was right; her mother was safe now. Nothing could ever hurt her again.

Lucy walked across the room's uneven stone floor to the cavernous fireplace, where her brother's cradle had been placed, taking advantage of what little heat was being given off by the fire smoldering there. She leaned over and studied his red, wrinkled features. He was so small. Fear shook her. Was he too small to survive? Could she and Marthe really keep him alive until Napoleon was defeated?

Lucy felt a sudden chill as she inexplicably caught the tantalizing scent of lilacs. It was a scent she always associated with her mother, but she hadn't smelled it in almost a year. The perfume her mother had brought to France had been left behind at an inn, along with most of their luggage, when hostilities had so unexpectedly broken out again.

Lucy's heart seemed to stop and then lurched into a slow, heavy beat as she felt the whispered softness of invisible lips brush across her cheek. Almost immediately, the sensation was followed by the firmer pressure of a kiss on her forehead.

Remember.

The soundless word echoed through the recesses of her mind, bringing an immense comfort in its wake.

"I will," she whispered, with a surreptitious glance at Marthe and the doctor, who were both busy by the bed. "I promise I'll get Vernon back to England, where he can take his rightful place as heir to the Earl of Langford."

Chapter One

Southern France, 1814

"Lucy! Lucy!" Marthe hobbled into the cottage, bringing an icy blast of air with her.

Lucy instinctively moved to block the draft from her sleeping brother's slight body.

"Le pauvre petit." Marthe peered down at Vernon's form huddled beneath the mound of rough blankets. His raspy breathing echoed loudly in the room's funereal stillness. "He sounds a little better," she offered with more hope than truth. "I have the dose from the apothecary." She handed Lucy the bottle she'd been clutching to her bony chest. "But the medicine, it matters not. *Le petit,* he is saved." Marthe offered the words like a priceless gift.

"Saved?" Lucy repeated in confusion. She was so tired—tired to the point where she found it hard to think clearly.

"Saved." Marthe nodded vigorously. "The English soldiers, they have arrived. They are in the village. With my own eyes I saw them. The innkeeper's wife says that the commander will arrive at first light tomorrow. She said he sent his aide to tell them that he would be setting up his command at the inn, and he's going to pay. Pay with gold, Maria says.'' Marthe shook her head in wonder. "These countrymen of yours, how they wage war. Imagine, paying the enemy for using his inn!''

"Tomorrow he comes?" Lucy ignored the thrifty woman's outrage. "You're sure?" After twelve years of waiting for Napoleon's troops to be defeated, she could hardly believe that it had finally happened.

"Tomorrow the commander comes," Marthe repeated. "Major Hart, Maria says his name is.'' She snorted derisively. "As if any soldier ever had a heart.''

"You said some of the English are already here?"

Marthe nodded. "Maria said that that rabble General Soult had stationed in our village were captured yesterday without a shot being fired.''

"Tomorrow the commander comes.'' Lucy repeated the words like a talisman, wanting desperately to believe they were true, but not quite able to do so. She'd waited so long. So very long. "When this Major Hart comes, I must talk to him. Tell him who we are so that he can..." She shook her head, trying to clear her clouded mind.

"Yes, you will see him," Marthe agreed. "But for now, you must sleep.''

"But I can't!" Lucy shot a panicked glance down at Vernon. Sometimes she felt that if she took her eyes off him for even a few hours, he'd slip away as her mother had all those years ago.

"I will sit with Vernon tonight," Marthe said soothingly. "You must rest so that you'll have your wits about you tomorrow. You'll need them to deal with the English," she added darkly.

Lucy smiled weakly. "You forget—I am English."

"Bah! What a thing to say about yourself. You have the soul of a Frenchwoman."

"Thank you." Lucy acknowledged what she recognized as a compliment of the highest order. "Often I feel more French than English. As if I dreamed the first thirteen years of my life." She glanced around the tiny cottage's single room. "Sometimes it seems as if this farm is the only reality in my life."

"You're just tired," Marthe said. "Go to sleep. I will guard our *pauvre ange.*"

"You're undoubtedly right. You usually are." With one last, worried look at her brother, Lucy started up the wooden ladder that lead to her pallet in the loft, while Marthe drew up her chair beside Vernon.

Once in the freezing attic, Lucy slowly unbuttoned her faded brown dress and stepped out of it. A wry smile curved her soft, pink lips. Once she got to England she was never going to wear gray or brown again. Ever. Slipping between the rough woolen blankets, she pulled them up around her ears and huddled into a ball, trying to get warm enough to sleep.

She blinked, focusing on the small wooden crucifix that hung over the washstand as she tried to remember her prayers, but she couldn't seem to concentrate. Her thoughts kept jumping around like water droplets on a hot iron skillet.

Why wasn't she more excited? She worried the question around in her mind. The English soldiers had come. After twelve years in exile, she could finally go home. She could redeem her promise and take Ver-

non back where he belonged. So why was she not
dancing around the room in delirious excitement?

She suddenly remembered something the curé had
once said in a Sunday sermon—that hope too long
deferred makes the heart grow bitter. Lucy grimaced.
If twelve years of trying to survive behind enemy lines
wasn't too long...

But it was more than that, she admitted. Despite
what Marthe had said, she wasn't really sure she believed that the English soldiers had finally prevailed.
She was almost afraid to believe it, because if Marthe
were wrong... Lucy closed her eyes on the appalling
thought and promptly fell asleep.

It was the sound of rain beating on the cottage's
slate roof that finally penetrated her deep sleep. She
burrowed deeper into her pillow in an attempt to escape the noise, but the pillow was too thin to muffle
the sound. Muttering in protest, she rolled over and
forced open eyes that felt stuck together. She propped
herself up on an elbow and peered blearily around the
dusky loft. The lack of a window made it difficult to
judge the time, but from the muted sounds drifting up
from the room below, she guessed it was morning.

Pushing aside the rough woolen blankets, Lucy
climbed out of bed, shivering as her bare feet made
contact with the cold wooden floor. An icy current of
air slithered up her chemise and she hurriedly broke
the thin layer of ice in the pitcher. Pouring some water into the chipped bowl, she hurried through her
toilette.

In deference to the occasion, Lucy put on her best
brown wool dress and pinned her long blond hair up
into a sleek chignon that emphasized her pallor as well

as her delicate beauty. Light-headed from a combination of hunger and hope, she hurried downstairs.

"Why are you so late, Lucy?" Vernon's querulous voice demanded. "I've been up forever. I want you to read to me."

"Do not nag at your sister," Marthe ordered. "She must go into the village just as soon as she eats her breakfast."

"I'm sorry," Vernon muttered contritely. "I didn't mean to complain. It's only that my head hurts and my throat feels all scratchy."

"Have you taken the medicine the apothecary sent?" Lucy asked anxiously.

"Yes, and it tastes nasty. I wish he'd sent me something to eat," he said wistfully. "Remember the Christmas before last, when his wife gave me a piece of candy?" His eyes brightened at the memory, sending a twist of pain through Lucy. Her memories of childhood Christmases were filled with every type of candy imaginable, and loving parents, laughing guests and presents piled high in front of the mantel. And all her brother had was the memory of a single piece of candy given two years ago.

Next Christmas! She pressed her lips together in determination. Next Christmas, they would celebrate in England at Landsdowne, her grandfather's principal seat. Then Vernon could begin to build happy memories of his own.

"Don't look so sad, Lucy," Vernon said hesitantly. "I didn't mean to complain. Truly, I didn't. I know how hard it is for you and Marthe to raise enough food for us. When I'm grown, I'll help. You'll see." He stuck out his thin chest in determination. "I'll find a way to buy horses to plow the fields, and then we can raise enough to eat every meal everyday. Enough to eat anytime we please. You'll see."

"I'm sure you will." Lucy's loving smile warmed her eyes to a cobalt blue. "You are a very resourceful young man. But for now you need to stay in bed where it's warm while I go into the village. Why don't you read some Voltaire while I'm gone and we can discuss it when I get back. Then you'll be prepared when the curé comes to hear your lessons."

"Voltaire!" Marthe snorted in disgust. "No good ever came of reading Voltaire. First, men read it, and then they want to fight someone."

"For what I've seen, men just want to fight, and any excuse will do," Lucy said ruefully.

"Like rats, men are a plague upon the earth," Marthe said vehemently.

"Me, too?" Vernon looked inordinately pleased to be considered a plague.

"Bah." Marthe handed him a steaming bowl of gruel. "You aren't a man, you're just a pesky boy. Now eat."

"I'll have mine when I get back." Lucy hurriedly wrapped herself in the voluminous folds of her threadbare, brown wool cloak, hoping it would protect her from the freezing rain.

It didn't. By the time she'd trudged the two miles into the village, the wind-driven sleet had penetrated her cloak, thoroughly chilling her.

Lucy paused in front of the dressmaker's shop and absently wrung out her skirts as she studied the inn across the narrow, muddy road. She felt a burgeoning sense of excitement as several soldiers, dressed in green uniforms that teased at her memory, came out of the inn and walked around the building toward the stables in the back.

Nervously, she chewed on her lower lip as she tried to decide what would be the best thing to do. She could go around to the kitchen door and try to ferret out information about this Major Hart from the innkeeper's garrulous wife, or she could simply march in the front door and ask to see the man. Indecisively, she shifted from one foot to the other.

"Hey, you there! Girl!" A rough, masculine voice yelled at her from across the street, and Lucy automatically turned toward the sound. It was all the encouragement the soldier needed.

"You looking fer someone, girl?" He swaggered across the road, his boots making sucking noises as they plowed through the worst of the mud.

Lucy pointedly turned her back on him and stared into the shopkeeper's window, pretending to be fascinated by the bonnet displayed there. To her dismay, the man sidled up alongside her.

"I got m'pay and I sure could use a woman. You look like you'd be a rare treat in bed with all that golden hair. I always did like golden hair."

Cautiously, Lucy eased away, trying to decide what to do. In her experience, soldiers were generally louts who felt they had a God-given right to take anything they wanted—be it goods or women. She glanced longingly at the inn. She refused to allow him to send her into retreat. Not this close to rescue.

"Ya understan' me, girl?" He edged close enough so that Lucy could smell the whiskey fumes that hung over him like a cloud, partially disguising the stench of his unwashed body. She swallowed uneasily as her empty stomach rolled in protest at the fetid odor.

"Go away!" She enunciated her words clearly and in English, so that he couldn't possibly misunderstand them, and then tried to walk around him.

"Hey! Don't go." The soldier grabbed her arm and forced her up against the wall of the building. "I got money. Half a crown."

"No..." She strained away from him.

"Trooper!" A deep voice aimed the word like a weapon at Lucy's tormentor.

The man let go of her with a haste that would have been laughable had Lucy been in the mood to be amused.

"Just talkin' to her, Colonel." The soldier scuttled backward. "Just talkin', that's all." He gave Lucy a frustrated glare and then scurried away. Like a rat looking for cover, she thought in disgust.

She let out her shaky breath and turned to thank her rescuer, but the words died unspoken on suddenly dry lips as she got a good look at him. He sat astride his huge gray horse with the natural arrogance of a man in total control of both himself and the powerful animal. He was bareheaded, and his short-cropped black hair framed a deeply tanned face, which was dominated by a slightly oversize nose and a piercing pair of coal black eyes. He was watching her with a speculation that made her feel far more threatened than the drunken soldier's attentions ever had.

She hurriedly dropped her gaze, breaking the unsettling contact, only to find her attention caught by his long, brown fingers. They were holding the black leather reins with a competence that made her realize that if he had been the one to grab her, escape would not have been an easy matter. She instinctively pressed back against the wall.

"That fool didn't hurt you, did he?" the man demanded in faultless French.

"Non, monsieur. Merci." Lucy edged along the building and then slipped around the corner, hurrying toward the back of the shop, wanting only to escape his notice. Her experience with men might be slight, but even she could recognize the air of ruthless command that the stranger wore like a cloak. Sending up a silent prayer that he wasn't the unknown Major Hart, she crouched down behind the dressmaker's woodpile and waited until she heard the sound of his horse's hoofbeats moving away. Just to be certain, she counted to a hundred before peeking around the side of the shop. The road was clear. Pulling her hood up over her head, she darted across the street to the inn.

She let herself in the front door and cautiously looked around. The taproom to her left was filled with shouting, laughing men, forgetting their cares in a flagon of ale. Dismissing them as unimportant, she turned her back on them and slipped down the hall to the inn's only private parlor, assuming that the commander would have appropriated it for his own. She was right. The door was ajar, giving her an excellent view of a middle-aged man sporting a bushy gray mustache and wearing a faded green uniform. He was shouting at a trembling young man who didn't look all that much older than Vernon.

Lucy felt a tremor of relief. Her rescuer wasn't the English commander. She wasn't going to have to deal with the unsettling stranger.

"Do you understand me, fool?" the older man demanded.

"Yes, sir." The young soldier gulped and his Adam's apple bobbed nervously. "It won't happen again, sir."

"It had better not!" the major barked.

"Yes, sir. Is that all, sir?"

"Isn't it enough? Get out of my sight."

The young man practically ran over Lucy in his haste to escape, but she barely noticed. She was feeling almost light-headed with relief. The major sounded so very…English. Like her grandfather when he was annoyed with someone. She took a deep breath and slipped into the parlor, closing the door behind her. She didn't want to be interrupted while she explained her circumstances to him. Nor did she want an audience.

The major had his back to her, shuffling through some papers on the scarred oak table he was using as a desk. He didn't seem to be aware of her presence. Finally, unable to wait a second longer, Lucy cleared her throat.

"Hmm?" He glanced up, frowning as he saw her. "What do you want, girl?"

"Passage back to England," she blurted out.

"So would I." He gave her a resigned look. "Take my advice and go home to your family."

"I want to, but to do that my brother and I need passage to my grandfather in England."

"What'd he do? Escape from Napoleon's army?" the major asked vaguely. "You'd do better to wait for him to come and get you."

"He doesn't know where I am." Lucy tried to keep her impatience out of her voice.

"You French—"

"English. I'm as English as you are. My name is Lucy Danvers and my grandfather is the Earl of Langford."

"Of course your grandfather's an earl." The major's disparaging gaze traveled over her threadbare cloak. "Fallen on hard times, has he?"

"I tell you I am!" A feeling of disorientation gripped her. Why was this man mocking her? He was supposed to commiserate with her over what had happened and assure her that he'd arrange their passage to England at the earliest possible moment. "My father was the Viscount Langford, and he brought Mama and me with him to France back in '02, when everyone thought the war was over. But it wasn't, and we were trapped. Papa was murdered trying to get to the coast, and Mama died when my brother Vernon was born," she explained, adding more details in an attempt to make him understand.

"See," she continued doggedly as he studied her with a kind of superior contempt that made her want to cringe, "this is my father's signet ring." She showed him the heavy gold ring, which she wore on a chain around her neck. "See, it has my family's crest on it."

"I don't know the Langford family crest, but even if I did, it doesn't prove anything. You could have stolen it or bought it. Or it could have been given to you by the man who killed the viscount."

"I have letters from the curé who buried my parents and from the doctor who delivered Vernon." Lucy refused to give up.

"Letters can be forged. And you French will lie about anything. Tell me, is there an Englishman about who can identify you?" he asked sarcastically.

"Englishmen have been in rather short supply around here the last twelve years," Lucy snapped, frustrated at having her story dismissed out of hand. Hastily, she bit back the furious words she wanted to throw at this smug, narrow-minded fool, knowing she couldn't afford to anger him. He had the power to arrange for her and Vernon to return to England. If only there was something she could add to make him believe her. But what?

"If I'm not English, where did I learn to speak it?" she finally asked.

"Many women learn to speak their protector's language."

"Protector!" Lucy repeated incredulously. "So far I've gotten precious little *protection* from His Majesty's forces."

The major ran stubby fingers through his gray hair. "That isn't what I meant, and I think you know it. Innkeeper!" He raised his voice to a roar. "Get your fat self in here."

"Yes, sir?" Pierre LeClerc came into the room and gave Lucy a speculative stare. "How is it that I might help you, sir?"

The major pointed at Lucy. "Who is she?"

"Lucia Delacoux, old Marthe Delacoux's cousin. She and her family came to live with Marthe many years ago, when the war drove them out of their own village. The soldiers killed her father soon after, and her mother, she died when the boy was born. May the good Lord have mercy on their souls." Superstitiously, he crossed himself.

"You're sure?" the major demanded.

The innkeeper blinked in surprise. "Of course I am sure. Ask my good wife, ask the dressmaker across the way, ask the apothecary, ask—"

"Never mind," the major snapped, cutting him off. "Get out."

"But of course, sir. Anything you desire, sir." The innkeeper bobbed his head, displaying the servility that a paying customer always brought to the fore. With a final curious look at Lucy, he slid out the door, closing it softly behind him.

"Major, if you would just listen to me," she said, forcing an even tone into her voice.

"No!" he barked. "I don't have the time to listen to you. Or anyone else, for that matter. I have to consolidate my troops' position. I have no time to waste listening to wild tales from the locals."

"It isn't a wild tale." Her voice rose despite her efforts to remain calm. This interview was not going at all the way she'd dreamed. For so many years, she'd believed that all she had to do was wait for the English to arrive, identify herself, and she'd be safe. Safe from Napoleon, safe from hunger and, most of all, safe from her fears about Vernon's health. But that wasn't happening. She shivered convulsively as fear flooded her mind, further chilling her body and making it difficult to think.

"Major, please—"

"No, no and no! I told you, I have no time for this. Dammit, woman, we're fighting a war here."

"But I'm not the enemy!" Her voice broke with the strength of her feelings. "I'm English, too."

"So you claim," he countered, "but it's far more likely you're just an adventuress." His eyes suddenly narrowed, making Lucy's stomach twist in sudden fear. "Or even a clever spy. I have no way of knowing."

"But—" she began desperately.

"And having no way of knowing," he continued inexorably, "your claim will simply have to wait until Paris is liberated. Then you can present your case at headquarters and they can decide what to do about it. I, however, have reached the end of my patience. Here." He reached into his pocket, extracted a coin and dropped it on the table. "Take this and go."

"I don't want your charity," she said through gritted teeth.

"That's all you're going to get. Take the coin and go or simply depart. I don't care which."

Lucy stared bitterly at the gleaming coin. Being offered charity—and grudging charity at that—from someone she'd pinned such hopes on galled her unbearably. She wanted nothing so much as to fling the coin in his face, but she knew she couldn't afford the gesture. That casually given coin would provide Vernon with food for weeks.

Swallowing the bitter taste of defeat, she reached for it with a jerky motion.

"I thought you'd see it my way," the major sneered. "You French are a canny lot when it comes to money."

Lucy drew herself up to her full five-foot-one-inch height and stared down her small, straight nose at him. "I shall not forget you, Major Hart." Her voice rang with the fervor of a vow. "I shall always remember your response to my plea for help."

For a moment, doubt shook him, and he eyed her uncertainly as she stalked out. What if she were telling the truth? The Earl of Langford was reputed to be an irascible old devil, and his son *had* been killed on the Peninsula back in '02. But then, that was common knowledge.

This woman had probably been hired as a serving girl to the viscount when he'd first come to France—that was probably it. The worry lines smoothed out of his face. That was undoubtedly where she'd learned such impeccable English. After all, everyone knew the French were a sly lot, always trying to turn events to their own advantage. The woman was nothing but a clever impostor, trying to use him to get to England. He sighed. Not that he blamed her. After all these years of war, this part of France was a ravaged land full of starving peasants. But that wasn't his concern, he reminded himself. Picking up a sheet of paper, he dismissed the incident from his mind.

Lucy did not have the luxury of being able to forget. Her body sagged slightly as she reached the front of the inn. The pride that had carried her out of the room was slowly seeping out of her, taking her small store of energy with it. She found it hard to remain erect. Wearily, she rubbed her fingers over the bridge of her nose and tried to think. What now? The question ricocheted through her mind, gaining force as it went. What should she do now? What could she do? She slumped against the wall, swallowing an overwhelming impulse to cry, to sob out twelve years' worth of fear and frustration and grief. But she couldn't afford the luxury of giving in to her feelings. She had to be strong. For her sake as well as Vernon's.

"*Mademoiselle?*" The deep, faintly familiar voice sliced through her despair, capturing her attention.

Lucy glanced up and found herself staring into a pair of gleaming black eyes. The eyes of the man who had rescued her earlier, she realized with a strange sense of detachment. It was almost as if she were standing outside her body, observing what was happening.

"*Mademoiselle?*" He frowned at her lack of response. His fingers closed around her fragile wrist, seeming to burn into her skin. "I'm Standen. Is something wrong?"

"*Non!*" She jerked away, and to her relief he made no attempt to restrain her.

Carefully avoiding contact with him, she slipped past his outstretched hand and hurried toward the front door. She didn't feel up to coping with any more problems at the moment, and somehow, on some instinctive level, she knew that this man had the potential to become a monstrous problem.

Lucy's breath caught in her throat as she stepped outside into the icy wind. She pulled her sodden cloak around her shoulders and, bending her head, walked toward the shops. With the unheard-of news that the English were paying cash for what they wanted, she was certain that every farmer in the area would have brought in hoarded supplies with the hope of selling them.

Even if she couldn't take home news that they were to shortly return to England, she could at least take home food, thanks to the major's guilty conscience. Maybe enough to help Vernon through this latest bout of illness. Her shoulders sagged beneath the weight of her problems.

Robert allowed the curtain of the taproom to drop back into place as the woman disappeared into a shop farther down the street. There was something about her that nagged at him. She looked half-starved, and probably was, he conceded. This part of France had been ravaged by the French army for years. That the peasants had managed to survive at all bore mute testimony to their tenacious hold on life.

Not that the woman had looked like a peasant. He absently ran his finger over his jawline. Her delicately carved features and extreme blondness seemed totally out of place among the much-darker faces of the rest of the population. Like a fine piece of porcelain sitting amid the tavern's heavy mugs.

"Colonel Standen, sir?" A visibly nervous, very young lieutenant was tentatively addressing him.

"Yes?"

"I told the major you were here, and he said to come right in. He's in the private parlor, sir." The young man led the way and, opening the door, gestured for him to enter.

"Colonel Standen, sir," the boy announced.

"Come in, come in." The major rose and shook Robert's hand. "Sit down." He motioned toward one of the rough wooden chairs in front of the blazing fire. "Sit down and warm yourself. Beastly weather, this. Just like the damn country." He turned and caught sight of the young man standing indecisively in the doorway. "Well? What do you want?" He glared at him. "Go on. Get out."

"Yes, sir. Of course, sir." The boy escaped with obvious relief.

"Bah!" The major snorted in disgust. "I need men to fight a war and what do they send me? Children! If they let them buy a commission any younger, I'll have to start making provisions for their nannies."

"Is there much fighting in the area?" Robert's eyes narrowed thoughtfully. "I thought the Frogs took to their heels without a battle."

"Most did," the major confirmed. "But they left a few stragglers to cause mischief. Now, what brings a member of Wellington's staff to this godforsaken spot?"

"Headquarters. Since I was traveling through the area on my way back to England, they asked me to bring you a packet of orders that they preferred not go through the regular channels."

"You checking up on the whereabouts of Soult's men?"

"No." A shadow darkened Robert's face. "I'm selling out and returning to England."

"Just when we've got them on the run?" The major was clearly shocked. "Why would you do a fool thing like that?"

"Personal reasons." Robert seemed to retreat behind an impenetrable wall of reserve.

Chapter Two

Marthe looked up from the blackened pot she was stirring as Lucy slowly pushed open the cottage door. The old woman gestured warningly toward Vernon, who was sleeping on the cot a few feet from the fireplace.

Lucy nodded and, setting her precious bundle of food on the heavy maple table, stripped off her drenched cloak. Meticulously, she spread it over the back of a chair to dry. Then, just as carefully, she slipped off her rough leather boots and set them in front of the fire, as if her attention to such inconsequential details could blot out the larger reality of the total and absolute failure of her mission.

"Drink this." Marthe handed her a steaming cup of herbal tea. "It would not do for you to be sick, too."

"Marthe, I didn't—" Lucy choked to a stop, the words she wanted to say seemingly unable to get past the lump in her throat.

"First drink, then talk, *ma petite choux*. The boy sleeps for now."

"For now," Lucy whispered bitterly. "He isn't better, but he sleeps for now. What is he supposed to do? Sleep his life away?" Her voice cracked in frus-

trated anger and she hastily took a swallow of the fragrant liquid, not even noticing when it burned her
tongue.

"Sit by the fire and warm yourself." Marthe urged
her onto the sturdy wooden stool close to the crackling flames.

Lucy complied, because it was easier to give in than
to argue. She briefly pondered the fact that she didn't
feel cold. She should. She'd just walked two miles in
a freezing rain and she was drenched. But she didn't
feel chilled. In fact, she didn't seem to feel anything.

It was as if her mind simply couldn't absorb any
more pain, and so had blocked out her body's discomfort. For so long her whole life had consisted of
finding ways to survive until the British troops came.
And now, after twelve interminable years, they had
finally come. But not in the guise of rescuing heroes,
as she'd always pictured them. They'd come as ordinary, overworked, exasperated men with problems of
their own. And they didn't want to hear about hers.

Vernon started to cough, and the harsh, hacking
sounds beat at Lucy's mind like physical blows. "Each
time he gets sick, the cough gets worse," she said
bleakly. "And he's so small. What does he have left to
fight with?"

"He has us," Marthe said fiercely. "We love him."

"And help is just across the Channel, even though
we can't get to it," Lucy muttered in an exhausted
monotone.

"They didn't believe you?" Marthe asked incredulously. "But the packet from the shop..." She gestured toward the table.

"Charity," Lucy said woodenly. "It was all they
were willing to give. And, God help me, I took it."

"But your father's signet ring, the letters! Can the *canaille* not read?"

"Can't. Won't. It makes no difference in the end. The result is the same." Lucy's shoulders slumped in defeat. "Marthe, what am I going to do? I can't wait till the Allies conquer all of France, if they ever do. And even if they should, how are we supposed to travel to Paris to present our case to headquarters?" she demanded in frustration. "If we had the money to travel, we could go to England now."

"Ah, money." Marthe grimaced. "Always and always it is the money. The good curé preaches that it is the root of all evil, but me, I think it is simply the root of all things."

"I have to get my hands on some soon. But how?" Lucy's frustrated gaze swept the barren room. "There's nothing left to sell. Nothing but Papa's signet ring, and we need that as part of the proof of who Vernon is."

"You showed the ring to the commander?"

"Of course I showed it to him. He believes I got it from the murderer."

"Bah! I would like to murder *him!*" Marthe snapped. "What about the way you speak English? Did the fool think you stole that also?"

"No, he thinks I learned that from my protector."

"What?" Marthe yelped and then hastily lowered her voice when Vernon stirred restively. "That misbegotten cur! That..." She sputtered to a stop as words failed her.

"Actually," Lucy said, as an idea born from the depths of her desperation began to take shape in her mind, "that may be the answer."

Marthe blinked in confusion. "The answer to what?"

"Obtaining money, of course. I was wrong. I do have something left to sell. Myself."

"No!" Marthe flatly rejected the idea. "Better we should..." Her voice trailed away as Vernon coughed again.

"Precisely." Lucy shrugged fatalistically. "Either we get Vernon to England or we watch him die, a little each day."

"What you would do, it is a sin," Marthe said uncertainly.

"Which is? Sell myself to save my brother's life or do nothing and let him die?"

"You are too clever for me to argue with, but I know it is a sin," Marthe insisted.

Lucy sighed. "Perhaps, but is it not the lesser of two sins? For a few minutes of my time, I can buy a lifetime for Vernon."

"Yes, but suppose you become *enceinte?* Then what?"

"Then I'll have to invent a French husband who died in the fighting." Lucy refused to dwell on the spurt of panic she felt at Marthe's words.

"But—"

"Marthe, I truly can't think of any alternative. I have to do it. I love Vernon. In some ways he's more like my son than my brother. And I gave my word to Mama that I'd get him back to England." Lucy's voice roughened at the memory, which, even after all these years, still had the power to hurt. "And a Danvers doesn't give up when things become rough."

"And things will become rough if you do this. Men are little more than beasts, pawing and panting at a woman. Disgusting, the lot of them...." Marthe's sigh echoed Lucy's sense of defeat. "But you're right, of course, *ma petite*. Vernon will die, and there is nothing else left to sell. When will you do this thing?"

"I think, as Shakespeare said, 't'were best done quickly."

Marthe frowned. "This man Shakespeare, he is a friend of your family?"

"No. He wrote plays a long time ago."

"Ah." Marthe nodded in satisfaction. "A dead man. The best kind."

"Dear Marthe." Lucy kissed her wrinkled cheek. "When we get to England—"

"No." Marthe shook her head. "I am too old to go anywhere. This is where I was born and this is where I will die. Here, among my flowers and my friends. You and Vernon, you are young and you are English. You will go home and, sometime, perhaps, you will come and visit with me?"

"Every year," Lucy promised. "And my grandfather will provide for you, as you have provided for us."

"If God so wills." Marthe crossed herself. "Now go change your wet gown. There is much to do. Night will be here before you know it."

Marthe was wrong. The time passed with an agonizing slowness, weighed down by Lucy's sense of fear and guilt and dread. Despite what she'd told Marthe, she knew full well that what she was going to do was wrong, and she shrank from the very thought. But she also knew that she had no real choice. Morality wasn't an abstract idea existing in a vacuum. Nor was it always black and white. Sometimes it was a murky shade of gray.

Finally, shortly after dark, Vernon slipped again into a light, troubled sleep, and Lucy felt it was safe to leave. She wrapped herself in her still-damp cloak and set out for the village, eager to have the whole distasteful experience over with.

Her steps slowed of their own accord as she approached the small cluster of buildings that comprised the village. Apprehensively, she pulled her cloak tighter around her thin shoulders and forced her reluctant feet forward. It had to be done tonight, she realized, urging herself on. Only an Englishman would have the money to pay her, and the English might leave at any time. From what she'd observed in the last twelve years, there didn't seem to be a great deal of reasoning to war. Soldiers appeared, indiscriminately caused death and destruction and then disappeared again, sometimes—if you were lucky—for months on end.

Lucy fixed her eyes on the flickering points of candlelight visible in the large, multipaned window of the inn's taproom. From where she stood she could see figures moving back and forth, but their features were indistinguishable. As she moved closer, she was able to make out details: the gleaming white apron of Maria LeClerc as she bustled around the room serving drinks, the shining buttons on the soldiers' uniforms. There did not appear to be any locals in the taproom, Lucy noted with a sense of relief. It would be hard enough to do what she had to do, but to do it under the shocked eyes of people she'd known and respected for the past twelve years would be intolerable.

She paused in the well-swept courtyard outside the window, trying to decide which of the soldiers would best suit her purpose. Her eyes narrowed thought-fully as she studied a man half turned away from her who was sitting alone at a small table beside the fire-place. His long fingers were cradling a glass of amber liquid and he was staring in rapt concentration at the dancing flames. His long legs were stretched out in front of him and the flickering light from the fire was reflected in the shine of his boots. He seemed to be isolated from the other men, not just from the fact that his uniform was of a different color. It was more than that. It was as if the man himself had withdrawn into a secret place where no one else could follow.

Lucy swallowed uneasily as she measured the breadth of his shoulders beneath his well-fitting blue coat. His body seemed so big, so powerful, when compared to her own slight frame, she thought ner-vously.

The man swirled the liquid in his glass, and there was a flash of greenish light as the flames were mo-mentarily reflected in the stone of the ring he wore on his right hand.

An emerald, Lucy realized. A very large emerald. It was the ring of an extremely wealthy man—a man who would be able to pay for what he wanted. But would he want her? Sudden doubt shook her. Most of the men in the village seemed to prefer plump, buxom, giggling young girls. Not overly thin, deadly serious spinsters of twenty-five.

But her father had adored her mother, she remem-bered, encouraging herself, and her mother had been neither plump nor buxom nor giggling. And this man was an Englishman like her father. Maybe English-men weren't like Frenchmen. Maybe their tastes were different.

Lucy waited until Maria had left the taproom and
then opened the front door and slipped into the inn.
There was no one in the hallway, but she could hear
Pierre LeClerc's voice in the kitchens yelling at someone. Lucy quietly moved toward the taproom. She
paused in the doorway and looked around, getting her
bearings.

Taking a deep breath, she let it out in a slow, steady
stream, trying to look as if she had a respectable reason to be there. She fixed her eyes on the blue uniform of the man she'd chosen to approach and headed
toward him, ignoring the various ribald comments that
followed her. In fact, she barely heard them. Her heart
was pounding so loudly that all she could hear was its
throbbing beat.

The man didn't move as she approached, and Lucy
walked around his table, faltering slightly when she
saw his face. It was the man who'd rescued her earlier, and she felt a flash of shame that momentarily
dimmed her determination. She hurriedly blocked out
the feeling. It didn't matter; he was still a stranger.
What mattered was that he could provide the means
for her to get Vernon back to England. Keeping her
mind firmly focused on that thought, she smiled at
him, her lips trembling ever so slightly.

The man didn't respond. He continued to stare into
the fire with rapt concentration. Lucy waited a moment longer for him to acknowledge her presence and,
when he didn't, she scrambled for a conversational
gambit. Her mind remained a discouraging blank,
however. She couldn't think of a single tactful way to
ask a complete stranger if he wanted to hire her body
for the evening. She swallowed a hysterical giggle.

There must be protocol to something like this, if only she knew what it was.

Finally, afraid that Maria LeClerc would return and order her out, Lucy cast subtlety aside and said, in her best imitation of the local peasant dialect, "I am Lucia and I am . . . lonely." She was unable to think of a word that adequately described the situation.

The man didn't seem to suffer from a similar lack of vocabulary. Nor was his French of the peasant variety, sounding instead as if it came straight from the Court of Versailles. "You are stupid," he said softly. "Go home to your family where you belong." His face twisted briefly, as if he were in pain.

I'm trying, Lucy thought with a flash of dark humor that added a flush to her pale cheeks. She gulped and started again. "I don't have a home and I find you very . . . exciting." She dredged the word up from the depths of her memory. Once, years ago, she'd heard one of the village girls say that to the baker's son, and the results had been totally unexpected. The young man had grabbed the girl's arm, pressed his wet mouth to hers and then pulled her behind a hedgerow.

It quickly became apparent to Lucy that this man's tolerance for excitement was much higher. He merely took a long swallow of his brandy and studied her over the rim of his glass. His dark gaze slid slowly over her face, examining each feature and heating the blood beneath her pale skin with a combination of embarrassment and shame and some other, far less easily defined, emotion. She locked the muscles in her legs to keep them from shaking and held herself rigid beneath his minute inspection. Finally, his eyes slipped lower, down over her shapeless cloak to linger on her small feet, peeping out from beneath the muddied hem of her shabby, dark blue dress.

Lucy's breath seemed to become suspended in her lungs when his eyes returned to her chest, as if he were curious about the size and shape of her. All she could think of was the way Marthe had taught her to tap and smell the melons in the marketplace, to determine which of them to purchase. She felt humiliated, but the feeling was not strong enough to extinguish the desperation that drove her.

"Sit down." Robert pointed to the chair across from him, and Lucy stumbled into it on legs that suddenly felt too weak to support her. Did this mean he was accepting her offer? she wondered. Or was he still in the considering stage? She swallowed uneasily as her empty stomach lurched beneath the force of the volatile emotions coursing through her. She desperately wished it were tomorrow and this whole frightful experience simply an unpleasant memory.

"When was the last time you had a meal?"

Lucy blinked in surprise at his unexpected question.

"A meal?" she repeated in confusion.

"Food." He gestured toward the serving dish in front of him. Most of a chicken, as well as a mouthwatering assortment of winter vegetables, was left on it. Beside the platter was an untouched apple tart and a jug of thick yellow cream. "Take the food and this—" he reached into his pocket and pulled out a shiny gold coin "—and go home to your family where you belong."

"I can't," Lucy blurted out in frustration. "I need—"

"To think," he said impatiently. "The war is almost over. You're going to want to marry. How can you if you become a prostitute?"

His blunt question hit her with the force of a blow, but she refused to let it fester in her mind. She knew she wasn't going to be here, if and when peace finally came. She was going to be living in England, where no one would ever know what had happened here. In England she would never see any of the villagers again. Just as she would never see this soldier again.

"I can offer you a bargain, a special price." Lucy tried to keep her voice low and seductive. "If you aren't interested..." She forced herself to scan the crowded room.

Robert's lips tightened as he stared at her in frustration. Didn't she understand that what she was about to do would forever place her beyond society's pale? She would be worse than dead as far as the village and probably her own family were concerned. She could never marry, and she certainly didn't look the type to make a success of being some man's mistress. He studied her delicate features, lingering on her hair, which gleamed like newly ripened wheat in the subdued light from the fire. Her mouth trembled, and he watched as she caught her lower lip between her small white teeth.

He felt an irrational gust of anger surge through him. If she continued on her present course, it wouldn't be long before her remote dignity and fragile delicateness would crumble beneath the incessant demands of an ever-changing stream of men. What she needed was a sharp lesson in the unpleasant realities of the profession she seemed hell-bent on enter-

ing. And it looked as if he were the man who was
going to have to give it to her.

Lucy jumped as he set his drink down on the table
with a thump. Her eyes focused on his long, brown
fingers, which were curled around the glass. His nails
were bluntly cut and, unlike most of the village men's,
immaculately clean.

He abruptly stood up, and she found her eyes on a
level with his muscular thighs, tightly encased in his
breeches. Nervously, her gaze skittered upwards, over
his flat stomach and past the breadth of his wide chest
until it finally landed on his face. His eyes were narrowed with the force of the emotion he was feeling.
But what emotion? she wondered uneasily. From the
tense set of his shoulders and the tightness of his lips,
she would have said anger, but why would he be angry? And if she was right and it really was anger,
would that anger translate into pain for her? Men were
much stronger than women. They could inflict pain at
will, and what she was about to do would leave her
very vulnerable to him.

But not as vulnerable as her brother was to the illness that had him in its grip. The thought steadied her
skittering nerves. All this man could do to her was inflict temporary physical pain. She would heal, but
Vernon might not.

Knowing that she had already made her choice, she
forced herself to put her hand in his outstretched fingers. They closed around her slim wrist like mana-
cles, leaving a feeling of impotent dread in their wake.

Without a word, Robert jerked her to her feet and
headed toward the stairs, making her trot to keep up
with his long strides. The thud of his boots on the
floor echoed through her mind like a death knell. The

sound drowned out the ribald comments from the soldiers, whose eyes followed them as they left. Lucy refused to look at them, keeping her own gaze fixed firmly on the floor.

By the time they reached his room on the second floor, she was out of breath. She sagged against the wall, trying to still her racing heart as he unlocked the door and pushed it open.

A short, thin man in a uniform was sitting in front of the blazing fire polishing a pair of boots, which he dropped when Robert strode into the room.

"Go have a pint, Jones," Robert ordered, while Lucy, after one quick look at the man's startled face, focused on the fire burning in the grate. "Be back in ten minutes."

"Ten minutes?" Jones cast a speculative look at Lucy, and then shrugged. "Yes, sir. Ten minutes."

Lucy winced as the door closed behind him with a disapproving snap.

"Now, to business." To her relief, Robert released her arm and strode over to the nightstand. He picked up a roll of bank notes lying there. "How much?" he barked out.

Lucy stared at the thick wad of bills. She'd been right, she thought. The English could afford to pay for whatever they wanted. But the realization brought her no sense of satisfaction, only a deep frustration that she should have to do this for so little when he had so much.

Perhaps, if she were to explain to him . . . A fugitive spark of hope flared briefly, only to die under the impact of his contemptuous stare. He wouldn't believe her, she realized. No more than the major had believed her. He might think she was simply trying to extort money from him and would tell her to leave. The prospect of having to go back downstairs to find another man who had both the money and the inclination seemed far worse than simply going through with what she'd started.

"Your price," he repeated.

"Twenty pounds." Lucy struggled to keep the tremor of uncertainty out of her voice. She had no idea if the amount was reasonable or not, but she and Marthe had guessed that it would take a little less than that to get her and Vernon to England.

"Twenty pounds!" Robert's dark eyebrows arched in surprise at how much she'd asked for, putting her very much in mind of the image of the devil on the icon that the curé displayed on the altar every Easter. She shivered and resisted the impulse to cross herself.

"Twenty pounds," Lucy forced herself to repeat more firmly.

"Very well, *madame*." He peeled off several notes and carelessly dropped them on the bed. Lucy watched them land with an impotent feeling of extreme frustration. Those few bills meant her brother's life and her freedom, and yet they seemed of little concern to him. She glanced at the roll of bills in his hand. It didn't look any smaller.

"Ah, no, my pretty." He followed her glance, but misinterpreted its cause. "Enough is enough. However—" his voice deepened perceptibly "—if you please me sufficiently, I might be inclined to give you more."

Lucy watched as his firm mouth lifted in a smile that held no humor. Please him? The words echoed ominously through her mind. How? Her knowledge of what went on between a man and a woman was limited to the hurried whispers of the village girls and to Marthe's oblique references to men and their disgusting demands.

Should she admit to total ignorance or try to follow his lead, hoping he wouldn't notice her ineptitude? She shifted uneasily. Unfortunately, he had the look of a man who didn't miss much.

"Well? Get on with it," he ordered. "My batman will be back in ten minutes."

Lucy stared blankly at him as she mentally scrambled for a course of action. Maybe she should start by kissing him?

Forcing herself to move closer to him, when every instinct she possessed was urging her to run, she covered the few feet separating them with jerky steps. When the tips of his boots were a scant inch from her own worn shoes, she paused. This close, she could actually feel the warmth of his body. It seemed as if tendrils of heat were curling around her, drawing her to him.

Holding her breath, she leaned closer, stood on tiptoe and hastily kissed him. Her aim was slightly off. Her lips landed to one side of his mouth, and the raspy, silken texture of his freshly shaved skin scraped over them.

Shaken by the encounter, she rocked back on her heels and peered up at him through her thick, dark blond lashes.

When he continued to merely stand there, completely immobile, Lucy decided something else was expected of her. Botheration! she thought with a flash of her normal spirit. Why didn't he help her? She couldn't do it all herself. Drawing on her observations of the flirtation that went on between courting couples in the village, she reached out and laid her palm against his chest. She could feel the slow, heavy strokes of his heartbeat through his chest wall. She flexed her fingers, feeling his wool uniform scratch her sensitive skin. When he still didn't move, she forced her hand upward until she reached his neck. Surprise stilled her exploring fingers as she absorbed the strange feel of his skin. It had a texture like roughly woven silk, only, unlike silk, it was warm. For a second, her natural curiosity drowned out her apprehensions and she ran her finger over his chin, stopping at the deep indentation in the middle of it.

His skin felt so different from hers. Her eyes focused on the dark pink of his lips. His mouth was bigger, too, and still curved in that humorless smile, which brought her apprehension flooding back. Her eyes skittered upward over his slightly oversize nose to become entangled in his gaze. His eyes gleamed with some suppressed emotion that both frightened and exhilarated her. It was as if, in some strange way, she possessed power, if only she knew how to use it.

Fascinated, she watched as his eyes came closer and closer, until they seemed to fill her whole field of vision, blotting out everything else.

She tensed as his arms encircled her and jerked her closer, up against him. Seconds later, his lips met hers with bruising force. His mouth pressed roughly against her lips, cutting the sensitive inner skin. Lucy instinctively tried to pull back, but his grip tightened, imprisoning her as his mouth ground against hers.

Vernon. She repeated her brother's name like a talisman against the pain the man was inflicting on her.

A feeling of disorientation shook her as he suddenly swung her up in his arms and carried her over to the bed. Unceremoniously, he dropped her onto the soft, fluffy feather mattress and followed her down. His hard body covered hers, pushing her deeper into the coverlet. She felt crushed by the weight of his body, and her loss of control panicked her. It took an enormous effort for her not to struggle as his lips captured hers again. Instead, she grimly braced herself to endure the assault.

At first his kiss was simply a painful repetition of the one before, but then, slowly, it began to change, becoming less domineering and more seductive. His lips brushed hers with feather-light strokes that sent shivers skating over her nerve endings. The sensation intensified as his lips traced across the petal-soft skin of her cheek and down to her earlobe, which he lightly bit.

Lucy could feel a strange trembling deep in her abdomen as wave upon wave of heat flooded through her. She didn't understand her uninhibited reaction and, in a way, it frightened her more than he did.

"Ah, my pretty." Robert's lips returned to her mouth, this time nibbling and caressing until, instinctively, it opened. His tongue immediately surged inside, to stroke along the line of her teeth.

All rational thought fled as an overpowering sense of excitement rolled through her. She forgot everything but the reality of what she was feeling.

Slowly, ever so slowly, an incessant banging on the door filtered through her absorption. She squeezed her eyes closed in a vain attempt to shut it out, but she couldn't. The pounding continued and was followed by the rattling of the door handle.

"Colonel, come quick!" Jones shouted. "Them troopers gonna kill 'emselves fer sure, and the major ain't nowhere to be found."

Robert raised his head and stared down into Lucy's flushed face. She looked as confused as he felt, he thought, disgusted at his lack of control. What had happened? All he'd meant to do was frighten her enough to send her back to her family, where she belonged. Instead, he was the one who had learned a lesson. Somehow, the minute he'd begun to kiss her, his original motivation had dissolved like morning mist in the noonday sun.

"Colonel?" his batman called. "I'se afraid they's gonna kill each other!"

"Let them," Lucy muttered, loath to let go of the totally unexpected sensations that gripped her.

"Colonel!" the batman yelled.

"Damnation!" Robert jackknifed up. If he waited much longer, Jones was liable to come in, and he didn't want to expose this surprising woman to his batman's curious eyes. "I'll be back," he muttered as he sprinted for the door, flinging it open.

"Come quick, Colonel," Jones urged. "One of 'em's already had his cork drawn, and t'other's got him a knife."

"I've a good mind to use it on him." Robert clattered down the steps, eager to dispatch the recalcitrant troopers and get back to the woman. He was on the bottom step when what she'd said finally registered. Or more importantly, how she'd said it.

She'd spoken in faultless, upper-class English. He frowned, wondering how she could have learned English in this very primitive part of southern France. And from whom had she learned it? The total lack of accent suggested it was her native tongue, but then her peasant French had been spoken with a fluency that had made him think she was a native. Who was she and what was she doing here?

"Colonel?" the batman began, only to be interrupted by the sound of gunfire. "I knew it," the servant said with gloomy satisfaction. "They's done kilt themselves."

Reluctantly, Robert headed toward the taproom. First he'd settle the dispute, then he'd unravel the identity of his mysterious, would-be courtesan. For the first time since his father's messenger had come to destroy his way of life, he felt a flash of interest in something besides the unfairness of fate.

She wasn't going anywhere, he told himself. These stairs were the only way down. "Stay here," he ordered. "Make sure that woman doesn't leave before I get back."

"Yes, sir." His batman promptly subsided on the bottom step, only too pleased to stay out of the line of fire.

The sound of the door closing behind Robert hit Lucy like a pailful of icy water thrown in her face. What was wrong with her? she wondered with appalled horror. Why had her body so suddenly turned traitor to her mind? It was as if she had a totally separate entity living within herself—one with the soul of a courtesan. If the man's servant hadn't returned ... She bit her lip at the galling memory of her uninhibited reaction to his kiss. It was one thing to sacrifice herself for her brother, but to enjoy that sacrifice made it seem so sordid.

The sound of gunshots from the taproom below quickly put an end to her musings. This wasn't the time to ponder the moral implications of it all; this was the time to escape while she could. That gunfire might mean that the French soldiers had returned, and even now were fighting with the English.

She grabbed her cloak from the floor and headed toward the window, intent on escaping before whoever won the fight came for her. Her gaze landed on the money her soldier had so casually tossed on the bed for her and, remembering where it had come from, she turned back to the nightstand.

The much-larger roll of bills was still where he'd set it. Lucy grabbed it up and extracted several more bills, then picked up the notes he'd given her.

He'd probably only gamble it away, and she had a much better use for it, she thought, appeasing her conscience. These few pounds would provide food and fuel for Marthe until her grandfather could send an agent to arrange matters. Tucking the money into her pocket, she tugged open the window and peered out into the darkness.

The room was at the back of the inn, facing the orchard. Directly below her was a lean-to built to hold wood and supplies for the kitchen.

Carefully lowering herself out of the window, she stretched until her toes touched the roof of the lean-to. An icy drizzle was falling, making the footing slippery, but Lucy barely noticed. Her sense of triumph drowned out every other emotion. She'd done it! She'd gotten the money she'd needed. She felt a faint sense of regret at the necessity of having to steal from the man, but she had long ago discovered that life wasn't played by a neat set of rules. The most important thing was to survive, and now, thanks to the colonel, she and Vernon and Marthe could.

Lucy dropped off the roof and landed on all fours in the freezing mud. Scrambling to her feet, she checked to make sure the money was still there, and then took off at a run through the orchard.

Tomorrow, she thought with a rising sense of excitement, tomorrow at first light she and Vernon would be gone.

Chapter Three

"I'm that sorry, Colonel." Jones slowly closed the
bedroom door behind him. "Proper slumguzzled, I
was. Who'd a ever thought a female would be climbing out a window like that? Ain't natural, I tell you."

"I'm not blaming you," Robert said impatiently.
"The thing now is to find her."

"Well..." Jones scraped a dirty fingernail over his
bristly cheek. "I been trying. All mornin'. But it seems
like nobody ain't never seen no yellar-haired female.
Of any age. A'tall. Asked everybody, just like you
said."

"Hmm." Robert frowned.

"Offered 'em gold, too, fer all the good it did."
Jones shivered. "Them Frogs just stared right through
me, every man jack of 'em. Wouldn't tell me nothing'—even that padre over at the church." Jones lowered his voice. "It was like she was a ghost what rose
from the dead last night and then went back to her
grave."

"Or like she's one of them and we're the enemy,"
Robert said dryly.

"I ain't no enemy! I'm an Englishman, bred and
born!"

Robert's lips twitched at Jones's aggrieved expression. "I'm not questioning your loyalty. I just wish you were a better spy."

Jones shrugged. "What we gonna do? We already asked everybody."

"Do what we should have done four hours ago. Continue on our journey."

"But we ain't found her yet and she stole from us," Jones insisted.

"And an odd sort of thief she was, too," Robert said thoughtfully. "What kind of thief only takes a fraction of the money available?"

"One that's all about in her head?"

"Or one who needed an exact amount for something and took only what she needed." Robert frowned. Who was she and why wouldn't the locals identify her either to him or to his less-formidable-looking batman? The villagers' refusal to betray her suggested that she was someone they knew, and knew well. But if she was indeed one of them, where had she learned her impeccable English?

Damn! He slammed his fist down on the dresser in frustration. He hated unsolved puzzles, but that's what the woman was going to have to remain. He couldn't linger in the village any longer. He should have left hours ago. He had a packet of information for the War Office, and his father was waiting for him at their town house in London.

Probably with a short list of eligible candidates for the position of his wife. He grimaced. He never thought when he'd so blithely made that promise all those years ago that he'd ever be called upon to redeem it. His brother Gervais had been in the prime of life.... And to think it had all come to this.

* * *

"Lucy, are we almost there yet? I'm so cold." As if to give added emphasis to his words, Vernon began to cough, a dry, hacking sound that promised worse to come.

"Soon." Lucy hugged his frail, shivering body closer to her, willing the jarvey's plodding horse to go faster. The heavy, misting rain had turned the London streets into a gray-shrouded world, muffling sound and blurring the outlines of the buildings. In the deepening twilight, very few people were abroad, preferring the comfort of their homes—no matter how humble—to the discomfort of the fickle March weather.

Lucy studied the slowly passing landscape with a feeling of disorientation. She had been a frequent visitor to London the first thirteen years of her life, yet she had recognized virtually nothing as they had driven through it. She had not felt the sense of homecoming she had expected. Nothing seemed familiar. Not the fashions, not the impatient crowds that had jostled them at the coaching house, and certainly not the stench of the rotting refuse lining the streets.

"I'm sorry, Lucy." Vernon drew a thin, raspy breath and determinedly pulled himself out of her arms. "I didn't mean to complain."

"Nonsense." She lovingly pushed a strand of his damp hair off his pale forehead. "Complaining about the weather is an English tradition. And even if it weren't, I feel the same way." She gave an exaggerated shudder. "In fact, sometimes I think I'll never be warm again. Or completely dry," she added ruefully. "One day I expect to wake up and find myself washed out to sea."

"If that were to happen, you wouldn't have to worry about it because you'd be drowned," Vernon, ever the pragmatist, pointed out.

Lucy braced her feet against the precious strong-box at her feet as the driver carelessly turned the corner, throwing them against the worn leather side of the open carriage. She wrinkled her nose as the smell of mildew became stronger.

"Lucy, is all of England like this? So big and noisy and smelly?"

"No, it's just because London is a big city. Paris would probably seem the same."

"I don't like it," Vernon blurted out.

"Landsdowne, the Langford family seat in Derby-shire, is absolutely beautiful." Unconsciously, her voice softened. "By next month there will be flowers blooming everywhere and acres of green lawns, and the home woods will be full of nesting birds."

"If we go there, can I have a horse?"

"A horse?" Lucy repeated uneasily, her mind filled with a vision of Vernon's broken body lying bleeding on the cobblestones. Despite his almost-constant ill-nesses, he was absolutely fearless.

"A big, black one with a shiny coat like that one we saw in the stable yard at the inn this morning."

"You mean the one that first tried to bite you and then tried to kick you?" Lucy asked dryly.

"That's the one." Vernon nodded happily. "I like a horse with spirit."

"I'd like a horse with intelligence, but I fear the two concepts are completely incompatible," she said tartly.

"Does that mean I can't have one?" Vernon's thin face fell.

"No, it means that first you'll have to learn to ride on a pony, and then you can—"

"'Scuse me, miss, but this here be the address you asked for." The driver sawed on his ancient nag's reins, pulling him to a stop. His gaze swung from Lucy's tattered cloak to the imposing stuccoed mansion in front of them. It rose three full stories and was topped by a series of dormers punctuating the gray slate roof. The waning light was reflected off the leaded glass of the six-foot-tall windows that marched across each floor, but the heavy drawn curtains seemed to shut out the world.

Nervously, Lucy's eyes swung to the massive black door. She unconsciously breathed a sigh of relief when she saw that the brass lion's-head knocker was in place. As she'd hoped, her grandfather had not changed his habit of spending the greater part of the year in London. She wasn't going to have to drag Vernon into Derbyshire in search of him. But at least she could if she had to. She drew comfort from the thought of the remaining money securely pinned to her chemise. She had sufficient funds left to provide them with food and shelter for several weeks, thanks to the colonel.

For a second the image of his dark face floated through her mind. His eyes were narrowed and his lips compressed in anger at her theft. Lucy breathed a silent prayer of thanks that the man was safely in France and she need never see him again.

"Miss?" The coachman's voice grew sharper. "Is this where you're awantin' to be?"

"Yes." Lucy banished disquieting thoughts of the enigmatic colonel from her mind. Picking up the strongbox in one hand, she grasped Vernon's cold fingers in the other and urged him out of the carriage.

She stumbled slightly on the slippery cobblestones as she stepped down and fell against the filthy side of the carriage, adding yet more mud to her bedraggled cloak.

"Come on, Vernon." Lucy tried to sound more confident than she felt. When she'd pictured herself coming home, the image had always included the vision of her grandfather hurrying down the broad steps toward her with open arms and a loving smile. The reality of the house's cold, repelling dignity fell far short of her dreams.

Telling herself that she was being ridiculous, that her grandfather could hardly have spent the last twelve years watching out the window in case she might suddenly appear, she handed a coin to the jarvey, squared her shoulders and turned to face the house.

When it became apparent that Lucy wasn't about to add anything to the agreed-upon price, the coachman shook the horse's reins and moved off down the street.

Vernon inched imperceptibly closer to his sister as they climbed the eight marble steps to the door. His thin, triangular face was pinched with cold and sudden uncertainty.

"He will want us, won't he, Lucy?" His anxious voice pulled her out of her preoccupation. "What if he doesn't want us? What if—"

"Our grandpapa will be overjoyed to see us." The absolute conviction in her voice momentarily soothed his fears. "In fact," she added, "once he finds out about you, he'll probably kill the fatted calf."

Vernon's eyes widened. "I hope not. I like calves. Marcel and I used to ride the ones his father had. At least, we did until those soldiers came and took them away."

Lucy gave him a swift hug. "Oh, Vernon, I do so love you."

Taking a deep breath to try to slow down the frantic beating of her heart, she reached for the brass knocker. For twelve years she'd prayed for this day, and now that the moment was finally here, she simply wanted to get it over with. Swallowing nervously, she banged the heavy knocker.

Nothing happened. She was about to knock again when the door slowly swung open, to reveal a bent, elderly man who stared down the length of his oversize nose at them.

"The tradesmen's entrance is to be found in the rear," he said reprovingly.

"Dear Fulton." Lucy gave him a misty smile. "You promised me a box of bonbons when I returned. Where are they?"

"What?" He leaned closer and peered myopically at her. "Miss Danvers? Is that really you?"

"Yes, and not before time, wouldn't you say?" She laughed at the incredible pleasure of finally seeing a familiar face. "And I brought back a surprise with me. Vernon, I would like to make known to you the mainstay of Grandpapa's staff, Fulton. Fulton, this is my brother, the earl's grandson, come home at last."

"Grandson!" Fulton repeated in shock as he glanced past her into the deserted street. "Your father—"

"Died before Vernon was born, and Mama shortly afterwards."

"Such sad revelations." Fulton rubbed his cheek with gnarled fingers that shook. "But he would go off to foreign parts, and your mother loved him so, she wouldn't let him go alone."

"Yes," Lucy said grimly. Her mother had loved her father, and in the end that love had cost her her life. Things would have been far better for her, as well as for her children, if she had merely been fond of him and had allowed him to go digging up Roman ruins on his own.

"But what am I thinking of to be keeping you standing on the stoop?" Fulton cried, breaking into her unhappy thoughts. "Come in. Come in." He looked around indecisively. "I'll have a fire lit in the drawing room and then—"

"No," Lucy said. "First we'll see Grandpapa and then we'll have baths, followed by something to eat."

"I don't need a bath, Lucy," Vernon grumbled. "I'm already all wet."

"Now, now, my boy. Being unwashed is all well and good in foreign parts, but you're in England now," Fulton said. "We have standards here. Cakes, too, and macaroons and gingerbread men," he added cunningly.

"And bilious stomachs," Lucy added in resignation.

"Why don't I take the young master down to the kitchens with me for hot chocolate and cookies? There's a warm fire there," Fulton said persuasively. "And I'll keep a careful eye on him."

To protect him from what? Lucy instinctively examined the butler's words for hidden meaning and then told herself that she was being ridiculous. There was nothing here to harm Vernon. She was simply so used to weighing her every word that she was reading meanings into Fulton's that had never been intended.

But it might be a good idea for her to see her grandfather alone first, so that she could tell him about Vernon. She didn't want to risk him being disappointed at Vernon's frailty and letting the boy see it. Vernon was already very sensitive about his physical limitations. It would crush him to think that his unknown grandfather had judged him and found him wanting.

"Perhaps you should take Vernon below stairs for hot chocolate," she agreed, not even bothering to question the strange notion of entertaining the heir to the house in the kitchens. Lucy smiled encouragingly at Vernon, who nodded happily, clearly willing to go with anyone who would feed him.

"Where is Grandpapa, Fulton?" she asked. "In his study?"

"No." Fulton shook his head sadly. "The earl rarely leaves his suite these days."

Lucy felt a sudden clutch of fear squeeze her heart. For so long now she'd held onto the thought of her grandfather as a talisman, thinking that if she could just reach him, everything would be fine. But he wasn't some kind of magical charm. He was simply a man. An old man. He'd be seventy-four in the fall, she remembered with a sinking heart.

"Is he ill?" she asked fearfully.

"Not exactly," Fulton replied slowly. "It's more like he's just sitting in his room waiting for notice to quit. He took it very hard when you and your parents never appeared on any of the lists of political prisoners. Everyone thought it meant that that monster across the Channel had murdered you. But now that you've come home and brought the earl a grandson, things will be different. You'll see." Fulton smiled in anticipation. "This house will be happy again, and *she* won't be having everything her own way.

"Now, you run along upstairs to your grandfather—" Fulton changed the subject before Lucy could ask who "she" was "—and I'll take care of young master Vernon. Are you hungry, my boy?"

"I'm always hungry," Vernon replied in perfect truth.

"Isn't that the way of young lads?" Fulton gave him an indulgent smile and Lucy felt a flash of pain. If only the aging servant knew. Vernon wasn't talking about the usual hunger-between-meals of a normal child. He was referring to the bone-deep hunger that came from never having enough to eat.

Lucy waited until Vernon and Fulton had disappeared through the green baize door in the back of the hallway before turning toward the stairs.

Feeling light-headed with anticipation, Lucy slowly began to climb them. The earl's suite contained a huge composite of rooms at the back of the second story. All she could remember clearly about it was the night many years ago when her grandmother had lain dying in the huge carved bed and she had walked across what had seemed like acres of carpeting to kiss her cold cheek. It was not a place she remembered with pleasure, and she wondered fancifully if it was symbolic that she should be reunited with her grandfather in the same room where she'd said her final goodbyes to his wife.

She turned at the top of the stairs and started down the long corridor. The set of cream-painted doors leading to the master suite seemed to glow in the flickering light from the candles in the wall sconces beside them. After twelve years, she was finally home.

Her breath caught in her throat and she began to run, unable to control her impatience a moment longer.

Her fist beat a rapid tattoo on the door's paneling. It was opened almost immediately by a paunchy, youngish man, obviously a servant, who glared incredulously at her.

"Who are you and what are you doing here, girl?" he demanded, but Lucy ignored both him and his question. Her eyes had discovered the hunched figure of her grandfather in the wing chair beside the fireplace. His hair was now totally white instead of the iron gray she remembered, and he seemed smaller, somehow, and far more frail than the memory she'd comforted herself with all these years. But it didn't really matter. Nothing mattered but that he was her grandfather. He belonged to her with the unbreakable ties of blood and love and law.

"Girl!" The servant pinched her arm painfully and she turned to him in exasperation.

"Let go of me, you mannerless jackanapes!" she said impatiently, and he did, taken aback by her tone and manner.

"Grandpapa!" Lucy called across the large room to the old man, who had so far ignored the altercation.

At her single word, his head snapped around and his face went chalk white.

"Lucy?" Slowly, he got to his feet and took a hesitant step toward her. "My precious little Lucy, is that really you? I never thought I'd see you again in this life." A tear slowly trickled down his wrinkled cheek.

Lucy gulped and lurched into his outstretched arms.

"Oh, Grandpapa, I've missed you. I'm so glad to be home."

"Where you belong." He enfolded her in a tight embrace that belied his frail appearance. "When I get my hands on that dolt of a son of mine—"

"Grandpapa." Lucy stepped back and took both his trembling hands in hers. "I . . . Papa . . . He's dead," she finally blurted out.

"Dead?" The word escaped in a long sigh, and he sank back down into his chair as if his legs would no longer support him. "How?" he finally asked.

"He was on his way to try to arrange passage for us to escape France when he was murdered for the money he carried."

"Poor Vernon." The earl rubbed his forehead with a shaking hand. "He was so smart about some things and such a dolt about others. And your mother?"

"She died an hour after the baby was born." Lucy swallowed hard. Even after all these years the memory of that awful day still had the power to hurt.

"What?" The earl's head jerked up at her words.

Lucy smiled, pleased to be able to give him some good news. "Vernon Adolphus James. That was the reason Papa was so desperate to get us home—because Mama was increasing. He said she'd never survive the winter at the primitive farm where we'd sought shelter." She sighed. "He was right. Mama lived just long enough to give birth to Vernon and then she died."

"And the boy?" he demanded.

"Marthe and I raised him."

"He's alive? Where is he?" The earl shot to his feet.

"In the kitchen, eating."

"You there, Ware," the earl barked at the man who was standing at the door staring at them. "Quit gawking at your betters! Get yourself downstairs and bring up my grandson." There was a world of satisfaction in the last two words.

"Grandpapa," Lucy said slowly once Ware had left, "Vernon is rather... frail."

"You mean he's sickly?"

"Yes," she admitted, "but I'm hoping that here in England, he'll grow out of it."

"You don't look too stout yourself, girl. How bad was it?"

"It wasn't all that bad." Lucy saw no reason to burden him with something that was already over. Something that wasn't his fault. "There wasn't enough food, but Marthe shared what she had with us. Grandpapa, Marthe is an old woman and she needs—"

"Anything she needs or wants is hers for as long as she lives," the earl vowed. "I can never repay her for her care of you and the boy, but I intend to try."

"Thank you, and please do something for the curé, too. He tutored Vernon twice a week from the time he was three."

"Something for the priest, too," the earl promptly agreed.

"He and the lawyer and the doctor all wrote letters saying that Vernon was Mama and Papa's son. There's also a letter Papa wrote to you right before he was killed."

"I'll read it later," he said gruffly. "Don't you worry none. I'll take care of everything. That damned Freddy won't step into my shoes now," he crowed in satisfaction. "Won't this put Amelia's nose out of joint. Maybe enough so's that she'll leave." He looked hopeful for a moment. "Maybe she'll even take that watering pot, Kitty, with her. Lachrymose females are

the very devil to live with. You remember that, girl,"
he ordered.

"I shall restrain all impulse to become a watering
pot when you are in the vicinity," she assured him.
"And by the way, exactly who are Freddy and Kitty
and Amelia?" The names sounded vaguely familiar,
but her memory couldn't supply any specifics.

"Relations," he said glumly. "Poor relations. Even
worse, they're dirty dishes. They're Evelyn's brood."

"Evelyn?" Lucy searched her memory. "Your
brother Evelyn?"

"Half brother," the earl corrected.

"I don't remember much about him," she admitted.

"That's probably because he wasn't the kind of man
one talked to young girls about," the earl said bluntly.
"He was a loose screw, not to wrap the matter up in
clean linen. He capped a long and dissolute career as
a gambler by getting himself shot by an outraged
player who caught him cheating." The earl shook his
head in disgust. "He was a disgrace to the name of
Danvers, and the only decent thing he ever did was die
and leave us all in peace."

"And his family came here to live with you then?"
Lucy asked, wanting to find out all she could about
the people who lived in the house.

"No, they went back to Evelyn's estate in Kent,
where they belonged. Snug little property our father
bought him in the hopes he'd turn respectable." He
snorted. "No chance of that. No, Evelyn's brood bil-
leted themselves with me a few years back when it was
time to launch Kitty into the ton. Amelia wanted to do
it from here, since she didn't have a house in London." He grimaced. "Seemed a reasonable request. Of

course, at the time I had no more than a nodding acquaintance with the damned woman. Once she moved in, I couldn't get rid of her. Even tried going to Landsdowne for a few months, but when I came back, she was still here. Kept saying that they ought to stay since your father was probably dead and Freddy was my heir."

He scowled. "Some heir. A dandified park saunterer with more hair than wit. I can hardly wait until Amelia returns from Brighton and hears about this. She'll be livid."

Lucy had opened her mouth to ask more questions when she heard the hesitant shuffle of Vernon's footsteps in the hallway.

The earl turned toward the door, his face white and his nostrils pinched with the strength of the longing that gripped him. Lucy sent up a fervent prayer that he would like Vernon. She knew that he'd do his duty toward her brother. He had always done his duty toward his dependents and he always would, but she wanted more than that for Vernon. She wanted him to be loved. To know the indulgence of a grandfather who thought you were absolutely perfect exactly the way you were. She had known that kind of love and she desperately wanted it for her brother.

Vernon hesitated in the open doorway, his anxious features relaxing a little as Lucy smiled warmly at him.

"Vernon, this is our grandpapa."

"How do you do, sir?" Vernon gave an awkward bow.

The earl swallowed several times and then cleared his throat. "Wonderfully well now that you and Lucy have come home to me. Come in, boy. Come in and let me see you. And you, send for Potter." The earl di-

rected the last command at Ware. "Tell him he needs
to figure out how to get aid to an old woman and a
priest in France."

"A Catholic priest?" Ware sounded shocked.

"That's the way they come in France, fool!" the
earl barked. "Now, get out and do as you're told."

With a look of acute loathing at Lucy, which the
earl missed because he'd already turned back to Vernon, Ware stiffly left, brushing past Vernon as if he
weren't there.

"Don't hover in the doorway, boy. Come over here.
My eyes ain't what they used to be."

Vernon slowly crossed the room, lured closer more
by Lucy's happy smile than by the order. He eyed his
grandfather uncertainly. The earl was totally outside
his limited experience with people.

"The spit of his grandmother," the old man pronounced in satisfaction. "Same eyes, same mouth, but
I'll bet he's got my pluck. Game as a pebble, ain't you,
boy?"

Vernon shot Lucy an imploring glance, uncertain of
how to respond.

"And smart." The earl didn't wait for an answer.
"You speak French, boy?"

"Certainly! All civilized men speak French." Vernon unconsciously echoed the curé's imperious tone,
as well as his prejudice.

"Ha! Arrogant little beggar, ain't he?" The earl
slapped his thigh in pleasure. "Reminds me of myself
at that age. I was sickly, too," he told Vernon.
"M'father despaired of me living long enough to inherit. That's why he married the second time—to get
himself another son. And you see what came of it?"

"No." Vernon looked thoroughly confused.

"Relations," the earl said gloomily. "Dirty dishes. Every family's got them. The trick is getting rid of them."

"Relatives?" Vernon looked intrigued. "You mean I have cousins?"

"More than likely they'll have you. All your live-long life they'll be hanging on your sleeve."

Vernon laughed. "Much good that'll do 'em. I haven't any money. Although Lucy does," he added thoughtfully. "Lucy's got enough that we can live for weeks. Eat, too."

"You and your sister can eat to your heart's content," the earl assured him. "And when I'm dead, you'll be a very wealthy young man."

"Thank you, but I'd as lief you didn't die yet," Vernon said anxiously. "Lucy'll share her money with me, and I never had a grandfather before."

"Bless your heart. I ain't had a grandson before m'self, and I ain't going nowhere yet. And Lucy's got more than a few paltry weeks' living expenses. Your sister is a formidable heiress."

Lucy frowned at him. "I am?"

"Of a surety. Your mama's dowry was left to her daughters, and you're the only one, so the whole hundred and twenty-five thousand pounds is yours. And do you remember your great-aunt Agatha?"

"How could I forget her?" Lucy asked dryly. "Papa used to say she had the disposition of a hangman."

"Really?" Vernon's eyes widened apprehensively. "Does she live here?"

"No, she lives in hell, if there's anything in what that clergyman spouts every Sunday," the earl said. "She's dead. Two years past. Left her whole estate in trust for Lucy, despite Bevis's trying to turn her up sweet. She said Lucy was the only one of her relatives who resembled her.''

Lucy chuckled. "I think that was an insult. In fact, I'm sure it was.''

"Probably." The earl's pale blue eyes twinkled. "But she cut up to the tune of eighty-six thousand pounds, as well as a considerable estate near Bath. Make a tidy little inheritance for your second son.''

Lucy felt her heart skip a beat as for one appalling second an image of the colonel's dark features superimposed on a small boy floated through her mind.

"Lucy isn't married," Vernon told the earl. "She's an old maid.''

"Not that old!" She forcibly banished the image. "And I'll thank the pair of you to quit arranging my future. I shall see to it myself.''

"See that you do it quickly," the earl said gruffly. "Pretty little thing like you needs a husband to take care of you.''

"I can take care of myself.''

"Then you can manage your own funds, too," the earl said, surprising her. "I'll have our man of business explain your investments to you.''

"Investments?" she asked weakly, beginning to feel overwhelmed. Her idea of an investment was smiling at the greengrocer so that he'd give her the freshest vegetables.

"Investments," the earl repeated firmly. "I never held with this modern notion that women couldn't understand money. Your grandmama knew as much about my financial affairs as I did. Maybe more. You'd better learn, too. That way you don't have to worry about anyone cheating you. You remember that," he ordered.

"I will. Is there anything else I can do for you?" she asked dryly.

"Pour the tea," he unexpectedly answered. "We need our strength, don't we, boy?"

"Yes, sir." Vernon nodded happily.

"We really ought to tidy up first." Lucy eyed Vernon's dusty face.

"Ah, Lucy," Vernon moaned. "I'm so hungry. All I had time to eat in the kitchen were two pieces of gingerbread and a cup of chocolate."

"Growing boys need lots of food," the earl pronounced. "Come along with me, Vernon. We'll tell Fulton to fetch us the best tea ever. Lucy, you can tidy yourself in the Rose Room if you must, but don't be long." He took Vernon's hand and urged him toward the door.

Lucy watched them leave and then went to the Rose Room at the other end of the corridor. She hastily washed her face in the stale water from the pitcher at the washstand, not wanting to wait while fresh water was brought up. She smoothed back a few strands of hair that had escaped from her chignon and frowned at her reflection in the cheval glass, remembering the last time she'd been in this room. It had been the night before they'd left for France, over twelve years ago. The face that had looked back at her from this same mirror had been younger, rounder and infinitely more trusting.

She bit her soft lip, deepening the pink color. She was only too aware of how much she'd changed over the years, but, somehow, she'd never given any thought to the fact that the people she'd left behind would have changed, too. It had simply never occurred to her that someone else might consider himself the earl's heir. She pressed her fingers to the bridge of her nose to try to dissipate the pain that was beginning to build behind her eyes.

For twelve years her every conscious thought had centered on the problem of getting Vernon home to England, and now that she'd finally done it, it appeared that her troubles weren't entirely over. There was still the problem of her cousin Freddy's blighted hopes for the earldom and his mother's anger.

Lucy straightened her shoulders. It was nothing she couldn't handle. If she could manage to keep herself and Vernon alive behind enemy lines for twelve years, she could certainly manage to soothe the ruffled feathers of a few importuning relatives. After all, even if she failed, there wasn't much they could do to her, she assured herself.

Chapter Four

Eager to show off her new finery, Lucy slipped through the half-open library door and glanced around the huge room, looking for her grandfather. She could just see the top of his white head above the green brocade wing chair, which faced the blazing fire. Vernon was sitting on the chair's arm with his back to her, his thin legs dangling over the side.

Lucy felt immense satisfaction at the trusting way Vernon was leaning against his grandfather. In just ten days a young boy starved for masculine attention and an old man desperate for a direct heir had developed a genuine liking for each other. A liking that Lucy had no doubt would, in time, deepen into love.

She walked across the thick Aubusson carpet, her silk slippers making no sound on the thick pile.

"What are you two finding so fascinating?" she asked, and then chuckled at their startled expressions when they turned and saw her.

"Lucy?" Vernon hopped off the arm of the chair and came closer to better study her appearance. "What happened to all your hair, and where did you get that dress? You don't look like yourself," he said, not sounding at all sure that he approved of the change.

"The hairdresser cut it. He said that this style is all the crack." Lucy self-consciously patted her short, tousled curls. She hadn't really had to hear the man's exclamation of delight to know that the style suited her. The curls softened her thin face and seemed to make her eyes even bigger. "And as for the dress, Madame LeFarge delivered part of my new wardrobe this afternoon." She twirled around, making the thin, blue silk skirt stand out. "I am complete to a shade."

Vernon frowned, looking for an instant like a disapproving father. "Where's the rest of your top?" He gestured toward the deeply scooped neckline—a neckline that had, in fact, caused Lucy a few qualms. But the dressmaker's assurance that the décolletage would, in fact, be considered moderate by the ton had reassured her somewhat.

"It's the fashion, m'boy," the earl said. "All the women wear their gowns like that. Your sister looks better than most. She looks like some sapscull poet's idea of a Greek goddess."

Lucy dropped a graceful curtsy. "If that was a compliment, dear sir, I thank you."

"All you need is a little more flesh on your bones. You're too skinny by half. The pair of you." He gave Vernon a possessive hug. "But we'll soon fix that, won't we, boy."

"I'll eat lots and lots," Vernon promised happily. "Lucy, did you know that I am the Viscount Langford? Grandpapa has a paper that says so." He gestured toward the thick sheet of vellum in the earl's hand that they'd been studying when she interrupted them.

"It's his christening certificate," the earl said with satisfaction. "The Archbishop of Canterbury issued it today. No doubt about who his parents were now. Not that I thought there'd be any trouble once I saw how his father handled the verification of the boy's birth." The earl chuckled with malicious glee. "Just wait till tomorrow."

"Tomorrow?" Lucy frowned uncomprehendingly. "What happens tomorrow?"

"Your aunt and her brood come back from Brighton. Back to a very different kettle of fish than when they left."

"I thought she wasn't due back for another week," Lucy said, feeling a prickle of unease.

"She wasn't, but she sent me a letter today. With postage due on it," he complained. "Just like her clutch-fisted ways. Said she had heard the most extraordinary rumors and was coming back to assure herself that they were unfounded."

"What's a 'strodinary rumor?" Vernon asked.

"You, m'boy." The earl cackled gleefully. "You are."

"I am?" He looked confused.

"What you are is the last of a long line of male Danvers, all of whom appear to be possessed of an unfortunate sense of humor," Lucy said tartly.

"Don't you dare turn Methodist on me, girl," the earl ordered. "I'm entitled to gloat a little. If you knew what I've had to put up with over the years form that woman and her brats..."

"Is she nasty?" Vernon looked worried.

"She sounds more silly than nasty," Lucy said reassuringly, hoping it were true. "We shall avoid her."

"You will not!" the earl barked. "This is still my house and it'll be the boy's after me. If Amelia doesn't like it, she can leave. It's not as if she has nowhere to go. Has a life tenancy at Freddy's place in Kent, and her widow's jointure. No call for her to stay here and make us all miserable."

"Perhaps not, but I think you ought to give her a chance to adjust first." Lucy tried to be fair. "She has suffered a major disappointment, and she is a close relative."

"Never lets you forget it, either," the earl grumbled.

"You don't want people saying you threw her out after she was kind enough to manage your home all these years, do you? It would be bound to reflect badly on Vernon and me." Lucy tried an argument that she thought he might accept. She wasn't sure exactly why she was defending a woman she didn't know and who would be bound to resent her and Vernon, but she herself had suffered so much in recent years that she didn't want to be the one to cause suffering in someone else if it could possibly be avoided.

"A damned poor job she made of running my home, too. Just didn't realize it when I spent most of my time in my suite." He glanced around the dusty library in disgust. "I pay for an army of servants. You'd think she could at least make sure they did their jobs."

"Perhaps the responsibility is getting to be too much for her," Lucy said soothingly, wondering about his so-called army of servants. From what she'd seen in the last week, the house was decidedly understaffed.

"Could be. She was complaining about how hard she had to work the very day she left for Brighton." The earl gave Lucy an innocent look that immediately put her on her guard. "And that being the case, it's our Christian duty to help her. You can take over management of the household."

Lucy blinked. "Me? I don't know how to run an establishment this size."

"Nothing to it," he said with a masculine arrogance that Lucy found exasperating. "You'll pick it up in no time. Nothing flighty about you. And it will be good practice for when you marry," he persisted.

"Marry?" Vernon's eyes widened apprehensively. "Are you going to get married, Lucy?"

"Not for years yet," Lucy said soothingly. "And it will be to someone you like."

"But will he like me?" Vernon looked worried.

"Certainly he will. You're a very likable boy. I like you. Marthe likes you. The curé likes you. Grandpapa likes you. Why shouldn't my future husband like you? Besides," she added more practically, "if he doesn't, I won't marry him."

"Ah, an independent woman!" The earl shook his head in mock sorrow. "It's an unnatural thing."

"Never mind the state of my mind. I'm more worried about the time. We're going to be late for this dinner you insisted I attend with you."

The earl looked surprised. "Of course, we'll be late. No one but cits and mushrooms are ever on time."

"Do you have to go, Lucy?" Vernon's tone was perilously close to a whine. "I don't like to stay by myself."

"What? A great boy like you, afraid?" the earl demanded.

"I'm not afraid," Vernon corrected. "I'm lonely, but I wouldn't be if I had a dog."

"Course not, you'd have fleas for company," the earl said.

"Maybe I could come with you tonight?" Vernon suggested.

"Children don't go to dinner parties. In fact, in the normal way of things, nobody under fifty ever goes to Chuffy's dinner parties. He's a dull old dog. Always reminiscing about the past and running down the government."

"But Lucy's only twenty-five," Vernon pointed out.

"True, but there's an excellent reason for Lucy to come tonight." The earl gave her a secretive glance that put Lucy forcibly in mind of Vernon planning some mischief. She felt a distinct twinge of apprehension. She was already nervous about her first foray into the polite world of the ton. The fear that her grandfather was planning something didn't help her frame of mind. She stifled a sigh. He really was a dear and she loved him, but he seemed to have a fixation on finding her a husband as soon as possible. She couldn't seem to make him understand that she didn't want the responsibility of marriage at the moment. Right now, all she wanted to do was to spend a few years with no more pressing concerns than what to order for dinner and how to cope with Vernon's latest start.

"The carriage is outside, my lord." Fulton spoke from the doorway.

"Thank you, Fulton." The earl got to his feet. "Come along, Lucy. There's a nasty wind blowing out there. Don't want to keep the horses standing."

"But—" Vernon began.

"Go to bed in ten minutes." Lucy gave him a hug.

"Ah, Lucy." He wiggled out of her grasp. "I'm too old to be hugged."

"Ha! A man's never too old to be hugged by a pretty girl," his grandfather corrected him. "Now mind what your sister said."

"I will," Vernon grumbled as they left.

"And remember that no matter how misinformed the other guests' comments are about the course of the war, you are not to tell them so," James Standen ordered. "And whatever you do, don't mention Prinny's extravagances or the Princess Caroline or old George's fits or—"

"Perhaps it would be better if you just dropped me off at my club?" Robert suggested without any real hope that his father would agree.

"Nonsense. Do you good to hold your tongue. You always were too outspoken. Your mother's fault. Thought the sun rose and set in the pair of you."

"While you, of course, were a monster of discipline," Robert said dryly.

"I tried," James defended himself. "But not much good came of it, what with your mother always cosseting both her sons. See what it leads to. No respect for your betters."

"Betters! My dear sir, allow me to inform you that the Standens have no betters." Robert imitated his uncle Herbert's gruff tones to a nicety.

James chuckled. "Good old Herbert. But never mind your sauce, boy. Herbert was right. The Standen name is one of the best in the land, and you have a duty to it now that Gervais is dead."

"Yes." Robert's clipped response held a volume of frustration and grief at his brother's senseless death.

"I miss him, too," James said gruffly, "but that doesn't change the fact that the line ends with you. It's your duty to marry and fill a nursery. You promised."

"I know," Robert said resignedly, feeling that youthful promise weigh heavily upon him. It should never have had to have been redeemed, he thought with an irrational flash of resentment toward his brother. If Gervais had married one of the many young women who had wanted to marry him, his father would now be indulging his grandsons and he would be in France with the army where he belonged. And where he would infinitely prefer to be. After five days spent attending a series of insipid social events, he was fast reaching the conclusion that this season's crop of young beauties didn't have a rational thought among them. How his father expected him to survive being leg-shackled to one of them... He shuddered at the very thought of being forced to share the rest of his life with a woman whose idea of conversation consisted of a nervous giggle, an incredulous "la, sir," or a blank stare.

His eyes narrowed as he suddenly remembered the soft luminescence of the deep blue eyes that had belonged to the woman in France. They hadn't been blank. They'd been lustrous and dreamy after he'd kissed her. Full of secrets. Secrets he was never going to be able to delve into, he thought in frustration.

"It won't be so bad, Robert," his father insisted.

"If the women I've met this past week are a fair sampling, it'll be worse," Robert contradicted him. "Maybe I should save us both a lot of time and effort and simply let you pick out my bride."

"Self-pity does not become you."

"Sorry, sir," Robert apologized, recognizing the legitimacy of his father's reprimand. "I'm simply blue-deviled this evening, but I'll do the polite, I give you my word. What hopeful chits are we looking at this evening?"

"No one at Chuffy's. He doesn't know any interesting females. Leastwise, none that you could introduce to your mother."

"Really?" Robert's eyes widened in surprise. His father's old friend, Lord Chuffington, had always seemed like the very model of moral rectitude.

"Never mind old Chuffy's peccadilloes. It's the rout we'll attend afterwards that should have lots of young hopefuls vying to catch your eye."

"Good Lord!" Robert looked horrified. "Does everyone know I'm looking to become a tenant for life?"

"Don't be a fool, boy. Your brother dies unwed and you immediately sell out and come home? Do you think they figure you've come to support me in my old age?" James snorted. "Of course they know what you're about."

"Damnation!" Robert swore succinctly.

"They're even taking bets about who the lucky bride will be. Odds in the clubs are leaning heavily towards old Grafton's daughter."

"Grafton's daughter?" Robert frowned. "I don't remember her."

"That's because you haven't met her. But you will. The family's in the basket, and Grafton's got her up for bids. From what I hear, she's a diamond of the first water. Some man'll have to come down heavy for her. Grafton probably figures you can afford her."

"I plan to marry an orphan," Robert said emphatically.

"You can marry anyone you want. Just do it quickly. I want to be dangling my first grandson on my knee by next Whitsuntide."

Robert sank back against the carriage's soft leather squabs, feeling hounded. But he knew his duty and he'd do it—no matter how painful he found the experience. Standens did not shirk their responsibilities, he reminded himself for at least the hundredth time since Gervais had died.

"Blanche will never find a husband for that branfaced daughter of hers," the plump Lady Denton gleefully assured Lucy.

"It's not like she had a decent dowry," Mrs. Peckenridge, who was seated on the other side of Lucy, agreed. "The family's all to pieces."

"How sad," Lucy murmured, not sure what kind of response was called for. She had no idea who these women were, nor did she know any of the people whose characters they'd been assassinating ever since they'd joined her ten minutes ago. The only thing she was certain of was that she didn't want to be here on the couch, trapped between them. Hating someone for good reason she could understand, but such generalized spite seemed incomprehensible to her.

"Sad?" Lady Denton stared at Lucy in astonishment. "Ebsen gambled the family fortune away at faro."

"Deep basset," Mrs. Peckenridge corrected.

"Then he deserves to suffer," Lucy said, "but I fail to see how his daughter is to blame. Yet it's her life that will be blighted by his imprudent behavior. One would have thought he would have had more sense."

"He's a man," Lady Denton said flatly. "They seldom show any sense. Not that you will have to worry." She tittered, and the sound grated annoyingly on Lucy's already tense nerves. "Not with your dowry. Why, I heard that it is in excess of a hundred thousand pounds." She gazed avidly at Lucy.

"Did you?" Lucy had no intention of satisfying the woman's curiosity. She found such prying vulgar in the extreme. In fact, she was beginning to think that her neighbors in the village in France had far better manners than the English aristocracy. They were certainly much kinder.

"Not that you'd have to worry, anyway," Lady Denton said enviously. "Not with the old earl's fortune." She tittered again. "Amelia is going to be so upset to have lost it for Freddy. To say nothing of poor Kitty."

Lucy bit her lip on the acid rejoinder she wanted to make. She was determined to behave with perfect propriety and she would. No matter what the provocation.

"For you to suddenly reappear, and with a little brother, too... Who does he look like?" Mrs. Peckenridge probed.

"Grandpapa swears he's the image of Grandmama." Lucy ignored the innuendo she suspected was there. "I think he looks more like Mama, particularly around his nose and eyes." She cast a harried glance around the large room, looking for her grandfather. He was standing by the fireplace, talking to a short, pudgy man in a snuff-stained neckcloth. How long would it be before dinner was announced and she could escape from this pair of old tabbies? she wondered, casting another furtive glance round the room.

"He isn't here yet." Mrs. Peckenridge misread her survey of the assembled crowd.

"He?" Lucy looked blankly at her. "Whom do you mean?"

Lady Denton tapped Lucy's arm with her ivory fan. "La, child, no need to dissemble with us. Only makes sense, you wanting to get a look at the best catch of the season. Be a perfect ninnyhammer if you didn't."

"I would?" Lucy asked, still having no idea whom they were talking about."

"Yes, indeed." Mrs. Peckenridge nodded her head in agreement. "My sister Trixie's husband's cousin was there when it happened, you know."

"No, I didn't know," Lucy finally said, since some type of reply was clearly expected.

"Yes, indeed," Mrs. Peckenridge repeated. "Helped to carry him home on a gate. Such a shock, for Gervais to be thrown like that. He was always such a bruising rider. Sad business, that." She shook her head.

"True," Lady Denton agreed. "Gervais was well liked. Fine old family. Rich enough to buy an abbey."

"I heard from my husband that old Standen sent for Robert before Gervais was even in his grave."

"Quite true." Mrs. Peckenridge nodded emphatically. "No title, of course, but they're one of the most respected families in England. Came over with The Conqueror, you know."

"It's a shame that Gervais couldn't have broken his neck last year," Lady Denton repined. "My Felicia would have been absolutely perfect for Robert."

"How very inconsiderate of him, to be sure," Lucy commiserated with a straight face.

"Quite. Not but what she didn't do very well for herself. She married a viscount, you know," Lady Denton related.

"How nice," Lucy murmured, wondering how any parent could judge the worth of a husband by his title and bank account and not by his character.

"Yes, Felicia—"

"Mr. James Standen and Colonel Robert Standen," the butler's voice intoned over the murmur of conversation.

Lucy turned toward the door, grateful for a respite from what passed for conversation with this pair. Her relief was short-lived. A tall, stocky man, his dark hair heavily streaked with silver, was greeting his host. The father, Lucy correctly assumed, and glanced behind him, curious to see the man at the center of so much gossip.

Her attention was momentarily caught by the intricate folds of his snowy white neckcloth before her eyes moved upward, to widen incredulously as the lines and planes of the man's formidable face suddenly formed a recognizable whole.

It couldn't be! Her heart began to beat with a rapid, heavy cadence and the air in her lungs seemed to be expanding, making it difficult for her to breathe.

No! Her mind screamed the denial. It couldn't be the soldier from the inn. It just couldn't.

Hastily, she dragged her gaze away from his features to the floral carpet at her feet, focusing on a tiny stain just above a yellow flower petal. It wasn't really him, she tried to tell herself. It was just her guilty conscience making her think she saw him.

She counted to ten, then forced herself to raise her head. To her horror, she found herself staring straight into a devastatingly familiar pair of coal black eyes, which were studying her with a puzzled curiosity but as yet no recognition. Her stomach lurched as she faced the inescapable fact that Robert Standen and the colonel she'd propositioned and then stole from were one and the same person. She felt like flinging herself down on the carpet and railing at the unfairness of a capricious fate. The man who had provided the means for her to get back to England was going to be the very same man who would destroy her new life.

Apprehensively, she glanced over at her unsuspecting grandfather. He was smiling unconcernedly at something one of the men had said. What would he do when Robert Standen denounced her as little more than a prostitute? she wondered in despair. That she wasn't one in fact as well as in intent was due only to the fight in the taproom. Not because she'd thought better of the idea.

She frantically tried to formulate a plan of action. What could she do? Pretend to have the headache and go home? No, she reluctantly discarded the idea. It would do her no good to run. She faced the unpalatable truth. London society was a closed world. Unless she intended to become a hermit, she would frequently be thrown into the colonel's company. There was nothing to do but to carry on as she was and pray that he didn't recognize her.

And if he did... She swallowed nervously. Not only would her grandfather's pride be devastated, but he'd blame himself for not having somehow rescued her. The knowledge of her social ruin would eat away at him, destroying his newfound happiness and his frail health. And the shame…! Lucy cringed inwardly. She knew she'd survive the gossip. She'd learned that one could survive almost anything if one had to. But her proud grandfather was quite another matter. Lucy gnawed on her lower lip. He'd never live down the public scandal. Not only might it kill him, it would follow her brother all of his life.

Perhaps she could appeal to Robert Standen's better nature… She stole another glance at him, but couldn't seem to get beyond the thrust of his jaw. He didn't look as if he had a better nature, she thought in despair. Or, if he ever had had one, it had been beaten out of him long ago by the horrors of war.

As she watched with a kind of helpless fascination his eyes meet hers again, narrowed and then suddenly opened incredulously. Lucy watched him turn to the woman next to him, who was simpering up at him in a most disgusting manner.

Robert said something to her and she turned and looked speculatively at Lucy before replying at some length.

Lucy couldn't hear what was being said, but she didn't have to. She knew that the woman was telling him all about the earl's long-lost grandchildren's miraculous return from France. There was no way he could fail to make the connection, she thought with a sort of fatalistic calm.

She lifted her chin. Since flight was impossible, she'd face him with the same grim determination she'd shown during her long years in France. Danverses didn't lack courage, she reminded herself. Intelligence, maybe. Luck, definitely, she thought with a flash of black humor, but they didn't lack courage. As her grandfather was fond of saying, they were pluck to the backbone.

The butler's voice announcing dinner interrupted her frantic conjectures, and Lucy forced herself to smile as her grandfather hurried over to escort her into the dining room.

"Enjoying yourself, my dear?" The earl studied her pale face with concern.

"Oh, yes," she lied. "It's just that it all seems so strange."

"It won't for long," he promised encouragingly. "Why, by the end of the season, it'll be like you'd never left England."

Lucy merely nodded. If he needed to believe that, she saw no reason to disillusion him, even though she knew it wasn't true. France had changed her. It had made her aware that life was a far more serious matter than the superficial, pleasure-seeking existence it was for the Lady Dentons of the world. Lucy knew that she could never be satisfied by an endless round of parties and gossip.

"I noticed that Robert Standen couldn't seem to take his eyes off you," the earl said in satisfaction.

If only you knew the reason, Lucy thought, biting back an hysterical urge to laugh. "Oh, which one was he?" she finally said.

"Minx, I saw you studying him when you thought no one was watching," the earl teased. "Do you want me to introduce him to you?"

"No! No," she repeated more softly, at the earl's surprised expression. "I think I need a little more town bronze before I'm ready to converse with such a paragon. Tell me about the little man you were talking to,

the one who looked like he'd been dipped in snuff,''
she said, changing the subject.

"Old Margate? It was a real shock to see him. Lord,
I thought he'd been put to bed with a shovel years ago.
I'm not sure where the time's gone." He shook his
head in disbelief. "I seem to have lost contact with
everyone. But I'll get out more now that I have a
beautiful gel to squire about."

He beamed at her, and Lucy smiled weakly back,
feeling a surge of guilt and despair at the pride in his
eyes. When he found out...

She shot a furtive glance at Robert, to find his cold,
dark gaze fixed on her. How long would it be before
he acted? And what form would that action take? She
swallowed uneasily. It seemed as if she were in France
all over again, at the mercy of forces she couldn't
control or even fully comprehend.

Her answer didn't come until well after dinner,
when the men finally rejoined the women in the
drawing room. With the vague intention of protect-
ing her grandfather, Lucy immediately went to sit next
to him.

At first Robert seemed to be ignoring her, but then
Lucy slowly became aware of the fact that each of the
conversations he engaged in served to move him closer
to where she was sitting.

She was forcibly reminded of the time the creek at
the bottom of Marthe's garden had flooded. Hour by
hour the water had risen, with an inexorability that
couldn't be denied. Nothing they tried had diverted it.
Robert was stalking her with that same relentless inevitability. Finally, when her nerves were stretched to
the breaking point, he reached the group she and her
grandfather were part of.

"Ah, Colonel Standen," the earl said, greeting him warmly, "allow me to make known to you my grand-daughter, Miss Lucy Danvers." The pride in his voice made Lucy feel faintly ill. "She just escaped from France, you know."

"No good ever came of visiting foreign places," Chuffy pronounced. "Englishmen belong in England."

Lucy barely heard the old man through the drumming of blood in her ears. Please, God, not here, she prayed. Don't let him say anything here in front of Grandpapa's friends.

"Good evening, Miss Danvers." Robert's deep voice held no more than the normal interest good manners dictated, and for a brief moment Lucy relaxed. Then he extended a hand to her.

She stared at it with the same fascination of a rabbit faced with a stoat. The last time she'd seen that hand it had been stroking her cheek, and she'd been mindless beneath the onslaught of pleasurable sensation it had caused.

The startled look on her grandfather's face at what he must consider her farouche behavior jarred her into some semblance of normalcy. Fatalistically, she gave Robert her hand.

It was a tactical mistake, she realized a second later, as the warmth from his fingers permeated her skin and skittered over her nerve endings.

Robert Standen wasn't going to have to denounce her, she thought grimly. Her bizarre comportment was going to tell everyone here that there was something between them. The thought made her stiffen her spine, and she managed a credible smile, though her eyes rose no farther than the cleft in his chin.

"Good evening, Colonel Standen," she managed to get out in a constricted voice.

"Yes, it is." His voice deepened imperceptibly.

Lucy tugged her fingers free and risked a peek upward into his watchful eyes.

"All this must seem very strange to you," he said.

"When I left England, I was still in the schoolroom, so it's merely new to me," she answered in the same polite vein, trying to read some significance into his question, but failing.

"You must find your granddaughter very changed after all these years?" Robert said to the earl, and Lucy felt a chill of fear feather over her skin at where his questioning might be headed.

"No," her grandfather said slowly, "not really."

Robert gave Lucy a practiced smile that didn't reach his eyes. "You must allow me to take you for a drive tomorrow, Miss Danvers, and we can compare our impressions of France."

"Thank you, but I promised my brother—"

"Nonsense," the earl said gruffly. "You go out and enjoy yourself, girl. I'll keep Vernon amused. Going to take him to see the menagerie at the Tower."

Her grandfather beamed at her, leaving Lucy with no option but to accept Robert's invitation. A bald refusal would lead to the very kind of speculation she was trying to avoid. It was clear that Robert Standen was determined to talk to her. Or, more likely, to rip her morals and her character to shreds. At least this way there wouldn't be any witnesses to his harangue. And maybe, just maybe, once he'd vented his anger he would leave her alone, she thought with a flash of hope. That hope wavered as she looked up into his night-dark eyes and saw the memory of what had happened between them burning there.

The colonel was not a man who would be easily dissuaded from his goal. The question was, what was his goal? Was it to simply tell her what he thought of her, or did he have a darker motive? Did he want revenge for what she had done?

Chapter Five

Lucy pushed the slice of gammon to one side of her delicate china plate and stared blankly down at the congealing flecks of fat through eyes that felt gritty from lack of rest. She'd spent the night tossing and turning, hoping for the oblivion of at least a few hours' sleep, but hadn't found it. Her frantic thoughts had kept her awake. And despite a night of worry about her dilemma, she hadn't been able to come up with a single idea for handling it.

She glanced out through the breakfast-room windows at the bright sunlight. Morning had not improved her perspective on the situation. Although a great deal of the reason that she hadn't been able to plan was because she didn't know what she was planning for, she admitted. She didn't know what Robert Standen was going to do. All she knew for certain was that he was angry. She shivered at the memory of his hard, unyielding face.

Perhaps after their ride this afternoon, when she had a clearer idea of what he intended to do, a counteroffensive would occur to her. Although...

She bit off an exclamation at the circular nature of her thoughts. She was simply going over and over the same ground without changing anything, except that each time she did so she became a little more frantic and her head hurt a bit more. At this rate, she'd be too ill to go for a ride at all.

Lucy brightened for a moment at the thought of a respite, before reluctantly rejecting the idea. If she refused to accompany the colonel, he might very well ask to see her grandfather.

She rubbed her aching forehead. That was a situation she wanted to avoid at all costs. She wanted her grandfather to be able to enjoy his new grandson as long as possible before he was forced to recognize just what price had been paid for his return.

"May I get you something else, Miss Danvers?" Fulton asked. "A muffin, perhaps?"

"Umm, thank you, no." Lucy smiled weakly at him. "I'm not very hungry this morning."

She checked the face of the small clock on the ornately carved marble mantel. "Has my grandfather rung for his breakfast tray yet?"

"No. He's still asleep. If I may say so, we below stairs are very pleased with how much better he looks since you and the young master have come home. That proud he is of you and the boy."

"Thank you," Lucy muttered, wondering how much time she had until the ax fell, severing that pride.

"Where is Vernon? Not out in the stables again, I hope?" she added anxiously.

"No, Miss Danvers. The viscount said he was going to have a battle with the lead soldiers up in the day nursery." Fulton smiled benevolently. "Apparently, he is in the final stages of working out a strategy Wellington can use to utterly defeat Napoleon."

"Good. That should keep him occupied," she murmured, suddenly remembering that her aunt and cousins were to return today. In the horror of rediscovering the colonel, she had completely forgotten about them. And there was something else... She frowned.

Mr. Potter, her grandfather's man of business! she finally remembered. Today was the day that he was to explain her inheritance to her. For a moment she was tempted to cancel the meeting, but she finally decided against doing so.

Not only would it help to fill her morning, but it was an event she could deal with—competently. And success begat success, she reminded herself. It had been one of the curé's favorite sayings.

Lucy determinedly straightened her shoulders. She'd cope with Mr. Potter this morning, and maybe it would be easier to cope with the colonel this afternoon. In the meantime, she would not dwell on the upcoming ordeal. Not only was doing so totally unproductive, it was making her headache worse.

"Fulton, I'm expecting Grandfather's man of business soon. When he arrives, would you direct him to the book room?"

"Of course, Miss Danvers, and there is no cause for concern." Fulton misunderstood her worried expression. "Mr. Potter is a gentleman by nature if not by fact."

While the opposite could be said for her nemesis, Colonel Standen, she thought grimly.

"Thank you, Fulton." Lucy took one last sip of her tepid coffee before leaving the breakfast room. She was crossing the entrance hall when she heard her name being softly called from above.

Pausing, she glanced up and saw Vernon's thin face peering down at her over the top of the railing on the third floor.

"Lucy! Guess what I am getting?"

A putrid throat, from the sound of it, she thought uneasily. "Why are you whispering?" she asked.

"Because I'm being quiet. Ware said that Grandpapa was still asleep and I was not to wake him."

"That's very thoughtful of you, and stop leaning over the railing like that or you will fall," she warned.

"Ah, Lucy, don't fuss. I can't fall. The railing is too high. Did you know what Grandpapa said yesterday?" he asked, and then rushed to answer his own question. "He said that we could go to Tattersall's this afternoon and buy me a pony. For my very own. To ride," he added, in case she hadn't properly grasped the significance of what he was saying.

And to fall off of, Lucy thought with an inward sigh. But she kept her worry to herself. She knew she couldn't keep Vernon wrapped up in cotton wool. She had to let him grow and explore his new world. She herself had learned to ride when she was a lot younger than he was now and had been none the worse for the experience, she reminded herself.

"I'd ask you to come with us, but ladies can't go to Tattersall's. Just us men," he added gleefully.

"Well, you men . . ." Lucy frowned as she heard a cracking sound that reminded her of rifle fire in the distance. A sound that had been heard with frightening regularity around the village in the past dozen years. She peered out through the narrow, leaded windows beside the front door, but the street was deserted at the unfashionable hour of eleven o'clock.

"Lucy!" Vernon's panicked voice echoed above her, and she glanced up, freezing at the sight that met her eyes. As if time and motion had slowed to a veritable trickle, she watched in helpless horror as the section of railing Vernon was leaning over bowed outward. Numbly, her mind registered her brother's terrified expression as she ran forward with the half-formed idea of trying to break his fall.

"Watch it!" A young girl's voice came from somewhere behind Vernon, and suddenly he was jerked backward, to disappear from sight as the railing broke loose at one end and swung precariously out into space.

The overwhelming sense of relief that engulfed Lucy made her feel light-headed, and she took several deep breaths in a vain attempt to slow her racing heart. She lifted her green silk skirts and hurried up the wide staircase, arriving at the third floor out of breath. She found her brother sitting on the worn carpet looking scared.

"Vernon!" Lucy gasped his name, torn between a desire to hug him because he was unharmed and an equal desire to smack him for frightening her so badly.

"I didn't mean to break it," Vernon yelped, hastily defending himself. "I didn't do anything but lean over it. Ask her." He gestured toward the young servant girl, who was nervously twisting a corner of her dirty apron between chapped fingers.

The girl ducked her head and mumbled, "I be Maggie, the tweeny, and it be true, ma'am. Him didn't do nothing. It just broke, all by itself."

"So I saw." Lucy smiled reassuringly at the maid. "We are indebted to you, Maggie. If it had not been for your quick thinking..." She shuddered at the horrible image of Vernon's broken body lying on the marble floor three stories below.

Maggie ducked her head in embarrassment. "It weren't nothin'. I was just up here emptyin' the chamber pots."

"Be that as it may, I shall not forget the debt," Lucy repeated. "And both of you, stay away from all the railings until the carpenter can check them over. Who is our carpenter?" she asked Maggie, intending to first tell him exactly what she thought of his slovenly work habits and then to dismiss him.

"That'd be Old Trimble," Fulton wheezed, arriving in time to hear her question.

"Sit down," Lucy hastily ordered the man, worried at his beet-red face. He was far too old to be racing up three flights of stairs.

"I'm fine, m'lady. Just a little short of breath." He sagged against the wall. "And this—" he gestured toward the gaping hole in the railing "—is not Trimble's fault. Leastwise, I suppose you *could* blame him for dying," he finished reflectively.

"The estate's carpenter died?" Lucy cut to the heart of the matter.

Fulton nodded. "Ten years ago come summer."

"And no one was hired to replace him?" she asked incredulously.

"No. The earl said that as far as he was concerned the whole—" Fulton cleared his throat, obviously censoring the quote "—house could tumble down around his ears before he would spend so much as a groat to repair it for that gapeseed."

Lucy frowned as she tried to relate what he was saying to what she already knew. "The gapeseed in question being my cousin Freddy?"

"Yes, the earl is not overly fond of his nephew." Fulton massively understated the case.

"I see. Would you please contact a reputable builder and have him repair the railing? At once. Then have him check over the entire house and make any repairs the two of you decide are necessary."

"Certainly, Miss Danvers. It shall be my first priority." He straightened up and adjusted his coat.

"And Fulton," Lucy said, "I see no reason to disturb the earl with what just happened."

"No, Miss Danvers, it would be a shame to worry him about something we can so easily handle ourselves. Come along, girl." He waved Maggie toward the back stairs.

"You aren't mad, are you, Lucy?" Vernon asked with an apprehensive glance at the broken railing. "It really wasn't my fault."

"I know." She tousled his silky brown hair, resisting the impulse to hug him. Vernon hated to be fussed over. "It was just an unfortunate accident, and as I told Fulton, I think we should avoid mentioning it to Grandpapa."

"Oh, no," Vernon agreed fervently. In his experience, adults tended to react to accidents in the strangest ways, and he didn't want to do anything to jeopardize the promised trip to Tattersall's this afternoon.

"I think I'll go back to my battle plans." He escaped before his sister could change her mind.

Lucy watched him disappear into the playroom with a feeling of relief tinged with frustration. It was ironic that after all the dangers they'd faced in France, the worst threat to Vernon's life had come once they were safely back in England.

In retrospect, it was beginning to seem as if France hadn't been quite as bad as she'd always thought. At least there the enemies had been clearly recognizable and the dangers predictable. She sighed as she headed back downstairs to the book room to await the arrival of her grandfather's man of business.

Mr. Potter arrived promptly. He was a plump, well-dressed, middle-aged man with a patronizingly avuncular manner that grated on Lucy's already raw nerves. She detested being treated like a half-wit simply because she was a member of the so-called weaker sex. From what she'd observed over the years, women needed the emotional fortitude of an ox in order to pick up the pieces after men created mayhem in the world with their eternal wars.

Fortunately, Mr. Potter was also a very astute man, and it took only one sharp setdown and several searching questions about her inheritance from her aunt Agatha for him to decide that perhaps the earl had known what he was about when he'd decreed that his granddaughter was not only to have the unrestricted use of her income, but was also to be allowed to draw freely on his own account to run the household.

His answer to her question about sums that had been allotted during each of the last twelve quarters to her aunt for household expenses was met with an incredulously raised eyebrow, although, to his relief, she didn't make any comment. Mr. Potter knew full well that the amounts paid would have been generous in a ducal household that entertained extensively. He'd long had his suspicions that Mrs. Danvers was diverting the money for her own use, but despite those suspicions, he had no desire to voice them. He'd learned early in his career that families tended to stick together, and even when they didn't, few people thanked you for pointing out that they were credulous fools. And since, like everyone else, he'd assumed that Mrs. Danvers's son, Freddy, would be the next earl, common sense had told him that he would be dismissed the minute Freddy inherited if he were so foolish as to accuse his mother of theft. Everyone knew that Freddy did exactly as she ordered.

But now, the earl's long-lost granddaughter, with her hitherto unsuspected brother, had come home to change everything. Suddenly, Mrs. Danvers was no longer in an impregnable position. He wished he could be a fly on the wall when this thin slip of a woman with the earl's sharp mind and tenacious determination faced the blustering Mrs. Danvers. Mentally, he rubbed his hands together in glee. For his part, he'd lay his blunt on Miss Danvers. From what was being said below stairs, the old earl fair doted on her and her brother. And everyone knew that he despised his sister-in-law.

It was with the hopeful thought that things might now improve in the earl's home that Mr. Potter finally gathered up his papers to leave, shortly after two.

Lucy was also in a sightly more positive frame of mind as she courteously thanked him for his patience and help. Her resources had gone from a handful of stolen bills to a respectable fortune by anyone's standards. She might still have the problem of Colonel Standen hanging over her head like the proverbial sword, but she was able to draw some comfort from the fact that she and Vernon and Marthe would never want for material things again.

Hoping to keep her mind off her upcoming interview with the colonel, she began to list things in the house that needed attention. She was only partially successful, and was about to try something else when she heard a loud, querulous voice out in the hallway.

She frowned. Her aunt had undoubtedly arrived and, while Lucy was not looking forward to the meeting, she had no intention of trying to avoid it. Some problems were best faced head-on, and she had the disheartening feeling that her aunt came under that category. Besides, she encouraged herself, this was her and Vernon's home, not her aunt's. According to the earl, her aunt had a perfectly good home of her own in Kent. If the woman wished to be unreasonable, she could go home and do so.

Pasting a welcoming smile on her face, Lucy opened the book-room door in time to hear her aunt demand to know where the adventuress calling herself Lucy Danvers and her baseborn brat were.

Lucy hung on to her determination to be polite with a supreme effort. She closed the book-room door behind her with a decided snap and slowly allowed her eyes to wander over her aunt's bulky frame, which was incongruously upholstered in a shiny, purple satin material. Glittering diamond drops hung from her ears, while three diamond brooches decorated her well-padded bosom. The total effect was one of too much money married to too little taste.

Amelia returned Lucy's scrutiny, seeming to find no pleasure in her niece's bottle green crepe de chine silk dress with its flattering Bishop sleeves. The woman opened her mouth, but before she could say anything, Lucy spoke.

"Good afternoon. You must be my aunt Amelia. I'm Lucy Danvers."

"So you say!" Amelia blustered. "How dare you come here and—and..." She sputtered to a stop as words failed her.

"You will find, my dear aunt, that I dare most things," Lucy said with a surface calm that was very thin. She didn't like acrimonious exchanges, but she wasn't afraid of her aunt. She had seen far too much of the seedier side of human nature not to recognize Amelia Danvers for exactly what she was: a selfish, greedy, grasping woman who might hate her, but who lacked the ability to do her any real damage because she had nothing Lucy wanted or needed. Nonetheless, Lucy felt a certain sneaking sympathy for her. It must be galling in the extreme to leave for a fortnight in Brighton thinking your son was heir to a wealthy earldom and come home to find out that he'd been dispossessed. If they were ever to reach any kind of understanding, then Amelia would have to learn that Lucy would not be bullied. And the sooner she learned it, the easier it would be on everyone's nerves.

"Kitty, my hartshorn!" Amelia moaned. "I feel faint." She began to fan herself agitatedly with one pudgy hand.

"Yes, Mama." The colorless voice issued from behind Amelia, and Lucy glanced curiously at the cousin she barely remembered. Kitty would be about twenty-three now, she realized, although she looked ten years older. Her light brown hair had been cut short and frizzed into a mass of tight curls, which made her plump cheeks appear fat. What little color had been in her pale face was leached out by the funereal black traveling outfit she wore.

"Here, Mama." Kitty uncorked a crystal bottle and waved it under her mother's quivering nostrils.

"I am going to faint." Amelia uttered the words like a threat.

"Please don't, Mama," Kitty said. "I couldn't carry you to the couch and Willie couldn't, either." She smiled gently at the bootboy, who'd opened the door for them and remained to watch the show with open-mouthed wonder.

"And that's another thing." Amelia's faintness disappeared in her outrage. "Where is Fulton?"

"I sent him on an urgent errand," Lucy said.

"You dared to send my butler away from his post?" Amelia exclaimed in an awful voice. "You dared—"

The doorbell interrupted her in midtirade and she turned to direct her fury at whatever hapless soul had been misguided enough to intrude.

"You! What do you want?" she demanded of the pudgy young man standing on the doorstep.

He frowned in obvious confusion and then looked over his shoulder to see if, perhaps, there wasn't someone else there.

"Don't want nothin'," he hastily disclaimed, once he'd realized that the question was, in fact, aimed at him. He handed the bandbox he was carrying to the footboy. "Live here, you know," he added, as if to clarify the matter.

"Not for long!" Amelia struck a dramatic pose worthy of Mrs. Siddons. "She—" Amelia jabbed a quivering finger at Lucy, who was hard-pressed to keep from laughing. Her aunt had obviously missed her calling. She'd been born to trod the boards at Drury Lane. "—She has come to usurp you."

Freddy considered the matter a moment and then said, "Can't have. She's a female. Ain't no such thing as a female earl. My brain-box might not be tight, but even I know that."

"Quite true," Lucy said cheerfully. "I take it you are my cousin Freddy?"

"That's right." Freddy glanced furtively at his mother and then gingerly accepted the hand Lucy held out to him.

"The problem is not her! It's that brat she calls her brother!" Amelia snapped at her son, who merely hunched his shoulders and looked miserable.

"My brother's claim to the earldom has already been verified. I'm sorry if it upsets your plans, but as our father's only son, Vernon is next in line to inherit," Lucy said flatly.

"She's right, you know." Freddy nodded ponderously. "Son does inherit from his father. Learned it at school."

"You are a dolt!" Amelia raged. "A bigger fool I have yet to meet."

"Mama—" Kitty began placatingly.

"Never claimed to be one of the cleverish sort like Oliver," Freddy insisted, with a mulish set to his mouth. "Ain't my style...at all."

"Unfortunately, we can all see your style." The earl's blighting tones brought the confrontation to an abrupt halt.

"I want to speak to you." Amelia recovered first from her surprise at seeing the earl out of his rooms. "This..." She gestured impotently at Lucy.

"I presume you are referring to my granddaughter?" the earl drawled. "Why, Amelia, I'm surprised at you. With your professed love of family, how could you have forgotten such an important member?"

"I've yet to be convinced that she really is Lucy Danvers," Amelia snapped.

"But then, it isn't necessary that she convince you, is it?" The earl's gentle voice in no way hid the steel beneath it. "Only I and my solicitors need to be convinced. And if we're satisfied, who are you to cavil?"

"Who am *I?*" Amelia's voice rose in frustration.

"Now, Mama," Kitty soothed, with a nervous look at the earl's tightening lips.

"I—" Amelia began.

"I beg your pardon for intruding, but the door was left ajar." Robert Standen's deep voice came from immediately behind Amelia. "Have I interrupted something?" His speculative gaze wandered over the suddenly silent tableau of people, all of whom were staring at him.

Lucy was strongly tempted to tell him yes. That he most certainly was interrupting something—her life and her peace of mind. But she didn't dare. She couldn't let her aunt catch even the slightest whiff of scandal or the woman would ferret out the whole story. Nor did she want Robert to know just how much she feared the disclosures he might make. The knowledge would only add to his power over her.

"Certainly not, Colonel." The earl beamed at him. "You're welcome twice over. For your sake as well as your father's. We were simply welcoming Amelia and her brood back from Brighton. Very vulgar of us to do it in the hall with the door open for any passerby to gawk at us, but the emotion of the moment overcame us."

Amelia studied Robert, her gaze lingering on the tailored perfection of his tightly fitted morning coat of Spanish blue. Her eyes narrowed speculatively as she caught sight of the single ruby nestled in the folds of his snowy white cravat.

"I don't believe we've been introduced," Amelia said, with a commanding look at her son.

Lucy stared at her aunt in surprise. The acrimonious exchange of a moment ago might never have happened. Now she was all polite-society matron.

"No good to look to me for an introduction," Freddy hastily disclaimed. "Don't know him." He eyed Robert's muscular build with a nervous eye.

The earl heaved a sigh and said, "Mrs. Danvers, make known to you Colonel Robert Standen. Colonel, Mrs. Danvers, my sister-in-law," he added, as if the relationship pained him.

Lucy watched in amazement as her aunt's pudgy features were suddenly wreathed in a smile.

"Colonel Standen, of course." Amelia beamed at him. "Your dear mama and I were bosom bows the year of our comeout. I had heard that you would be returning from the Peninsula to comfort your father in his hour of loss, but I didn't know that you'd already arrived."

"His loss, too." Freddy unexpectedly spoke up. "Only makes sense," he added, when everyone stared at him. "He's a member of the family. If his father had a loss, stands to reason he did, too."

"Quite true, Cousin Freddy," Lucy finally said, when everyone else merely continued to stare at him.

"This jokesmith is my son." Amelia shot Freddy a glare that promised retribution later. "And this is my daughter, Mrs. Kitty Whitney." Amelia tugged the shrinking Kitty forward.

Charmed was the only word that Lucy could clearly make out from Kitty's muttered reply to Robert's polite acknowledgment.

"Come into the drawing room, Colonel, and have a cup of tea with us," Amelia urged.

"Some other time, Mrs. Danvers. Miss Danvers is promised me for a drive in the park," Robert said.

Lucy fatalistically accepted her cloak from the helpful bootboy. "Shall we go then, sir? You won't want to keep the horses standing in such a brisk wind," she said, eager to get Robert away from both her aunt and her grandfather before he inadvertently or on purpose said something to make them suspicious.

Superstitiously, she touched the wad of bills she'd hidden in the inner pocket of her gown. Please, God, let him accept the return of his money and an apology, she prayed. Please don't let him ruin our new life.

"Why, a drive is a wonderful idea," Amelia enthused. "This spring air is positively invigorating."

"Eh?" Freddy stared at her in confusion. "No such thing. It's damned cold out there. Said so yourself. Complained about it all the way from Brighton," he finished triumphantly.

"Now, Freddy, no more of your funning." Amelia's laugh sounded forced. "A drive is exactly what Kitty needs to clear away her megrims. I'm sure she'd love to go with her cousin and the colonel."

"No, I wouldn't." Kitty seemed to shrink visibly.

"Delightful though the idea is, I'm afraid that my curricle only seats two," Robert said coolly.

"Only two?" Amelia managed to invest the words with all sorts of sordid insinuations. "As Lucy's chaperone, I'm sure I couldn't allow—"

"Oh, cut line, woman!" the earl snapped.

To Lucy's relief, Robert opened the door for her before Amelia could respond, and she hurriedly slipped outside. Being alone with the colonel might be fraught with hidden dangers, but at least there was only one of him and she knew exactly what she was facing. Back in her grandfather's house there was a horde of people, all with their own causes to advance.

Lucy scrambled up onto the high curricle seat without waiting for Robert Standen to assist her. She didn't want him to touch her. For some reason, the feel of his warm, callused fingers against her smooth skin made it difficult for her to think. It was not a sensation she liked. Losing control was dangerous, both to herself and to those who depended on her. And yet Robert Standen made her do it so very easily. For some reason, all of her careful plans came to naught the minute he appeared. And the frightening thing was, she didn't know why. All she knew was that it had to stop.

Lucy arranged her silk skirt around her feet, then cast a cautious eye toward the groom, perched in the elevated seat behind her. How could she broach the subject of what had happened in France with his eager ears there to drink in every word? The tale would be all over town by nightfall.

She watched with a reluctant admiration as Robert vaulted into the curricle with the grace of a natural athlete. Lucy braced her feet against the floorboards as his action tipped the seat toward him. She had a brief glimpse of a blue-clad sleeve as he reached behind her to take the reins from the groom before the faint fragrance of sandalwood teased her nostrils.

He competently threaded the black leather reins through his tanned fingers. Within seconds, he had the horses under perfect control. As he probably had most things in his life, she thought uneasily.

"I won't need you for the rest of the afternoon," Robert told the groom, tossing him a coin. It glittered brightly for a second in the afternoon sunlight before the man caught it with a grin.

Lucy waited until he had jumped down and headed toward the corner. "Colonel Standen—" she began slowly, as Robert guided the spirited animals into the light traffic around Grosvenor Square.

"So formal, and under the circumstances, too," he said dryly.

"Yes, the circumstances." Lucy made no attempt to deny knowing his meaning.

"Were unique."

"For me, perhaps," she said wryly, "but, somehow, I doubt that they were for you."

"Spirit." He gave her a mocking smile that made her long to smack him. "I like that in a woman. Or a horse," he added mendaciously.

"Your likes and dislikes are of no concern to me, sir."

"I hope you'll reconsider." His firm lips lifted in a smile that deepened the feeling of impending disaster that had dogged her since the moment she'd seen him standing in the doorway last night. "It wouldn't bode well for our future relationship."

"We aren't going to have a future relationship," she said, praying it was true. "Any more than we had a past relationship."

"How soon you forget," he said, with a sorrowful look that was belied by the wicked gleam of amusement in his eyes. "I must endeavor to be more memorable in the future."

"My dear Colonel Standen—"

"Now that's a promising start." He nodded encouragingly.

"I..." She had to swallow her hasty rejoinder as they passed within a foot of an open carriage, and a middle-aged woman gave Robert a beaming smile. To Lucy's relief, he didn't stop the curricle to speak, as the woman clearly wanted him to.

"Smile at her," Robert murmured softly, "or she'll have it all over London by nightfall that we were arguing."

"That story would at least have the saving grace of being true, which is more than can be said for most of the gossip I was entertained with last night," Lucy said tartly.

"I couldn't say. The main topic of conversation in the group I was in was you. How the earl's long-lost granddaughter had miraculously escaped from the French and returned, bringing back a hitherto unknown brother with her."

"Vernon isn't the least bit unknown. It was only the English aristocracy that was unaware of his existence and, contrary to the ton's beliefs, they do not constitute the whole civilized world. Or even the most important part of it."

Robert chuckled at her annoyed expression. "Have your years in France turned you into a Republican?"

"No!" Lucy said vehemently. "The revolution brought that Corsican adventurer to power, and whatever else the Bourbons might have been, they resisted plunging the whole country into an endlessly bloody war.''

"It isn't going to be endless. Our English soldiers are about to put a finish to it, while I'm tied here in London, listening to a lot of clodpolls who know nothing about the war tell me what the army is doing wrong."

"Don't let me keep you here." Lucy smiled sweetly at him.

"You aren't the problem, although you're part of the solution.''

"Were you a cryptographer for the army?"

He frowned uncomprehendingly at her. "No, why?"

"Because while your words are all part of the English language and I understand each one individually, taken as a whole they don't make any sense.''

"I was in the cavalry.''

Lucy smiled blandly at him. "That explains it. You were kicked in the head by a horse.''

"I must have been, to be about to do what I'm going to do, and all because of a promise." He glared at her.

"You have my sympathy,'' Lucy said truthfully. "Promises can be the very devil to keep. And, if you don't, you feel guilty.''

"Which is precisely why I intend to do this.''

Lucy stared blankly at him. "Do what?'' she finally asked.

"Marry you, of course.'' He smiled gently down into her shocked face.

Chapter Six

"Marry you!" Lucy stared at him in astonishment.

"Very good." Robert Standen gave her a condescending smile that infuriated her. "You seem to have grasped the basic concept. What a comfort it is to know that you aren't lacking in intelligence."

"Unfortunately, I cannot take similar comfort. You must be all about in your head if you think I'd marry you!" Her tone was all the more vehement, because for one wild moment she'd actually been tempted. Tempted by the memory of his arms holding her tightly against his hard body. By the recollection of his warm lips trailing liquid heat over her quivering skin.

Lucy swallowed uneasily as her breathing shortened and a flush heated her pale skin at the evocative memories. Then she emphatically denied them. The feelings Robert had aroused were dangerous. Indulging them could lead to her submerging her own personality in his. It could lead to love, and that could lead anywhere. It had led her mother to France and her death in a tiny stone cottage.

No, love was a cleverly baited trap that she wanted no part of, Lucy thought grimly. Not with Robert

Standen or any other man. When she married, as she undoubtedly would, it would be to a man she respected but was able to keep at an emotional and mental distance.

"I realize that a show of maidenly modesty is considered de rigueur in these matters, but all things considered, I think you can dispense with it," Robert said, breaking into her thoughts.

"I am not being modest. I am stating a simple fact. I will not marry you."

"Why?" he asked, as he turned the carriage into Hyde Park. To Lucy's relief, this early in the afternoon it was populated mainly by nursemaids and their charges. His unexpected proposal had left her much too agitated to try to exchange polite conversation with curious strangers.

"Because I do not want to get married," she finally said.

"Is it the married state in general you object to or is it me in particular?" he asked, still in that calm voice that Lucy mistrusted. She would have expected him to be angry at her flat refusal to fall in with his plans, but he seemed more curious than annoyed. Somehow, her conversations with this man never seemed to follow the direction she'd decided upon beforehand, as they did with other people. He always managed to divert her from her chosen path.

"I'm sure you would make an unexceptional husband," she said carefully. She didn't want to be totally frank, for fear of making him angry enough to strike back. She shivered. Something he could do with devastating accuracy because he knew her secret.

"Then it must be the married state you hold in aversion," he concluded. "One wonders why? It cannot be that you object to the physical intimacies involved. You seemed quite taken with them, as I remember.''

"Be quiet!" Lucy glanced around, afraid someone might overhear him. Fortunately, no one was near.

"My nanny always said, 'Tell he truth and shame the devil.'"

"An entity I am sure you have more than a nodding acquaintance with," Lucy was goaded into retaliating. "I have refused your kind offer, and as an officer and a gentleman you should now accept my response and change the subject."

"What strange ideas you have of the conduct of officers and gentlemen," Robert marveled. "I must remember never to allow you to be alone with one after we are wed."

"We are not going to be married." Lucy carefully enunciated each word.

"It says little for our future harmony if you persist in contradicting me. Has no one ever told you that men have a superior intellect?"

"Than what? Their horses? Never mind," she rushed on when he opened his mouth. "If your intellect is so superior, it can surely understand the word no. And I want to return home."

"You're simply nervous," he said, making no attempt to turn the carriage. "You must marry sometime. So why not to me? Can it be that you haven't been in London long enough to find out just how wealthy I am? Or how much wealthier I'll be when my father dies?"

The cynical edge to his voice unexpectedly made Lucy want to comfort him. To tell him that he had much more to offer a woman than just money. That he was also well-favored physically, quite intelligent, and that he seemed to have a purpose in life, unlike most of the idle young men she'd met since her return to London. But she firmly stifled the impulse. She couldn't allow herself to begin to worry about him, she reminded herself. Robert was a threat to her future as well as to her grandfather's health. The thought stiffened her resolve.

"Have no fear, Colonel. Your fame—or perhaps I should say your infamy—has gone before you. I was regaled with your life history, your enormous financial worth and your reason for selling out and returning to England in the time it took for you to be announced and to greet your host. However, since I do not need your money and don't want your hand..."

"Actually, I had the impression while I was kissing you that you wanted a great deal more than my hand." His eyes gleamed wickedly as they slowly traveled down over her flushed cheeks to focus on the soft swell of her breasts beneath her clinging cashmere cloak.

Lucy took a deep breath as a strange sensation swirled through her. She could feel her breasts begin to tingle, and the sensation frightened her. What was it about this man that affected her so? she wondered in confusion. She didn't even like him overmuch.

"No," Robert continued with satisfaction, "that part of our marriage will present no problem."

"I have the money." Lucy tried a different tack, pulling the roll of bank notes out of her reticule and shoving it at him.

Robert raised his eyebrows in mock surprise. "My dear, I know nothing of the ideas you picked up in France, but in England it's not necessary to pay one's husband to do his duty."

Lucy gritted her teeth together and counted to ten slowly. She would have felt much better if she could have treated his attempt at levity with the contempt it deserved, but she didn't quite dare. She simply didn't know him well enough to predict how he might react. Finally, she unclenched her jaws and said, "I am very sorry for what happened. And being sorry, I want to return the money to you that I—"

"Stole," he finished.

"I did not steal it," Lucy insisted. "I simply borrowed what I needed."

"You stole it," he repeated. "What I find curious is that you did not take it all."

"I took what I needed. But I'm not a thief," Lucy insisted, trying to make him understand.

"Certainly not a common one," Robert agreed. "Tell me, why did you not simply ask for help in getting home?"

"I had already tried that. The commander said I'd probably learned English as the mistress of some Englishman," she said bitterly. "That's what gave me the idea of—"

"Embarking on a life of prostitution."

"It wasn't like that," Lucy muttered.

"I know," he conceded, surprising her. "While you were being regaled with my matrimonial prospects, I was receiving all the details of your triumphant return from France with your young brother."

"I am fast coming to the conclusion that London society needs something to fill its time," she said tartly, hating the thought of complete strangers discussing her.

"They already have something. Gossip," Robert said dryly.

"I meant something constructive. There's certainly plenty of scope. I have never seen so many beggars since I came to England. In France, we helped each other."

"We do in villages here, too," Robert said. "It's only in the anonymity of the large cities that people turn their heads to another's plight. But as much as I would like to discuss economic and social reform with you, I have an appointment in—" he pulled his watch out of the fob pocket of his flowered silk waistcoat "—forty-five minutes, and I want this settled. I shall insert a notice of our engagement in the *Morning Post* and we will be married at the end of the season," he decreed.

"This may have escaped your notice, Colonel Standen, but you are no longer in the army, and I was never under your command."

"On the contrary, my dear, you most assuredly were under me," he purred. "And very delightful I found the experience, too."

Lucy closed her eyes and tried to picture the serene statue of the Virgin Mary that stood in the village church back in France. Robert Standen might have no notion of proper conversation between a gentleman and a lady, but she did, and she refused to descend to trading insults, no matter how clever the innuendo. Besides, she thought with a flash of grim humor, he seemed to be so much better at it than she was.

"You can't want to marry me. You hardly even know me." She tried logic, since a flat denial wasn't working.

"I don't want to marry anyone," he agreed. "Women have their uses, but they have a distressing tendency to become dead bores within a month."

"Probably a reflection of the company they keep."
Lucy gave him an impossibly innocent smile.

Robert ignored the gibe. "I promised my father that
I would marry, and sire children to continue the line."

"Children are in the hands of God," Lucy pointed
out.

"God helps him who helps himself," Robert countered piously. "And I wish you would cease interrupting me. It is not a desirable trait in a wife."

"How fortunate for you that I am not going to be
your wife."

"If you refuse to marry me, I shall inform your
grandfather of exactly why it is imperative that we do
so. At once." With military directness, he aimed for
her most vulnerable point.

"You can't." Lucy felt a cold chill feather over her
skin at his implacable expression. Robert looked absolutely pitiless. "Grandfather is an old man and he
hasn't been well. If he knew how I got the money to
travel home..." She shivered at what the shock might
do to him.

"I can and I will." Robert refused to allow himself
to be swayed by the fear he could see in her eyes. He
wasn't threatening her with lies, he told himself, salv-
ing his uneasy conscience. It was the truth. Every word
of it. And she was going to have to marry sometime;
all women of breeding and fortune did. It was the only
avenue open to them. So why not here and now to
him? He'd be a good husband. Once she'd provided
him with the heirs he needed, she could go her own
way.

He wouldn't interfere with her life. Much. And he'd
be the one to introduce her to the delights to be found
in bed. He shifted restlessly as he remembered the soft

yielding sound she'd made when he'd kissed her. That was the only good thing about having to saddle himself with a wife, he thought. He would be able to make love to Lucy Danvers. This time without any interruptions.

"But..." Lucy twisted her fingers together as she tried to think of an argument that might sway him. "But you can't want to marry me," she finally blurted out, "not after what I did."

"On the contrary—" he lightly flicked her cheek with his forefinger, and the scent of his leather driving glove filled her nostrils "—that's a point in your favor. Several, in fact."

"What?" She stared at him. "Are you daft, man? I propositioned you!"

"In order to save your brother, which shows loyalty. Not a common trait among women."

"Or men," she muttered, thoroughly confused by his response.

"It also showed a great deal of ingenuity and perseverance," he continued. "All traits I want in the mother of my children."

"Vernon." Lucy latched onto the thought of her younger brother. "I can't marry you. Vernon needs me."

"I have no objection to his living with us, although I suspect your grandfather might," Robert said. "His every second sentence last night was about the boy."

"And Grandfather won't want me to marry so soon."

"Wrong. He all but asked me last night if I wanted to marry you. I told you I'm a very eligible *parti*." He gave her a smug smile.

Lucy's conciliatory manner slipped substantially under the maddening impact of his smile. "If you want to live long enough to redeem your promise to your father—"

"Delightful as exchanging witticisms with you is, I must point out that we have arrived at your home." He pulled the horses to a stop. "And while I hesitate to bring your aunt's vulgar manners to your attention, she is watching us from behind the curtains."

Lucy glanced up at the sitting-room window in time to catch a glimpse of her aunt's face before it moved out of sight. "She's probably worried about my reputation," she said, trying to smooth over Amelia's snooping.

"No, she's probably worried that you might manage to leg-shackle me before she can figure out how to nab me for her daughter."

"That's absurd! She doesn't even know you."

"She knows my income," Robert said cynically. "I'm a realist. I know what's important to a vast number of women. I could be the greatest villain unhung and it wouldn't matter. My fortune and my name would make me respectable to even the highest sticklers."

"You're not a realist, you're a cynic," Lucy protested.

Robert studied her for a long moment, his expression enigmatic. "And you are a rather strange mixture," he finally said. "So practical about some things and so naive about others. I'm quite looking forward to initiating you into the workings of society. Among other things." His lips lifted in a sensual curve that sent a shiver of awareness through her body.

"No!" She raised her voice in repudiation of her feelings. "I do not want to marry."

"Neither do I." He transferred the reins to his right hand and picked up her hand with his left, closing his fingers around hers. His possessive gesture filled her with a confusing mixture of emotions.

"So why should we each marry someone else and make two other people unhappy?" he asked whimsically.

Lucy bit her lip as she tried to come up with a reason that he would accept. Time, she finally decided. She needed time. In time, surely she could come up with a convincing argument. But she had to stop him from making a formal announcement in the meantime, because once they were officially engaged, they were as good as married.

"I need time," she said, trying not to sound as desperate as she felt.

"Time for what?" He gave her a long, thoughtful look.

"Time to get used to the idea. Time to—to become better acquainted," she finally said. "I know virtually nothing about you. Come to that, you don't know me, either."

"I know that behind your fragile blond exterior lies a very determined, very intelligent and, I suspect, a very passionate woman. I will not be manipulated, Lucy."

Robert's voice hardened, and she barely repressed a shudder. She was so vulnerable on so many fronts. Vernon, her grandfather, her own reputation... The world of the *haute ton* was the world she was going to have to live in, and it was a very unforgiving place to those who flaunted its rules, no matter what the reason. If Robert Standen revealed to anyone what she had done in France, society would close its doors to her. Her life here would be over before it ever began, she thought bleakly. Not even her grandfather's wealth and title could salvage her reputation.

Robert watched the fear chase across her features, and a sense of impatience shook him. Why was she carrying on so? He was offering her marriage and all the money she could ever want. So why wasn't she jumping at the chance? Every other woman he knew would be. But then, Lucy Danvers was not at all like the pampered, spoiled beauties who filled the drawing rooms of his father's friends. Lucy was a unique creature: very feminine, with the more masculine virtues of loyalty and intelligence. He wanted her for himself. And he would have her, he vowed. But it might not be wise to push her too far too fast, he realized, reining in his sense of impatience. She was already under a great deal of pressure. Maybe he should loosen the trap a little, while she adjusted to the idea.

"Tell me, how much time do you need?" he asked.

"Just until the season is over," Lucy hurriedly suggested. "Just one season, to help Vernon adjust to his new life, and to allow me to begin to feel at ease in society. Then I can begin to think about the future."

"You don't need to think about the future. As your husband, I'll see to it," he said. "However, I can sympathize with your desire for time to become better acquainted with me."

"Oh, but..." Lucy began, and then fell silent, realizing that she could hardly say what she truly thought. That in her opinion, they already knew each other far too well.

"Therefore, I will court you during the season, and we shall announce our engagement once it is over."

Lucy stared blankly at the horse's shiny flank as she considered his offer. It wasn't what she wanted, but, on the other hand, it circumvented an immediate engagement. This way she had several months to convince him that she would make him a terrible wife. At the very least, she had gained a reprieve.

"Thank you," she finally murmured, and then hastily scrambled down from the carriage, knowing he couldn't stop her without his groom there to hold the horses' reins. She didn't care if he thought her rag-mannered or not. At the moment her only concern was escaping from him, so that she could fully consider this latest threat to her future.

"Thank you for the drive," she said over her shoulder as she reached for the door knocker.

"The pleasure was all mine, Miss Danvers." Robert's infuriating chuckle followed her through the door, which Fulton had opened immediately.

Just you wait, Lucy thought. He might have the upper hand at the moment, but she had bested him once before and she would again, she vowed, as a feeling that bordered on anticipation flooded her.

"Did you have a nice drive, m'lady?" At her grim expression, Fulton looked uncertain.

"Yes, thank you." She smiled at the old man. She didn't want him saying anything to her grandfather that would lead to awkward questions, which would in turn lead to lies on her part. She stifled a sigh. When she'd arrived in England, she had thought her days of lying were over. But it appeared they weren't. Her love for her grandfather and her fears for her own future happiness had enmeshed her in a web of deceit, and

God only knew where it would lead. As long as it didn't lead to the altar...

"I had a lovely drive in this glorious spring weather," Lucy elaborated. "Have the earl and Vernon returned from Tattersall's yet?"

"No. The young master said he intended to examine every single pony for sale to make sure he found the right one," Fulton said indulgently.

"Then I think I'll go to my room for a while. Would you please have a pot of tea sent up?" Lucy started toward the stairs, only to stop at Fulton's cough.

"No tea?" she asked.

"Oh, no, not that. It is just that Mrs. Danvers expressly requested that I ask you to join her in the drawing room when you returned."

"After I have tea," Lucy said, feeling she needed to recover from her encounter with Robert Standen before she faced her aunt. She didn't know what Amelia wanted, but, brief though her acquaintance with the woman was, she was willing to bet that it would be a trying interview.

"She said immediately," Fulton reported unhappily, giving Lucy a shrewd idea of who would bear the brunt of her aunt's anger if she did not comply. "And your cousin Bevis is here," he added as inducement.

"Does he live in London?" Lucy asked curiously.

"Yes. He has a bachelor's establishment in St. James Street. He comes by every week or so. The earl is always glad to see him."

Lucy chuckled. "Then Bevis must have changed a great deal. I remember a grubby little schoolboy with a penchant for playing nasty tricks."

"Boyish pranks," Fulton corrected gently. "I'm sure he would be pleased to renew your acquaintance."

"And I his." Lucy was curious to see what kind of man Bevis had turned into. As the only surviving grandchild of the earl's only sister, he had received frequent invitations to stay at Landsdowne during school holidays. Only four years younger than he, Lucy remembered him as a boy whose pockets had always been full of wet, slimy things and whose goal had seemed to be to make her life miserable. She had always breathed a sigh of relief when he had left, although her parents, particularly her father, had not shared her aversion to him, she remembered. They had seemed quite fond of him.

Lucy paused in the doorway of the drawing room and glanced around. Her aunt and Kitty were sitting on a sofa, facing the man across from them. Lucy had no trouble recognizing the boy in the man, even though Bevis's once-plump cheeks were now lean and his chin more pronounced. His gleaming chestnut hair was arranged in the Brutus style and his Egyptian brown morning coat and fawn-colored trousers were fashionable, without adopting any of the extremes that her cousin Freddy seemed to favor.

Bevis glanced up, and she caught a glimpse of speculation in his brown eyes.

"You must be my cousin Lucy." He rose. "What a pleasure it is to see you again after all these years." He smiled warmly at her, and Lucy found his undemanding approval soothing after the unnerving encounter with Robert Standen.

"You must think me remiss in welcoming you back," he continued, "but I only returned to London this morning and found the story of your miraculous escape on everyone's lips."

Lucy smiled as she gave him her hand. "Hardly an escape. The English troops simply drove Napoleon's soldiers out of that part of France, leaving Vernon and I free to go. Which we did before the fortunes of war could turn again." She deliberately tried to make their return sound commonplace. She didn't want anyone asking questions, the answers to which might prove embarrassing.

"But surely it must have been more exciting than that?" Bevis sounded disappointed.

"Not unless you consider traveling with a young boy who is constantly carriage-sick exciting," Lucy replied.

"Don't be disgusting," Amelia snapped, "and sit down. It's rude to loom over people."

"Many things are rude, Aunt Amelia." Lucy refused to be intimidated. She had already suffered one defeat today, at Robert Standen's hands. She wouldn't allow herself to be bullied by her aunt.

"Vernon was very excited about buying a pony," Kitty offered into the uneasy silence that fell after Lucy's words.

"I'm sorry I missed meeting the new viscount," Bevis said, with a malicious glance at Amelia. "I'm quite looking forward to making his acquaintance. Perhaps I could take him riding in the park once he finds his pony?"

"I'm sure he would enjoy that," Lucy said truthfully.

"Freddy can take him riding." Amelia glared at Bevis.

"Our Freddy?" Kitty's disbelieving gasp was drowned out by Bevis's crack of laughter.

"Freddy is the most cowhanded man in England," he stated bluntly.

"Nonsense!" Amelia's ample bosom swelled with indignation. "Freddy knows all the manly accomplishments."

"Maybe he knows them, but he hasn't yet acquired them," Bevis countered.

"And to think that when I was in France I used to yearn to be back in the bosom of the family," Lucy said dryly.

Bevis laughed. "Ah, but distance lends enchantment. And now that I've welcomed you home, I must go."

He got to his feet with a lithe grace that Lucy couldn't help but admire. It was hard to believe that he and Freddy were both limbs from the same family tree. A fact Amelia was having trouble dealing with, too, Lucy thought shrewdly, as she noticed her aunt's tight-lipped expression.

"I hope I will have the pleasure of seeing you at the Alverson's ball tomorrow evening, Cousin Lucy?" Bevis asked.

"You will see all of us," Aunt Amelia pronounced, and Bevis, with a laughing glance at Lucy that invited her to share the joke, left.

"He was a rude boy, and he's grown into a forward man," Amelia pronounced.

"I've always rather liked him," Kitty offered.

"And we all know about your taste in men." Amelia aimed the words at Kitty, who turned pale and subsided into her chair with a stricken look on her face.

Not all of us, Lucy thought in frustration, wishing she understood the hidden currents swirling through the family. There were thirteen years of events, secrets, laughter and hopes that they had all shared and she hadn't. She might be a member of the family by birth, but most of the time she felt like a stranger, scrambling to make sense of half-formed sentences and vague references.

Lucy rubbed her head, which was beginning to ache. She desperately needed a peaceful hour alone in her room to allow her jumbled nerves time to return to normal. Unfortunately, she wasn't likely to get it, from the look on her aunt's face.

She stifled a sigh. Given her aunt's character, this confrontation was probably inevitable. And, that being the case, she might as well face it now, leaving her free to deal with other, more pressing, problems. Such as her sudden acquisition of an unwanted, although thankfully unannounced, fiancé.

"I wish to speak to you, Lucy," Amelia began.

"Oh, Mama." Kitty sighed.

"About Robert Standen." Amelia ignored her daughter's imploring look.

"Robert Standen?" Lucy repeated, wondering for one horrible moment if Robert might have told Amelia about his intention of marrying her.

"Well you might be embarrassed." Amelia nodded her head mendaciously. "Putting your relatives to the blush with such hoydenish behavior."

"Hoydenish behavior?" she asked, fearful of what her aunt might know.

"Going driving alone with Robert Standen in such a manner."

Lucy breathed an inward sigh of relief when she realized that her aunt had no idea she and Robert had met in France, in circumstances that would be sordid enough even for Amelia's love of scandal.

"Grandpapa thought it was unexceptionable behavior," Lucy replied. "Was he wrong?"

"He's a man," Amelia pronounced.

Lucy nodded. "An unarguable statement, but it doesn't answer my question."

"Given your circumstances, it is vital that you avoid the appearance of being fast." Amelia tried another tack.

"Aunt Amelia, I'm curious. What do you fear Colonel Standen might do to me in an open carriage in Hyde Park in the middle of the afternoon? While my personal acquaintance with rakes and debauched men is nil, every Gothic novel I have ever read has a dark, stormy night and a crumbling ruin as a prerequisite for seduction."

"Lucy Elizabeth Mary Agatha Danvers!" Amelia seemed to swell with outrage. "Such talk is outside of enough."

"Forgive me, Aunt, but you brought the subject up, and I can't help but wonder why you did?"

"Why, she asks?" Amelia addressed the fireplace. "After all I have done for this family, she questions why I would try to guide her?"

"Quite right." Lucy took advantage of the opening Amelia had unwittingly provided. "You have done too much in my absence, and now that I have returned, you should no longer be obliged to do so. I will take over running the household."

"But..." Amelia spluttered.

"There's no need to thank me." Lucy gave her an innocent look. "I consider it my responsibility to make sure that we do not take advantage of your good nature any longer. And now that we've settled that, I think I shall retire to my room to rest before supper. Good afternoon."

Lucy nodded to her stunned-looking aunt and her cousin, who was eyeing her with sudden respect, and escaped.

"Ah, Mr. Danvers." Mr. Goldring glanced up as his harassed-looking office clerk ushered Bevis into his crowded office. "How good of you to come to see me. Sit down, do." He gestured toward an oak chair in front of his massive desk.

Bevis glanced disdainfully at the dusty piece of furniture before gingerly sitting on the edge of it. "I have come to see you on a matter of business."

"Ah. Dare I hope that you have come to repay your loan? Or, perhaps, even the interest that has been due this last quarter?" The man's voice hardened. "I should so hate to find it necessary to begin the totally distasteful task of foreclosing on your estate."

"That won't be necessary!" Bevis snapped. "I have found a way to raise the ready and a whole lot more besides."

"And how might that be?"

"Not how. Who," Bevis corrected. "The who being my cousin Lucy, newly returned from France."

"Ah, yes." Mr. Goldring looked thoughtful. "The heiress who escaped from Napoleon. Yes, indeed. Her dowry would definitely solve even your pecuniary difficulties."

"Quite."

"And she has agreed to have you?" Mr. Goldring asked suspiciously.

"Her grandfather, my uncle, prefers that she marry in the family, and she always was a biddable little thing." Bevis stated what he hoped would be the earl's wishes. "That only leaves my cousin Freddy and myself as contenders for her hand. It should be easy for a man of my address to capture the affections of an aging spinster with no town bronze or social experience." Especially when that man had easy access to the earl's home and she had a little brother he could bear lead, he thought in satisfaction.

"What a fortunate set of circumstances, to be sure. And why have you come to tell me of your good fortune?"

"I want you to wait ninety days before you take any action on the overdue mortgages."

Mr. Goldring's smile had no roots in humor. "Ah, but I find myself asking why I should accommodate you."

Bevis glared at him. "Because, damn you, if you do, I'll add twenty-five percent to the total of the mortgages when I pay them off."

Mr. Goldring peered off into space for a long moment. He could almost find it in himself to feel sorry for this spinster cousin of Bevis's, but business was business, after all. "Very well," he finally said. "Twenty-five percent for ninety days grace. And not one second longer."

"No need to worry." Bevis got to his feet. "I doubt it will take me two weeks to bring her to the sticking point."

Chapter Seven

Interest on consols. Lucy added another notation to the list of things she wanted to discuss with Mr. Potter when he arrived, but her mind wasn't really on the state of her finances. It was too taken up with the emotional tatters of her life.

She stared blindly at the crackling fire in the book-room grate, which was battling the chill of the early spring day. How could her life have disintegrated to such an extent in such a short time? she wondered in frustration.

She shoved her fingers through her short curls, dislodging the blue ribbon threaded among them. Frustrated, she tossed it onto the gleaming surface of the mahogany desk. If she refused to marry Robert Standen, he would tell everyone what she had done and she would become a social outcast. Worse, her grandfather's pride would be shattered, and at his age, the blow would undoubtedly prove devastating. And Vernon would carry the scandal for the rest of his life.

On the other hand, if she yielded to Robert's blackmail and married him, her own future would be socially safe, but emotionally bankrupt. Robert didn't want a wife to share his interests, because from what she could see, his only interest was in war. That and tormenting her, she thought grimly. No, Robert Standen didn't want someone to share his life with. He only wanted someone to bear his children. He wanted some self-effacing drab who would agree with everything he said and never ever have an opinion of her own.

Lucy shuddered at the thought of living such a life. For her, it would be like living behind enemy lines again—always having to watch her every word, never daring to do anything to call attention to herself.

She pressed her soft lips together in determination. She hadn't escaped from Napoleon only to fall into another trap. Because that's what marriage to the autocratic Robert Standen would be—a trap with no hope of escape, short of death.

Lucy rubbed her fingertips across her forehead. She couldn't marry him. She simply couldn't endure a lifetime of being a cipher for an opinionated husband.

The problem was, how was she going to avoid it? At the moment, Robert seemed to hold all the cards. The only one she had was time, and she didn't have much of that. The season would be starting in a few weeks, and by the end of May... She swallowed uneasily. At the end of the season he would announce their engagement, unless she could somehow convince him that they would not suit...

But how could she do that? She stared at the portrait of her parents hanging over the mantel. What options did she have? She tried to think logically, instead of simply reacting to the sense of panic that filled her.

She could do nothing and hope that Providence would come to her rescue. But it had been her experience that just hoping things would right themselves never worked. One needed to do something. Something constructive.

But despite the fact that she'd worried the problem around in her mind all of last night, she hadn't been able to think of a single solution that was both moral and legal. She let out her breath in a drawn-out sigh.

She knew that her main attraction for Robert was that she was readily available and that he could marry her without having to go through the elaborate courtship rituals any other hopeful debutante of their class would expect. That and the fact that he would not have to bother to tone down his autocratic manner with Lucy or make any concessions to her needs and wants. Any accommodations made in the marriage would be made by her.

So what could she do? She traced over the marquetry design in the desk top. A flat refusal to marry him was out of the question. What was needed was a subtle chipping away at his idea that she would make an easily manipulated wife. She had over two months, she encouraged herself. Over two months in which to make him realize that any one of the multitude of starry-eyed young misses decorating this year's marriage mart would be infinitely less trouble in the long run than she.

She could do it, she encouraged herself. She would just have to be very careful to do so without angering him to the extent that he might want revenge.

"Mr. Potter," Fulton intoned from the doorway, and Lucy gratefully abandoned her thoughts in favor of a topic that was both impersonal and nonthreatening.

"Good afternoon, Mr. Potter." Lucy smiled at him. "Thank you for coming so promptly. I have a few questions for you about my inheritance."

Her few questions generated a few more, and it was almost an hour later before she clearly grasped exactly how her investments worked.

"Do you understand, Miss Danvers?" Mr. Potter peered anxiously at her over the top of his spectacles.

"I think so. There is so much to absorb all at once." She smiled ruefully at the man of business. From his bald head to his pointed chin, he reminded Lucy of one of the little elves that had decorated the nursery walls when she'd been a child.

"You really don't need to learn all this," he assured her. "Once you marry, it will be your husband's duty to manage your inheritance."

"From what I've observed so far of the typical society husband, he would be more likely to throw it all away at the gaming tables than to manage it," Lucy said tartly.

"Yes, well..." Mr. Potter took off his spectacles and polished them on his somber waistcoat, obviously torn between the undeniable truth of her words and his bone-deep conviction of the superiority of men.

"Not all men gamble," he finally compromised. "Your cousin Freddy doesn't."

"He doesn't?" Lucy asked, suddenly realizing that Mr. Potter undoubtedly knew all of the family secrets. If she weren't too obvious about it, perhaps she could find out a few things about her relatives. "But Freddy looks so fashionable, and gambling is all the crack..."

A pained expression flitted across Mr. Potter's face. "Far be it from me to criticize my betters, but your cousin has adopted the extreme of fashion. He is what is commonly known as—" he lowered his voice and, leaning closer to Lucy, whispered "—a dandy."

"Is that bad?" Lucy encouraged him to expound on the subject.

Mr. Potter pressed his fingertips together as he considered her question. Finally, he said, "Possibly not at Mr. Danvers's age. It is only to be expected that the young will adopt absurdities of one sort or another. Why, when I was a lad, I actually once wore a tinted wig," he confessed sheepishly.

"Really?" Lucy blinked at his bald head, totally unable to picture him as either young or in the grips of the dictates of fashion.

"Really." He nodded emphatically. "And as you can see, I suffered no lasting damage."

"Quite true. It's just that Freddy seems so—so different from, say, that Colonel Standen, who I was introduced to at Lord Chuffington's dinner party."

"Different is not quite the way I would describe him, Miss Danvers," Mr. Potter said dryly. "Colonel Standen is a dedicated army officer with enormous wealth at his command. And will have even more when his father dies."

While poor Freddy had merely a competence. Lucy felt a flash of sympathy for her cousin. So many people in English society seemed to judge a person's worth by how much money he had and very little else.

"Surely the colonel has some vices," Lucy said encouragingly.

"He doesn't suffer fools gladly, and his years in the army have made him believe that his orders should be carried out instantly," Mr. Potter replied.

"I see," Lucy said slowly. Mr. Potter's impression of the colonel tallied with her own, except it would appear that Mr. Potter had not had the misfortune to run into his ruthless side.

"I—" She broke off as the book-room door suddenly opened and Vernon erupted into the room.

"Lucy! Lucy!" he gasped, grabbing the end of the desk as he struggled to draw sufficient air.

"Slowly," Lucy said soothingly, "and when you catch your breath, apologize to Mr. Potter for interrupting us."

"Sorry, Mr. Potter," Vernon said to the man, "but this is important. Cousin Bevis invited me to go to Astley's Royal Amphitheater with him this afternoon." He hopped up and down on his stick-thin legs. "Please say I can go, Lucy. Please," he begged.

"Yes, Cousin Lucy, do say he may come." Bevis's warm drawl came from the open doorway.

"Good afternoon, Bevis." Lucy smiled warmly at him. "I didn't realize that you were here. Allow me to make you known to Mr. Potter."

"We have met, Miss Danvers," Mr. Potter said stiffly. "And since we have concluded our business, I shall be leaving. Good day." He smiled at Lucy, and with a distant nod at Bevis, left the room.

"I don't think that Mr. Potter likes you, Cousin Bevis." Vernon's frank words echoed Lucy's thoughts embarrassingly.

"He used to handle my father's affairs, but when I inherited, I found it necessary to turn him off," Bevis said carelessly.

"Oh." Vernon immediately lost interest, but Bevis's response bothered Lucy. Why had he dismissed Mr. Potter? From what she had observed, Mr. Potter was intelligent, loyal and very discreet. He had served her grandfather for over thirty years, and she knew her grandfather trusted him implicitly.

"Lucy?" Vernon's impatient voice distracted her. "Please say I may go? Please?"

"Well..." Lucy looked at Bevis. His brown eyes were warm and his mouth lifted in an infectious smile that made her want to smile back. At least she had one relative who didn't resent her existence, she thought ruefully.

"If Cousin Bevis doesn't mind," she finally said.

"He doesn't. He said so." Vernon jumped up and down in joy.

"Wear your new duffel coat," Lucy ordered. "It might be spring, but that wind has an unpleasant bite to it."

"Ah, Lucy!" Vernon stomped out of the room to get it.

"It is very kind of you to give my little brother such a treat, Bevis," Lucy said sincerely.

"I'm not doing it for his good opinion, but for yours," Bevis said candidly. "I'm hoping you'll feel so grateful that you'll favor me with the first dance at the Alverson's tonight."

"I shall look forward to it," Lucy replied truthfully. Her cousin Bevis would be an undemanding, entertaining companion. Unlike the colonel, who was sure to be there.

"Here I am, Lucy." Vernon ran back into the room, dragging his coat behind him. "Can we go now, Cousin Bevis?"

Bevis laughed good-naturedly. "I think we had better, before you expire from excitement."

Lucy walked them to the front door, then stood on the steps watching as Vernon scrambled onto the seat of Bevis's high-perch phaeton. She bit her lip to keep back the stream of warnings she wanted to call after him about the dangers of leaning out of sporting vehicles.

There was no need, she assured herself. Bevis was a sensible man. He wouldn't let anything happen to Vernon.

As she started to close the door, she caught sight of a vaguely familiar curricle moving down the street toward her at a spanking pace, and she squinted in the bright sunlight, trying to see it more closely.

She suddenly recognized the driver's broad shoulders, even though he was too far away for her to see his features. It was Robert Standen. Hurriedly, she stepped inside and slammed the heavy door, hoping that he was simply passing the house on his way to somewhere else.

"Is something wrong, m'lady?" Fulton looked at her in surprise.

Yes, Lucy thought grimly. The something wrong bears the name of Robert Standen, and he's probably coming to torment me again.

"Umm, no," she finally said, as the butler studied her worriedly. "I just saw a carriage turn into the square and..."

The forceful sound of the knocker banging against the door startled her and she jumped.

"Just a moment, please," she said when Fulton started toward the door. "Give me a moment to get up to the drawing room. I don't want our guest to think that I'm in the habit of standing in the hall waiting for visitors.''

''Certainly, m'lady.''

Lucy hurried up the stairs, reaching the drawing room just as the rapping started again. The man had absolutely no patience, she thought in exasperation. He'd probably chivy his poor wife into an early grave.

''There you are.'' Her aunt looked up from the tambour frame she was working on and stared at Lucy, studying her pale blue silk morning dress. ''An unexceptional gown,'' she finally pronounced, ''but you really must try to adopt a more ladylike manner. Ladies do not rush into rooms. They glide. Isn't that right, Kitty?''

''Yes, Mama,'' Kitty agreed, in a colorless voice that piqued Lucy's curiosity.

Was Kitty truly as vapid as she seemed or was she simply following the line of least resistance? Lucy surreptitiously studied her cousin, who was concentrating on her netting. She was wearing an obviously expensive, ill-fitting black dress that drained her skin of all color, giving it a grayish cast. How recent was Kitty's bereavement? Lucy wondered as she sat down in the chair across from them.

''I'm very sorry to see you're wearing black,'' she said gently.

''For my husband.'' Kitty's voice was barely audible.

''I didn't know,'' Lucy said.

''No way you could have. You were in France,'' Amelia stated flatly. ''Besides, it all happened three years ago. Time enough to let go of the past and look to the future. Who was at the door?''

"I came up before Fulton answered it," Lucy said truthfully. "Perhaps it was simply someone coming to see Grandpapa," she added hopefully.

"Colonel Standen." Fulton's stentorian tone dashed her hopes.

"Ah, Colonel, do come in." Amelia's face was suddenly wreathed in smiles. "We are so glad to see you." She poked her daughter as Kitty continued to net.

"Thank you." Robert glanced at Lucy's frozen face and his eyes gleamed with suppressed laughter. "It's gratifying to be so welcome."

Lucy forced a polite, meaningless smile to her lips, resisting the impulse to tell him where she wished he was. It was far too dangerous to risk provoking him in public. If she made him angry, he was quite capable of announcing their so-called engagement, knowing that she couldn't deny it. Apparently, this was his opening move in the courtship he'd threatened her with yesterday.

"Kitty," Amelia ordered, "do ring for fresh tea. I am persuaded that a hot cup is exactly what the colonel wants after that brisk wind. Do sit down, Colonel," the matron continued. "I was just telling my dear Kitty that it was time we saw about getting her a new wardrobe now that she's out of mourning." She gave a titter of laughter. "Time for her to be looking around for a new husband."

"Mama!" Kitty gave a strangled gasp from between bloodless lips and cast an anguished look at Lucy.

Feeling sorry for her cousin as well as embarrassed by her aunt's heavy-handed matchmaking, Lucy attempted to change the subject.

"Nonsense, Aunt Amelia. This is 1814, not the Middle Ages. There are other things for women to do besides spend their lives catering to some man's idiosyncrasies." Lucy offered Robert the first hint that she would not be a conformable wife.

"Such as?" Robert asked with a grave courtesy that Lucy instinctively mistrusted. "I can think of several alternatives to marriage, but I doubt if they are the ones to which you refer."

"Undoubtedly." Lucy gave him a limpid smile. "We have such dissimilar tastes."

"Oh, not entirely." Robert's black eyes focused on her mouth, and Lucy could almost feel the warmth of his kisses. "For example—"

Lucy hastily interrupted him, afraid of what he might reveal. "I could retire to Derbyshire and write novels."

"Novels!" her aunt gasped, torn between outrage at the improper turn the conversation had taken and the hope that her niece's radical views would give the colonel a disgust of her.

"Yes." Lucy elaborated on her theme. "The type of books that the Minerva Press publishes. Where the poor heroine has to suffer through the machinations of the dastardly villain to finally emerge triumphant in the end, having thoroughly vanquished him." She gave Robert a bright, glittering and totally false smile.

Robert returned the smile with a gleam of white teeth. "You do realize that you are discussing fiction and not real life, do you not?"

"What a very droll idea, to be sure." Amelia tried to take control of the conversation. "If you aren't careful, Lucy, you will shock the colonel."

"You underestimate me, Mrs. Danvers," Robert said blandly. "Like most men, I prefer a challenge."

"Wrong! Most men prefer money." Lucy's true feelings slipped out.

"Lucy Danvers, that was totally uncalled for!" Amelia sounded shocked at such plain speaking.

"But she's right," Kitty added, surprising Lucy.

"Kitty! Have your wits gone begging?" Amelia glared at her daughter. "Colonel Standen will think you are a bluestocking."

"Nonsense," Lucy said, rushing to her cousin's defense. "He will think she is a woman of common sense who knows what she's about."

"And honest." To Lucy's surprise, Robert helped to defuse her aunt's anger. "Since you are now out of mourning, Mrs. Whitney, would you save me a dance at the Alverson's ball tonight?" he asked the shrinking Kitty.

"Certainly she will." Amelia threw a triumphant look at Lucy, who determinedly suppressed her feeling of uncertainty at Robert's unexpected invitation to her cousin. Her concern was because Kitty was no match for Robert mentally or emotionally, she told herself.

"And you, too, Miss Danvers." Amelia's smile faded as Robert turned to Lucy. "Will you save me a waltz?"

"I cannot waltz," Lucy said, pleased to be able to turn him down.

"That is not an insurmountable problem. You seem intelligent enough to master the basic steps." He gave her a condescending smile that made her long to smack him. How dare he patronize her! Especially when there was nothing she could do about it—at least not while her aunt was watching them so avidly.

"I am intelligent enough to learn," she replied tightly. "What is lacking is incentive."

"I have already said I'll dance with you." He grinned at her, and Lucy suddenly found her attention caught again by the gleam of white teeth against tanned skin. How much of his swarthy color was natural and how much of it caused by constant exposure to the peninsular sun? The thought unexpectedly flittered through her mind. Her eyes dropped to the pristine whiteness of his neckcloth. Would the skin on his body match his face or would— She caught her imagination up short, truly horrified at herself. What was the matter with her—fantasizing about a man's body? She was behaving like a trollop. How could one kiss have so unhinged her?

"I'll play the piano while you practice," Kitty said kindly, seeing the flash of uncertainty on Lucy's face but misunderstanding the cause.

"Thank you, Mrs. Whitney," Robert said before either Amelia or Lucy could veto the idea. He stood and held out his hand. "With Mrs. Whitney to provide the music and myself as sacrificial victim—"

"I thought that was my role," Lucy muttered under her breath.

"—I predict you'll be waltzing by this evening," he finished.

Kitty seated herself at the small rosewood piano and began to play a lively tune. Knowing there was no graceful way to escape the ordeal, Lucy decided to try to master the steps as soon as possible. After all, she encouraged herself, how hard could it be to learn a dance?

Her first suspicion that it was not going to be as easy as she thought came when Robert put his arm around her and pulled her against him.

"What are you doing?" she gasped, with a quick look at her aunt. To her surprise, her aunt merely looked disgruntled, not shocked.

"Trying to teach you the waltz. It seems to be my lot in life to lead you through new experiences," he murmured near her left ear as he pulled her closer still.

His warm breath stirred the tendrils of hair on her forehead and her skin tightened. The feel of his hard fingers burned into her back and she instinctively swayed forward, only to find her nose pressed up against the crisp folds of his neckcloth. The material scraped abrasively against her face and she hastily jerked back.

Lucy took a deep, steadying breath, trying to regain control of her erratic breathing, but it proved to be a mistake. This close to him she could smell the scent of sandalwood clinging to his skin.

She glanced up and her attention was caught by the dark sheen of the emerging beard beneath his skin. Her fingertips began to tingle as she remembered the raspy texture of his cheek. This is awful, she thought in despair. Somehow, it didn't seem quite decent to be so physically aware of a man.

It was guilt, she tried to tell herself. Guilt about what had happened in France. That was why she was so sensitive to him. Once her sense of guilt dissipated, so would her intense physical reaction.

"It is usual for both parties on the dance floor to move," Robert whispered, his warm lips inches from her forehead.

Lucy glared up at him in frustration. She had always wanted to marry a man with a ready sense of humor, but she hadn't expected to be the source of his amusement.

"Follow my steps," he ordered. He moved at the same instant she did and Lucy tripped over his feet. She fell forward, finding herself pressed up against him from shoulder to thigh. The result was electrifying. Her breasts swelled, her mouth dried and her palms became sweaty. She closed her eyes in dismay. This was never going to work.

"Really, Lucy, how can you be so clumsy?" her aunt snapped.

"Perhaps the colonel is not the best teacher." Lucy made a bid to end the torture.

"Colonel Standen was on Wellington's staff, and everyone knows that all his officers are expert dancers." Her aunt smiled ingratiatingly at him, and Lucy wanted to scream. How could her aunt toadeat him so?

"Perhaps what is needed is for Miss Danvers to first observe the waltz being performed," Robert unexpectedly suggested. He turned to Kitty. "Mrs. Whitney, would you be so kind as to dance with me so that your cousin may see the steps?"

He held his hand out to her, and Kitty stared down at it in dismay. It was almost as if she were afraid to have him touch her, Lucy thought. Could her cousin know something about Robert that she didn't? Something that might have occurred on one of his leaves home?

Robert ignored Kitty's obvious reluctance and took her in his arms. "If you would just walk through the steps with me, Mrs. Whitney...and pay attention," he said to Lucy.

Lucy smiled limpidly. "Never fear, I intend to watch you very closely."

Robert raised his dark eyebrows at her double-edged remark, but he held his peace. Instead, he slowly guided the visibly reluctant Kitty around the room in what appeared to Lucy to be a very graceful dance.

Finally, after two circuits of the room, he released Kitty, who immediately scurried to the safety of the piano, and turned back to Lucy. "Do you think you can do that?"

"I can try." She waited with a vague sense of excitement that she refused to acknowledge as he put his arms around her.

"Simply count. One and two and..." He began to move as he had with Kitty, and this time Lucy was able to follow him. She wasn't as graceful as her cousin had been, but neither did she stumble over his feet as she had before. In fact, she decided as he swung her around in a graceful arc, she could become quite fond of waltzing. Maybe she was becoming debauched, she thought uneasily. First, she had lost herself in a stranger's kiss, and now she found pleasure in swirling around the floor in his arms.

"Bravo! Bravo!" Her grandfather's pleased voice came from the doorway, and Lucy stumbled slightly as she turned. Robert steadied her against his body for a long moment, before stepping away.

"You looked so very graceful dancing, Lucy." Her grandfather beamed at her. "Just like your mother used to."

"Thank you. But...you don't think that waltzing is a trifle...fast?" she asked, with the half-formed idea that if he said yes, she would have an excuse to avoid the disquieting sensation of being in Robert's arms.

"Nonsense," the earl scoffed. "It is graceful and beautiful, and our English moral fiber is strong enough to withstand its effects. Right, m'boy?" he shot at Robert.

England's moral fiber might be strong enough, but she had grave reservations about her own, Lucy thought grimly.

"Lucy, I can't find Vernon. Where is he?" the earl went on.

"Bevis was by earlier and took him out. They left about half an hour ago."

"Bevis!" Amelia repeated in amazement. "Took the boy on an outing with him? What can he be about?"

"Kindness to a young relative?" Lucy suggested, rather surprised at her aunt's reaction. Was she trying to nab Bevis as well for the reluctant Kitty? Or did her aunt know something about Bevis that made him an unsuitable companion for a young boy? Lucy felt a dull ache start to throb behind her eyes. She, more than most, knew that a warm smile and a pleasant demeanor could mask almost anything.

"Better Bevis than that fop you call a son, Amelia," the earl snorted.

Lucy felt some of her tension fade at his words. That must be why Amelia didn't like Bevis—because the earl obviously preferred him to Freddy. It was jealousy that had colored Amelia's reaction, not anything Bevis had done.

"Glad I found you, m'boy." The earl turned to Robert. "Need someone I can trust to take care of a small matter for me. It'll give you a chance to take Lucy for a drive, too."

Lucy felt her cheeks flush with color at his blatant attempt at matchmaking. She was beginning to have a great deal of fellow feeling for Kitty.

"A pleasure of the highest order, sir," Robert said, and Lucy cringed at the laughter behind his smooth words.

"I think I have the headache," she muttered.

"You should lie down at once or you will miss the ball tonight." Unwittingly, her aunt became her ally.

"Nonsense!" the earl proclaimed. "Quacking oneself never answers. The fresh air will blow away your megrims, m'girl. Go get your bonnet while I give the papers to Robert."

"Yes, sir." Lucy gave in, telling herself that being alone with him wouldn't be as bad as being in public with him. At least then she wouldn't have to worry about his unexpectedly announcing their engagement.

Chapter Eight

Recognizing the futility of the heated debate on the necessity of maintaining the army's supply lines, which Robert was waging with the elderly official they had delivered her grandfather's missive to, Lucy took the opportunity to study the first government office she'd ever been in.

She was not impressed. Books and papers had been stacked on every available bit of table space, as well as most of the floor. Scores of maps detailing what she assumed were past and present campaigns were pinned to the walls, and a thick layer of dust covered everything.

She glanced down in annoyance at the smudges on the hem of her new dress. Lord Alridge didn't need more military data; he needed to be taught the rudiments of cleanliness, she thought in disgust. This office was a disgrace.

"Too damned expensive by half." Lord Alridge's suddenly raised voice bounced off the walls, and Lucy turned her attention from the inadequacies of his housekeeping to the man himself. "You military types have no understanding of what's happening here at home." Lord Alridge's multiple chins trembled in anger. "The government has exorbitant expenses right here in London."

"Ah, yes, I was reading about Prinny's latest purchases for his Brighton Pavilion in the *Political Register* just the other day." Robert's clipped voice sent a shiver of apprehension through Lucy. Uncertainly, she studied his taut features. His face was pale with the strength of his feelings and his eyes were seething pools of dark fire. Her gaze slipped lower, over his rigid jaw, past the corded muscles in his neck to his hands, which were clenched into fists. He was absolutely furious, she realized with a sense of shock. Robert Standen, who always seemed so in control of himself, was perilously close to losing his temper entirely.

"Heh! Soldiers, you call yourselves!" Lord Alridge snorted. "Why, in my day soldiers lived off the land. Why don't you do that, instead of always whining for more and more supplies that we can't afford to send you?"

"I can answer that." Lucy hurriedly entered the conversation before Robert could give voice to what she very much feared would be a rude comment. Her grandfather had asked them to deliver a message to Lord Alridge, not make an enemy of him. "English soldiers cannot live off the land, because French soldiers got there first. They carried off everything they could find. And since it is spring, the new crop hasn't grown enough for the English to steal it."

"Steal!" Lord Alridge's jowls wobbled in outrage. "I will have you know that England is at war with France. It is far from stealing to take from the enemy."

"The ones you are proposing to take from are the farmers and the villagers." Lucy began to lose her sense of detachment at the man's complete insensitivity to the peasants' plight. "They didn't declare the war and most of them are not fighting in it. They're simply the prey of both sides."

"That's the way of wars," Lord Alridge said dismissively.

"It's a bad way," Lucy insisted.

"You're a woman. Women don't understand," he said condescendingly.

"We understand death and destruction and starvation, which is what wars always bring in their wake," Lucy said, trying to make him understand what to her was so clearly obvious.

"Nonsense! Pretty gels like you should be thinking of beaus and parties, eh?" He winked at Robert, who stared back at him with all the interest of an entomologist faced with a rare insect specimen.

"Maybe women should think about the war," Lucy snapped, furious at his condescending dismissal of her viewpoint, "since you here at Whitehall do not seem to be."

"Oh, I say now." Lord Alridge looked offended.

"What you say is arrogant nonsense!" She stalked out of his office, far too angry to remain. The damned fool! She marched down the narrow hallway, ignoring a junior clerk, who scurried to get out of her way. How could that sapscull have been fighting Napoleon all these years and still have absolutely no concept of the horrors of war? Insulated in his snug little office, he made decisions that cost people like her parents their lives, and he told her she didn't understand!

She shoved the door open and stepped out into the bright afternoon sunshine.

"Were you planning on driving away without me?" Robert caught up with her at the bottom of the flag-stone steps.

"Being a woman, I can hardly be expected to plan ahead, can I?" she snapped back, and then fell silent as the ridiculousness of the situation suddenly struck her. She had entered the conversation in the first place only to stop Robert from insulting her grandfather's friend, and then she had done so herself.

Robert gestured to his groom, who'd been patiently walking the team of chestnuts while they were inside.

"It's a good thing for Lord Alridge that women can't plan ahead." Robert chuckled. "If they could, his mother would never have married his father, for fear of producing just such a jingle-brain."

"Now that's a solution. If all the women of the world simply refused to have anything to do with the men, there would not be sapsculls like him."

"There would not be people, period." Robert helped her into the carriage and then, tossing a coin to his groom, told the man to return home.

"Why do you do that?" Lucy watched the groom disappear into the crowd at the end of the street.

"Do what?" Robert muttered, his attention focused on the large number of pedestrians who seemed to be intent on walking in front of his skittish horses.

"Dismiss your groom every time I come for a ride with you."

"I find a third party a hindrance to conversation." He breathed a sigh of relief when he cleared a closed carriage by inches. "Especially one who is liable to repeat everything he hears. Rather like that old fool we just left." His voice hardened.

"Yes, Lord Alridge is a fool, isn't he?" For once she found herself in complete agreement with Robert. "How could anyone have given that man a responsible position?"

"He probably got it as repayment for a favor to Prinny," Robert said in disgust. "How we're supposed to win in the field, with men like that in charge of our supplies..."

"They can't all be that bad. I remember that Grandpapa used to be very active in the government when he was younger," Lucy offered.

"Yes, but for every competent man like your grandfather, there are twenty incompetent cronies of the prince to be dealt with."

"That's because most of the competent men want to dress up in a pretty uniform and go charging off to war," Lucy said tartly. "Taking care of supply lines seems pretty tame when weighed against the thrill of a cavalry charge."

"It's only thrilling until you have actually been in one. Until you've held a friend in your arms while he screams out in agony from the lance through his chest," Robert said, sounding unbearably tired.

Compassionately, Lucy covered his clenched fist with her fingers and squeezed gently, wanting to console him. Alone among her acquaintances in London, Robert Standen knew the horrors of war. Like her, he had lived through the death and destruction.

"He who does not learn from the past is doomed to repeat it," she said.

"Accurate, but not original." Robert flashed her a crooked smile, and she hastily pulled her hand back.

"I know. One of those old Greeks probably said it. They never seemed to do anything but stand around and say profound things that defenseless schoolchildren would ever after be forced to commit to memory."

"Doing so is good for you," Robert insisted. "It broadens the mind."

"Rote memorization stifles the mind. Which brings us full circle to Lord Alridge. You ought to do something about him," she said slowly, as an idea occurred to her.

If she could get Robert interested in trying to change Lord Alridge's antiquated ideas on conducting war, it might fill up some of his free time. In fact, as stupid as Lord Alridge had seemed to be, the task might well consume all of Robert's waking hours, which would leave him with little time to court her. It would also give him an interest in something besides getting her to the altar.

A sudden sense of excitement gripped Lucy. If she could get him involved in the government, he might well decide that what he really wanted was a political hostess for a wife.

Yes, indeed, she thought happily. That might well be the answer to all her problems. Robert could marry someone else, and they could just be acquaintances. Or maybe, in time, friends. He'd make a good friend, she thought wistfully.

"The Crown frowns on murder, which I very much fear is the only thing to do with Lord Alridge," Robert said glumly.

"Not necessarily. Did you notice how fat he was?"

"Notice!" Robert snorted. "How could one fail to hear the creak of his Cumberland corset every time he moved?"

156 Suspicion

Lucy giggled. "Is that what that noise was? I thought he had some exotic affliction in his joints. But that proves my point."

"What point?" He checked the horses as a small boy dashed into the street.

"On how to influence him," Lucy said patiently. "From what he said, it is clear he spends a great deal of time listening to people who are unsympathetic to the problems the military faces. What you need to do is to give him the army's side of it."

She eyed him thoughtfully for a long moment and then said, "It's a shame you didn't lose an arm in the war."

"Lose an arm!" He stared at her. "Why?"

"Because it would give you credibility as a military hero," Lucy explained. "Everyone would fuss over you, and you could be brave and forbearing, and lobby for the military."

"You are all about in your head," Robert said flatly.

"No, I'm simply an astute judge of human nature. I don't suppose you have any medals you could wear?" she asked hopefully.

"You suppose right," he said dryly. "One does not wear military medals on civilian clothes."

"Pity. Well, food might work as well."

He frowned uncomprehendingly at her. "On my clothes?"

"No, in Lord Alridge's mouth. Would you please pay attention?"

"I'm trying, but your thought processes—if one can call them that—bear a striking resemblance to the Gordian knot."

"Then I will state the problem in terms even you can understand. You need to convince Lord Alridge and ministers of his ilk that it is in England's best interests to support the troops in the field. The most practical way to accomplish that is to wine and dine them, and then, when they're feeling relaxed, slip in a few facts."

"It won't work."

"How do you know until you've tried it?" Lucy countered.

"It's..." He gestured impotently and the horses danced sideways as the reins jerked. He quickly brought them under control again. "It's demeaning to go begging to a bunch of political hacks."

"War itself is demeaning to everyone connected with it," Lucy argued. "It seems to me the least you can do for your friends still fighting in France is to help where you can."

"Why do you care what happens to the military?" Robert asked suspiciously.

"I don't," she said candidly. "From what I've seen, the color of the uniform a soldier wears makes no difference. If he shoots you, you're just as dead. And a lot of the people getting shot are innocent bystanders, like my parents were."

Robert gave her a lopsided smile that she found strangely comforting. "You are right, of course. There are no winners in war, only survivors. Although your idea..." He lapsed into silence as he considered it.

They reached Grosvenor Square a few minutes later, and Lucy hastily scrambled down from the carriage. She purposely didn't answer his parting remark, "See you at the Alverson's ball tonight," as she hurried up the stairs to the door.

She didn't want to see him there, she told herself, ignoring the traitorous thought that tonight he would hold her in his arms again and she would feel the same inexplicable flood of sensations she had earlier.

"Lucy! Lucy!" Vernon came clattering down the stairs at breakneck speed as she entered the house. "Astley's was splendiferous. It was the most fabulous..." He lapsed into a replete silence as words failed him.

Lucy smiled down into his animated features as a feeling of peace settled over her. Whatever problems she might be experiencing in England were worth it to see Vernon thriving so.

"And not only that, but Grandfather says he wants to see this marvel and he is going to take me back next week," Vernon concluded. "And Cousin Bevis is a wizard. He knows lots of things."

"Does he?" Lucy climbed the stairs beside him. "Such as?"

"Men kind of things." Vernon puffed out his thin little chest in self-importance.

Lucy swallowed her laughter. "I see," she said seriously. "Well, at the moment I'm interested in some tea. Would you like to join me in the drawing room?"

"No, I'm going to write a letter to the curé and then, when Grandpapa gets up from his nap, I'm going to play chess with him. He says he's going to teach me the moves."

"I don't suppose you told him that the curé taught you the moves seven years ago, or that he said you were the best player he had ever faced?" Lucy asked dryly.

"Grandpapa didn't ask," Vernon said innocently, "and I would hate to put myself forward."

"You'll put yourself in the nursery at this rate," Lucy warned.

"Ah, Lucy, I'm too old for the nursery. Grand-papa says I need a tutor."

"You definitely need something," she said wryly. "Now run along and write your letter. Be sure to give the curé my regards."

"I will." Vernon scampered off to the study.

Thoughtfully, Lucy made her way to the drawing room. Her brother was changing, expanding and developing. It was as if the freedom and safety of London was allowing him to finally become the person he had been meant to be.

Lucy came to a sudden halt after entering the room, and the conversation going on there stilled. She found herself the cynosure of three pairs of eyes—Freddy's, Kitty's and a strange young man's.

At least her formidable aunt wasn't here, Lucy thought with some relief.

"Good afternoon, Lucy." Kitty smiled shyly at her. "Do come in so we can make Lord Oliver known to you."

Lucy watched as a blond man about Freddy's age, wearing a carelessly knotted Belcher tie and a wrinkled, dark blue coat with some sort of stain on the lapel, rose to his feet and sketched her a graceful bow.

"Miss Danvers, this is Lord Oliver, a very old friend of Freddy's," Kitty offered.

"Went to school together." Freddy turned so that he could see Lucy without his high shirt points interfering with his vision. "Eton, then Oxford."

Lord Oliver stared blankly at her for a few seconds and then suddenly demanded, "What time is it?"

Lucy blinked. "Time? Um—" she glanced at the carriage clock on the mantel, "—shortly before three."

"I'll miss it," Lord Oliver muttered, and, without so much as a goodbye, rushed out, trailed by the anxious-looking Freddy. The latter paused momentarily in the doorway.

"Must forgive Oliver, Cousin Lucy. He's a dashed clever cove, you know," he said, and then hurried after his friend.

"Apparently not clever enough to have learned any manners," Lucy said in amusement.

"Actually, I don't think he was ever taught any," Kitty said seriously. "He's the youngest son of the Duke of Acton, and his parents have spoiled him outrageously because he really is very clever. Most of the time I can't even understand him. Would you like some tea? It's still hot."

"Yes, please." Lucy accepted a cup and sat down, wondering if Kitty were simply more at ease in her company now or if it was because her mother was absent.

Lucy sipped the fragrant brew while she tried to think of something innocuous to say. She wanted to avoid inadvertently sending Kitty into a paroxysm of nervousness again.

"Is Aunt Amelia at home?" She finally decided that sounded harmless enough.

"Mama is resting, to conserve her energies for the ball tonight." Kitty's lips trembled. "Poor dear, she's hoping that my appearance at the Alversons's tonight will convince one of the patronesses of Almack's to give me vouchers."

"You? I can understand some high sticklers having doubts about the years I spent in France, but you—"

"Ah, but you are the granddaughter of an earl and very wealthy in your own right, while I am a penniless blot on the family honor."

Lucy was taken aback at the depth of bitter despair she heard in her cousin's voice.

"Has no one told you about me yet?" Kitty asked harshly. "You went to that dinner with Uncle Adolphus. I'm surprised the old tabbies didn't whisper about me."

"They were too busy quizzing me about what I did in France to even think about telling me anything."

Kitty sighed. "They will. Believe me, they will. You can live down a scandal only if you have pots of money and a title."

"I see," Lucy said slowly, not seeing at all, but not wanting to add to the pain Kitty obviously felt.

"I might as well tell you myself. At least then I shall be sure you know the whole sordid truth."

"Kitty, if you don't want me to know..."

"I never wanted anyone to know," Kitty said sadly. "I wanted to keep all the shame and embarrassment locked deep inside, so that no one would point and titter at me behind my back." Her voice broke. "A few don't even wait until I'm past.

"The truth of the matter is that at seventeen I fell in love." Kitty stared blindly at the Romney portrait of her grandmother hanging over the fireplace. "I had been reading Gothic novels for years, so I had no trouble at all recognizing a hero when I met him. Thomas Whitney was his name. He was so handsome! What I should have remembered is what our vicar used to say, 'Handsome is as handsome does.'"

Lucy murmured sympathetically when Kitty lapsed into silence.

"My mother was against the match, but I knew she wanted me to marry a very fat, very boring, very wealthy baron three times my age. Uncle Adolphus said Thomas was a scoundrel, but then he hates Freddy, and Freddy is very nice," Kitty said fiercely.

Lucy nodded in agreement. She didn't know if Freddy were nice or not, but he was certainly harmless.

"In short, we decided to confound my relatives and elope. Yes," she said when Lucy winced, "now I know how ill-advised it was, but then it seemed so wonderfully romantic. Two star-crossed lovers thwarting the plot against them. We left for Gretna Green, but a snowstorm stranded us at a tiny inn just over the Scottish border. We shared a room for three days before they caught up with us," she said baldly.

"When Uncle Adolphus told Thomas that my dowry was only three thousand pounds, and that he had no intention of allowing him to hang on his sleeve..." Kitty's voice trembled at the memory. "Thomas said he didn't want to marry me, after all."

"After...?"

"Yes. After. Uncle Adolphus finally paid him to marry me. It was a disaster," Kitty said bleakly. "We weren't welcome in society, so we went to Tunbridge Wells where, between drunken sprees, Thomas gambled away my dowry and Uncle Adolphus's bribe.

"Then, after about eight months, he finally got himself killed in a duel over some lightskirt, and I came to live with Mama and Uncle Adolphus."

"Oh, Kitty, I'm so sorry," Lucy said. "I know it's inadequate, but—"

"You're sorry?" Kitty laughed shakily. "You've just returned from thirteen years in French captivity and you feel pity for me?"

"Not for you," Lucy said slowly. "For what happened to you."

Kitty blinked in surprise. "You know, Cousin Lucy, you are a very unusual woman."

"I am what circumstances have made me," she replied, knowing full well that if the story of her misadventures with Robert ever became known, she would suffer a far worse social ostracism than Kitty had.

"And now Mama wants to force me into a second marriage," Kitty said bitterly. "All because Freddy is no longer—" She broke off in sudden confusion.

"To be the next earl," Lucy finished for her. "Actually, Aunt Amelia is right. An establishment of one's own is definitely preferable to living as a permanent guest in a relative's house. For both of us."

"I know that, but I would bring nothing to a marriage but a tarnished reputation," Kitty wailed. "Sometimes I feel—"

She broke off as a muffled, crackling sound echoed in the hallway.

Lucy jumped to her feet, having no trouble recognizing the sound for exactly what it was.

Fearfully, she rushed out into the hall, with Kitty right behind her. They met Fulton at the head of the stairs.

"What was that?" he asked fearfully.

"A gunshot." Lucy sniffed, smelling the acrid odor of gunpowder.

Kitty glanced apprehensively up the broad staircase toward the bedrooms on the third floor, but nobody was visible. Apparently neither Amelia nor the earl had been woken from their naps.

"The study." Lucy suddenly remembered that Vernon had gone there to write his letter. She raced down the hall, trailed by Kitty and the panting Fulton. Unceremoniously, she shoved open the door, to discover her brother standing beside the large mahogany desk, a still-smoking dueling pistol in his trembling hand.

"I didn't do anything!" Vernon blurted out, his face white and pinched.

Lucy fearfully ran her shocked eyes over his shaking body, looking for gaping wounds. When she didn't find any, she sagged against the doorframe in relief.

Fulton and Kitty peered around her into the room.

"I was just looking at it," Vernon tried to explain. "I picked it up and it went off." His voice had a raspy quality that Lucy heard with dread. She had to calm him down. If she didn't, within minutes he would be gasping for air, each breath an agonizing ordeal.

"Vernon," she said, purposefully keeping her voice light, "if you ever touch one of Grandpapa's dueling pistols again, I shall wring your neck and tack your lifeless body on the stable door to frighten the varmints away."

"Actually, after a day or two, the smell would frighten everyone away." Kitty followed her lead.

"True." Lucy watched as the color slowly began to seep back into Vernon's face. "I guess I won't do that, after all. I will settle for your word of honor that you will never touch a gun again unless there is an adult present."

"I promise." Vernon sighed, and Lucy silently echoed the sound, this time from relief that the rasp seemed to be fading from his voice.

"If you will let me have that, Cousin Vernon?" Kitty held out her hand for the pistol he was still clutching. "My late husband was very fond of dueling pistols, so I'm used to them," she explained to Lucy.

Vernon handed her the gun, seemingly grateful to be rid of it.

"Perhaps you should go down to the kitchen with Fulton and get something to eat and a cup of hot chocolate," Lucy said, wanting to remove him from the source of stress as soon as possible.

"Yes, you come with me, Master Vernon. Cook just made a fresh batch of ginger-nuts." Fulton urged him toward the door.

"Fulton?" Lucy called after him.

"Yes?" He turned.

"I don't wish for my grandfather, or anyone else, for that matter, to be told of this unfortunate incident."

"As you wish, Miss Lucy, but it seems a bit havey-cavey to me," he muttered. "His lordship has always been most particular that no loaded guns be kept in the house. Even at the hunting box, he never broke that rule. And now..." Fulton shook his head. "It would kill him if anything were to happen to the lad."

"It wouldn't do much for my peace of mind, either," Lucy said dryly as he left.

"They were both loaded." Kitty looked up from the mahogany case that held the second dueling pistol. "Now, why would anyone load a dueling pistol and then leave it out where it could cause a nasty accident?"

"Accident?" Lucy felt the hairs on the back of her neck lift as she suddenly remembered Vernon's near fall from the third floor. She had labeled that an accident, too, but two in little more than a week seemed highly improbable. Especially considering the fact that Vernon had never been prone to mishaps.

Of course, there were far more opportunities for accidents in this big house than in Marthe's tiny cottage. And Vernon's health—and curiosity—was improving almost daily. But still... Lucy bit her lip nervously. Two accidents that could have had fatal consequences in one week? That was stretching coincidence too far. But why would anyone want to deliberately harm Vernon?

Because he is the heir to the earldom. Her shocked mind automatically supplied the answer.

"There." Kitty finished unloading the second pistol, and began repacking them in their case. "Whoever left these down here should be shot with one of them. Everyone knows that the first thing a boy is likely to do when he discovers a gun is pick it up."

"They aren't normally left on the desk?" Lucy tried to keep her suspicions out of her voice. Kitty wasn't stupid. If she realized that Lucy suspected it wasn't an accident, she would also realize that her brother had to be the prime suspect, and she would warn him.

"No." Her cousin picked the case up and returned it to the top shelf of the mahogany escritoire. She frowned. "Uncle Adolphus must have had them out for some reason, although it's unlike him to be careless. But he is getting older."

"Yes," Lucy murmured, much more concerned that someone seemed determined that Vernon not get any older.

* * *

"Have some of this." Oliver ladled out a cup of the steaming punch the waiter had just served. "Nothing beats The Three Lions's punch. It'll put the heart back into you."

"Not enough blue ruin in the whole of London to do that." Freddy gloomily accepted the cup and took a sip, choking when the force of the liquor hit the back of his throat.

"Not blue ruin." Oliver took a more cautious sip. "Best rum to be had. Straight from the Americas."

"Maybe that's where I ought to go," Freddy muttered.

"The Americas!" Oliver stared at him in horror. "Why would you do a daft thing like that?"

"To escape." Freddy took a second swallow. This time it went down much easier, for his throat was becoming numb.

"That is a frightful waistcoat." Oliver looked askance at Freddy's jacket. "But it's not bad enough to hide yourself away in the Americas."

"Frightful?" Freddy was momentarily roused to defend himself. "I'll have you know it's all the crack."

"If you say so." Oliver's doubts were clear in his voice. "If it ain't the waistcoat that's cast you into the dismals, what is it?"

"Everything," Freddy moaned.

"The first step in solving a problem is to identify it," Oliver said reprovingly. " 'Everything' is not specific."

"It's my cousins from France, Lucy and Vernon."

"Not very French names."

"They ain't French," Freddy said in exasperation. "They've just lived in France for years. Never even knew about the brat at all till he showed up. You must've heard. The story is on everybody's lips."

"I never listen to gossip," Oliver said. "And I still don't understand. You don't like these cousins?"

Freddy reflected for a moment. "Wouldn't say that exactly. Don't really know 'em. Lucy's a trifle quiet, but the brat's a cheeky little devil."

"They all are," Oliver assured him, remembering his own brother's sons.

"Problem is, the brat's now m'uncle's heir. Cut me out of the succession and my inheritance," Freddy said, quoting his mother.

"He did not *cut* you out," Oliver objected. "The earldom was always his, and his father's before him."

"But I didn't know about it," Freddy objected.

"It doesn't matter. The earldom was never yours," Oliver insisted. "I cannot see what the fuss is about, anyway. Your uncle is likely to live forever. They always do when you want them to die."

"Don't like him, but I can't say as I want him to die. Don't even want the title. Not really. It's just that when he thought me the heir, he made me an allowance. M'mother says he's bound to remember and cut it off, and then where will I be? I've no blunt of my own."

"Come live with me," Oliver offered. "I have lots of room."

"Ain't nobody's charity case," Freddy said reproachfully.

"Oliver, you sly dog." A young, dapper-looking man slipped into the seat beside Oliver. "And Freddy, old man, what brings you down here?"

"Drink," Freddy said succinctly.

"Ah, yes, drink." Barney eyed the brew longingly.

Oliver obligingly handed him a cup, which he promptly drained and held out for a refill.

"It's been a long morning. This 'having a position' isn't what I thought it'd be," Barney complained. "Somebody's always wanting you to be doing something. Think they own you, body and soul."

"Why do it?" Oliver asked curiously.

"Need to live, old boy. We weren't all delivered into the world hosed and shod like you and old Freddy here."

"Not me," Freddy said glumly. "Been dispossessed."

"That's right. I heard about it the other day. Hey, landlord," Barney suddenly yelled. "Bring some food over here." He turned back to Freddy. "Everyone was talking 'bout it ... Tell you what," he suggested, "I'll have my uncle get you a position in the treasury department, too. We've been damnably busy what with minting all the new gold sovereigns to replace the old guineas." He nodded importantly. "Have to coordinate the shipments. No easy task, that."

Freddy shuddered. "Ain't my cup of tea."

"It's like a game," Barney insisted. "Thinking up ways to disguise the shipments. Why, we're sending one up by your uncle's country seat next week, and you know what we're going to disguise it as?"

"What?" Oliver asked, when Freddy merely stared into his punch.

"As a grain shipment." Barney beamed at them. "My idea. Nobody'll ever suspect a thing."

"Guards'll give it away," Oliver said.

"No guards. Just an outrider. Nobody will suspect a thing," he repeated. "That gold'll be as safe as a baby in its mother's arms."

Oliver snorted. "Never met old Freddy's mama, have you?"

"I tell you, nothing can go wrong. Now give me some more of that punch and I'll tell you how we're shipping the stuff to Bristol." He lowered his voice conspiratorially. "We had to find three lightskirts for that one."

Chapter Nine

"The dress is lovely, Miss Danvers." Simms, Amelia's fashionable dresser, ran an assessing eye down Lucy's white gown of sarcenet with its over-dress of shimmering white satin. She frowned slightly as she considered the deeply cut Austrian neckline. "It needs something more," she muttered.

"Yes, a few yards of lace to fill in the bodice." Lucy studied herself uneasily in the mirror. This gown was cut even deeper than the one she had worn to Lord Chuffington's dinner party, and that one had given her distinct qualms. After years of wearing dresses that buttoned to her chin, she simply didn't feel comfortable with such a large portion of her chest exposed.

"No, Miss Danvers, what it needs is a necklace," Simms declared.

"Which I don't have," Lucy said unconcernedly. The small bits and pieces of jewelry her mother had taken to France with her had long since been sold to buy food and pay the doctor. And while Lucy remembered magnificent pieces that her mother had worn to parties while they had still been in England, she had no idea where they were. Nor did she care. At the moment, simply being home was enough.

"But people will think—"

"That I choose not to wear any jewelry," Lucy said. "The whole upper ten thousand probably know my dowry to the last shilling. They know that if I wanted to wear jewels, I could do so."

"Yes, my lady." Simms pursed her lips disapprovingly. "If you say so."

"I do." Lucy smiled at the aggrieved little woman and picked up her beaded reticule. "Thank you for helping me dress."

"Mrs. Danvers told me to. Not that I minded," she added frankly. "You are a credit to my skill."

"Thank you," Lucy repeated. Then she went in search of her grandfather, to say good-night to him before she left for the ball. She found him sitting in front of a roaring fire in the library, reading the *Political Register*.

The earl looked up as she came in. "Ah, Lucy. I thought you were Ware."

"I haven't seen him." She tried to keep her dislike of the man out of her voice—dislike that she knew was mutual. Ware bitterly resented her and Vernon's advent into the earl's life because it had greatly diminished his own influence. But while she had no doubt that her grandfather would dismiss the man if she were to complain about him, she was reluctant to do so.

Ware had, from all accounts, served the earl well these past years, and because of that she felt he should be given a chance to work through his jealousy, if he could.

"Come closer and let me look at you," the earl ordered.

Lucy obeyed, twirling around when she reached him. The overskirt swirled out in a cloud of silvery white satin, rustling delightfully.

"Hmm." The earl stroked his chin consideringly. "It needs something. A little sparkle, I think." He uncannily echoed Simms's opinion. Picking up a flat leather box from the table beside him, he handed it to her.

"Here," he said gruffly. "I gave this to your grandmama when your father was born, and she was going to give it to you as an engagement gift. Might as well have it now as later."

"Later?" Lucy eyed him uncertainly. "What do you mean, later?"

"Ha! Think I don't have eyes in my head to see that Standen's boy is smitten?"

"Colonel Standen is merely being kind." Lucy couldn't decide whether she wanted to laugh or cry at his erroneous assumption.

"To himself," he cackled. "Quite a feather in your cap to have attached him this quick, girl. All the gels are on the catch for him. Stands to reason. He's got breeding, money—"

"As well as a nasty habit of barking out orders as if he were still in the army."

"Bah, you're a clever woman. You'll soon change that."

"How? By murdering him?" Lucy asked wryly.

The earl heaved an aggrieved sigh. "By guile, girl. Women are born with it. Use it to your advantage."

"I still think murder would be far more efficient." Lucy opened the case and gasped at the glittering array within. The dark green gleam of emeralds enhanced by the dazzle of sparkling diamonds momentarily blinded her.

"Grandpapa, it's beautiful," she said reverently. She picked up the heavy necklace with its rows of alternating gems that narrowed down to an emerald pendent the size of her thumbnail. The huge gem seemed to glow with an inner fire.

"The setting is a little old-fashioned," the earl offered hesitantly.

"I don't think so." Lucy kissed his wrinkled cheek. "I think it is absolutely perfect, and every time I wear it, I'll think of you and Grandmama."

"Thank you." He beamed at her. "Put it on, girl, and let me see what it looks like."

Lucy obediently fastened the necklace around her slim neck. It felt icy cold and very heavy. Almost oppressively so, as if it were more than just a collection of gems and metal. As if it carried with it the weight of her responsibility for her grandfather's happiness and her brother's safety. She stared somberly at her reflection in the pier glass. Loving someone seemed to bring with it nothing but worries.

"Try the earbobs, girl," the earl said, breaking into her uneasy thoughts.

Lucy obediently put them on. Then she stepped back to study her reflection. The jewels added a maturity to her slight figure and a regalness to her appearance that bolstered her self-confidence.

"Perfect!" The earl rubbed his bony hands together in glee. "You look fit to marry as high as you please. But mind you, stay away from that dissolute brood of King George's," he ordered. "I won't have you bringing any of that ilk into the family." He scowled darkly. "There's bad blood there. You mark my words."

Lucy chuckled. "No royal dukes. Nothing but a good Englishman."

"Like Colonel Standen," the earl said, belaboring his point.

His continued harping on marriage reminded Lucy of what Kitty had said earlier, and she decided to try to help her cousin.

"Grandpapa, I'm a bit nervous about going to this ball tonight. I wish Kitty were going to be with me," she said, carefully laying the groundwork.

"She is. Amelia said so." He scowled. "Nobody gainsays that woman."

"But Kitty doesn't want to be there," Lucy said. "The moment Aunt Amelia's back is turned, Kitty will hide in the ladies' retiring room or with the dowagers. But if she were on the catch for a husband, she wouldn't do that. She would stay and be company for me, and I wouldn't feel so conspicuous."

"Kitty already had a husband."

"No, Kitty had a youthful mistake," Lucy said seriously. "She picked a husband with her heart and not with her head."

"Very French." Her grandfather nodded approvingly. "Tell me, if you feel that way, girl, why don't you accept Standen? Your head should be telling you that you won't find a better catch."

"For one thing, I haven't been asked." She kept her voice level with an effort. She dearly wished that he would quit singing the man's praises. If he knew what she knew about his precious Robert Standen . . .

"Irritability is one of the first signs of love, girl," he said slyly.

Lucy gritted her teeth and slowly counted to ten. Somehow, when she had longed to see her grandfather, she'd forgotten how exasperating he could be.

"If Colonel Standen is such a fantastic catch, I'll come to see it," she said.

"If some gel quicker off the mark doesn't leg-shackle him first," the earl grumbled.

Lucy tried to imagine any woman forcing the formidable Robert Standen to do anything he didn't want to and failed completely.

"Nonetheless, who I marry must be my own choice," she said. And it would be, Lucy thought with grim determination. Somewhere in England there had to be a man for her. A kind, gentle man whom she could like and respect. Someone who would share her interests. Someone who would treat her like a rational human being with a mind of her own instead of as a simpleton who could only obey orders. And, most importantly, someone who would never threaten her hard-won self-sufficiency.

"I could find a husband faster if I had Kitty to go to all the parties with me," Lucy persisted.

"I ain't stopping her." The earl sniffed.

"What is stopping her is the lack of a dowry!"

"I gave her a dowry. I even paid that Captain Whitney to marry her."

"Yes, you did your duty," Lucy agreed, "but can you not find it in your heart to be kind to her?"

"To one of Amelia's brats?" The earl looked astonished at the idea. "Can't abide the woman. Never could."

"I understand your feelings," Lucy said in perfect truth, "but Kitty is not an extension of her mother. She's a person in her own right."

"She's a watering pot," the earl grumbled. "Give me one good reason why I should squander my blunt on her again."

"Because you dislike Aunt Amelia."

"Huh?" The earl frowned at her. "Girl, you were too long with them Frogs. You ain't making any sense."

"Yes, I am. Think a minute. If Kitty marries, she'll leave here, and if she leaves, Amelia will have to go with her."

The earl stared blankly at Lucy for a second, and then a huge grin spread over his face.

"Girl, I'm proud of you. You got a mind that Italian fella would have been proud to claim."

Lucy frowned uncomprehendingly. "Italian? What Italian?"

"You know, that Maca-something-or-other."

"Machiavelli. Thank you, I think," she said dryly.

"It's perfect," he chortled. "Absolutely perfect. Don't know why I didn't think of it m'self. A woman can't refuse to go with her own daughter. Maybe she'll even take that damned Freddy with her." His expression brightened further.

"Freddy would do better to cut free from his mother's leading strings and set up his own establishment."

"Damned if I won't do it." He didn't seem to hear her. "I'll give her—"

"Ten thousand pounds," Lucy inserted.

"Ten thousand pounds!" the earl howled. "If you knew how heavy I had to come down for the first marriage—"

"Ten thousand pounds. She's a Danvers. She can't go to her husband in her shift."

"I don't care how she goes as long as she goes."

"Ten thousand," Lucy repeated inexorably. "That's not enough to tempt the fortune hunters, but it's enough so that she can hold her head up."

"You ain't at all like your dear mama," the earl said in frustration. "She would never have argued with me."

"True." Lucy smiled gently at him. "I'm exactly like you."

"The devil you are. I don't squander my blunt."

"Think of it as buying peace of mind."

"I—"

"Ah, ha! Here you are." Amelia's shrill voice preceded her portly frame into the room.

"Where else should I be but in my own library reading my paper?" The earl glared at his sister-in-law.

"I have been waiting for Lucy in the drawing room." Amelia returned his glare. "We shall be late."

"Good. She can make an entrance," the earl declared.

"It's vulgar to draw attention to yourself," Amelia decreed.

"I've always known that son of yours was vulgar," the earl said. "Never thought to hear you agree with me, though."

Amelia opened her mouth to blister him, but her breath caught on an audible gasp as Lucy turned, and the candlelight was caught and reflected by the magnificent necklace she was wearing.

Amelia pointed a quivering finger at it. "What is that?" she demanded.

"Are you blind, woman? It's a necklace," the earl snapped. "I gave it to Lucy to mark the occasion of her first ball."

"Those jewels belong to the estate!" Amelia's heavy cheeks quivered with outrage. "You can't give them to anyone."

Lucy felt a shiver of apprehension as her earlier fears came rushing back. Why was Amelia so eager to make sure that all the entailed property remained intact? Freddy was no longer the heir, Vernon was. Unless...unless those accidents hadn't really been accidents, and Amelia was planning on disposing of Vernon? Then it would matter to her if Lucy had a valuable necklace that belonged to the estate, which would ultimately come down to her son. Lucy stifled a sigh. There was no way she could know the truth. And until she somehow figured it out, all she could do was keep Vernon close to her.

"Don't be daft, woman! Those gems ain't part of the entail. I bought those baubles from Rundel and Bridges nigh on to fifty years ago. Bought 'em for my own dear Margaret, and she wanted 'em to go to Lucy. Wanted all her jewelry to go to Lucy, and it will!" His face was beet-red with anger. "Margaret put it in her will and there ain't a damned thing you can do about it."

"And what about your precious grandson?" Amelia sneered.

"He don't like to wear fancy jewels. Unlike that fop of yours."

"Kitty, there you are." Lucy, catching sight of her cousin hovering nervously in the doorway, used her as an excuse to break into the escalating argument. "I was just telling Grandpapa how glad I am to have you going about with me."

"How kind." Kitty's soft voice was barely audible as she slipped into the room.

Lucy's eyes widened as she got a good look at her cousin's gown. The deep caramel color was an excellent choice, but the style was an unmitigated disaster. It seemed to Lucy that the dressmaker had covered every square inch of material with a profusion of frills and furbelows and ruffles until the original line of the dress, if indeed there had ever been one, had been lost. The overall affect was to make Kitty look like a well-stuffed cushion.

"Ten thousand won't be enough," the earl muttered in an aside to Lucy.

"What did you say?" Amelia glared at the earl, daring him to criticize her taste in gowns.

"Grandpapa was just saying that he's decided to give Kitty a dowry," Lucy offered placatingly.

"Might as well go bail for a few gowns while I'm about it," he grumbled, "or we'll be dished up before we even begin. But mind you—" he glared at Amelia "—Lucy gets the final say on them."

"That's very kind of you." Amelia seemed to choke on the words. "But as her mother, I'm sure I know what is best for my daughter."

"Not if that thing she's wearing is any indication, you most certainly do not . . ." the earl countered.

"Grandpapa!" Lucy frowned at him.

"It's all right, Cousin Lucy." Kitty sighed. "It's no more than the truth, after all."

"The only truth is that that gown ain't to your style." The earl moderated his stance under Lucy's minatory eye. "All them—" he gestured toward the flounces "—things make you look—"

"Fashionable, but not elegant," Lucy broke in, afraid that he might blurt out the truth. Honestly, she thought in exasperation, her grandfather had absolutely no tact. "You would appear better in a more mature style instead of the *jeune fille* look."

"That's the ticket," the earl said happily. "You don't want to look like mutton dressed for lamb."

Lucy winced, but to her relief, Kitty seemed more amused than angered.

"Indeed I do not, Uncle Adolphus. And I do thank you for your offer of a dowry."

"My duty as head of the family. Besides, it's cheap at ten thousand."

"Ten thousand!" Kitty looked shocked. "But—"

"You're a Danvers, gel. You might have had a wastrel for a father, but your blood's good."

"That's very generous of you, Adolphus." Amelia eyed him suspiciously.

"I know." He smiled smugly at her. "Just see that you find her a proper husband this time."

"It wasn't Mama's fault." Kitty unexpectedly sounded belligerent. "She liked Thomas less than you did."

"Then listen to her this time," the earl snapped. "Now go away. I'm an old man. I need my peace, which I ain't going to get with a parcel of blamed females naggin' at me." He shook open his paper with a decided snap.

Lucy chuckled. "Good night, you frail old man." She kissed his cheek. "And thank you for the necklace."

"Good night, Uncle Adolphus," Kitty echoed. "Thank you for the dowry."

"Just hope it pays off," he muttered, and retired behind his paper.

"Arrogant old..." Amelia muttered under her breath as she urged Kitty out the door. "Don't dawdle," she told Lucy. "We'll miss the opening dance."

Which would give her a brief respite from the threat of having Robert's arms around her, Lucy thought nervously. A respite from worrying about the strange emotions that being held close to him seemed to cause.

Perhaps it wasn't the man, but the dance, she considered. Maybe any personable man she waltzed with could invoke those sensations. Lucy chewed her lower lip, trying to decide if this were preferable or not. Not, she finally decided, sighing. The alternative made her seem like a lightskirt, and a half-witted one at that.

"Now remember," Amelia repeated, keeping up a running dialogue, "you are not to waltz with anyone unless one of the patronesses of Almack's first gives you permission."

"Permission?" Lucy asked in confusion. "I thought the reason for going to the ball was to dance."

Amelia heaved a sigh. "The reason for going to the Alversons's ball is to be seen by the upper levels of society. As for dancing, you may dance any dance but the waltz. For that you must await permission."

"I see," Lucy said, seeing nothing of the sort. Polite society seemed to be full of pitfalls for the unwary. But at least this particular rule meant that she could avoid having to deal with the sensation of being in Robert's arms. So why wasn't she relieved?

In an uncertain frame of mind, Lucy climbed into her grandfather's luxurious carriage and leaned back against the soft leather squabs for the short ride.

There was a great deal of bustling activity around the entrance to the Alverson mansion, and they had to wait almost twenty minutes to reach the front door.

Once Lucy had passed through the receiving line, she followed her aunt into the ballroom and looked around curiously. It was a fascinating sight. A fountain had been set up in the middle of the room and colored water sprayed into the air. There were flowers everywhere, their heavy perfume clogging the hot, stuffy atmosphere. Hundreds of yards of a pale pink material had been draped from the center of the ceiling to give the illusion of being in a tent. But the most enticing sight was the multicolored gowns the women wore. As the dancers dipped and twirled to the steps of the dance, the light from what seemed to be thousands of candles was reflected off their jewels. They looked like gigantic flowers that had suddenly been imbued with life and were celebrating the gift with movement, Lucy thought fancifully.

"Stop air dreaming," Amelia said, hissing under the cover of her fluttering fan. "Maria Sefton is coming toward us. I have hopes she will give us vouchers for Almack's."

Lucy blinked and refocused on the elegantly dressed woman in yellow silk approaching them. She was middle-aged and slightly plump, but far more importantly from Lucy's point of view, she was smiling at them—a real, warm, welcoming smile.

Lucy smiled back.

"My goodness, Lucy." Lady Sefton blinked in surprise. "When you smile like that you are the image of your mother. I would recognize you anywhere. Welcome home."

"Thank you," Lucy said sincerely.

"We are all pleased to welcome Cousin Lucy back into the bosom of her family." Lucy jumped slightly as Bevis appeared out of nowhere to stand beside her.

"La, Bevis, what brings you here?" Maria Sefton asked slyly. "Pretty tame entertainment for you. Nothing but cards, for chicken stakes."

"Why, the company, of course, my lady." He smiled at Lucy, his eyes warm and full of admiration, which Lucy found very soothing.

"Oh, ho!" Maria chuckled. "Sits the wind in that corner, does it?"

"Perhaps, like most hardened bachelors, all it takes in the end is a smile from the right woman," Bevis replied gallantly.

"Her money certainly doesn't hurt." Lucy heard the muttered comment issue from a group slightly behind her, but other than unconsciously raising her chin, she didn't respond.

"And you've brought your daughter with you, Amelia," Maria said, rushing to fill the awkward silence. "Good evening, Kitty."

"Good evening, m'lady," Kitty mumbled, looking as if she would rather be anywhere than where she was.

"Yes, it is long past time my daughter assumed her rightful place in society," Amelia stated.

Before anyone could respond to the comment, the orchestra struck up a waltz. "Dear Lady Sefton—" Bevis gave her a coaxing smile "—could I possibly trespass on your kindness even further and ask you to present me to my cousin, Lucy, as a desirable partner for the waltz?"

"Naughty boy." Maria Sefton tapped him on the arm with her ivory fan. "The season has yet to properly start, and Miss Danvers has not even made an appearance at Almack's."

"I quite understand," Lucy hastened to assure her. As far as she was concerned, the patronesses could withhold permission indefinitely.

"Modesty in an heiress." Maria Sefton nodded approvingly. "It deserves a reward. You have my permission to dance, my dear."

"Thank you." Lucy smiled weakly and stole a glance around the crowded room as Bevis led her out onto the dance floor. She didn't see Robert anywhere, but that didn't mean he wasn't there. There were so many people jammed into such a small space that it was impossible to see them all.

"Who are you looking for?" There was the faintest edge of pique to Bevis's voice.

"The Prince of Wales," Lucy lied. She could hardly tell him that she was searching for another man. It would be bound to annoy him, and she didn't know what his reaction would be. Any more than she knew what was behind his sudden fit of gallantry in claiming that he was captivated by her charms. Lucy sighed. At least with Robert she knew what his motives were. She knew exactly what he wanted from her. She had no intention of giving it to him, but she knew. And in knowing, there was a kind of security.

"The prince won't be here until much later." Bevis took her in his arms and began to move to the waltz. "He's probably engaged with Mrs. Fitzherbert," he added acidly.

Lucy ignored his comment, her entire concentration focused on not falling over his feet and disgracing herself. Once they had circled the floor and she'd gained a little more confidence, she began to notice other things, such as the pressure of Bevis's hand on her waist and the heat from his lean body. She could smell a scent of some sort, one which was stronger than she liked but not oppressively so. Lucy stared straight ahead at his chest, counting the folds in his elaborately arranged cravat. It was gleaming white and his dark blue coat molded his broad shoulders in a way that bespoke the work of a master tailor.

Taken as a whole, Bevis was a superbly turned out specimen of masculinity. So why did she have no more reaction to him than she had to the seventy-eight-year-old priest who had tutored Vernon in France? She gnawed on her lower lip, trying to puzzle it out. It didn't make a great deal of sense. Unless, perhaps, she responded so strongly to Robert because he represented a threat to her peace of mind? She regretfully discarded the idea. She'd reacted that way to him back at the inn in France, when she'd thought she was never going to see him again. She stifled a sigh. Her life seemed to have far more questions than answers lately.

Across the room, Robert gestured toward Lucy. "There. That's Lucy Danvers."

"And who is the man she's dancing with?" his father asked.

"Her cousin Bevis." Robert felt a flash of annoyance at the proprietary way Bevis was holding her.

"He seems to be viewing her with more than cousinly interest."

Robert's eyes narrowed as he watched Bevis smile at Lucy. Was that simply family feeling or was his father right? Was there something deeper behind Bevis's ingratiating manner? Something that might possibly threaten his own plans? He felt a ripple of unease disturb the initial pleasure he'd felt at the sight of Lucy.

"What do you know about Bevis, sir?"

His father absently rubbed his forefinger along his jawline. "Not much," he finally said. "He's far too young for my set, of course, but one does hear things. Seems to like to play deep. Very deep. But I never heard of him not paying when he loses. Nor have I heard anything that would suggest he fuzzes the cards. Fact is, never heard much of him at all. Do you want me to ask around?"

"No," Robert said slowly. "He's not a threat to my plans to marry Lucy."

His father chuckled. "Aye, but what about the young lady's plans? It's possible that she might have a few of her own."

"She'll marry me," Robert said flatly.

"Be a good thing if she will have you." His father nodded. "Fine looking gel, excellent family, considerable heiress. Yes, it's a good choice you've made, m'boy. Couldn't have picked better myself. You spoken to the earl yet?"

"No," Robert murmured. "I want to give her a chance to get to know me before I make a formal declaration." He hedged the truth.

"Bah! I have no patience with all these newfangled notions. Plenty of time to get to know her after you've wed. Don't waste time." He dug an elbow into Robert's white satin waistcoat. "Remember, I want grandchildren by next year."

"Yes, sir," Robert muttered, as a sudden warmth shot through his body at the very thought of children in connection with Lucy. At the thought of her soft, pliant body arched beneath him at the peak of her pleasure. At the thought of her soft lips, red and moist from his kisses. At the thought of hearing once again the soft yearning sounds she had made when he'd kissed her.

Soon, he promised himself. Soon she would be his, and in the meantime, it wouldn't hurt to steal a kiss or two. After all, he fully intended to marry her, he thought, stifling his qualms of conscience.

The music finally ended. Robert nodded to his father and then began to make his way through the crowd, intent on reaching her before someone else claimed the next dance.

"—And get a drink." Robert arrived in time to hear Bevis's suggestion.

"May I have the next dance, my lady?" Robert perfunctorily asked as he took her arm.

"I was about to take my cousin for a glass of lemonade." Bevis's voice had a decided edge to it.

"Suppose we allow your cousin the choice." He smiled at Lucy, and she watched the upward lift of his lips in unwilling fascination. Their movement carried her eyes to the tiny silver lights dancing in the center of his night-dark eyes. Her breathing seemed to shorten as a band tightened around her chest.

What she felt was fear, she tried to tell herself. She was afraid of what Robert might say and who he might say it to if she refused to dance with him. But she knew in her heart that it was more than that. Much more. The man himself seemed to hold an irrepressible magnetism for her. He intrigued her on some level that Bevis could never reach.

Her cousin might be the nicer person, but Robert was the challenge. Defeating him engaged her senses on every level. Her mind never wandered when he was around. A sense of anticipation began to spill through her.

"Lucy?" Bevis sounded querulous.

"Thank you for the dance, Bevis, but I'm not really thirsty, and I did promise the colonel a dance," she said.

For a brief second, so short that she wasn't entirely sure she hadn't imagined it, an ugly expression hardened Bevis's face. Then it was gone, if indeed it had ever existed, and he made her a graceful leg.

"The pleasure of our dance was all mine, Cousin. Perhaps later you will again do me the honor."

"Of course," Lucy murmured, already dismissing him from her mind as the orchestra began to play and Robert reached for her.

Chapter Ten

Frustrated, Lucy threw her quill down on the muddled mess her aunt claimed were the only expense records for the household for the last five years. She bit off a furious expletive as the spattering ink added yet another series of splotches to the virtually indecipherable pages.

Sighing, she reached for the pen and then paused as she saw Vernon trying to sneak past the open bookroom door. Curious as to the reason for his furtive manner, she quietly got up and walked over to the doorway. At lunch her brother had gobbled his food in his haste to return to the stables in the mews behind the house, where the head groom had promised him a second riding lesson. That had barely been an hour ago, hardly enough time for his newfound fascination with horses to be sated.

He had far too much free time on his hands, she admitted. And now that his health was improving by leaps and bounds, far too much energy to invest in schemes that had an unfortunate tendency to go awry. She shuddered at the memory of the dueling pistols. It was all right when he was with their grandfather, but even though the earl's health seemed to be improving, along with his grandson's, there was no denying the fact that he was over seventy. He simply did not have the stamina to keep up with a boy of eleven. And she had the stamina, but not the time. What with trying to run the household, oversee the renovations of their wardrobe, participate in the incredible amount of socializing that seemed to be part and parcel of the London scene and trying to hold Robert at bay, she was being run off her feet.

Maybe she should consider her grandfather's idea of a tutor, she thought. She would, just as soon as she was sure that Vernon's accidents really were that. At the moment, she wouldn't feel safe introducing a stranger into the household.

Lucy emerged from the book room as Vernon reached the stairs. She grimaced as she took in the rip in the seat of his pants and the mud on the back of his jacket.

"Vernon Danvers, when will you have a care for your clothes? You look like a shagbag."

"Aw, Lucy," he moaned.

"Turn around and let me assess the damage."

"Aw, Lucy," he repeated.

"Now, young man."

Vernon slowly turned, and Lucy gasped in horror at the sight of the blood trickling from his nose. A raw, angry-looking scrape covered his left cheek, and the bump on his forehead was already beginning to turn purple.

"What happened?" she demanded as a wave of fear chased over her, making her skin feel too tight for her body. Not another accident, she thought in disbelief.

"Nothin'." Vernon wiped the blood away with the back of his sleeve.

"Nothing?" Lucy repeated incredulously. "You sneak into the house looking like you have been set upon by footpads who robbed you and left you for dead, and you tell me nothing happened?"

"What's going on out here?" The earl came out of the library, his eyes narrowing as he spied Vernon's battered condition.

"Now see what you did." Vernon eyed his sister reproachfully.

"It's what I am going to do that you should be concerned about." Lucy snapped, her fear making her short-tempered.

"Don't fuss, girl," the earl ordered. "Give the boy a chance to explain."

"I came off," Vernon muttered, ducking his head.

"Came off what?" she demanded.

"Buccilous."

Lucy let her breath out with a long sigh of relief as she realized that there was a perfectly reasonable explanation for Vernon's disheveled appearance. A beginning rider falling off his horse was something she could easily accept. It happened to everyone, herself included. Her feeling of relief was short-lived as Vernon launched into a defense of his pony.

"It wasn't Buccilous's fault," he insisted. "Freddy drove into the courtyard just as I was getting off after my lesson, and Buccilous was startled and reared, and I came off."

"Freddy?" Lucy repeated slowly, as all her half-formed fears came rushing back to torment her.

"That cowhanded looby!" the earl said scathingly. "Damned lucky he didn't run over you, m'boy." He grasped Vernon's chin and tipped his head back to study the damage. "Not too bad," he declared.

Lucy carefully studied Vernon's face. Her grandfather was right. It was mostly surface gore. This time. She bit her lip uncertainly. Would there be a next time or was she imagining plots where there was simply incompetence and coincidence?

"What is all the fuss down here? You are disturbing my guests in the drawing room." Amelia stomped down the stairs. "I might have known." She eyed Vernon with revulsion. "What have you been doing?"

"Your caper-witted son drove into the courtyard and startled Vernon's pony," the earl snapped.

"Where else would Freddy stable the carriage?" Amelia asked, rushing to his defense.

"True," Lucy agreed, trying to be fair. "London is not really the place for Vernon to learn to ride. There are far too many things to distract his pony."

"Lucy!" Vernon eyed her with dismay. "I got to learn. Everyone else my age is already a bruising rider."

"Well, you have certainly got the bruises," she said dryly.

"Lucy, you can't—"

"Your sister is right, m'boy," the earl admitted. "I wasn't thinking. London has a scarcity of soft grass to land on."

"I learned to ride at Landsdowne," Lucy told the disappointed-looking boy.

"And that is where Vernon will learn the basics," the earl pronounced. "We will go to Landsdowne for a few weeks. That should be long enough for you to learn how to stay on, m'boy. Once you've done that, you can practice mornings in the park here in London with one of the grooms. Now go wash the blood off and dispose of those ragged clothes. Ask Ware to help you."

"Thank you, Grandpapa." Vernon beamed at him and then pounded up the stairs.

"You cannot mean to go down to Landsdowne with the season about to start?" Amelia demanded incredulously.

"Only thing to do," the earl insisted. "You heard the boy. He wants to learn to ride."

"You are spoiling him outrageously," the matron snapped.

"No concern of yours," the earl shot back. "Didn't ask you to go to Landsdowne. Stay here and try to find a husband for poor Kitty."

"No." Lucy suddenly spoke up.

"No what?" The earl frowned at her.

"Don't refer to Kitty as 'poor Kitty.' She isn't. She has a dowry and a family and, as far as I can tell, is healthy. 'Poor Kitty' conjures up visions of invalids reclining on sofas, wasting away."

"Just as soon not call her anything," the earl grumbled. "Just as soon not even see her. Just as soon not see any of them."

"The feeling is mutual." Amelia glared at him.

"I wish the two of you wouldn't do this," Lucy said tiredly. "You are setting a terrible example for Vernon with your continual brangling. Now, about going to Landsdowne..." she continued, once the two combatants had reduced their hostilities to glares.

"Season won't start proper like for a couple of weeks yet," the earl said. "And Landsdowne is pretty this time of year."

Amelia contented herself with a contemptuous snort.

And Landsdowne didn't contain Robert Standen's disturbing presence, Lucy thought. Maybe away from him, she could manage to put her reaction to him into perspective. And there was also the fact that if Robert wanted to marry at once, he might well set his sights on less-elusive quarry. The realization sent a disquieting sensation feathering through her mind. She didn't want to think about him marrying someone else. Of him touching someone else as he'd touched her. Not wanting to examine her unexpected feelings, she focused instead on her grandfather's plan.

"I think it's an excellent idea," she said, "and I would love to see Landsdowne again."

"We'll get up a party," the earl said, and Lucy tensed at his words as an awful premonition of impending disaster popped full-blown into her mind.

"What kind of a party?" Amelia voiced Lucy's fears.

"A congenial party. Not the kind you would know about," the earl snapped.

"Grandfather!" Lucy said reprovingly. She was beginning to feel a sneaking sympathy for her aunt. It was no wonder Amelia was irritable if she had been subjected to these constant insults for the years she'd lived here. What Lucy did not understand was why she stayed. Perhaps Amelia's widow's jointure wasn't sufficient to lease the type of establishment in London that she felt was her due. It was obvious to Lucy after only a few weeks that London was a ruinously expensive city.

"We'll invite a few people," the earl announced, beginning to plan.

The doorbell rang and Lucy swallowed a giggle as they all turned toward it, waiting like statues while Fulton emerged from behind the green baize door to answer it.

"Good morning, Fulton." Robert Standen stepped into the hall, blinking as he found himself the focus of three pairs of eyes. His attention skimmed over Amelia, rested briefly on the earl and then paused to linger thoughtfully on Lucy. He studied the way the soft jaconet of her rose morning dress clung to her breasts.

Lucy's mouth suddenly felt dry under his scrutiny. She shortened her breathing in an attempt to control her instinctive reaction, but from the gleam that suddenly lit his dark eyes, she was sure she had not been successful.

"Is something amiss?" Robert finally asked.

"Not at all. Not at all." The earl beamed at him. "We were just discussing taking a houseparty to Landsdowne, my estate in Derbyshire. We shall leave tomorrow and return in two weeks. You and your father are invited, of course. Isn't that right, Lucy?" The earl smiled slyly at her.

Lucy gritted her teeth against an almost overwhelming desire to throw something. So much for her plan to force some distance between herself and Robert. Now she was even more firmly caught in his trap. It would be almost impossible to avoid him at Landsdowne. She would be virtually living in his pocket.

"My father is promised elsewhere, but I accept with pleasure." Robert gave Lucy a smug smile that made her long to do him a physical injury.

"How nice," Amelia simpered. "Kitty will be so pleased to hear you will be among the company. She is so looking forward to the party." Amelia ignored the earl's outraged expression at her including herself. "Why don't you join us for tea while I tell her the happy news?"

"Another time, perhaps," Robert said. "Miss Danvers is promised to me for a drive."

"I see." Amelia shot Lucy a frustrated glare.

Lucy wished she could tell her aunt that the drive certainly had not been at her instigation. Robert had simply informed her during one of their two dances at last night's rout that he would call to take her for a drive this afternoon. And as much as she had wanted to treat his self-assurance with the contempt it deserved, she didn't dare.

"Excellent, excellent," the earl approved. "Fresh air and all that."

It was the "all that" that worried her, Lucy thought glumly as she accepted her cloak from the smiling Fulton and allowed Robert to usher her out of the house. She felt as if she were caught in a snare that was slowly tightening around her, pinning her in place until her captor came to claim his prize.

Lucy scrambled up into Robert's curricle and then waited until he'd once again dismissed the smiling groom.

"Why do we always go for a drive?" She huddled deeper into her deep blue, terry poplin cloak as a brisk gust of the fresh air her grandfather had praised threatened to freeze her ears.

"To escape, of course." He tightened the reins and the horses danced sideways before stepping forward at a quick walk. "If we stay in your drawing room, your aunt will throw her daughter at my head."

"You aren't irresistible!" Lucy snapped, annoyed at his observation, especially since it was no more than the truth. Her aunt's determined pursuit of him would put anyone to the blush.

"No, but my money is," he shot back.

"Not to me. I have pots of my own," she said smugly. "Besides, Kitty is not trying to lure you into marriage. And anyway," she said hurriedly, when he opened his mouth, "you can hardly blame my aunt for trying to arrange an advantageous marriage for her only daughter. It's not her fault she doesn't know what you're really like. Maybe if you would stay for tea a few times you'd put her off."

"Don't you believe it. She wouldn't be put off if she found I were a lecherous gambler. With enough money, all sins are forgiven."

"You can't have that much money!" Lucy said tartly. "Who is that?" She suddenly changed the subject as she saw a vaguely familiar man of about sixty gesturing to them from a carriage just inside the park gates.

"A friend of my father's." Robert obediently pulled to a halt beside the man's carriage.

"Good afternoon, Mr. Corstairs. May I make Miss Lucy Danvers known to you?" Robert said politely.

"No need, m'boy." He chuckled and his oversize paunch bulged out between his tight pantaloons and his brilliantly colored floral waistcoat. "I met the young lady at Chuffy's t'other night. Always make it a point to meet the pretty gels." He wheezed at his own wit. "Quite a difference between tooling around the park with her on your arm and participating in that fiasco on the Continent, ain't it? If Wellington knew what he was about, you would have been home doing it long before now."

"Wellington is not the problem!" Robert exclaimed, hotly defending his commander. "The problem is the sapsculls in the War Department who foul up our supplies, muddle our orders and leak our plans to the enemy."

Corstairs bristled. "My son works in the War Department."

"If the War Department worked at all, Wellington would have routed that vulgar Corsican years ago," Robert replied, giving vent to his frustration.

"Hotheaded cub!" Corstairs muttered, and with a glare at Robert, drove off.

Robert watched him leave, and then turned to Lucy. "You were wrong," he said.

"About what?"

"About how I should tell people the facts about the war when they criticize Wellington. I told Corstairs what the real problem was and he didn't listen, he just got angry," he said in frustration.

"I think I should have been a little more specific with my instructions," Lucy said wryly. "I forgot you have been in the army all your adult life."

Robert frowned. "What does that mean?"

"It means that your method of communicating with people is to issue an order and then expect them to jump to obey. It is not an approach that works well in civilian life. Especially not when the civilian in question has a son whom you are casting aspersions on."

"I was not! His son couldn't possibly be in a position of power. Not if he's as stupid as his father."

Lucy cast her eyes heavenward. "Lord give me strength."

"Now what?" he asked in resignation.

"You don't have a diplomatic bone in your body."

"Thank you."

"That was not a compliment!" she said tartly.

"Diplomats are vultures."

"And you think you're going to do the army's cause any good by putting people's backs up?"

"Every word I said was the truth," he insisted.

"If people feel threatened or angered by what you are saying, they are not going to even listen to you, let alone agree."

"But if I can't disagree with them, what's the point in trying to tell them the truth about the Peninsular War? They already have the wrong idea."

"Sneak the concepts in. Don't hit them over the head with them," Lucy said.

"As you pointed out, I'm a soldier, not a diplomat."

"You aren't a soldier anymore. You sold out and now you are a civilian."

Robert sighed. "Yes."

"And since you can't help Wellington on the battlefield, you will have to do it here in England."

"By pouring the butter boat over to a bunch of dolts who owe their positions to patronage?" he asked scathingly.

Lucy switched tactics. "Tell me, Colonel, how do you plan a military offensive?"

"Robert, I am called Robert," he said in exasperation.

"You are called lots of things," Lucy replied primly. "That is no reason for me to sink to the level of repeating them."

He grimaced. "Perhaps there is something to be said for languid debs after all."

"From your point of view, perhaps, but not from theirs."

"You forget that I have that all-important ingredient in a husband—money."

"How you do prose on about your money," Lucy said reprovingly. "Puffing up one's consequence is vulgar, Aunt Amelia says."

"And ignoring the facts is stupid," Robert countered. "One should always assess an enemy's strengths and weaknesses."

"If you view your future wife as an enemy—"

"The other side, then." He swung the carriage into one of the park's many narrow byways. "And, since I don't have a title, my money is my major asset."

Lucy studied him from beneath her lashes. His eyes were narrowed against the bright sunlight, a sunlight that gilded his taut features and added bluish highlights to his inky black hair. His lips suddenly compressed as the horses shied away from a squirrel, scrambling across the path in front of them.

Lucy shivered as she remembered the impact of his lips pressed against hers. Remembered, too, the feeling of helplessness she had experienced at being held captive by the confining weight of his hard body. But rather than frightening her, the sensation had exhilarated her. Probably because she had known even then that she wasn't really a captive. Robert would have let her go if she had struggled. He wasn't the kind of man to physically harm a woman. He might well drive her to Bedlam with his eternal orders, she thought ruefully, but he would never abuse her.

"Why are you studying me like that?" he asked, once he had the horses under control again.

"I was thinking that you would make a perfect character from one of Mrs. Radcliff's novels," Lucy lied, having no intention of letting him know that she found him physically appealing. "I'm just not certain if you're the villain or the hero," she added thoughtfully.

"Really?" The corner of his well-formed mouth lifted in a wicked grin. "And what's the difference?"

"Well, you understand that I have not had the opportunity to read very many of them, but from what I can tell, the villain is a lot more inventive. He is also ruthless, while the hero is nauseatingly good."

"You think being good is nauseating?" Robert eyed her curiously.

"A man who always did and said the proper thing at the proper time would be impossible to live with."

"You don't want a perfect husband?"

"Of course not," she said promptly, "because I'm not perfect. I have faults, so I need a husband who will overlook them in exchange for my overlooking his."

"Hmm." Robert brought the team to a halt on the deserted path as he considered her words. "That opens up some intriguing possibilities."

Lucy frowned at him. "I don't see how."

"I was referring to your desire for a husband with faults." He transferred both reins to his left hand, and suddenly reaching out, grasped her chin in his right hand.

Lucy instinctively leaned back, but his hand tightened, and the narrowness of the seat prevented further retreat. She took a deep breath and the smell of leather from his gloves filled her nostrils, making her vividly aware of his masculinity. She swallowed uneasily as his face came closer and closer, until it filled her whole field of vision. His black eyes were so dark they seemed to have no pupils, and she could see the long, sooty sweep of each eyelash. The very faint aroma of sandalwood, which she had come to associate with him, drifted into her lungs, heating the air in them.

"What are you doing?" Lucy winced as she realized the stupidity of the question. It was obvious to the meanest intelligence what he was doing. What wasn't so obvious was why. She tried to think, but the pressure of his fingers on her soft flesh and the warmth of his breath as it wafted across her sensitive cheek was causing her skin to tighten.

Lucy shivered convulsively as his lips brushed hers, and she instinctively leaned forward. Finally, his mouth pressed against hers and she felt a dry surge of heat, followed by a tingling awareness that pierced her like thousands of tiny needles. A whirling sensation swirled through her mind and Lucy grasped his forearm to steady herself as the world suddenly tilted on its axis.

It started to rock as Robert began to outline her lips with the tip of his tongue. But to her intense disappointment, he suddenly jerked back. A moment later, the jingling sound of harnesses penetrated her absorption. Robert quickly snapped the reins and the chestnuts started forward at a brisk walk.

Lucy stared down at her hands, surprised to find them clenched into fists. She took a deep breath and then a second, fighting to relax her tense muscles. She ran her tongue over her mouth, somehow expecting to find it different, changed by his brief kiss. But it was unchanged. She jumped slightly as a carriage driven by a somberly dressed man overtook them.

"That man almost saw what you were doing." Lucy launched an attack in the hopes that it would disguise just how absorbed she'd been in his kiss. "Do you know what would have happened if he had?"

"What *we* were doing," Robert corrected, "and yes, I know. You would have been hopelessly compromised and I would have had to declare our engagement at once instead of waiting until the end of the season. In fact..." He eyed her narrowly for a second and then, stopping the horses, deliberately tied the reins onto the seat.

"What are you doing?" Lucy squeaked as he reached out for her.

"Taking advantage of your idea." His arms closed around her and he pulled her up against his chest. "You know, my dear, if you had changed your mind about marrying me, all you had to do was say so. It wasn't necessary to lure me to a deserted spot and cast out lures."

"Cast out lures!" Lucy sputtered. "Why, you conceited—"

Robert's mouth cut off her flow of invectives and his hot breath mingled with hers. As his tongue surged inside her mouth to stroke over hers, Lucy shuddered convulsively. Desire slammed through her, obliterating rational thought. She was fast losing all sense of who and what she was. The only relevant thing in her whole universe was Robert. The feel of his hard lips, the clean warmth of his skin, the musky scent of his body....

The very depth of her response terrified her, effectively drenching her reaction in the cold light of reason. Desperately, she jerked back, horrified that her body could have so quickly gained ascendancy over her mind. That she could have so quickly forgotten the dangers of allowing herself to respond so wholeheartedly to a man. To any man, but especially to one like Robert Standen. With Robert she could never maintain any emotional distance. With him, there could never be a lukewarm, pleasant relationship. All he had to do was touch her and she seemed to become someone else, someone who bore no resemblance to her normal, level-headed, cautious self. And it had to stop. She firmly squelched her feeling of regret.

"Lovemaking would appear to be one area where we are in perfect agreement." Robert unexpectedly accepted her retreat and untied the reins, urging the horses forward.

"No, we—" Lucy began, and then faltered to a stop under his level gaze. "You, sir, are not a gentleman."

"If that kiss brands me so, then what does it label you?" Robert retaliated with devastating accuracy.

Lucy winced at the direct hit.

"We seem to have wandered rather far afield," she finally said, having no intention of exploring the thought further. She was already feeling shaken enough.

"Do you always ignore subjects you don't want to deal with?"

"I do when the only solution that springs to mind is both immoral and illegal," she snapped. "Now then, before you decided to..." She gestured helplessly with one slender hand.

He grinned at her. "Kiss you. You have been overlong in France if you have forgotten your English to that extent."

Lucy closed her eyes and counted to ten, both infuriated and intrigued by Robert. He was turning out to be far less rigid than she'd originally thought, although no less ruthless.

And now she couldn't even hope to make him lose interest in her while she was hiding in Landsdowne. He would be right there, and the old house was full of nooks and crannies for him to catch her in. A fugitive ray of excitement colored her mind and she grimaced in annoyance. She was beginning to feel as if she were fighting both him and herself.

Chapter Eleven

"Good morning, Freddy." Lucy winced as her unexpected appearance in the breakfast room caused her cousin to choke on the coffee he was drinking. "I'm sorry." She gave him a sympathetic smile. "I didn't mean to startle you."

"Wasn't expecting anyone this early. Mean to say..." He sputtered to a stop, his eyes widening in horror.

"What is it?" Lucy moved closer to the protective bulk of the sideboard as she hastily scanned the floor for any unpleasant creatures that Vernon might have introduced into the household.

"My neckcloth!" Freddy choked. "I got coffee on it." He raised anguished blue eyes to Lucy.

"You did?" She stared at him, nonplussed at his violent reaction.

"Yes," he groaned. "Look!" He pointed one slender finger at a faint brown spot that marred the otherwise snowy perfection of the cloth.

"You can hardly see it," Lucy offered, not sure what kind of response was called for.

"Hardly!" His pale eyes bulged.

There was a lot of his mother's love of the dramatic in Freddy, Lucy suddenly realized. "If it bothers you, why don't you just change it?" she tried again.

"It took me almost three hours to get the proper effect. It's my own design, you know," he confided. "All the crack, I assure you. I call it Variations on a Waterfall."

Lucy simply stared at him, unable to believe that anyone, let alone a grown man, would spend three hours tying a bit of cloth around his neck.

"There's nothing for it." Freddy heaved a huge sigh, reminding Lucy of Vernon in one of his martyr moods. "I shall simply have to change it. I cannot possibly be seen in public like this. Oliver will understand why I'm late."

Lucy stifled a smile as her cousin, with one last reproachful look at her, left. From what she had observed of Lord Oliver, he wouldn't even notice if Freddy was late. Picking up a plate from the sideboard, she ran a cursory eye over the selections of breakfast dishes. A sense of satisfaction filled her. Since she had taken over the running of the household, no more fatty gammon and skimpy plates of eggs were served at breakfast. Now, both the quality and the variety of food was excellent, and the overall cost was but a fraction of what her aunt had claimed to have spent.

Lucy helped herself to a baked egg, added a muffin and sat down.

"Is there anything you wish, Miss Lucy?" Fulton asked, appearing in the doorway.

"Just coffee, thank you." Lucy waited until he had poured it and then dismissed him. She found it disconcerting to try to eat while the servants stood around and waited on her. She felt as if she ought to gulp down her food so as to release them from their vigil.

As she reached for her coffee cup, she noticed a half-folded piece of paper lying beside Freddy's empty plate. Curious, she looked at it, her eyes widening when she realized that it was a dunning notice from Freddy's tailor—a dunning notice for what seemed to her to be an astronomical sum. Lucy raised her eyebrows, wondering how anyone could possibly spend that much on clothing. Or why a merchant would allow that large a bill to accumulate. Her first thought was that the tailor must know that Freddy had ample funds to pay for it when it was finally brought to his attention. She frowned as another, less palatable explanation occurred to her. Perhaps the tailor had assumed that her grandfather would pay the bill even if Freddy couldn't, since Freddy was his heir.

Lucy frowned as she considered the possibility. Freddy might well have problems meeting this bill from his own income. His father had been a second son and his mother was not from a wealthy family. Although it was possible that Freddy had inherited money from another relative, as she had done. . . .

But what if he hadn't? The thought nagged at her. Suppose he didn't have the funds to pay this exorbitant bill. Suppose he had assumed that eventually he'd have her grandfather's money at his disposal. And when she had come home so unexpectedly with Vernon, he'd had to face the fact that he no longer would. What had his reaction been? Had he decided to remove the only obstacle between him and the very wealthy earldom? Lucy felt a clutch of fear tighten her stomach as she remembered how Vernon had been thrown because Freddy had driven up and startled his pony. Could her cousin have done it on purpose, hoping the results would be more serious?

She nervously chewed on her lip as she reconsidered Vernon's accident in this new light. Freddy lived in the house. It would have been an easy matter for him to load the dueling pistols and leave them out, knowing that they would hold a fascination for a young boy, one that would probably override any warnings he'd been given about the dangers of touching guns.

Lucy stared down at her breakfast, which had suddenly become tasteless. Freddy hadn't been at home when the railing had broken and Vernon had almost fallen to his death, she reminded herself. But he could have damaged the rail some time ago in the hopes that the earl himself might be the victim, hastening his own inheritance of the earldom.

Just how pressed did her cousin feel by this bill? She had discovered that many of the ton put off paying their bills for years and felt no compunction about it. Freddy could well be one of their number. Or he might feel that if he were to give it to the earl, the old man would eventually, after he'd ranted and raved, pay it rather than see a close relative tossed in the Fleet. And he'd probably be right, Lucy conceded. Her grandfather might dislike Freddy, but he'd hate having his name dragged through the courts. She sighed. Taken as a whole, the notice seemed an insufficient motive for murder.

She rubbed her shaking fingers over her forehead and tried to think. If someone really were trying to kill Vernon, and those weren't just accidents, then she had to do more than simply try to keep her brother close.

She had to find out who was behind the plot and unmask him. She stared down into the dark depths of her coffee. The question was, how?

She couldn't ask her grandfather for help. He was too old and still far too weak to cope with her suspicions. And, anyway, what could he do? No more than she could, she thought grimly.

Even if she were to go so far as to call in Bow Street, they would be bound to point out that she had no proof that anything other than a series of coincidental accidents had occurred. It was even possible that Freddy had, in fact, loaded the dueling pistols at some time in the past and had then forgotten about them. The railing could have simply weakened with age. Fulton had said it had been years since anyone had done anything around the estate in the way of repairs. And it could well be that Freddy had driven up quite innocently just as Vernon was receiving his riding instruction. As Amelia had been quick to point out, where else would he drive his carriage but into the stable yard?

Underlying that bit of logic was the fact that Lucy simply couldn't believe that Freddy, who didn't seem to care about anything other than the cut of his coat, would stoop to murdering for money.

But she had been ready to engage in prostitution for money. The unwelcome thought intruded relentlessly. That was totally unlike her, but her need had overridden her normal scruples.

Lucy ran a finger over the final sum at the bottom of the tailor's bill. Did Freddy feel his need justified removing Vernon from his path? Or had her years of hiding in France made her imagine plots where none existed?

Lucy grimaced as her thoughts kept circling round and round, and what she knew chased what she suspected but couldn't prove. Didn't want to prove, she admitted. She didn't want it to be true. She didn't want to believe that someone was really trying to kill her young brother.

She took a drink of coffee, swallowing it along with the acute sense of frustration that clogged her throat. It was all so unfair. Instead of being able to relax and enjoy life in England, with only the normal day-to-day problems that everyone else coped with, she was having to deal with a man who knew her worst secret and was prepared to reveal it if she refused to marry him, as well as what might be a plot to kill her brother. Lucy sighed again. Viewed in retrospect, France didn't seem so bad after all.

Refusing to give in to her mounting sense of fear, she forced herself to calmly consider who could be behind the plot—if, indeed, there really was one. Lucy pushed her plate away and took another sip of her now-tepid coffee as she considered what she actually knew as fact. It was pitifully little.

Logically, Freddy was the most likely villain, because he had the most to gain by Vernon's death: he would once again be heir to the earldom and all its resources. She slowly swirled her coffee around in the delicate porcelain cup. Even so, she couldn't see Freddy as a murderer. He was too... She groped for a word to describe her impression of her cousin and finally settled on *ineffectual*. She simply didn't believe that he had either the backbone or the wit to cold-bloodedly plan and carry out a murder.

But his mother did. Lucy felt a chill slither down her spine as she remembered the fury in her aunt's voice when she'd questioned the validity of Vernon's claim. Yes, Lucy conceded, her aunt not only had the backbone for murder, but she was devoted to the betterment of her offspring. And things didn't get much better than having her son inherit the earldom.

Not only that, but she already knew that her aunt's basic sense of integrity was malleable, to say the least. Lucy remembered what she was virtually certain were falsified entries in the housekeeping books. Over the years Amelia must have channeled thousands of pounds of the earl's money into her own accounts. But did her willingness to steal from her brother-in-law necessarily translate into a willingness to kill Vernon? Lucy tried to be fair.

Amelia might well have justified the thefts in her mind by telling herself that it would all belong to her son someday anyway, and that Freddy certainly wouldn't begrudge her the money. Which was perfectly true, Lucy admitted. Freddy appeared to be unable to refuse his mother anything. In fact, Vernon was far more independent than Freddy.

If it wasn't Amelia and it wasn't Freddy, then who did that leave? Lucy thought hard, knowing how important it was that she weigh all the possibilities. Bitter experience had taught her that danger could come from any direction, no matter how unlikely it seemed initially.

There was Kitty, of course. Being sister to an earl would put her in a far better position on all counts. But Kitty didn't seem to want to even go out into society, let alone cut a dash through it. Not only that, but the earl had provided her with a dowry, making it possible for her to remarry if she chose to do so. No,

Kitty's main concern seemed to be staying out of the limelight. Hardly the attitude of a murderess.

So who did that leave? Lucy ran through the list in her mind. The only other family member in residence in London was Bevis, and it couldn't be him. He was the only son of the earl's sister, which left him out of the succession. Bevis had nothing to gain by disposing of Vernon.

Lucy sighed, wishing she had someone to confide in. Someone like Robert, to whom a murderous plot or two was undoubtedly nothing out of the ordinary. Not after years of campaigning on the Continent. But she just couldn't do it. Not only was the habit of secrecy too deeply ingrained, but she didn't want to give Robert anymore information. Look how he'd used what he already had.

"Mr. Bevis Danvers." Fulton's voice registered an ever-so-slight disapproval. Clearly, in his view, gentlemen did not intrude at breakfast, even if they were relatives.

"Ah, good morning, Cousin Lucy." Bevis smiled at her.

Lucy looked up into his warm, twinkling brown eyes and some of the tenseness drained out of her. Bevis seemed so blessedly normal. So far removed from the problems she had so unexpectedly found herself grappling with.

"Please tell me that you don't share Fulton's antiquated view of proper behavior?" Bevis smiled charmingly. "After all, I haven't broken all the rules of polite society. I've only bent one, and as my excuse, I claim the privilege of family."

"It's all right, Fulton." Lucy smiled at the butler. "I'm sure my cousin had a compelling reason for calling before breakfast."

"Expedience," Bevis admitted ruefully, sitting down beside her. "I want to take you driving this afternoon, so I needed to ask you before Colonel Standen calls." For a second Bevis's features hardened, and Lucy blinked, having the eerie sensation that she was seeing another person entirely. But almost immediately his expression cleared, and she told herself not to be ridiculous, that she was imagining plots and enemies behind every bush.

"Of course I'll go for a drive with you," Lucy said, not responding to his comment about Robert. In truth, she was grateful for the invitation. Bevis seemed to be the only person around her who wasn't demanding something from her. "I also want to thank you again for your kindness in taking Vernon to see the bareback riders at Astley's."

"But Cousin Lucy, I only asked Vernon to please you," Bevis said candidly. "Your return from France is the most exciting thing to happen in our family in years." He laughed maliciously. "Although the fury your brother's existence caused in Aunt Amelia's breast is a close second."

"I'm sure Aunt Amelia feels just as she ought to," Lucy said, unwilling to openly criticize her. She didn't trust Bevis not to repeat what she said.

He chuckled. "Oh, Cousin, what a plumper! You know full well that Aunt Amelia would consign Vernon to perdition if she could. But your kind heart does you credit. It's one of the many things I lo—like about you." His eyes glowed with a sudden fervor that Lucy couldn't possibly misread.

Once her first rush of purely feminine pleasure that this very experienced man found her attractive faded, she felt a definite frisson of unease. Why did he find her attractive? she wondered. Why was he making her the object of his gallantry? Unless the attraction was not so much her as her dowry... She considered the comment she'd overheard at the ball. Could Bevis be short of funds? Or was he simply trying to be kind to her? She considered the last idea for a moment before dismissing it out of hand. Bevis had made several cutting remarks about various people, comments that had shown a callous disregard for their feelings.

No, Lucy thought. Bevis didn't act out of casual kindness for others. He acted for a reason. Although, perhaps, all he wanted was to set up a flirtation with her. After all, she was this season's prime heiress. It might appeal to his sense of vanity for it to be seen that she preferred his company to that of Colonel Standen. And while that was a very shallow motivation, if it were true, it was essentially harmless.

"Has my compliment really thrown you into so much confusion?" Bevis teased.

"You underestimate me," Lucy replied gently. "However, you haven't underestimated my desire for a drive in this beautiful spring weather before we leave."

"Leave?" Bevis's voice sharpened.

"Yes," Lucy answered. "We leave for Landsdowne early tomorrow."

"With the season about to start?" For a second he sounded like Amelia.

"We'll be back in a few weeks."

"You see me desolate at your desertion," Bevis mourned. "I've a mind to beg an invitation."

"I doubt the party would be to your taste," Lucy said.

Bevis's eyes narrowed. "Party?"

"A very ill-assorted one, I'm afraid, consisting of Aunt Amelia, Kitty, Freddy, Lord Alridge, Colonel Standen—"

"Colonel Standen?" Bevis frowned. "Why did you invite him?"

"I didn't," Lucy replied, trying to conceal her annoyance at his questioning. "Grandpapa did. If you wish to take him to task about whom he invites to his home..."

Bevis threw up his hands in horror. "Not I. I'm not so brave. Nor am I usually so clumsy. I did not mean to give offense. It's just that I'm not used to thinking with my heart."

He gave her a glowing smile, which she didn't believe for a second. Some deep instinct told her that Bevis's head would always rule his heart.

"If you would take pity and invite me along?"

"Certainly you may come." Lucy gave the only answer possible. Bevis was right about one thing, she admitted to herself. The party was going to need all the diversions it could get. Her aunt would spend her time mourning the loss of the earldom, Kitty would try to avoid everyone, Freddy's concern would be with the cut of his coat, and she very much feared that Robert's main topic of conversation would be on the necessity of her marrying him—as soon as possible.

"Thank you, Cousin Lucy." Bevis smiled with satisfaction at the invitation. "Till this afternoon, then." He got to his feet with seeming reluctance.

"Till this afternoon," Lucy agreed.

* * *

"Freddy, I have just been to see the most marvelous invention!" Oliver slipped into the empty wing chair beside the morose-looking Freddy. He ignored the annoyed glance from a fellow member of Brooks's, who was reading a racing form. "Absolutely fantastic!"

"Humph!" The disgruntled member got to his feet and, with a glare at the oblivious Oliver, stomped out of the room.

"Tell you, Freddy, mechanics is the future."

"I haven't got a future," Freddy said heavily.

"Eh?" Oliver looked more closely at his friend, noting his mournful expression and, even more ominous, his wilted shirt points.

"Everyone says so," Freddy muttered. "M'mother, m'uncle, Kitty, m'tailor—"

"Who wants the opinion of some upstart tradesman?" Oliver scoffed.

"Wants his money," Freddy continued. "Says I owe him thousands and thousands of pounds. Says I haven't paid him in years and years." He shook his head. "Never thought it would amount to all that. I mean, what choice did I have? One must keep up appearances. Don't see why he had to send me a bill now." Freddy took a gulp of the brandy he was holding. "Never did before."

Oliver considered the matter a moment and then said, "It's 'cause of that cousin of yours. Vernon."

"Can't be," Freddy objected. "Just a boy. A shagbag of a boy. He couldn't be in debt to my tailor."

"That's not it. It's because he's come. You see," Oliver elaborated at Freddy's blank look, "before, you were your uncle's heir, and everyone knows the old boy's swimming in lard. All the tailor had to do was to wait until the earl stuck his spoon in the wall and you would have had plenty of money to pay him. And to keep buying from him for the rest of your life. But now, you ain't the heir. The boy is. He gets the money, not you, and so the tailor wants payment right now."

"Vulture." Freddy took another gulp of brandy. "Damned bloodsucker."

"They all are." Oliver dismissed the merchant class. "No help for it, just have to change tailors."

"Change my tailor?" Freddy's eyes fairly bulged in horror. "Nugent is the best there is."

Oliver shrugged. "Then pay him."

"Can't." Freddy seemed to shrink down into the huge wing chair. "Told you, got no money. M'mother says t'marry an heiress." Freddy shuddered. "But then, what would I do with her once we was riveted?"

Oliver rubbed the side of his nose thoughtfully. "No reason to live in her pocket. But as to that, what heiress are you going to marry? They're thin on the ground this season, you know."

"M'mother says I should marry m'cousin Lucy," Freddy confided.

"Lucy?" Oliver frowned. "Don't mean to put a rub in your way, but from what I hear, Standen's interested there. Mean to say, if Standen wants her, she's not going to have you."

"M'mother says that she owes it to me," Freddy repeated. "Says that her coming back with the boy took away my inheritance, so she should marry me to share her dowry."

"Certain amount of logic to that," Oliver agreed. "Course, it wasn't your cousin's fault that you thought you were the heir. Mean to say, she never asked to be kept there by them Frogs.''

Freddy nodded morosely.

"Don't mean no offense, but living with your cousin couldn't be as bad as living with your mother.''

Freddy shuddered. "True. M'mother, she nags. Or yells. And nothing makes her happier than having something to complain about. Lucy's a quiet little thing. She ain't forever pitching at a fellow, but that don't mean I want to get leg-shackled to her.''

"Still the problem of Standen," Oliver reminded him. "He's got lots of address, money, a uniform.''

"He don't wear a uniform," Freddy objected.

"Don't matter." Oliver nodded sagely. "He did, and women love a uniform. Don't know why, but there it is.''

"M'mother says that I should pop the question when we're at Landsdowne.''

Oliver looked shocked. "Never say you're going into the country at this time of year?''

"Only for a couple of weeks. M'uncle's got some kind of maggot in his brain. Nothing for it, but he needs to go." Freddy eyed Oliver with a look of sudden hope. "You could come and support me in my hour of need.''

"Glad to," Oliver lied manfully.

Freddy drained the last of his brandy and announced with unwanted firmness, "I'll do it. I'll get myself leg-shackled to m'cousin.''

"That's the ticket, and then we can leave her somewhere and be comfortable again." Oliver raised his glass. "To success.''

"To survival," Freddy amended.

Chapter Twelve

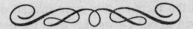

"Wells?" Lucy poked her head out the traveling carriage and called up to the driver, "Stop at the top of the next rise, please."

"Yea, m'lady."

"I am chilled to the bone and parched for a hot cup of tea. Why are you delaying us?" Amelia demanded.

"It's only for a moment," Lucy replied. "I want Vernon's first view of Landsdowne to be from the hill, where he can see his whole heritage spread out in front of him."

"It is a lovely view," Kitty hurriedly inserted, when her mother's lips tightened ominously.

"Can I see the stables from there?" Vernon focused on what interested him.

"No. Nor can you smell them, thank goodness." Lucy smiled at him. "They're hidden behind the stand of beech trees."

"Landsdowne is one of the premier homes in all of England." Amelia fixed Vernon with a beady eye, and he scooted closer to Lucy. "Although I much prefer the countryside in Kent around my dear Freddy's estate to this...wasteland." She gestured toward the rugged landscape. "You must come and visit us, Lucy," she graciously added.

Lucy noticed Kitty's start of surprise at the invitation and felt surprised herself. Why had her aunt suddenly extended what appeared to be an olive branch, when she had been aggressively antagonistic toward her thus far? Could Amelia finally be becoming reconciled to the facts as they were instead of as she wanted them to be? Or was her aunt the one behind Vernon's sudden rash of accidents and perhaps thinking it would be easier to arrange a final, fatal one on her home ground? Lucy didn't know, but it was a risk she wasn't prepared to take.

"That sounds like a lovely idea," Lucy prevaricated. "Perhaps next year, when Grandpapa has regained his health and Vernon is feeling more the thing...."

"I'm fine, Lucy," Vernon insisted. "I hardly ever cough any more and..." He paused as the coach came to a sudden halt. "We're here." He shoved open the carriage door and tumbled out before it came to a full stop.

"Such an impetuous child." Amelia sniffed in disapproval. "My own dear Freddy had far more decorum when he was that age. He was such a dear, sensitive boy, and he grew to be such a distinguished man. Some girl will be very fortunate to get him for a husband."

Freddy might make an unexceptional husband, but Amelia as a mother-in-law would be enough to put off the most determined bride, Lucy thought wryly.

At the sound of approaching hoofbeats, Lucy hurriedly climbed out of the carriage, wanting to make sure that Vernon didn't get too close to the rider.

"Lucy, look!" her brother yelled, and the four carriage horses shifted restively. "It's Cousin Bevis. Cousin Bevis!" He waved his hands.

"You're frightening the horses," Lucy said, to the coachman's obvious relief. "He'll reach us in a few minutes whether you shriek or not."

"I was not shrieking," Vernon insisted with injured dignity. "I was..." He fell silent as he turned and suddenly caught sight of the sprawling mansion in the middle of the valley below them. The brilliant afternoon sunlight glinted off scores of windows, engulfing the red brick house in a patina of golden warmth. Acres of immaculately groomed lawn extended in all directions and a neatly graveled drive lined by huge copper beeches led to the marble portico.

"It's so big," Vernon said uncertainly.

"That's because it used to be a priory," Lucy explained. "Hundreds of monks lived there."

"Really?" Vernon was duly impressed. "And they gave it all to us?"

"Not exactly," Lucy said dryly. "When Henry VIII confiscated all the church lands in England, he gave this to the third Earl of Langford."

"Why'd he do that?"

"Family tradition has it that it was a reward for murdering several people Henry wanted disposed of."

"That doesn't sound very honorable," Vernon said slowly.

"The strong have always taken from the weak." Bevis arrived in time to add his opinion. "And the monks were very weak."

"No one who walks in the path of the Lord is weak! And he who would do ill to the clergy is thrice damned.'' For a second, Vernon sounded exactly like the curé.

"Acquit me, young fire-eater.'' Bevis lifted his hands, palms up. "I didn't do it. It all happened a long time ago.''

"As you say, Cousin Bevis,'' Lucy agreed. "And both the victims and the victors have long since gone to be judged. I didn't know that you were traveling behind us, Bevis,'' she added, changing the subject before Vernon could argue the point. "I thought you were coming with Grandpapa's party yesterday.''

Bevis grinned ruefully. "I changed my mind when I discovered that your grandfather had invited Lord Alridge to accompany him. I hope I'm as well mannered as the next man, but the thought of spending two days closed up in a carriage while Lord Alridge complained about the failures of the Allied commanders in the Peninsular War and Uncle Adolphus complained about the failures of modern society was more than I could countenance.''

Lucy laughed. "I can enter into your sentiments exactly. It was all I could do the other night to keep my tongue between my teeth when Lord Alridge began to lecture Colonel Standen on how to fight the war.''

Amelia stuck her head out of the carriage window and glared at the three of them. "I am freezing!'' she snapped.

"Sorry, Aunt Amelia, we're coming.'' Lucy forced the polite words out, while wishing the blasted woman had chosen to stay in London. "Back into the carriage, my lad.'' She tousled her brother's silky hair.

"Ah, Lucy, it's so stuffy in there,'' Vernon moaned.

"Why don't I take him up in front of me?" Bevis suggested. "It's only a short distance, and we'll be in sight of the carriage the whole way."

"Please, Lucy!" Vernon begged. "It's such a stupendously wonderful horse."

"No horse is stupendously wonderful," Lucy said dryly. "They are smelly, overgrown brutes with the intelligence of garden slugs. But since you have not as yet discovered that for yourself, you may go."

"Thank you, Lucy." Vernon ignored her disparaging words and held out a hand to Bevis, who pulled him into the saddle with a supple movement that made Lucy suddenly realize that for all his slenderness, her cousin was a powerful man.

Bevis settled Vernon in the saddle in front of him, and at the boy's urging, nudged his horse into a gallop. Lucy stared after them for a second to make sure that Vernon was being held securely and then climbed back into the carriage.

"I hope I don't catch an inflammation of the lungs from this inconvenience." Amelia sniffed.

"Now, Mama," Kitty murmured placatingly.

"We'll be at Landsdowne in a few minutes, Aunt Amelia, and then you may retire to your room with a hot posset." Lucy leaned back against the squabs and let her sense of homecoming drown out the carping sound of her aunt's voice. With luck, Amelia might really take to her bed and leave the rest of them in peace for a few days.

Although peace and Robert Standen's presence seemed an incongruous combination. Lucy felt an unexpected frisson of anticipation slither through her. Things seemed to happen around him...

As long as those things didn't happen to Vernon. She frowned, and lapsed into her own disquieting thoughts of how to deal with the problems she faced. Problems that seemed to have no answers. Probably because she didn't as yet know all the questions, she thought in frustration.

What she needed was some kind of plan to lure Vernon's attacker—if there was an attacker—out into the open, because at the moment all she was doing was reacting to events after they occurred. But what kind of plan would work, and how could she carry it out herself?

She bit her lip. She needed help. But who? Since she didn't know who was behind the plot, whom could she trust? An image of Robert's dark features formed in her mind. His dark eyes were hard and purposeful, the muscles in his firm jaw corded and his lips pressed together. She could trust Robert not to harm Vernon but could she trust him to do as she wanted? She didn't know. Robert had his own agenda, and she wasn't quite sure exactly where Vernon fit into it. No, it would be better to handle the problem herself, she decided, as the habit of years of trusting no one won out.

The carriage came to a stop in front of Landsdowne and Lucy hurriedly stepped out of the carriage, to find that Fulton, who had traveled down with a few of the other servants the day before, was there to greet her.

"Welcome home, Miss Danvers, Mrs. Danvers, Mrs. Whitney," Fulton beamed at her as he accepted her cloak and passed it to a waiting footman.

"I am not feeling at all the thing," Amelia announced. "I shall go directly to my room. Come,

Kitty." Amelia, trailed by her daughter, started up the stairs.

"I'll have tea sent up," Lucy called after her, and then turned to the butler.

"Thank you, Fulton. Is my grandfather here?"

"Yes. His party arrived yesterday afternoon. He spent the morning closeted with his bailiff, and then, after luncheon, he went to his room to rest."

"And Lord Alridge?"

"Also resting. Colonel Standen has also arrived. I'm not sure where he is."

Probably somewhere where he isn't supposed to be, Lucy thought in resignation. No doubt she'd find out in good time. His good time, not hers.

"Has my brother come into the house yet? He rode on ahead with Bevis."

"No, Miss Lucy." Fulton winced as the young footman dropped a bandbox he was carrying in from the carriage. "They would no doubt have gone directly to the stables. And knowing the young master, he will stop to examine the points of every animal there," the butler said indulgently. "Would you like me to send someone for him?" He glared at the clumsy footman.

"No, that's not necessary." Lucy gave the visibly nervous young man a smile. "You have more than enough to do, and Vernon won't thank me for dragging him away from his precious horses. I shall be in the library. Would you ask the kitchen to send up a tray of tea to my aunt and one for me and then have the housekeeper wait on me at her earliest convenience?"

"The tea will be there very shortly, but as for the latter, I regret that it is beyond my power to do," Fulton said.

"Beyond..." Lucy frowned uncomprehendingly at him. "You mean she isn't here?"

"Bloody right, she ain't 'ere," the footman muttered, and then blushed scarlet when he realized that he'd been overheard.

Fulton gave him an exasperated look and then turned to Lucy. "I regret to say that Mrs. Compton suffered a seizure November last and expired."

"Expired?" Lucy repeated, wondering why she hadn't been replaced.

"Dead, mum," the helpful footman offered.

"We do not require elaboration from such as you," Fulton said repressively. "As you can see, m'lady, the staff is in sad disarray."

"What about the under-butler?"

"Alas, he also died. Several years before her. All that's here is a skeleton staff that takes care of the house and Mr. James. The bailiff," he added, at her blank look. "The earl has not been here in years. He said that he couldn't bear to come. That he was haunted by what could have been."

"I see," Lucy said slowly.

"I have already sent to London for Cook, and she should be here by tomorrow morning. In the meantime, we shall contrive to be comfortable with the undercook."

"I am sure we will. When Vernon returns from the stables, would you direct him to the library, please?" Lucy said, and then made her escape.

She slipped through the heavy, carved, ten-foot-tall door and pushed it shut behind her. She leaned against it and, closing her eyes, breathed a sigh of relief. At last, she thought. A moment to herself, free from her aunt's constant carping.

"I feel exactly the same way."

Lucy's eyes flew open as Robert's deep voice ripped through her fragile sense of peace. Her head snapped around and she discovered him seated in a wing chair beside a blazing fire. His gleaming boots were propped up on a footstool, a leather-bound book was in his hand and a crystal glass half full of wine was on the table beside him.

"Has two days in a carriage with your aunt addled your wits?" he asked in tones of polite interest when she didn't respond.

No, the sight of you has, Lucy thought. She continued to study him in an attempt to figure out exactly why he seemed to have that effect on her. While he was the epitome of the elegant male, from the curl of his gleaming ebony hair to the lie of his perfectly cut coat of dark blue superfine, he was nowhere near as fashionable as her cousin Freddy. Nor was he as polished in his address as her cousin Bevis. But somehow he seemed more quintessentially masculine than either of them. Her eyes measured the width of his shoulders, which his form-fitting coat only served to emphasize. And he was very strong.

Lucy suppressed a shiver and moved away from the door as he raised his wineglass in a mocking salute and took a long swallow.

Lucy watched helplessly the way his tanned throat muscles moved as he drank, and rushed on, "I have some advice for you. Look for a wife elsewhere."

He gave her a lazy grin that infuriated her. "Why should I go to all that trouble when you have already fallen into my hands like a plum, ripe for the picking?''

''I have not!''

He shrugged. ''True. I suppose it would be far more accurate to say that it was my bed you fell into, but being a gentleman, I wasn't going to bring that up.''

''Will you forget that!'' Feeling driven, she grabbed a crystal goblet from the sideboard, splashed some of the burgundy into it and took a gulp. The liquor warmed a path to her stomach and revived her somewhat.

''But, sweetlings, how can I?'' Robert asked in seeming confusion, which didn't fool her for a minute. He knew exactly the effect his words were having on her.

''The very memory of the feel of your soft lips trembling against mine and the frantic beating of your heart as it pounded against the palm of my hand...'' His voice dropped, deepening and becoming huskier.

Lucy felt its timbre reverberate through her, making her uneasy and on edge. There was a heavy, leaden sensation growing deep in her abdomen and it frightened her.

''I can hardly wait until I can caress your breasts again,'' Robert murmured. ''Until I can rub my palm over the curves and knead the rosy tips with my fingers....''

Lucy gasped at his evocative images. Her breathing was developing an uneven cadence and her face felt flushed. Flushed with embarrassment at his highly improper words, she told herself. She stared at him from beneath eyelids that suddenly felt too heavy to stay open, and tried to think, but she couldn't. Her mind was too busy trying to absorb the feelings seething through her.

"And after I've caressed them, I want to take them into my mouth and suckle on them."

Lucy gasped as she felt her breasts swell beneath the onslaught of his words. His outrageous words, she thought, trying to focus on the undeniable fact.

"No," she muttered, and then repeated the denial more strongly. "No! You should not say such things to me."

"Why ever not?" His dark brows arched questioningly. "We are to be married. Indeed, we're as good as married. Making love is a central part of marriage. I quite look forward to it."

"This whole conversation is highly improper," she said, falling back on the conventions.

"At least it's just a conversation. So far." He gave her a wolfish smile that sent a very confusing mixture of anticipation and apprehension through her.

"You, sir, are no gentleman."

"Then we are an excellent match, because you, my dear, hardly fit society's notion of a proper lady."

Lucy winced as his shaft struck home.

"Then why marry me?" she wailed. "Maybe I really have the soul of a harlot? Maybe underneath my ladylike facade I'm completely immoral."

He grinned at her. "The possibility quite excites me."

"Maybe I shall completely disgrace you. Maybe—"

"My dear fiancée..."

"Don't call me that!" she cried, goaded beyond endurance.

"I will call you anything I please, and I'm beginning to find these missish vapors of yours tedious in the extreme. Part of fighting any battle is knowing when you have been defeated."

"I have not been defeated," Lucy muttered. "I have merely suffered a temporary setback. I will come about."

"You will come at my bidding." His calm assurance infuriated Lucy, all the more so because she knew he was right. And what was worse, he knew it, too. He held all the trump cards. There was very little she could do other than try to convince him to change his mind, and so far her efforts on that count had been a dismal failure.

Unless... She suddenly remembered the fleeting idea she had had of marrying him off to another woman. But to whom? What kind of woman would appeal to him?

"Have you ever been in love?" she asked curiously.

"Of course," he answered promptly. "Many times. There was a nursery maid who used to feed me sweetmeats whenever I was in disgrace."

"Which I would imagine was all the time," Lucy said tartly, having no trouble picturing him as a small, mischievous boy with tousled black curls, black eyes, a rumpled cotton shirt and muddy nankeens. Would his son look like that? she wondered. Or would he resemble his mother? Telling herself that it was totally fruitless to speculate about his offspring, she took another sip of her wine.

"What I meant was, have you ever been in love as a man loves a woman, not cream-pot love?"

"Cream-pot love being how a woman loves a man," he gibed, and then continued before she could give voice to the retort burning on her lips. "As for that…" He stared off into the distance, as if seeing an image painted there. "There was a diamond of the first water my first term up at Oxford. Fiery red curls, bright brown eyes and not a single freckle to mar her perfect ivory skin."

Lucy resisted an impulse to rub the six freckles that decorated her own small nose. "She sounds rather theatrical," she muttered.

"Oh, very," he promptly agreed. "She was playing the lead in some farce or other. Then there was Belinda." He heaved a huge sigh that reminded Lucy of the farce he'd just alluded to. "I met her at a gaming hell in London and wanted to set her up as my mistress. Unfortunately, the Captain Sharp who owned the establishment had already relieved me of my next quarter's allowance, so I couldn't afford to."

Lucy tried to imagine Robert as an impressionable youth ripe for the plucking and failed miserably. "What did this Belinda look like?"

"Glossy black curls, deep blue eyes, white skin, plump arms, very lush—"

"That proves it." Lucy cut into his disturbing memories. "I am not at all in your style."

"I am nothing if not adaptable."

"What you are is impossible." She poured herself some more wine and gulped it down.

"And you are going to be foxed very shortly," he warned. "That is not orgeat you are drinking."

Lucy drained the glass, taking an inordinate amount of pleasure in the small act of defiance. "You forget, sir. I have lived in France for the past thirteen years. I know all about wine and I have no intention of becoming foxed, as you so gallantly predict. I know exactly what my limits are.''

"You'd do better to know what my limits are."

"I have no intention of doting on you! I ..." She paused as she caught sight of Vernon through the window that faced the south lawn.

"What is it?" Robert turned and looked out.

"Vernon." She frowned. "Without a hat or muffler. He probably left them in the stable."

"Hmm, making his escape into the home woods, it appears."

"The wind will give him the earache," she said worriedly. "Or a cough."

"Don't fuss," Robert ordered. "You'll turn the boy into the kind of adult who is always quacking himself."

"I am more concerned that he should live to turn into any kind of adult."

"Lucy—" Robert's hand closed over hers as she started to raise the sash "—there are many ways to die. If you aren't careful, you will kill the boy's zest for life."

"You don't understand," she muttered, as the heat of his warm skin seeped into her slim fingers.

"I understand that you are in England now. You're not the only one with the boy's best interests at heart. Do you think your grandfather would object to him slipping his leash to roam the home woods? Even without a coat?"

"No," she answered honestly. "Leastwise, he never used to when I did it."

"Then let the boy be," Robert ordered.

"No." Lucy shook his hand off. He didn't know about Vernon's ill health. No one fully understood but her. She finally managed to open the sash and stick her head out, only to find that Vernon was no longer in sight. He had been swallowed up by the thick trunks of the centuries-old trees.

"Now see what you've done," she snapped as she hurried out of the library, intending to find her brother. But once she'd given vent to her feelings of frustration by slamming the door behind her, she paused and thought for a moment. Maybe there was something in what Robert had said. Maybe she was stifling Vernon. His health had been much better since they'd arrived in England. And he couldn't come to harm in the woods, even if those accidents weren't really accidents. The woods were far too open for an attack. Anyone trying to harm him would be clearly visible to a number of people.

Besides, she thought practically, Freddy wasn't at Landsdowne yet, and as for the others...

"Fulton?" she called as she saw the butler emerge from the saloon. "Where are my aunt, Kitty and Bevis?"

"Mrs. Danvers and Mrs. Whitney went directly to their rooms to rest, and Mr. Bevis has just gone up to his room to wash away his travel stains."

"Thank you," Lucy said slowly. Everyone was accounted for. Vernon was safe—at least from human harm. It remained to be seen if he was safe from illness. She sighed unhappily. Despite her impulse to go find him, she knew Robert was right. She should allow Vernon a little more freedom. At least when it was safe to do so.

* * *

"Very tolerable brandy, this." Oliver held the glass up to the light streaming in through the taproom window and studied the deep amber color critically. "Don't see why we stopped here, though. Could have easily reached your uncle's in another hour."

"Know it." Freddy heaved a despairing sigh. "But they're all there by now."

Oliver looked up from his study of the brandy and asked, "All who?"

"M'family," Freddy said gloomily.

"Dash it! It's your family home. Where else would your family be? Besides, that's why we're going. So you can toss the handkerchief at that cousin of yours."

Freddy moaned and drained the last of his brandy.

"Promised your mother you would," Oliver reminded him. "Devilishly awkward things, promises. But there it is. No hope for it. 'T'were done, t'were best done quickly.'"

"Huh?" Freddy stared blankly at him.

Oliver shrugged. "Read the line in a play once. Seemed appropriate somehow."

"Did the play tell you how to go about popping the question?"

Oliver frowned. "No, as I remember it was all about murder."

"Oh, they must've already been married. Thing is, how do I make up to m'cousin so's she'll want to marry me?"

"Don't know. I ain't in the petticoat line."

"Me neither. What am I to do?"

Oliver rubbed the side of his nose. "Have four sisters."

"I noticed."

"One can't help but notice," Oliver said tartly. "They're into everything. No common sense. I was never so glad of anything as when Mama fired off the last one and she took."

"Hmm," Freddy murmured sympathetically.

"Couldn't help but notice what my sisters liked in a suitor."

"Yes?" Freddy looked up in sudden interest.

"Flattery and lots of compliments. Empty the butter boat over your cousin. Tell her how much you admire her. Keep thinking about how much you need the ready. Your cousin has the biggest dowry of all this season's chits. Of quite a few seasons," he added reflectively.

"Yes, there's the rub." Freddy so far forgot himself as to run his fingers through his carefully disarranged locks. "Got no way to live without m'uncle's allowance, and he's bound to stop it once he remembers to."

"Welcome to live with me," Oliver reminded him.

"No." Freddy squared his buckram-padded shoulders manfully. "Ain't nobody's charity case. I'll marry m'cousin."

"Before you ask her, you ought to read her sonnets to her beauty."

"Sonnets?" Freddy's pale blue eyes bulged.

"Sonnets," Oliver insisted. "My last sister took a spotty-faced coxcomb who wrote odes to her left eyebrow."

"Maybe I could find a position...." Freddy's chin sunk into his elaborate neckcloth.

Oliver studied him a moment and then asked, "Doing what?"

"Well ..."

"I'll write the poem," Oliver offered. "You just have to read it. You can do that—you're a Danvers, after all. There was a Danvers at the Battle of Bosworth Field," he said encouragingly.

"Umm. Edmund Danvers. He got himself killed, too. Oliver, do you really think Lucy'll have me?"

"No telling what maggot a female might take in her brain. In fact, I have m'doubts that they think at all. M'sisters don't seem to."

Freddy got to his feet, staggering slightly as the effects of all the brandy he had drunk hit him. "Let's go on to Landsdowne," he announced. "Go and get it over with."

Chapter Thirteen

"Fulton." Lucy leaned over the ornately carved banister on the first-floor landing and peered down at all the activity in the hallway below. Fulton was directing the deposition of what seemed like a mountain of luggage.

Curious, she hurried down the wide staircase and skirted the stack. "What is all this, Fulton?" she asked.

"Mr. Freddy has arrived."

"I see." Lucy eyed the pile of trunks and boxes in fascination for a moment and then asked, "Has my brother returned to the house yet?"

"He came in about an hour ago for biscuits and milk. I believe his plans then involved returning to the home woods, where he was engaged in a battle against Napoleon," Fulton said.

Lucy smiled at the thought that at last Vernon was free to indulge in such blessedly normal boyish pursuits. But he had been outside the better part of the afternoon already, and it was beginning to get cooler. It was time for him to come inside. Besides, she thought with a feeling of unease that she tried not to allow to grow into fear, Freddy was now here and the rest of the house party was undoubtedly beginning to stir. If there really was a plot against Vernon, she wanted him where she could watch him while the others were out and about.

"If any of our guests should ask for me, I've gone to fetch Vernon and will be back shortly."

"You, Miss Lucy?" Fulton looked shocked. "I shall send a footman."

"Nonsense. I rather fancy a breath of fresh air after that long carriage ride."

"Then a footman will accompany you," Fulton amended.

"No, he won't," Lucy corrected. "I don't need an escort on my own land."

"As you wish, Miss Lucy." Fulton's disapproval was no less apparent for being unspoken.

Lucy stifled a sigh as she headed toward the side entrance by the library. She was beginning to have a great deal of fellow feeling for Vernon's desire to escape occasionally. During the long years in France she had virtually forgotten how very many dos and don'ts there were governing acceptable behavior in the polite world. Especially don'ts. But only the very highest sticklers could find anything amiss in a grown woman walking near her house on her own property without the ubiquitous escort in attendance.

Lucy borrowed from the cloakroom a serviceable brown wrap that she suspected had belonged to her grandmother, instead of waiting while her own was fetched from her room. She slipped it over her shoulders and was fastening the ties when she heard her name being called.

"Ah, Cousin Lucy, there you are." Freddy hailed her from the small sitting room next to the cloakroom.

She stopped, blinking as the full glory of his waistcoat assaulted her eyes. She could almost hear her grandfather muttering counter-coxcomb.

Seeing her reaction, but misunderstanding the reason, Freddy preened a little.

"I hope you had an uneventful trip, Cousin?" Lucy asked politely.

"Uneventful!" Freddy shuddered. "Simply shocking, the condition of the roads. I vow I was tossed around like a piece of flotsam on the tide. Every bone in my body was jarred."

"Perhaps a rest before dinner?" Lucy edged away.

"Oh, pray don't leave yet," Freddy blurted out. "I haven't told you yet that—" he gulped and furtively glanced down at the piece of paper in his hand "—that you appear like a vision of celestial beauty."

Lucy looked at her cloak, which had lost any pretensions to fashion at least twenty years ago, and then peered back up at him in disbelief.

"I mean—I mean you would look like a vision of celestial beauty if you didn't look like a dowd in that thing." He pulled a lace-trimmed handkerchief out of his pocket and mopped his damp forehead.

"Thank you, Freddy." Lucy was able to keep all but the very faintest tremor of laughter out of her voice. "I shall treasure the compliment all the more for it having come from someone of your obviously refined taste. Now, if you will excuse me..."

"Yes, of course. But the thing is, Cousin Lucy, I have to tell you. I brought Oliver with me."

"And he is very welcome," Lucy said honestly. If Freddy had someone to pass his time with, it would be one less guest she would have to try to figure out amusements for.

Freddy glanced down at the paper in his hand again and then muttered, "Until later. I shall count the minutes until I see you again."

"Quite," Lucy said dryly as she made her escape. What was going on? she wondered. Why was Freddy behaving so out of character? He'd always been polite to her, but it had been the strangled politeness of a man who didn't have the vaguest idea what to say to her. Or, she strongly suspected, to any other woman.

So why the clumsy attempt at flirting now? And why with her? Lucy sighed. She didn't have an answer for Freddy's odd behavior, but one thing she was certain of: her Aunt Amelia was somehow behind it, and it boded no good.

"Is that frown directed at me?" The sound of Robert's deep voice sent a shiver of awareness through Lucy and she turned as he emerged from the library.

"You give yourself too much importance. I hadn't even seen you lurking in the doorway," she said repressively. Her words were more a rejection of what he made her feel than the man himself. "I was thinking about other things."

"Unpleasant things, judging from your fierce expression."

"Not really. Just about Freddy."

"Ah, vacuous thoughts." Robert grimaced. "That lad needs the discipline of the military."

"But could the military survive him? They already have enough problems coping with Napoleon's starts."

"Where are you off to?" Robert suddenly seemed to notice that she was wearing a cloak.

"Out to find Vernon. He hasn't returned yet."

"I'll come with you." Robert fell into step beside her.

"I'm flattered," Lucy muttered, not sure even in her own mind whether she wanted him along or not. Somehow, whenever Robert was with her, she had the most disconcerting habit of forgetting all about what needed to be done and dwelling on what had already been done. Such as the memory of their kisses.

A flush burned across her cheekbones and her heart lurched into a slow, heavy rhythm at the thought that maybe he wanted to accompany her in order to find a private spot away from the other guests' prying eyes in order to kiss her again.

"I wouldn't take my desire to accompany you as a compliment." His prosaic words returned her heartbeat to normal. "I'm afraid that if I remain any longer, I'll come to blows with that imbecilic sapscull."

Lucy chuckled. "You'll have to be more specific. 'Imbecilic sapscull' doesn't necessarily distinguish one guest from another at this house party."

"The sapscull in question is Lord Alridge."

"Yes, he is, isn't he? But..."

She tripped over a root as they entered the woods and Robert grabbed for her. He caught her upper arm and jerked her back against his body. It was like hitting a wall. There was nothing soft and yielding about any part of Robert Standen. Except, perhaps, his lips. She glanced up at his firm mouth, her gaze lingering on the dusky pink of his lower lip as she remembered the feel and taste of it.

She wanted to relive the experience, she admitted honestly. She wanted to press her mouth against his. To feel the brand of his tongue as it traced her lips. She clenched her hands into fists. Her fingernails dug into her palms, and the tiny pain released her from the sensual spell that had momentarily held her in thrall.

She was becoming far too aware of him, and it had to stop. Total absorption in a man could lead to love, which in turn could lead to the total submergence of her being and the suspension of her common sense. Love had led her mother to her death and had condemned her brother and her to years of deprivation and terror. She would never fall in love, Lucy told herself emphatically. She would make sure of it by marrying a man that she liked—but only liked. Not someone like Robert, whose character was full of unexpected depths that could drag a woman down into them, drowning who she really was.

She stifled a sigh. If only she could figure out how to make him go away quickly—because the more she got to know him, the more she was fighting her own desires as well as his.

"Are you all right?" Robert frowned at her fierce expression. "Did you twist your ankle?"

Lucy took a deep breath and hastily stepped away from him. "I am fine, and a gentleman never refers to a woman's body parts," she added primly. She marched into the woods, moving among the ancient tree trunks.

"Really?" Robert appeared to be giving her words serious consideration as he followed her. "I could understand your outrage if I had been so gauche as to comment on the exquisite shape and texture of your breasts, but—"

"Colonel Standen! How dare you?" she de-manded, but her outrage lacked any real conviction. What he had said was outside of enough, but some-where deep inside her she was both proud and de-lighted that her body gave him pleasure. And her pleasure bothered her far more than his improper teasing ever could.

"But Lucy—" he gave her a look of injured inno-cence "—I just told you that I wouldn't dream of mentioning your breasts."

Lucy closed her eyes, knowing she was being made a May-game of, and also knowing that continuing to object wouldn't help the situation. Instead, she de-cided to try the curé's remedy for dealing with exas-perating people and began to recite the Hail Mary.

"What are you muttering?" Robert asked.

"A prayer for the repose of your sense of decency, since it seems to have met with an untimely death," she said with a pious glance heavenward.

"Do you have papist leanings?" he asked, when he finally recognized the prayer.

"No, I'm really a devotee of the ancient Druids, who Grandpapa says used to live in the vicinity. I par-ticularly like their practice of sacrificing irritating people." She gave him a broad smile and let her gaze slowly wander from his shining Hessians, up past his biscuit-colored pantaloons, over his waistcoat, to come to rest on his twinkling black eyes.

"Sometimes," she confided, "I think that the old ways are best."

"I'm a fair-minded man. I don't hold the fact that you think against you." Robert gave her a conde-scending smile. "Bruton may have castigated you as a bluestocking, but I never would."

"Why'd he do that?" Lucy demanded.

"Far be it from me to indulge in tittle-tattle, but if you will tell your dinner partner that it wasn't pride he had an excess of, but hubris..." Robert's eyes gleamed in honest amusement. "I think the thing that annoyed Bruton the most was that he didn't have the vaguest idea what the word meant."

Lucy grimaced. "Yes, that was badly done of me. It just slipped out. I can only plead extenuating circumstances. But if you had been forced to have just spent the better part of an hour listening to that pompous, smug, self-satisfied fop..."

"For shame," Robert mimicked the man in question to a nicety. "And him a member of the Devonshire Brutons, with three thousand pounds a year. Where is your respect?"

"One earns respect," she insisted.

"You, my dear, would have made a damned fine officer."

Lucy glanced up into his suddenly serious eyes, wondering what he'd meant. She was about to ask when she heard running footsteps coming toward her from deeper in the woods.

Robert turned toward the sound. "Your brother, I presume, hoping to make it home and secret away his treasures before some adult tries to dispose of them."

"How do you know?" Lucy asked curiously.

"I was a boy once."

Robert would make a good father, Lucy suddenly realized. He was disciplined enough himself to teach values and to develop his children's characters. But he was also sympathetic toward a child's need to occasionally escape adult authority and simply enjoy being young and free.

Lucy stopped as, instead of Vernon, a young boy suddenly emerged from the trees to their right. His rough woolen clothes identified him as the son of one of her grandfather's tenant farmers, probably trespassing. Lucy expected him to bolt when he caught sight of them, but to her surprise, he didn't. He raced up to them and practically fell at her feet.

Robert reached out and steadied the boy.

"I—he. . ." the boy gasped.

"Take a deep breath, then tell us who you are," Robert ordered.

"I be Jem, your worship, but you gotta help me. Please, I can't get him out of the trap."

"Trap?" Lucy frowned at him. "You haven't been snaring rabbits, have you?"

"Course not, miss." The boy glanced worriedly over his shoulder. "They transports a body fer that, you know. 'Sides, no need. Ol' Marson, he ketches the rabbits and gives 'em to the vicar. He gives 'em to everyone what likes 'em. Ol' Marson, he'd fair skin us alive if'n we was to set a snare, cause it might catch the earl's young quail. But that ain't of no matter. I tell you, I can't find Ol' Marson, and ya gotta help 'em."

Lucy searched her memory and came up with an occupation to match the name. "Ol' Marson is the head gamekeeper?"

"Aye, come on." The boy so far forgot himself as to grab Lucy's hand and tug her forward. "I told you. He done stepped in a trap. We was sneaking through the woods to deliver a secret message to Wellington. I didn't do nothin' to make it happen." His young voice rose in sudden fear.

"You went for help for your friend," Lucy soothed as she hurried along behind him. "That was very practical of you."

"Ain't 'xactly m'friend." The boy gulped. "Never clapped m'peepers on him afor. He's from up there." He gestured in the direction of the big house.

"Vernon!" Robert's hard voice echoed Lucy's sudden clutch of fear. "Hurry up, boy."

"He's over here." Jem rounded a huge tree trunk, and Lucy almost fell over her brother's hunched figure. His thin shoulder blades were jutting against his stained cambric shirt and there were tears smeared across his dirty cheeks.

Lucy felt the hairs on the back of her neck lift in horror as she saw the huge steel trap that was clamped around Vernon's beloved new boots right above his ankle. Instinctively, she reached for the support of the tree as a feeling of light-headedness swept over her. All her doubts about what was happening had been answered in one fell swoop. They hadn't been accidents. Gothic as it seemed, someone really was trying to kill a defenseless little boy. Her fingers clenched, scraping over the rough bark of the tree, and the sensation helped to steady her thoughts. Vernon needed her. She took a deep breath. First she'd rescue him and then she'd worry about the future.

"Don't move, Vernon," Robert ordered. "The only reason that thing hasn't snapped your foot off is because the log it's fastened to has gotten caught in it." He stripped off his coat and carelessly dropped it on the ground.

"Lucy, I didn't mean to do it." Vernon manfully gulped back his tears. "I didn't think there'd be traps here. There weren't in France," he added on a plaintive wail.

"There didn't used to be any here, either," Lucy said, trying to calm him.

"Nope, not never." Jem nodded vigorously. "Ol' Marson, he says the earl up at the house always said that a man's life ain't worth no rabbit. Not like some of them swells thinks."

"Life?" Vernon muttered, while Lucy watched impatiently as the good-size branch Robert was bending finally broke free with a snap that sounded like a pistol shot to her overwrought nerves.

"Uh-huh," Jem elaborated ghoulishly. "Traps like that there, they chops your leg off, and if'n you don't die from the bleeding, then the fever gets you. You was lucky," Jem added. "Him what set the trap didn't know nothin' 'bout it."

"He'll know to leave them alone when I get finished with him." Robert's hard voice sliced angrily through the still air.

Using the stout branch as a lever, he pressed down on the trap's release mechanism. There was a sudden click and the trap sprung open. Vernon jerked his foot out and Lucy grabbed him, hugging his shivering body against her own violently trembling one.

"I ain't no baby, Lucy," Vernon protested.

No, Lucy thought in despair. You're the object of some madman's murder plot. She swallowed the bitter taste of fear that filled her mouth, then watched helplessly as Vernon tried to put his weight on his injured foot. She'd been so sure that bringing him to Landsdowne would make it easier to protect him, but it hadn't. It had simply provided the murderer with far more opportunities to execute his plot.

And what could she do about it? she wondered in despair. She could hardly keep her brother under lock and key in his room.

She watched as Robert bent over to examine Vernon's leg. He tried to pull off the boy's boot, but stopped at Vernon's involuntary gasp of pain. His thin face had turned chalk white.

"We'll have to cut it off," Robert said.

"No!" Vernon wailed. "Not my new boots!"

"I'll buy you another pair," Lucy promised.

"Here." Jem pulled a wicked-looking knife out of his pocket. "You can use this."

"Thank you," Robert said with grave courtesy. Taking the razor-sharp blade, he carefully began to slit the leather.

Lucy held her breath, fearful that the knife might slip and cut Vernon, but Robert's hand was steady as he meticulously worked his way to Vernon's ankle. Handing the knife back to the hovering Jem, he carefully peeled the ruined boot off Vernon's foot.

Lucy sucked in her breath in a horrified sound as she saw the violent, purplish bruising around his ankle. She waited anxiously as Robert gently poked and prodded the maltreated flesh.

"Ain't no skin broke," Jem offered encouragingly.

"And no bones," Robert stated. "Just bruising."

"Just bruising!" Lucy repeated incredulously as some of her fear bubbled out, finding a target in his words. "He looks like he was trampled by a herd of horses and you say—"

"Coulda lost his leg." Jem's dispassionate voice immediately sobered her.

"Yes, you are right, of course. I am sorry. I'm a little upset. Actually, I'm a lot upset," she said grimly.

"I'm sorry, Lucy," Vernon said with a gulp.

"I'm not upset at anything you did, Vernon," she assured him. "I'm upset at myself. I should have realized—"

"Hey there, you varmints. What d'ya think you're doin'?" An elderly man came running through the trees toward them, brandishing a shotgun. "If'n I've told you once, I've told you a hundred times..." His voice trailed away as he got close enough to see them clearly.

"See here, Jem." He spoke to the one person he knew. "You ain't been apesterin' the quality, has you?"

"No," Robert answered for him. "Jem has been of inestimable help to us. And you are...?"

"Marson, sir." The old man touched the brim of his cap respectfully. "I be the earl's head gamekeeper. Not that we have much game to keep these days." He sighed. "We..." He stopped as he caught sight of the trap at Robert's feet.

Reaching down, Marson picked it up, his face turning a dark red as he studied it. "And where did this come from?" He glared at Jem, who nervously scooted behind Lucy.

"We don't know," Lucy said. "Nor do we know who set it."

"Someone set it from sheer cussedness," Marson said through clenched teeth. "Ain't no other reason. Traps like this ar'only good fer killin' and maimin'."

"Men being the primary target, I take it?" Robert asked.

"They's called a mantrap. Some landowners use 'em to make sure the villagers don't do no poachin' on their land. We don't do that round these parts. No one does. Not even that jumped-up mushroom from Birmingham what built the house over t'other side of the village. Ain't hardly human. Vicar won't like it.''

"Where would a man buy one?" Robert asked.

Marson removed his battered wool hat and scratched his balding head. "Not 'round these parts. No shops sells 'em. And it's new." He gestured toward it. "No rust. Not a'tall. It's fresh set."

"But is it one or one of many?" Lucy looked around her, wondering how many more of the deadly things might be hidden beneath the thick scattering of leaves under the trees.

"An interesting point." Robert's speculative gaze followed hers. "Marson, how many men can you hire for tomorrow morning? Say, at first light?"

Marson squinted off into the distance, spat and then said, "As many as you is needful of. Too early fer spring plantin', and the winter work, it be already done. Farmers be grateful for a chance to earn a shillin' or two.''

"Fine, hire everyone you can and comb these woods and the surrounding grounds at first light. If there are any more traps, I want to know about them. In addition to ten shillings a man, I shall pay ten pounds apiece for each trap found."

"Ten pounds!" Marson's eyes bulged. "Yes, sir. I'll tell 'em." He touched the brim of his hat and then rushed away.

"And be careful where you put your feet," Lucy called after him. "We can't count on being lucky twice."

"I guess I'll be leavin', too." Jem started sidling away from them.

"Don't move." Robert barked out the order, and Jem froze. "We will leave together and you will walk behind me. Exactly behind me." Robert pinned the boy with a stabbing glance. "Do you understand?"

"Yes, sir, your worship, sir." Jem bobbed his head nervously. " 'Xactly behind you."

Robert reached down and scooped Vernon in his arms and then turned to Lucy. "I'll go first, you follow, then Jem."

"No, I'll go first and sweep the leaves away with a stout stick," Lucy said.

"You can't—"

"You can't see clearly while you're carrying Vernon," she insisted, picking up a thick branch and starting forward. Robert grumbled, but to her relief, he fell into step behind her.

Their return was much slower than the outward trip. Once they had reached the safety of the lawn, Jem turned toward home, while the three of them slipped inside the house through the side door.

"Ware?" Robert caught sight of the earl's secretary at the other end of the hall.

"Yes, Colonel Standen?" Ware walked toward them with a reluctance that Lucy found irritating.

"Where is the earl?" Robert asked.

Ware frowned as he took in Vernon's tear-streaked face and badly bruised foot. "The earl is still resting. The trip tired him. He should not be disturbed by boyish pranks." He looked down his nose at Vernon.

"Boyish pranks?" Lucy exploded. "Why, you sanctimonious—"

"Nor shall we disturb him." Robert cut her off. "Vernon has merely fallen out of a tree. Please ask Fulton to send hot water to the viscount's chambers—at once.'' His voice sharpened when Ware merely stood there.

"As you wish, sir,'' the servant agreed in a tone of voice that left no doubt that he considered such a task beneath him. Stiffly, he turned and stalked toward the back of the house and the kitchens.

"Go into the library and wait for me, Lucy,'' Robert ordered. ''I'll be down as soon as I have seen Vernon into bed.''

"No, I—'' Lucy began, not wanting to leave Vernon alone.

"Don't fuss, Lucy,'' Vernon said happily. ''Maybe the colonel will tell me if he's got any battle scars. Will you?'' he demanded.

"No, brat, I won't. I'll be back shortly,'' Robert told Lucy.

"All right.'' With an encouraging smile for her brother, who didn't seem to notice, Lucy slowly made her way to the library.

Once there, she couldn't relax enough to sit down. Her mind was teeming with questions—questions that fed her sense of fear and dread. She didn't know what to do. At the moment, her only coherent thought was to pack up and run back to France and Marthe. At least there the enemy had been easily identified by the uniform he had worn and by the contempt he had exhibited toward the general population. There the enemy had inflicted pain and suffering only if you were so unwise as to get in his way. Here the enemy was stalking them. Following them with deadly purpose.

Lucy paced nervously across the Axminster carpet, her short, jerky steps matching her frantic thoughts. She swung around as Robert opened the door.

"I left him in the capable hands of my batman, who knows enough bloodthirsty stories to satisfy even Vernon."

Lucy chuckled weakly. "He'll like that."

Robert paused in front of the long, leaded-glass windows and studied Lucy with a narrow-eyed expression that did nothing to ease her nervousness.

"Suppose you tell me what's going on?" he finally said.

Lucy nervously twisted her fingers together, filled with an intense longing to do just that. To tell him everything. To share the burden of worry with someone strong enough to help. But she just wasn't sure...

"If you don't, I'll have to go to the earl," Robert replied promptly. "I'll tell him what happened."

"You can't! He isn't strong enough to be told that..."

"That someone is hunting people in his home woods?"

"Maybe..." Her voice trailed away.

"Maybe what?" Robert demanded. "Maybe you know what our hunter was after? Or, perhaps, who he's after? Certainly not any of the men in the party," he continued inexorably, when she didn't reply. "It's the wrong time of year for hunting, so none of them would have had any reason to be out there. And the women would hardly be walking in muddy woods on a raw spring day. He couldn't have been trying to kill Marson," Robert continued inexorably. "Not only is it far too much trouble to go to to get rid of a gamekeeper, but, according to Jem, Marson is well liked."

Lucy closed her eyes. "I've already thought of all that," she said tiredly.

"Then who was the target? A young boy who would predictably head for the woods as soon as he could? Is that it, Lucy? Is someone trying to kill Vernon?"

Lucy stared into his taut face, her gaze locking on his intense black eyes. She could trust Robert. She felt a feeling of peace seep through her mind. She couldn't trust herself to marry him, but she could trust him to help her in this. He might know where to start to unravel this fiasco. So tell him, her mind ordered her tongue, which felt frozen to the roof of her mouth.

"Is that it, my poor sweet?" His unexpectedly gentle voice warmed her frozen heart and she nodded.

Taking a deep breath, she added, "I wasn't sure until today. I thought the other times might have been accidents. Actually, I wanted to believe that the other times *were* accidents, and they could have been. But after that trap..." She shuddered.

"What happened before?"

Lucy told him, counting the incidents off on her fingers.

"Hmm." Robert walked over to the sideboard and poured two glasses of wine. He handed one to Lucy and began to sip the second as he walked back to the window and stood, staring blindly out at the bucolic scene.

Hungrily, Lucy watched as the late-afternoon sunlight pouring in through the old-fashioned panes of glass was broken up into shards of multicolored light, which drenched Robert.

He looked exactly like the representation of the Archangel Michael in her childhood prayer book, she thought fancifully. If only he truly had the power to wave his celestial sword and vanquish the wicked.

"Any of those incidents taken by themselves could have been accidents," he finally said. "But so many in such a short time... And when they were followed by today's... Someone wants Vernon dead. The question is who?"

Lucy sighed. "Yes, indeed, who? We certainly aren't spoiled for choice. At first, I thought that Freddy was behind it, because he inherits if Vernon dies, but then..." She gestured vaguely.

"But then common sense got in the way?" Robert asked dryly. "Freddy is about as unlikely a murderer as I have yet to meet."

"I know, but what about his mother? I think she resents Vernon more than Freddy does."

"Possibly, but she would have needed help to set that trap. She came down with you, remember. Not only that, but she could hardly buy a mantrap without someone becoming suspicious. And if she had had help, there would have been a stranger lurking around the estate. A stranger who would have been noticed."

"True," Lucy conceded. "Kitty is another unlikely suspect. Especially considering the fact that Grandfather is giving her a dowry. If something were to happen to Vernon, Grandfather might very well renege on his promise. Particularly if the something were suspicious."

Robert frowned thoughtfully. "You're probably right. Besides which, Kitty appears to want nothing more out of life at the moment than to be left alone. I don't believe that she would do anything to draw attention to herself.... There's your cousin Bevis," he continued.

"But what's his motive?" Lucy shrugged. "He can't inherit the earldom no matter what happens to Vernon. And he's been very nice to him."

"I saw him playing faro at Watier's earlier in the week and the play was very deep."

"Did he lose?"

"No," Robert admitted. "He won. That time. But the thing about gambling is that one's luck never holds. If that session I saw was typical, your cousin will be under the hatches in a few years."

Lucy sighed. "Which could well account for his sudden interest in me and my dowry. But it still isn't a motive for killing Vernon."

"Perhaps, but there are several things I want to check out before we dismiss him as a suspect."

"Something occurred to me when Ware met us at the door earlier," Lucy said slowly. "Ware does not like us."

"He's jealous of you," Robert corrected. "Until the pair of you came, he controlled access to the earl. He was the earl's main contact with the outside world. Now, all of a sudden, he has been relegated to a rather minor role. But as to whether he would stoop to murder..."

Lucy grimaced. "I know. It seems highly unlikely, but then the whole thing seems unlikely."

"Perhaps the plot is more devious. Suppose the idea is to kill Vernon and make it look like Freddy did it? Then the courts would remove Freddy from the succession by the time-honored method of hanging, which would leave whom to inherit the earldom?" Robert asked.

Lucy searched her memory, but couldn't remember the name of her grandfather's closest male relative after Freddy and Vernon. "I don't know," she finally said. "The family Bible would tell us."

"Where is it?"

She sighed. "I don't know that, either. I could ask Fulton. He would know."

"Why don't you do that while I find the bailiff and warn him about the traps."

"Fine," Lucy said with a sense of relief. Suddenly she felt much more hopeful about finding the killer. She wasn't alone anymore. She had Robert to help her.

Chapter Fourteen

"Here you are, Miss Lucy." Fulton handed her the heavy family Bible. "The earl had it in his sitting room."

"Thank you for finding it for me." She clutched the oversize book to her chest. "If anyone should want me, I shall be in the library." Lucy hurried toward the library, hoping it wouldn't take Robert long to find the bailiff. Somehow, she felt safer when he was near. As if his very decisiveness could protect Vernon, even if she couldn't.

To her dismay, as she passed the open door of the morning room, her aunt called out to her.

"So there you are, Lucy. Where have you been all afternoon?"

"Oh, here and there," she murmured, not sure how to respond to Amelia's aggressively friendly tone.

"Sit down." Her aunt gestured toward the wing chair across from her. "The fire is very welcome this late in the afternoon."

"Yes," Lucy agreed as she came farther into the room, curious about Amelia's attitude. She gingerly sat down on the chair and waited to see what her aunt would say.

"And how is your dear little brother?"

Lucy's eyes flew to her aunt's face as the question sent a chill down her spine. Amelia's features were bland, her lips arranged in a meaningless smile, but her eyes were watchful. But watching for what? Had her aunt finally faced the fact that Vernon wasn't going to go away and that it would be better for her as well as for Freddy and Kitty if they were all on good terms with the next earl? Or was there a deeper, more ominous significance to the question? Could her aunt be the one responsible for the mantrap that Vernon had stepped into this afternoon? Could her question reflect her growing impatience to find out if anything had come from her plan yet?

Lucy clenched her teeth in frustration at her lack of any real knowledge upon which to base a conclusion. She felt helpless, as if she were engaged in a game of blindman's buff with an armed enemy.

"Vernon's fine, Aunt Amelia," she finally said. "He spent the afternoon exploring the home woods with the son of one of Grandpapa's tenant farmers." Lucy carefully watched for any reaction to her mention of the woods.

"A propensity for low company is to be abhorred in a gentleman," Amelia pontificated, sounding more like her normal self. "I hope you sent the young person on his way and punished Vernon."

"Do any of the local gentry have sons Vernon's age?" Lucy sidestepped the question.

"Society around Landsdowne has degenerated in recent years. Our neighbors are little more than jumped-up mushrooms and cits trying to buy their way into polite society." Amelia sniffed disparagingly. "We don't want to be inviting those kind here...

What is that you are clutching?'' She frowned myopically at the book Lucy was holding.

''The family Bible.''

''You shouldn't be carrying it around. It is very old and very valuable. It should be left in its case in the library.'' She moderated her reprimand slightly with an acidulous smile that only increased Lucy's sense of disquiet.

''I wanted to look at our family tree,'' Lucy said, just as it occurred to her that Amelia, with her inveterate love of gossip, probably knew more about their relatives than her grandfather did.

Lucy opened the Bible and then swallowed, as tears suddenly clogged the back of her throat when she saw the fresh entries beside her parents' names. She reached out and traced over the crisp black lines with a trembling finger. Somehow, seeing the dates of their deaths written in the Bible made it seem official.

''Most regrettable,'' Amelia surprisingly stated. ''Your father might have been an impractical air dreamer and your mother a lovely wigeon, but they did not deserve their fate.''

''How many of us do?'' Lucy's voice cracked as she thought of the danger Vernon was facing.

''True.'' For a moment Amelia looked old and careworn. ''But we must all of us cut our coat to fit the cloth. We . . .'' She paused as her son sidled into the room, followed by Oliver. ''Freddy, my dear boy,'' she said in greeting, ''what have you been doing this afternoon?'' She asked the question Lucy wanted to.

''Been dashed well busy,'' he complained. ''But we finished it.'' He gestured with the thick piece of vellum he was carrying. ''Even copied it out in a clean hand.'' He looked at Lucy as if for approval.

"How nice," Lucy said, hoping it was an appropriate response. Somehow, the written word and Freddy did not sound like a complementary alliance.

"Want to read it to you." Freddy cast an imploring glance at her, and Lucy wasn't sure if he wanted her to say yes or no.

Amelia took the decision out of her hands. "Of course, dear boy, do read it."

"Yes, Mama." Freddy so far forgot himself as to tug on his intricately tied cravat. "It's a poem. We call it 'Ode to Feminine Pul-Pulcra...'" He gulped and cast an anguished look at Oliver, who leaned over and whispered something in his ear.

"'Pulchritude,'" Freddy repeated. "Means beautiful, don't you know. Don't know why he couldn't have just said beautiful." He shot a reproachful glance at Oliver.

"Pray continue, dear boy," Amelia urged. "I can hardly wait."

Neither can I, Lucy thought ruefully. So far her day had been dominated by fear and worry. A little light relief in the guise of her cousin masquerading as a poet would be a welcome change.

Freddy gulped, took two deep breaths and then began to read in a singsong voice, "Your beauty fills me with a sense of awe. The exquisite perfection of your eyebrows are a visual delight to my starved senses. Your rosebud lips—"

"What are you doing, reading warm poetry to Lucy?" The earl stalked into the room. "And you, Amelia, are you so lost to propriety that you would allow such a thing?"

"It wasn't a warm poem, Grandpapa." Lucy came to the defense of her appalled-looking cousin.

"Freddy would never subject a lady to anything vulgar."

"Indeed not!" Freddy assured her. "Not at all the thing. Besides, ain't in the petticoat line."

"We know that, dear boy," Amelia said soothingly. "Which makes your capitulation all the more remarkable." She gave Lucy an arch look.

Lucy stared blankly back, trying to organize Amelia's sudden friendliness and Freddy's attempt at poetry into something that made sense. Surely her aunt wasn't trying to suggest that Freddy had developed a lasting passion for her? Or any other kind of passion, for that matter? The only strong feeling Lucy had ever seen him show had been directed toward his clothes.

"Ah, so that's your game, Amelia." The earl reached a similar conclusion. "You'll catch cold at it."

"I don't know what you mean," Amelia snapped, twin spots of red staining her sallow cheeks.

"Mama didn't help me, Uncle Adolphus," Freddy said. "Oliver did."

"Humph." The earl glared at Oliver, who merely smiled back. "Cork-brained, the pair of you."

"Never claimed to have a lot in my cock-loft, but Oliver is a clever cove. Everyone says so," Freddy said, loyally defending his friend.

"I don't," the earl grumbled.

Lucy, eager to end the exchange before her grandfather baited Amelia into an argument, changed the subject. "I was just looking at our family tree, Grandpapa. The Danvers seem to be dying out. You, Vernon and Freddy seem to be the only male members left."

"Not quite." The earl looked over her shoulder, peered at the Bible a moment and then pointed to a faded, crabbed entry. "There's Bartholomew Danvers." He shook his head. "Asked him to visit a few years back when there was only Freddy between him and the earldom. Hard to believe he's a Danvers. There's an odd kick in his gallop, make no mistake."

"Oh?" Lucy asked encouragingly. Maybe this was the link she was searching for. "In what regard?"

"He said I was goin' to hell," Freddy confided. "Said thinking about your clothes was a sin. Said I should have my mind on a higher plane, like the plight of my fellow man. So I tried. Told him his coat gave him a very off appearance and offered to give him m'tailor's direction. But he took it amiss."

"Cousin Bartholomew took everything amiss," Amelia said tartly. "Things like fires in the grates, food on the table. Never saw such a pinch-penny in my life."

"He didn't have any money of his own?" Lucy asked.

"You're out there," the earl said. "His father was well to grass, and old Bartholomew never spent a groat he didn't have to. Then he got religion . . ."

"The kind that finds fault with people," Amelia said.

Freddy nodded vehemently. "Was enough to turn one into a heathen."

"Always thought his mother played his father false," the earl said reflectively. "Ain't like no Danvers I ever saw. We may have had our failures—" he fixed Freddy with a minatory eye "—but Bartholomew was the first Bible-thumping Methodist we ever produced."

"It's true," Amelia said, ignoring the slight to her son. "He actually told Lady Jersey that she was dressed like—" she lowered her voice "—a harlot."

Lucy, remembering the semitransparent gown that Lady Jersey had been wearing at the Alverson ball, wondered if there might not be something to this unknown relative's strictures.

"And he wanted me to invite some of m'friends over for a Bible reading." Freddy saved the worst to last.

"No doubt about it." Lucy swallowed a grin. "He sounds perfectly depraved."

"And it's the worst kind of depravity," the earl grumbled. "The kind that you're supposed to admire. Never saw such a fellow for turning virtue into vice."

"Fortunately, he felt the same way about us," Amelia said. "He cut his visit short and returned to Scotland."

"In my carriage," the earl related, with an anger that hadn't abated after four years. "Too nip-farthing to pay his own post fees."

"Sounds like the loan of the carriage was a small price to pay to get rid of him." Lucy got to her feet. "I think I'll return the Bible to the library."

Freddy, in response to a nudge from his mother, jumped to his feet and said, "I'll...accompany you."

"Oh? Do you intend to get a book to read?" she asked, trying to hide her annoyance. She wanted to find Robert and share what she had learned about this hitherto-unheard-of Cousin Bartholomew and discuss where he might fit into their list of suspects, something she could hardly do in front of Freddy.

"Grandfather has an excellent collection of Latin tomes," she added for good measure.

"Tombs?" Freddy looked worried. "Ain't that where they bury coves?"

"Only intellects are buried in tomes," the earl snipped. "You haven't a thing to worry about."

Freddy took a deep, steadying breath. "Come anyway."

"Why don't you stay and read me the rest of your poem?" the earl suggested, smiling nastily at him.

"For shame, Grandpapa," Lucy chided him. "And you a sportsman, too."

Freddy, after a quick, whispered consultation with Oliver, said, "Oliver and me are going to write another poem instead." With a harassed look at the earl, he followed the oblivious Oliver out of the room.

"I don't know why you must be so unkind to poor Freddy," Amelia snapped at her brother-in-law.

"I would enlighten you, but since it only lacks two hours of dinner, there wouldn't be time."

Lucy shook her head and walked out of the room, leaving the two oldest members of the house party bickering like members of the nursery set.

She found Robert in the library, in the process of sending a letter. She stepped inside the room, leaving the door open a crack to observe the proprieties, and watched as he folded the thick sheet of vellum. His long fingers competently dripped some sealing wax on the closure, and Lucy felt a totally unexpected surge of warmth course through her body at the memory of those same fingers touching her. She tilted her head back and studied him through her long lashes. His dark green jacket molded his powerful shoulders, and she ran the tip of her tongue over her suddenly dry lips as she remembered the feel of those muscles beneath her questing fingers.

"Why are you lurking in the doorway?" Robert demanded. "Have you the headache?"

"I never have the headache. Despite extreme provocation." She gave him a significant look as she carefully placed the Bible back on its stand.

"Good." He grinned at her, and Lucy's heart unexpectedly flip-flopped. "A wife who always had the megrims would drive a man to drink."

"Oh, dear." Lucy gave him a weak smile. "I seem to have spoken too soon. I feel a spasm coming on."

"Or to murder," he amended.

Murder? The dark word scattered all her thoughts of teasing. "I found out who inherits after Vernon and Freddy, and he doesn't seem a very likely culprit."

"Who?"

"A Bartholomew Danvers from Scotland. As far as I can tell, he's the only thing that my aunt and grandfather have agreed upon since I arrived home."

"How so?"

"That the man is a sanctimonious, Bible-thumping bore with a substantial fortune of his own. Moreover, he's a nip-cheese."

"Sounds like the type who drives you to murder, not commits it," Robert said. "I shall confirm their view of him with Potter when I write to him later. I want him to check out a few facts for me. And I want his opinion on an idea I have."

"What idea?"

"I would rather not say until I'm sure. I don't want to impugn anyone's reputation on a guess. First I'll see what Potter can find out for me, then, depending on his information, I'll share it with you."

"You don't want to slander anyone?" Lucy repeated incredulously. "You are perfectly willing to blackmail me into marriage, but you don't want to slander anyone?"

"A man's reputation—"

"I am more concerned with the rest of my life!"

"Hush." He reached around her and gently closed the door. "Your grandfather will hear you."

"Not him," she said dryly. "He's in the morning room maligning poor Freddy."

"Freddy carries his own armor. He's an amiable fool."

"Not entirely," she said smugly. "Freddy wrote me a poem."

"Freddy can write?" Robert repeated in mock surprise. "And the Bible claims that there's no new thing under the sun."

"Not when it comes to greed." Lucy heaved a sigh. "I am fast coming to the conclusion that Freddy has joined the ranks of men wanting to marry my dowry."

"I don't want your dowry." Robert lightly ran the tip of his forefinger along her jawline.

Lucy's eyes widened as the skin on her cheek seemed to tighten.

"In fact, I don't give a damn about your dowry." Robert's voice somehow seemed huskier, and she took a deep breath to try to counter the strange sensations flooding within her. It proved a mistake. The smell of sandalwood drifted to her nostrils.

Lucy's muscles locked as his fingers began to trace over her soft lips. She gulped as a shower of sparks permeated her flesh, making it tingle.

"You mustn't do this," she muttered, trying to concentrate on something other than the way her traitorous body was reacting to him.

"Why not?" His whispered breath touched her soft lips, and she felt the heat of his body engulf her. She wasn't sure which of them had moved, but suddenly his mouth was a scant inch from hers.

"Because if someone should walk in on us and see us..."

"Kissing," he finished.

"We are not kissing," she muttered, putting her hands on his shoulders, intending to push him away. But, as with so many of her intentions where he was concerned, it came to naught. Her fingers seemed to stick to the smooth texture of his coat.

"But we will be." Robert's mouth lightly brushed against her lips, and Lucy lost all thought of resistance. She sagged against him with a sigh of pleasure. As if to reward her capitulation, his tongue darted out to trace her bottom lip, and her mouth instinctively opened.

A shudder took her as his warm tongue surged inside, to find and stroke hers. Heat seemed to be pouring from him, engulfing her in a raging inferno of seething emotions. Dimly, she realized that her response was more intense than the last time he had kissed her. More intense and much more pleasurable.

She moaned when he raised his head, leaving her feeling bereft.

"Ah, Lucy, my sweet." His warm, wine-flavored breath wafted across her face, escalating the sense of yearning that filled her. "You are so soft." His hard lips began to string kisses over her cheekbone, pausing to lightly brush her quivering eyelid.

Lucy reached up and laid her palm against his cheek, relishing the texture of his skin. He felt so quintessentially masculine, she thought, rubbing her hand back and forth over his jaw. She shivered at the prickly sensation.

"You feel so different from me," she murmured abstractedly. "So hard where I'm soft. So scratchy where I'm smooth."

"So flat where you're curved." His hand unexpectedly closed with unerring accuracy over her breast.

Lucy jerked at the intense surge of longing that moved through her. It seemed to sear her skin, heating the thin silk of her dress. She pressed forward against his hand, gasping when her movement intensified the sensation. Robert began to rub his palm in a circular movement, and Lucy could feel her breasts swelling, the nipples hardening. She was having trouble breathing, but she didn't care. Nothing mattered but that he continue what he was doing. But to her massive disappointment, his hand stilled.

"No," she murmured in protest, blinking in an attempt to bring his face into focus. He looked subtly different somehow. His features seemed harder, sharper. His eyes glittered as if with a fever, and his lips were curved in a sensual twist that found an echo deep within her.

She frowned, while the fact that he was glaring at the door finally penetrated the sensual haze that fogged her mind. Languorously, she turned her head slightly, freezing when she realized that there were voices in the hallway.

With more haste than finesse, she scrambled away from him and grabbed hold of the edge of the desk, to keep from falling when her wobbly knees wouldn't support her.

"What..." Her voice came out as a croak and she closed her eyes in chagrin.

"Don't look so shattered," Robert ordered. "Perhaps I shouldn't have kissed you like that, but—"

"Perhaps!"

"Oh, cut line, woman." Robert shoved his fingers through his ebony hair, and Lucy took perverse pleasure in the fact that they were shaking. It only seemed fair, considering her own reaction.

"It isn't as if we aren't going to be married."

"That doesn't matter," she said primly. "You still shouldn't have kissed me."

"Then you shouldn't have flirted with me."

"Me? Flirt?" She glared at him, her frustrated desire finding an outlet in righteous anger. "I was not flirting with you!"

"You *were* flirting," he insisted. "The way you laugh at me with your eyes... You may not be doing it on purpose, but you are doing it all the same. All I can think about is the taste of your lips and the feel of your bare skin and—"

"Stop it!" she hissed, not sure whether she was madder at him or herself. "I don't want this."

"You would rather be repulsed by my embrace?" he asked dryly.

Lucy stared at him in frustration. "It might be better," she muttered. "At least then—"

"Then what?" Robert's eyes narrowed speculatively.

"Oh, I say. So sorry. Didn't mean to intrude," Lord Alridge broke in. "Although it isn't at all the thing to close the door with just the two of you in here," he said reprovingly.

"Vernon must have shut it when he left and we didn't notice." Robert lied with a prompt smoothness that Lucy couldn't help but admire, even though she knew it was not a desirable trait in a husband.

"Boys will be boys, eh, Miss Danvers?" Lord Alridge came into the room. "Fine lad, your brother. Put heart back into Adolphus. Don't mind telling you I was that worried about him. He seemed to lose interest in everything these last few years. Different now that he's got the boy."

"And me?" Lucy asked dryly, wondering if anyone in this benighted society valued women for anything other than their ability to produce an image in some man's likeness. Or as a partner in sensual games the scope of which she only dimly perceived, she thought, with a wary glance at Robert.

"Certainly, certainly," Lord Alridge hastily agreed. "I only meant an heir, you know. Every man should have an heir, eh?"

Lucy opened her mouth to tell him exactly what she felt every man should have, and then firmly pressed her lips together again. What was the matter with her? She never used to indulge in temper tantrums, and she'd never before pursued lost causes, which the meanest intelligence could see that trying to convince Lord Alridge that there was some worth to the feminine half of the population would be.

She swallowed uneasily. It was as if her association with Robert were freeing parts of her that she had buried so deeply and so long ago that she had forgotten they'd ever existed.

"Allow me to walk you to the stairs, Miss Danvers." Robert took her arm. "Sir." He nodded to the elderly man before exiting.

"It isn't necessary to hold on to my arm as if I'm about to make a bolt for freedom," Lucy said, once they were in the hall and Lord Alridge could no longer hear them.

"I was afraid that you were going to throw something at him, and think of the scandal if you were to hit him." Robert's voice was threaded with laughter.

"It isn't funny," she insisted. "I managed to survive a war and raise Vernon, and yet to that old idiot..." Her voice trailed away in frustration.

"Rather like when that old idiot told me how Wellington was fighting the war all wrong?" Robert gave her an innocent look.

"That's different."

"I don't see how," he insisted. "Stupidity is stupidity and frustration is frustration."

Lucy glared at him for a second and then, unexpectedly, the humor of the situation struck her and she chuckled.

"The difference, my dear sir, is that one is my frustration and the other is yours."

"Mine is more important."

"Only to you," she shot back.

"To you, too, if you want to see the war ended speedily."

Lucy sighed. "Of course, I do. We can begin our plan to try to influence him at dinner tonight."

"How?" he asked.

Lucy thought for a moment and then said, "I think you should pick out one point that you want to make—"

"I'm certainly spoiled for choice," he said dryly.

"—and make it," she concluded.

"I already tried that."

"No, you ordered him to adopt your point of view, which put his back up. Keep reminding yourself that you aren't in the army anymore. People don't have to follow your orders."

"You're saying that I should just say something and expect him to believe me?" he asked skeptically.

"If it were me, I'd couch my comments in terms of 'those dolts over in the War Department may think whatever, but we experts on war know...' The thing is to try and make him identify with you as one of the knowing ones. From there, it's a short step to him really believing you."

Robert eyed her thoughtfully. "You are a very astute judge of human nature. At the very least, you would make a fantastic political hostess.

"I'm beginning to think that I have chosen far better than I thought," he murmured. "I am a very understanding man."

"Of what? Your own viewpoint?"

Robert eyed her for a moment and said, "Some may castigate my tendency to assume leadership, but you and I know that I'm really very understanding."

Lucy grinned at him. "That approach doesn't work on me. I not only wrote the script, but I can also recognize a plumper when I hear one. Now, if you will excuse me, I want to check on Vernon before I dress for dinner." She turned and hurried up the stairs.

Robert watched her go, prey to a number of emotions, namely elation that she had finally trusted him enough to share her worry over what was happening to Vernon, and a seething sense of unfulfilled desire.

He wanted to make love to her. He needed to make love to her, and not in hurried little snatches. He needed a whole, long night. He firmly reined in his thoughts, as he could feel his body reacting to his need. Perhaps a brisk ride in the chill air would help, he decided, heading up to his room to change.

Oliver watched Robert disappear up the stairs through the slight crack in the study door and then turned to his friend, who was slumped in his chair wearing a harassed expression. "Don't mind telling you, Freddy, I don't like the looks of this."

"Don't like what?" Freddy muttered.

"The colonel and Miss Danvers together. They don't act like strangers." Oliver's eyes narrowed thoughtfully. "You have formidable competition for her hand there."

"M'mother says she'll have me," Freddy announced gloomily.

His friend frowned thoughtfully. "Might be best to put it to the touch soon," he finally said. "If you wait, she might begin to compare you to him."

"I'm more fashionable."

"Keep telling you, women like a uniform and money and titles."

"He ain't got a title."

"Neither do you," Oliver said bluntly. "Nor much chance of one. Little chap's thin, but he's wiry. No hope he'll stick his spoon in the wall just to suit you."

Freddy looked startled at the idea. "No call for the aggravating little beggar to put a period to his existence on my account. Already told you, I don't want to be an earl anyways. All them matchmaking mamas after you, and my own mama always pitching at me about dignity and what's due my name.''

"She does talk in flowing periods." Oliver eyed him in sympathy. "Not at all a restful kind of person."

Freddy shuddered. "Should say not! She's not at all happy about how I muffed the poem...."

"My fault." Oliver rubbed his nose reflectively. "Shouldn't have used *pulchritude*. Forgot myself."

"Wish I could forget."

"Once we get you safely riveted, you can forget all about your mother and Lucy," Oliver said to comfort him.

"How should I go about asking for her dowry?" Freddy asked.

"Hand," Oliver corrected. "You should ask for her hand. Actually, first you should ask your uncle for permission to pay your addresses to her."

"No!" Freddy paled. "M'mother says Lucy is her own mistress. Says we should settle it between us first and then tell the old devil. Says he'll let m'cousin do whatever she wants."

"Probably right," Oliver agreed. "Does seem to dote on her."

"How do I ask her, Oliver? What do I say?"

"Never done it myself," Oliver admitted, "but I do remember what my sister said when Farley proposed to her. Said he told her he couldn't live without her. Told her she was the very breath of his life."

"He really said that?" Freddy looked shocked.

"Umm." Oliver nodded. "Women expect it. Don't mean nothing. Just say it."

"Won't remember all of it." Freddy's chin sunk into his neckcloth.

"We'll write it out and you can memorize it," Oliver said bracingly. "Nothing to it."

His only answer was an anguished groan from Freddy.

Chapter Fifteen

"**I** am sure you won't mind just a hint, Lucy," Amelia said the moment Lucy returned to the drawing room. "I don't know what passes for manners in France, but here in England the hostess does not disappear after dinner and leave the guests to their own devices for almost half an hour."

"Mama," Kitty murmured placatingly.

"Guests?" Lucy frowned. "The men have not as yet rejoined us, and I think of you and Kitty as family who would understand that I wish to check on Vernon before he goes to bed."

"You spoil the boy," Amelia continued. "Vernon has had too much petticoat rule altogether. He needs a man's influence. My own dear Freddy has a marvelous way with children."

"I'm sure he does." Lucy kept her doubts to herself in the interests of peace. Her own observation was that Freddy viewed Vernon rather as he would a wild beast: interesting, but potentially dangerous and best left alone.

"I knew that you would appreciate my dropping a word in your ear." Amelia nodded in self-satisfaction.

"Now then, what have you planned for the rest of the evening? The men should be rejoining us shortly."

"Planned?" Lucy repeated blankly. She had been so worried about Vernon's accident that she hadn't given a single thought about what she was going to do with this misassortment of guests tonight.

"Have you no ideas at all?" Amelia demanded.

Lucy forced herself to concentrate. It all seemed so ridiculous. She was worried about preventing a murder and her aunt was concerned about entertainment.

Unless her professed interest in entertainment was just a blind, Lucy thought uneasily. Unless... Stop it, she commanded herself, pulling her imagination up short. She had to halt this endless speculating. It was simply making an already tense situation worse. Her wisest course of action would probably be to protect Vernon with every means at her disposal, while Robert instigated inquiries. In the meantime she would try to treat her relatives normally. Despite the fact that, from what she had observed so far, only Bevis seemed to fit her definition of normal.

"No, Aunt Amelia, I must admit that I don't have any entertainment planned. Perhaps you could advise me?" Lucy said, knowing full well that her aunt liked nothing better than telling people what to do.

"Certainly." Amelia nodded with regal condescension. "I would be only too happy to give you the benefit of my own extensive experience. Since this small party is mostly family, I think we may be a little more informal than would normally be the case. Perhaps we could begin with Kitty playing the harp." Amelia gave her daughter a fond smile and received a glassy-eyed stare of horror in exchange.

"No, we could not!" Kitty gasped. "I haven't played the harp since before . . . in years."

"But you would make such a delightful picture leaning over the gilded harp with the candlelight reflected off your red satin dress," Amelia coaxed.

Reflected off the ells of flounces and ruffles that made Kitty's already plump frame seem three stone heavier, Lucy thought, wishing that the dressmaker she had taken her cousin to before they had left town would hurry with their order before she earned a reputation as a dowd. Lucy knew only too well that once the ton made up its mind about something, it was almost impossible to change it.

"A delightful idea, Aunt Amelia, but I noticed just this afternoon when I was in the music room that the harp was out of tune," Lucy lied, having no idea what kind of repair it was in. "All Kitty's notes would be flat, which would be bound to give her playing a very off cast." She embroidered her lie when Kitty gave her a look of undying gratitude.

Amelia sniffed disparagingly. "How very like Adolphus to allow everything to go to rack and ruin. Very well then, we shall play whist."

"Lovely," Lucy muttered, hoping she wouldn't be required to make up a fourth. She wasn't that fond of card games in the first place, and as distracted as she was by what had happened this afternoon, she doubted she could keep her mind on the play.

"I—" Amelia began, only to break off as Fulton threw open the salon doors for the men. "Remember to smile at Colonel Standen, Kitty," she whispered warningly to her frightened-looking daughter.

Lucy bit back an instinctive protest at her aunt's blatant matchmaking. How could Amelia pursue

Robert simply because he had money and a secure social position? she thought in frustration. Where was her common sense? The colonel would make a terrible husband for the shy, retiring Kitty. His brisk manner would terrify her, which in turn would exasperate Robert and make him even more brusque. They would be caught in a vicious cycle that would only get worse as time passed.

Kitty needed a gentle, soft-spoken man who would provide a great deal of emotional support, while Robert needed... Lucy frowned thoughtfully. Robert needed a wife as strong as he was. One who would stand up to his autocratic pronouncements. Someone who wouldn't be afraid to tell him when he was being unreasonable. Someone who could help him adjust to civilian life. Someone who would give him children.

Lucy felt a flush stain her pale cheeks at the memory of his lips moving across her skin. But not her! She instinctively rejected the shimmering tingle of awareness that always seemed to bedevil her when she thought of him. Robert had too many unexpected twists and turns to his character. There was too much danger of her losing her own identity in his. Of her succumbing to that most deadly of all maladies, love.

She needed to marry someone like...like who? She frowned as she watched the men enter the salon.

There was Freddy. He was certainly amiable and he would never touch her heart. Nor would he ever involve her in any social scandals. And she didn't think he had any vices, unless you counted lack of intelligence a vice. Lucy stifled a sigh as she watched him mince across the room. No, the idea of marrying Freddy was insupportable. He was like a bumbling puppy one was fond of, but didn't take seriously. And marriage was a very serious business.

There was Bevis. Lucy continued her inventory, watching as he laughed politely at something that her grandfather had just said. He was also very amiable, and he laughed a lot more than Freddy, but, somehow, the laughter never seemed to reach his eyes. It was as if he were always watching the people around him to see how they were reacting to his show of good humor. And then he would modify his response, depending on theirs.

Lucy nibbled on her lip. Robert was a man who behaved in a predictable manner, regardless of other people's reactions. What Robert thought and felt was relatively easy to figure out. Whereas what Bevis thought was a mystery, she admitted, as she realized that he never seemed to put forth an opinion of his own. He merely reflected back what the people around him said, or what was expedient. Lucy shivered. The woman who married Bevis was liable to find that the man behind the facade was something else again. Or, even worse, that the social posturing was all there was.

"Are you sickening for something?" Robert's voice jolted her out of her preoccupation, and she looked up to find him beside her. His eyes were narrowed thoughtfully as they studied her. "You are pale," he finally said.

"I am not sick, and I am always pale. It's a trait much admired among the upper ten thousand." Lucy gave him a mischievous smile. "Freddy told me so."

"Your cousin Freddy is a dolt." Robert sat down on the sofa beside her.

"But a very pleasant guest for all that." Lucy glanced across the room, to where Amelia was bullying her son into forming a fourth at the whist table.

"Your grandfather doesn't think so."

"No," Lucy said slowly. "He seems to hold Amelia and her children in the greatest aversion."

"Seems to?" Robert's dark brows lifted.

"All right. He can't abide having them in his house," Lucy conceded.

"Having met Mrs. Danvers, I can enter into his sentiments," Robert said. "In fact, the thought of having her as a mother-in-law would put off the most devoted suitor."

Lucy sighed as his assessment of the situation eerily echoed her earlier thoughts.

"I just checked on Vernon." Robert lowered his voice. "He was trying to teach Jones chess."

Lucy smiled. "I know. I was there just a few minutes ago." She frowned. "His foot looks even worse than it did earlier."

"The bruising is coming out," he said dismissively. "I also managed to speak to Marson before dinner. He has virtually every able-bodied man in the village hired. They will be here at first light."

"What did Marson tell them?"

Robert looked blankly at her. "What do you mean, what did he tell them?"

"About how there happen to be mantraps in the home woods? I mean, mantraps aren't like having a mouse in the pantry that you need help to get rid of. People are bound to wonder."

"And we can't stop them from wondering. Or from drawing their own conclusions. All we can hope is that they'll keep them among themselves."

"As long as they don't worry Grandpapa."

"I shouldn't think they would. In the normal way of things, he rarely sees his tenants, and the whole search should be over long before he is up. I'll have a word with Marson and the bailiff first thing tomorrow and warn them to be sure not to mention it."

"And I've already warned Vernon to tell Grandpapa that he wrenched his ankle in a rabbit hole. If we just knew who was behind this . . ."

"We'll find out." The conviction in his voice comforted her. "But until we do, Jones is going to stay as close to Vernon as a sticking plaster."

Lucy shivered involuntarily at his implacable expression. Robert would be an enemy who would ask no quarter and give none. She couldn't have chosen a better ally, she thought. Despite all her problems, a feeling of peace stole over her. It was a feeling that suffered a jolt when she looked up and saw Lord Alridge making his ponderous way toward them.

"Lord Alridge is going to join us," she whispered.

"Thank you for the warning." Robert started to rise, but Lucy surreptitiously yanked on the tail of his evening jacket.

"This is no time to run," she hissed.

"I was thinking more in the line of a strategic withdrawal," Robert grumbled as he sat back down.

"This is a chance for you to try to influence his thinking," Lucy muttered.

"I told you, he doesn't think, he reacts," he whispered back, and then fell silent as Lord Alridge reached them.

"Ah, my dear Miss Danvers, what a fair vision you are," he said with a heavy-handed gallantry that somehow suited him. "If I had met someone like you when I was young, I wouldn't be alone today." He lowered himself into the chair across from them.

"It's never too late to find love, sir," Lucy said. "And just think of the reward of a full nursery to brighten your old age."

Lucy was hard-pressed to squelch her laughter at the horrified expression on his face. "No, no," he said. "Everything to its own season, and I fear that my season is past. Not that I mind, but—"

"How wise." Lucy decided that it was time for the silent Robert to practice his diplomacy. "Colonel Standen and I were just discussing the war in France, and I was telling him how very knowledgeable about the situation you are, sir." She smiled at him.

"Humph." He shot Robert a wary glance, no doubt remembering some of Robert's earlier caustic comments.

"Indeed," Robert said in the silence that followed, "I am constantly amazed at how many of our ministers seem to have no more real understanding of how a war is waged than Lucy's young brother. And to think that they are responsible for making decisions that may cost thousands of our soldiers their lives."

"Shocking! Positively shocking!" Lord Alridge murmured, perfectly willing to believe that someone else was incompetent. "It is what comes of Prinny giving appointments to his cronies," he added virtuously, conveniently forgetting how he had gotten his own.

"Worse than shocking, it's a national disgrace," Lucy said. "Why, do you know that some ministers actually don't understand the absolute necessity of getting the pay to our troops in the fields?"

"No!" Lord Alridge said, hoping that she hadn't heard of his own speech on the subject in the House of Lords just last month.

Lucy nodded vehemently. "I can see that you are as outraged as we are. Why, can you imagine how our poor soldiers must feel, risking their lives to defend England and then having some minister sitting safely in London saying that it really isn't convenient to get their pay to them?"

"Terrible thing." Lord Alridge shook his head.

"And very dangerous," Robert threw in. "Men die if they aren't supported in the field."

"And almost every family my grandfather knows has brave sons fighting in the Peninsular War," Lucy added. "Think of what a comfort it is to their families to know that men like you are championing their cause at Whitehall."

"Yes, indeed, I am." Lord Alridge nodded at them. "Happy to do it. Brave sons and all. Ah, there's your grandpapa. I want to tell him all about Warton's latest start." He heaved himself to his feet and waddled off, to the accompaniment of his creaking corsets.

Robert watched him go with a sardonic expression on his face. "Exit, one fool," he said, misquoting Shakespeare.

"One fool who has just had the germ of an idea planted in his head," Lucy corrected.

"Where it will no doubt expire from loneliness!"

"Patience," Lucy consoled. "Wars aren't won in a day. It will take time to sway him to your way of thinking. We shall simply continue to advocate at every opportunity we have, the necessity of paying the soldiers in the field, and by the time we return to

London, he will think that it was all his idea in the first place."

"Provided I don't strangle him in a fit of frustration first."

Lucy grinned at him. "Well, the spectacle would solve my problem of entertainment for the house party, but I wish you wouldn't."

Robert grinned back. "I know. The church frowns on bloodshed."

"Ha! Historically, the church has caused a lot more bloodshed than it has prevented. What I was referring to was the difficulty we would have in explaining his body."

"Tell me, Lucy, has it occurred to you yet that neither of us is entirely comfortable with society's rules?"

"It is only because I was in France for so long. Once I have had a chance to get used to things, society's strictures won't seem quite so silly," she said, hoping it was true.

"Would you care to place a small wager on it? Once one's eyes have been opened to the inanity of the way society operates, it's impossible to go back to being blind to it."

"But it's still possible to function effectively and very happily in that society," Lucy insisted. "Absolutely every society has its absurdities. My village in France did. Your military did."

"That's different," Robert objected.

"No." Lucy grinned at him. "That proves my point."

"Cousin Lucy," Bevis called from across the room. "Come and partner me in a game of whist. Kitty has the headache and wished to retire."

Robert chuckled. "Kitty is obviously a woman of good sense. I wish I would have thought of that excuse first."

"Me, too, but I suppose as hostess I'm not allowed that subterfuge. Although, perhaps I can use the time to try to find out if any of the players knows anything about that mantrap in the woods this afternoon."

"Excellent idea," Robert said with approval, and Lucy felt a small glow of pleasure. "When people are concentrating on one thing, quite often they will say something without thinking. While you're doing that, I'll try to find out if anyone else knows anything pertinent."

"Cousin Lucy?" Bevis's voice was developing an edge to it, and Lucy stifled a sigh as she got to her feet, reluctant to go. She enjoyed conversing with Robert more than anyone she knew. He talked to her, not at her, as so many of the men she had met recently seemed to do. What's more, he talked about ideas and events instead of limiting his conversational offerings to extravagantly elaborate compliments that no woman of even moderate understanding would believe.

"Tomorrow?" Freddy looked hopefully at his mentor.

"No!" Oliver emphatically dashed his hopes. "We have been here four days already."

"But we ain't leaving for another week."

"Ain't the point, dear boy. Point is that Bevis is courting your cousin just as hard as he can trot. And what's worse is the way she looks at Colonel Standen. Not only that, but ain't you noticed how the pair of them keep having private conversations that stop when someone else joins them? And how taken Colonel Standen is with her brother? Seems to always have him near him."

"Maybe he likes the little beggar," Freddy offered doubtfully. "They say there's no accounting for taste."

"More likely, Standen's trying to make sure the little chap is in his corner before he pops the question to Miss Danvers. Anyone can see she positively dotes on the boy. Tell you, Freddy, there's no time to lose. Do you know your speech?"

"My dear cousin Lucy, you must be aware of... My dear cousin Lucy, you, um... Better take it along." Freddy pushed the crumbled sheet of paper up his coat sleeve. "Just in case," he said when Oliver frowned.

"Buck up, old man. Remember your Caesar. 'We who are about to die salute you.'"

"Huh?" Freddy looked startled.

"Latin. Learned it at school."

"Did not," Freddy said with utter conviction.

"Never mind. Not important."

"That's why I didn't learn it," Freddy said smugly as he followed Oliver out of his bedroom. They paused at the head of the broad staircase, and Oliver surreptitiously leaned over the railing and peered down into the hallway two stories below. It was empty.

"Lucy there?" Freddy asked.

"Course she ain't. It's dashed cold in that hall. Likely she's in the book room, going over menus and the like. That's what my mother does this time of the morning. Come on." Oliver clattered down the stairs, trailed by Freddy, reluctance visible in every move he made.

As Oliver had predicted, Lucy was indeed in the book room. She glanced up from her account books as they came in and smiled at them, wondering about Freddy's harassed expression.

"Good morning," she said. "I trust you passed a restful night?"

"No," Freddy began.

He was overridden by his friend's, "Yes." Before Lucy could respond, Oliver added, "I must go," and then left.

She frowned in confusion and looked questioningly at Freddy.

He stared back at her. His round face was red and there was a decided film of perspiration on his pale brow.

What was going on? she wondered.

Freddy walked around the desk, planted his stocky body in front of her, took a deep breath and blurted out, "My dear cousin Lucy, you must be—be aware of..." He took a sustaining gulp of air and hurried on, "Of the tender feelings that I hold you...I mean, for you. Your—your womanly...is such as to raise the finer emotions in any man. Indeed, so it is with me. I find myself fathoms deep in love with you," he rattled off in a desperate monotone. "I shall be—be..." His anguished expression made Lucy want to comfort him much as she would Vernon.

To her surprise, he pulled a crumpled sheet of paper out of his sleeve, glanced at it and hurriedly added, "Desolate if you won't consent to become my wife. I shall cherish you forever." He reached forward to take her in his arms, but Lucy hastily jerked sideways. Freddy tried to adjust, but all he managed to do was to poke himself in the eye with one of his high shirt points.

"Ouch!" He rubbed his reddened eyelid, momentarily forgetting that he was supposed to be professing his undying love.

His mournful expression added the final touch of absurdity. Trying not to giggle, Lucy asked, "Did you hurt yourself?"

"Don't think so." He didn't sound any too certain. "But my heart will be broken if you won't consent to be my wife."

"Nonsense," Lucy said briskly. "You don't really want to marry me."

"I know that," Freddy muttered. "Don't want to marry anyone."

"Then might I point out that proposing to a woman could be dangerous to your bachelor status?"

"Dangerous not to. Have to marry you," Freddy said miserably. "Got no choice."

"I have a choice," Lucy said gently. "And even though I am very fond of you as a cousin, I have absolutely no desire to marry you. I assure you, we would not suit."

"Mama says we would." Freddy delivered the opinion in funereal tones.

"Your mama is wrong," Lucy said firmly.

"Mama wrong?" Freddy's eyes bulged at the traitorous thought. "No. Mama's never wrong." He took a step toward Lucy, but didn't see that the desk's bottom drawer at her feet was open, and tripped over it. His jacket caught on the edge of the desk and ripped.

Lucy felt a surge of pity for him as he surveyed the damage with an appalled expression.

"Maybe it could be mended?" she offered.

"Mended? I am a leader of fashion! I don't wear mended clothes. Dash it all, anyway! Rather be rolled up," he muttered, and bolted from the room.

Poor Freddy. Lucy watched him go with sympathy. He really needed to learn to tell his mother that he was a grown man and would make his own decisions.

"What have you done to poor Freddy?" Robert asked as he walked into the room a moment later. "He just rushed past me, looking positively distracted."

"I'm the one who should be looking distracted." Lucy mentally weighed the pleasure she felt at seeing Robert and found it deeper and richer than it had been just a few days ago.

"I take it that fair Lochinvar has finally screwed his courage to the sticking point and proposed marrying your dowry."

Lucy grimaced. "His mother is the one turning the screw. It would appear that both of my proposals to date have come at the behest of the suitors' parents."

Robert's deep laugh was infectious. "I don't know why you should find that surprising," he said. "No man with an ounce of common sense would willingly enter into parson's mousetrap without a good shove from someone. Marriage is first and foremost a female institution."

Lucy frowned at him. "Why would you say that?"

"Because all the advantages accrue to the woman, of course."

"All the..." Lucy sputtered in disbelief.

Robert reached out and felt the side of the teapot sitting on the desk in front of her. It was cold. He sighed and insisted, "They do."

"Of course they do. Women lose the right to manage their own properties, have no legal redress if their husband abuses them or their children, or wastes the money she brought to the marriage, and she's supposed to pretend not to notice when her husband indulges in an affair. You, my dear sir, have a very strange idea of what constitutes an advantage."

"Is that what you're afraid of?" Robert studied her narrowly. "Losing control? I have already told you that you may have unqualified use of your dowry as well as what I settle on you. We can even have the solicitors put it into writing. As for the rest—" his lips lifted in a slow, sensual smile that sent an involuntary curl of excitement through her "—I give you my word that I will never play my wife false."

"I'm sure that will be a great comfort to her."

"And I hope a great pleasure," he slipped in, and Lucy felt a flush stain her cheeks.

"And I will never beat our children, no matter how much they deserve it."

"I was speaking generally," Lucy said, making a bid to change the subject.

"If you don't want to talk about the terms of our marriage, why did you bring it up in the first place?"

"You may have eschewed physical violence, but I never did!" she said dryly.

"The uncertainty about your marital status is giving you the megrims." Robert's eyes danced with glee. "Believe me, once you allow me to announce our engagement, you will feel much more the thing. You also won't have to deal with fools like Freddy."

"Freddy is not a problem," she said.

"And you are the kind of woman who likes a challenge," Robert said with a shrewdness that made her uneasy.

"Speaking of a challenge," Lucy said, gladly changing the subject, "have you managed to discover anything more about Vernon's attacker?"

The teasing light in Robert's eyes was suddenly doused. "Not yet." He walked over to the fireplace and stared down at the blazing logs. "Although Bevis's man tried to convince Jones to sneak out after Vernon fell asleep last night and go into the village with him."

Lucy felt a clutch of fear twist through her stomach. "Which would have left Vernon unprotected so that he could be killed in his sleep?"

"Possibly, but it hardly seems likely. All the other attempts have had the look of accidents. They were set up so that Vernon triggered them while the villain was elsewhere. What kind of accident could anyone arrange to happen to a boy sound asleep in his own bed?"

Lucy shuddered. "I don't know, but anyone diabolical enough to use a mantrap on a child is capable of anything."

"A valid point, but that invitation last night could have simply been a desire for Jones's company. And Jones is a very entertaining drinking companion," Robert added fairly. "Lucy, have you considered the idea that our villain is someone who hates the earl and is striking at him through Vernon?"

Lucy ran her fingers through her short curls in frustration and forced herself to consider the idea. "It's possible," she finally said. "But who could hate Grandpapa that much? Most of the servants have been with him since before I was born, and besides, what could they be so angry about? The only cause for anger that I can see is the fact that Aunt Amelia has treated them very shabbily these past few years. But in that case they would be angry at her, not him."

"True," Robert conceded. "It's just that I'm running out of ideas. Perhaps, when Potter is able to complete those inquiries I asked him to make . . ."

"How much longer do you expect it to take?"

"I hope to hear something tomorrow. The following day, at the latest. I was very specific about the urgency of the situation, and Potter seems to be an astute man. In the meantime, we must continue to keep Vernon close to one of us at all times."

"Thank goodness for the weather." Lucy glanced at the window, where rain was beating against the panes. "It makes it easier to keep him safe in the house. Safe!" She suddenly grimaced. "Do you know how long and how hard I prayed to be safe in England?"

Robert walked over to her, automatically avoiding the open desk drawer, and put his arm around her, pulling her up against his hard chest. His hold was comforting, encouraging, and Lucy drew strength from it.

"Don't despair yet, my dear." His arms tightened and her nose was crushed up against the starched folds of his neckcloth. It smelled of sunshine, soap and sandalwood. Lucy found it an infinitely soothing combination.

Perhaps the curé was right, she thought dreamily. Perhaps trouble shared really was a trouble halved. But while it was acceptable to share her troubles with Robert, she was in distinct danger of beginning to depend on him to solve her problems, and that way led to disaster. Forcing herself to step back, she gave him a crooked smile and asked, "When should I despair?"

"If Potter doesn't manage to discover anything in London, then you can worry."

Lucy grimaced. "No, then I can worry more."

Chapter Sixteen

"No more! Do you hear me?" The earl's loud voice roared down the hallway and seeped under Lucy's bedroom door.

Lucy's first terrified thought was that, somehow, despite her and Robert's attempts to protect Vernon, his attacker had struck again and her brother had been hurt. Wrenching open her bedroom door, she ran down the hall, following the sound of her grandfather's voice. When she realized that the voice wasn't panic-stricken but furious, and that it was coming from Freddy's room and not her brother's, Lucy felt almost light-headed with relief. She leaned against the wall and took several deep breaths as her heartbeat returned to normal.

She wondered whether it would be kinder to try to deflect her grandfather's anger from her hapless cousin or whether it would be kinder to go away and pretend she hadn't heard the argument. Frowning, she moved closer to the half-open door and peered inside.

Her grandfather was standing by the bed, yelling at Freddy. Her cousin was slumped against the wardrobe, a piece of yellow-and-puce-striped silk clutched in his trembling fingers and an expression of outrage on his round face. There was a third occupant in the room, her brother. He was leaning up against the heavy mahogany bedpost, a smug look on his face.

Lucy had no difficulty recognizing the expression. Vernon had been up to mischief. And this time, part of the blame was hers, she admitted. Normally, on such a beautiful spring day, he would have been outside playing any number of harmless games. But with a murderer loose, she didn't dare allow him outside. He had to remain inside where he was relatively safe from attack. And where the opportunity for mischief from boredom was infinitely greater. Lucy sighed and walked into the room.

Vernon turned at the sound and quickly assumed a pitiful expression.

"Lucy," he wailed. "Freddy beat me."

"That's going to make two of us if you don't cut line, young man," Lucy said dryly.

"You don't understand, Lucy," her grandfather said.

"Quite true," she agreed. "So why don't you explain it to me."

"Freddy did beat Vernon." The earl glared at the appalled-looking Freddy. "And I will not tolerate it. The minute we return to London I want that—that cabbage-head out of my house!"

"Freddy beat Vernon?" Lucy repeated disbelievingly, and then turned to study Vernon, who suddenly looked uneasy. "I fail to see any bruises. With what did he beat you?"

"I didn't—" Freddy began indignantly, but Lucy held up a silencing hand.

"Vernon hasn't answered me yet. Well?" she continued, when Vernon shuffled his feet. "With what did Freddy beat you?"

"His hand," Vernon muttered, "and he didn't exactly beat me."

"He has no right to touch my grandson," the earl snapped.

"What exactly did Freddy do to you, Vernon?" Lucy refused to be sidetracked.

"He smacked me on my seat," Vernon admitted.

"How many times?"

"Once," Vernon mumbled.

"I see. I take it the provocation for this beating—" she gave Vernon a long, thoughtful look "—is that waistcoat Freddy is holding?"

"Should say so," Freddy burst out. "That limb snuck into my room and spilled chocolate on it. It's ruined. Look." He held it out so that she could appreciate the full enormity of the outrage. A dark brown stain did, indeed, mar the silk.

"Ruined," Lucy agreed. "Vernon—" she turned back to her brother "—why did you spill chocolate on it?"

"I didn't mean to," Vernon defended himself. "I heard Freddy tell Oliver about his new waistcoat and I pretended I was a spy and snuck in here to see it. There was a cup of cold chocolate on the bureau, and when I heard Freddy coming back, I jumped and knocked it over. And then the chocolate spilled on it, and Freddy came in and—"

"And gave you a well-deserved smack," Lucy finished, much more concerned with how he had managed to escape Jones's watchful eye.

"He has no right to hit my grandson," the earl insisted.

"Come to that, the little scapegrace had no right to come sneaking into my room," Freddy, with unaccustomed assertiveness, pointed out.

"Your room?" The earl's face turned an alarming shade of red. "This is my house and someday it will be his." He gestured toward Vernon, who couldn't resist a slight smirk.

"Whom the house belongs to is irrelevant," Lucy said. "The fact is that a gentleman does not sneak into a guest's room for any reason. Nor does he damage a guest's property and then try to weasel out of the consequences." She frowned at her brother. "I am deeply disappointed in your behavior, Vernon Danvers."

Vernon gulped and glanced down at the floor.

"You owe your cousin an apology for your absolutely unwarranted invasion of his privacy," Lucy continued.

"An apology?" the earl repeated incredulously.

"Are you saying that what Vernon did was the act of a gentleman?" Lucy asked him, refusing to back down. She couldn't allow the earl to indulge Vernon to the extent that he came to believe that his was the only view that mattered. That the rules of common courtesy didn't apply to him. She loved her brother far too much to allow his basic sense of fair play to be warped.

"Well . . . no," the earl finally admitted, under her level stare.

"Then an apology is due. Vernon?" She nodded at him.

"I'm sorry, Cousin Freddy," Vernon muttered. "I shouldn't have come into your room even if I was playing spy. And I'll buy you a new waistcoat."

"I'll pay for it," the earl snapped.

"No, thank you, Grandpapa." Vernon manfully squared his thin shoulders. "Lucy's right. It wasn't a gentlemanly thing I did, so I'll pay for the waistcoat. I got lots of my pocket money left. I'll go get it." He scurried out of the room.

"I say, no need to pay for it. I haven't yet," Freddy said ingenuously.

"No doubt!" the earl snorted. "Well, you may have cozened Lucy, but not me. I meant what I said. When we return to London, I want you out of the house. Hear me!"

"Grandfather, that's not fair," Lucy said, defending the stricken-looking Freddy.

"Don't have to be fair. I own the house. Can have who I want living in it, and I don't want him." With a last glare at his nephew, he stomped out.

Lucy released her breath with a long, shuddering sigh. "I'm sorry this happened, Freddy. I'll talk to him later. Once he's had a chance to calm down a little."

Freddy echoed her sigh. "Won't do no good. He don't like me. Never has. Won't change his mind now."

Fearing he was right, but not wanting to say so, Lucy gave him an encouraging smile and left in search of Robert. She wanted to see if he had any ideas for keeping Vernon occupied indoors.

Freddy also left, hoping to find Oliver. He found him in the library poring over a sheaf of papers.

Freddy closed the door behind him and burst into speech, "Oliver, it happened."

"Hmm?" Oliver muttered without looking up.

"Oliver, listen to me. This is important. M'uncle has forbidden me the door of the London house. Said I had to move out. The very day we return."

Oliver frowned. "Shabby thing to do. Why?"

"'Cause that little blighter, Vernon, ruined my new waistcoat!"

"Don't mean to impugn your taste, Freddy, but the little chap may have done you a favor. Ghastly color for a waistcoat."

"I was going to set a trend," Freddy said with injured dignity.

"Oh, that explains it." Oliver nodded sagely. "Plain to see you weren't following one."

Freddy sank down into the wing chair opposite his friend. "What does it matter?" he muttered. "Got no place to keep it anyway."

"Keep telling you, you can come live with me. You'll be as comfortable as fleas on a dog."

"And I keep telling you, I won't become your pensioner." He groaned. "Almost wish m'cousin Lucy had accepted me."

"No, you don't," Oliver said with conviction.

"You know what I really wish?" Freddy finally said after a long silence. "I wish we could get that gold."

Oliver looked confused. "What gold?"

"The gold from the mint that Barney said they were shipping past the estate on the twenty-fifth, remember? And today's the twenty-fifth. Almost like it was meant to be. If I had all that gold, I wouldn't have to worry about m'uncle." Freddy smiled wistfully at the thought.

"Might have to worry about the excisemen, though," Oliver pointed out.

"Can't be much of a threat," Freddy objected. "They've never stopped the smuggling and it's been going on for years and years."

Oliver frowned. "Maybe it's the runners that catch highwaymen."

"Never caught Dick Turpin. He's been free for a hundred years or so."

"Dash it all, Freddy, can't have been. Men don't live that long. Turpin's only a legend, anyway."

"Don't care. I mean to get that gold," Freddy added in a burst of bravado.

"Hmm." Oliver squinted into the fire as his agile mind sorted through the difficulties inherent in such a scheme.

"Have to take the whole wagon," he said.

"Why? Don't want the wagon. Want the gold."

"That much gold'd be heavy. Too heavy to carry on a horse."

"We could take some horses from the stable," Freddy suggested.

"Take too long to transfer the gold from the wagon to the horses. Besides, the grooms would get suspicious if we were to take out a bunch of horses late at night— Or any other time, for that matter. Have to take the whole wagon and hide it somewhere until the uproar dies down."

"Will it?" Freddy asked anxiously.

"Bound to. The treasury has lots of gold. Stands to reason. Look how Standen's always going on to Alridge about how they haven't paid the troops in the field for months. They'll probably just stamp some more coins," Oliver assured him. "Problem is, where can we hide a good-sized wagon where no one will stumble across it?"

Both men stared into the fire for a long minute, and then Freddy burst out, "M'father's broken leg."

"You feeling all right?" Oliver eyed him worriedly.

"It's the answer!" Freddy literally bounced in his chair.

"And what was the question?"

"Where to hide the wagon. We'll hide it in the cave where m'father broke his leg when he was just a boy like that limb Vernon. I've been there, years ago. It has a wide entrance, not too steep, over hard stone. We can drive the wagon in, unhitch the horses and let someone find them miles from the cave." Freddy peered hopefully at his friend.

Oliver eyed him with sudden respect. "You don't get many ideas, Freddy, but when you do, they're bang up to the nines. But what about the guards?"

"Guards?"

"Don't mean to cast a rub in your way, Freddy, but ain't to be supposed they'll just hand the gold over simply because we ask for it."

"Remember, Barney said there was only the driver and one guard."

"Still got to dispose of them," Oliver pointed out.

"Dispose?" Freddy's pale blue eyes bulged. "You mean kill 'em?"

"No need to snuff 'em out." Oliver rubbed the side of his nose reflectively. "Just meant we got to put 'em out of the way. Perhaps the element of surprise?"

"Ain't a surprise," Freddy objected. "I know all about it."

"Not you, them. We could lie in wait and jump out at them. Then we could truss them up and leave them on the side of the road."

Freddy glanced outside, where a brisk wind had started up. "Kind of cold at night," he offered. "They might freeze."

Oliver shook his head. "It's not that cold. They'll be fine until the morning, when they'll be found."

"Suppose so." Freddy dismissed the driver and guard from his mind, preferring to dwell instead on the tantalizing thought of the gold that was soon to be his. "I'll buy my own house," he said.

"No. Wouldn't be smart to be sporting that much blunt so soon after the robbery. Better to just rent rooms. I know of a snug little place over in St. James's Street you can get. Emmick rented it 'fore his father had that last seizure and cocked up his toes. Suit you right down to the ground."

"Right down to the ground." Freddy sighed happily as he leaned back in his chair, contemplating the future bliss of being independent of both his uncle's vile moods and his mother's constant reproaches.

Lucy had to wait almost an hour and a half until Robert finally returned. She tried to concentrate on a list of menus, but couldn't. Her mind kept wandering, wondering where Robert was and what he was doing and worrying about what the murderer was plotting next.

"What's the matter?" Robert's voice from the doorway took her by surprise and she turned with a jerk, her heart speeding up at the sight of his broad-shouldered frame filling the doorway.

His dark hair was disheveled from the wind and one errant strand had fallen over his forehead. As she watched, he impatiently brushed it back and then came into the room, closing the door behind him.

Robert studied her for a moment and then said, "Has anything happened here? You look faintly... worried. Is something wrong with Vernon?"

"No. Vernon is having a riding lesson with Jones," Lucy said, watching as he perched on the edge of the desk. She instinctively followed the movement of his leg as it swung back and forth. The light from the fire reflected off the gleam of his highly polished boot. Her eyes wandered upward over his bent knee to linger on the fawn-colored material of his pantaloons, which hugged his muscular thighs. Lucy watched as those muscles bunched and then relaxed with each swing of his foot, and her mouth suddenly went dry.

Why was she so fascinated with his body? It didn't seem decent, somehow.

"Poor Lucy, have you had a bad morning?" Robert's gentle voice made her feel cherished. It made her feel as though someone cared about her as a woman, and that was an idea almost as seductive as his body.

"Freddy was the one with the bad morning," Lucy said. "Grandpapa lost his temper and told him that when we return to London he has to move out of the house."

"Given the way your grandfather feels about him, it was inevitable. The only question was when would it happen."

"Perhaps, but I would have preferred that the impetus hadn't been Vernon's fault. And it was his fault."

"It might well be a blessing in a very thin disguise," Robert said. "Having rooms of his own will remove Freddy from your grandfather's constant disapproval as well as his mother's domination. The freedom may well be the making of him. Besides, it also serves to remove him from your brother's vicinity. Not that I really believe that Freddy had anything to do with the attacks, but if I'm wrong, then he will no longer have access to the boy.''

Lucy sighed. ''You're probably right. And it's not as if a set of rooms will cost him a great deal. While I don't put much credence in Amelia's claims to his being plump in the pocket, Freddy was the only son, so he must have inherited at least a competence.''

''And if he does outrun the grocer, no doubt his mother will help him.''

''Of course.'' Lucy brightened as she suddenly remembered all those thousands of pounds that her aunt had diverted from housekeeping over the years. She not only had all that, but she had her widow's jointure, too. ''It won't do any harm to at least see if it answers. If it doesn't, I don't doubt I can depend on his mother to let me help.''

Robert ran his hand around the back of his neck in frustration. ''I wish all our problems could be so easily solved. I spent a totally fruitless morning.''

''Doing what?''

''Visiting Mr. Cushing. The upstart mushroom from Birmingham Marson referred to,'' he added at Lucy's puzzled look.

''Oh, him. What happened?''

''His social background may be suspect, but he certainly isn't. I didn't even have to figure out how to lead into the subject of mantraps. He brought them up. Asked me who was trying to put the little lad below ground.''

Lucy winced, and Robert put his hand over hers and squeezed it comfortingly.

"I didn't even try to deny it. I told him we didn't know and asked him if anything unusual had happened in the village recently. Or if he'd noticed any strangers."

"And?" Lucy urged when he fell silent.

"He said that the only thing unusual had been the mantrap and the fact that the earl was in residence. He also said that it had been almost a year since a member of the family had been near the place."

"A year?" Lucy frowned. "But I'm almost positive Fulton said that it had been many years since Grandpapa had been here."

"Your grandfather wasn't here. Just Bevis and his man."

"Bevis? Why would Bevis come to Landsdowne?"

"I don't know for certain, but I spoke to the bailiff when I got back and he said that Bevis simply appeared one day about fifteen months ago, spent several weeks here and then left."

"Strange," Lucy said thoughtfully. "Bevis does not seem to me to be the kind of man who would enjoy a few solitary weeks in the country."

"He wasn't planning on spending his time alone," Robert said dryly. "Which is how he happened to come to the attention of Cushing. According to him, Bevis made suggestions of a highly improper nature to the daughter of one of Cushing's tenants. The girl told her father, who told Cushing, who confronted Bevis and threatened to write to the earl. At which point, Bevis suddenly remembered a pressing engagement elsewhere and left. This is the first time he's been back since."

"Interesting," Lucy murmured. "But why did he come here in the first place?"

"A repairing lease?" Robert suggested. "He could have been temporarily out of funds. Or he could have become involved in something unsavory and wanted to play least in sight for a while."

"It couldn't have been much of a scandal or Aunt Amelia would have known all about it," Lucy said slowly.

"True. I'm more inclined to lean toward the temporarily out-of-funds theory myself. Especially having seen how deep he plays."

Lucy made an exasperated sound. "Which brings us full circle. It's a motive for his pursuit of my dowry, but not for murdering Vernon."

"I know." Robert reached out and pulled her unresisting body against his.

Lucy swallowed uneasily, wondering why Robert had such an unsettling effect on her senses. Her mind had no answer. Indeed, it didn't seem capable of answering anything; it was too busy trying to deal with the sensory overload caused by being so close to him. Caused by the feel of his hard, muscular thighs pressing tightly against her legs. Their heat seemed to be burning through her thin Indian muslin gown, penetrating her skin and flooding her body. Freeing it of the restraints of society and common sense.

She didn't care that being so close to him was frowned upon. She didn't care that she might well be inviting future problems. All she cared about was the here and now.

His hands speared through her curls and he tilted her head back. Lucy looked up into his gleaming black eyes and felt excitement lurch through her at the hunger she could see reflected there.

"You are an incredibly beautiful woman." His warm breath caressed her lips, making them feel dry.

Lucy instinctively ran the tip of her tongue over her lips and then repeated the action more slowly when she saw the longing in his dark eyes as they followed her action. It gave her a feeling of power that this experienced man should find her so enthralling.

She put her hands on his shoulders, and the smooth wool of his coat scraped tantalizingly across her fingertips. She flexed her hands, digging her fingertips into the material to discover the heavy muscles of his shoulders.

Not for Robert was buckram padding necessary, she thought dreamily. Nature and an active lifestyle had forged his hard, muscular body. It was a body she wanted to touch, to explore. Strangely enough, this bit of self-knowledge didn't shock her. Society's rules were fast coming to have no relevance when applied to her and Robert. The only thing that seemed to matter was what she felt.

Her hands slid up over his shoulders to caress the warm, supple skin of his neck. The ends of his hair pricked against her fingertips, fueling her sense of anticipation. She watched with an eager inevitability as he came closer still, until finally his warm mouth brushed against her lips.

Lucy sucked in her breath at the contact, and his fingers gently threaded through her blond curls, holding her head as he pressed forward. Her mouth opened, and his tongue was quick to take advantage of it. It surged inside. Lucy shuddered at the sensation and her arms tightened, pressing her soft breasts against his chest.

A small whimper of longing bubbled up in her throat at the feel of his hot tongue stroking over the line of her teeth. She wanted more. Her fingers rubbed across his cheek and its texture intensified her longing. She wanted much more, she admitted with a total lack of self-deception. She wanted to fully experience everything possible between a man and a woman. To experience it with Robert Standen.

Chapter Seventeen

"Oliver?"

"Hush!" Oliver hissed with a furtive glance up the road. "Someone might hear you."

"Hear me?" Freddy repeated incredulously. "Nobody could hear me in this downpour. I'm drenched. Water's running down m'neck and m'boots are full of mud. Think they're ruined. Can't see t'tell for sure. Can't see the end of m'nose."

"No moonlight is all to the good," Oliver insisted. "Lessens the risk of us being seen."

"Shipment probably won't come anyway. Ain't never going to come. Been sitting here three hours now. Know what I think? I think Barney was having a May-game of us. M'boots'll never be the same. Don't know what m'man's going to think."

"It's not his place to think," Oliver said, dismissing Freddy's long-suffering valet. "It's his...ssh! Listen to that!"

"Don't have to shush," Freddy complained. "I wasn't the one talking. You was." He shifted his weight, trying to escape the water that was beginning to pool in the ditch he was crouched in. It proved impossible, and the cold liquid soaked his jacket. He heroically suppressed a sneeze and listened. Suddenly, he heard what Oliver had: the steady clip-clop of horses' hooves, accompanied by the creak of their leather harnesses.

"You remember what it is that you're supposed to do?" Oliver asked.

"Get on my horse, charge the wagon, fire just one of the dueling pistols over their heads and let you do the talking." Freddy rattled off his hard-learned instructions.

"Don't forget your mask." Oliver wrapped his own sodden piece of black silk around his face and then pulled the ancient cavalier's hat they'd found in the attics a little lower over his forehead.

Freddy followed suit, shivering as the icy material felt like clammy fingers on his face. Somehow, at this moment, abject penury seemed preferable. To say nothing of safer.

Determined not to fail Oliver, he untied his horse from the tree behind him and scrambled astride it with more speed than finesse. He unwrapped one of the earl's prized dueling pistols from its protective covering and apprehensively took up his position by the side of the road.

He squinted through the darkness, trying to see Oliver, who had taken up his assigned spot on the other side. But because of the lack of moonlight, all he could make out was a slightly darker shape between two of the trees that lined the roadway.

Freddy waited fatalistically as the gold wagon came closer and closer, until he could see the blurred outline of the horses and hear the chatter of the driver talking to the outrider. He was determined to fulfill the role Oliver had assigned to him. By the time the wagon had reached the spot directly in front of him, the thundering of his own terrified heartbeat had all but drowned out the sound of the horses' hooves.

Taking a deep, steadying breath, Freddy aimed the pistol over the horses' heads and fired.

"Stand and deliver!" Oliver roared out the command, but in the ensuing melee, no one seemed to hear him.

The six oversize horses, frightened out of their somnolent state by the sound of the gunshot, first plunged, then reared and leapt forward, jerking the heavily loaded wagon behind them.

There was a confused shout from the outrider, a shot fired over Freddy's left shoulder and then the sound of horses running in panic. Freddy hurriedly moved his own mount out of the way of the runaway team. Oliver muttered a curse and raced after the wagon.

Confused, since this last had not been included in the instructions Oliver had drilled into his head, Freddy looked around, trying to decide what he should do. To his right, he could hear the rapid tattoo of a single horse's hoofbeats retracing the way the wagon had come, while to his left was the sound of the thundering gold wagon, heading away from him.

Not knowing what else to do, he followed the habit of a lifetime and raced off after Oliver.

He finally caught up with him a half mile down the road. Oliver had managed to catch the team. He was holding the bridle of the lead horse while the horses shuffled and blew in unhappy discomfort at their unexpected exertion.

"It's me, Oliver," Freddy hailed him. "The outrider took off in the opposite direction, so I followed you."

"Probably gone for help," Oliver guessed. "How long do you figure it will take him to get back to the village and raise the militia?"

Freddy considered a moment and then said, "It's six miles back, and this late at night, he'd have to find someone to do it. Late as it is, it might take awhile."

"Who's the local justice of the peace? Your uncle?"

"No, Squire Lestings is. But they won't find him. He always goes to London for the season. Bound to have left already."

"Good," Oliver muttered in satisfaction. "By the time that outrider locates help, we'll have the wagon safely hidden away and the horses already turned loose. Rain will cover any tracks they might leave.

"Here. Give me your horse's reins and get into the box and drive the wagon. I'll stay by the leader's head and make sure they don't bolt again."

Happy to leave the decision-making in Oliver's hands, Freddy hurried to do as he'd been told. He clambered onto the wagon seat and groped around in the darkness for the dangling reins.

"All set," he finally said. Clucking to the horses, he started the restive team moving.

"Oliver?" he said after a few minutes.

"What?" his friend muttered abstractedly, his attention focused on the side of the road so as not to miss their turning in the darkness.

"Was just wondering what happened to the driver. I couldn't've shot him, could I?" Freddy swallowed against the suddenly sick feeling in the pit of his stomach.

"Don't be a sapscull. You shot over the horses' heads. Don't you know anything about trajectories?"

"No," Freddy said simply. "Never heard of 'em. There!" His voice sharpened in excitement as he recognized the cluster of oaks by the side of the road. "Turn off past them and we'll be at the cave in a few miles."

"If nothing goes amiss, we'll be home before dawn." Oliver sighed. "I could use a brandy."

"Could use a whole damned keg of brandy," Freddy muttered. "Going to buy me one, too. From the innkeeper in the village. He gets it straight from France."

Freddy lapsed into silence as he began to picture all the other things he was going to buy with his suddenly acquired wealth. Visions of flowered waistcoats and multicaped driving coats with mother-of-pearl buttons the size of saucers filled his mind.

"There. That's it, ain't it?" Oliver pointed to his right.

"Uh-huh." Freddy came out of his reverie. "The cave's just up that incline." He urged the horses forward, their hooves clattering over the loose shale as they entered the cave. Within minutes, they were entirely concealed within the antechamber.

Oliver dismounted, tied both of their horses to the back of the wagon and then groped around in the darkness near the cave entrance, trying to locate the lanterns they'd secreted there earlier in the day.

"It's very dark in here, Oliver," Freddy said, unable to entirely keep the quaver out of his voice. "I thought it was dark out in that pouring rain, but this..." He shuddered. "This is dark dark."

Oliver paused in his attempts to light the lantern, looked around and then said, "Yes, you could almost say it's stygian dark."

"Maybe *you* could," Freddy objected, "but I couldn't. Don't know what it means."

"Means dark. Very dark." Oliver finally managed to get the lantern lit. A soft glow illuminated the area around the entrance. He hurried to pick up the lamp and moved farther into the cave.

Freddy carefully drove the horses after him. "Then why don't you just say dark?" he complained, climbing down from the wagon. "No need to use some break-jaw word nobody has ever heard of. I already know you're smart. Smartest man I know."

"Smartest man I know, too," Oliver, not given to false modesty, agreed.

Freddy accepted the lantern and held it aloft while Oliver worked on getting the second one lit. "Never would have figured out how to arrange all this myself," he admitted fairly.

"Always glad to help a friend." Oliver grunted in satisfaction as the second lantern blossomed with orange light.

"I swear this damned cave gets bigger every time we come here. And colder. I—" Freddy broke off, peering fearfully into the darkness at the edge of the lantern light.

"What's wrong?" Oliver turned from his contemplation of a particularly interesting formation on the cave's floor and frowned at Freddy, who was shaking.

"What was that?" Freddy asked.

"A stalagmite."

"Not that!" Freddy interrupted him. "The noise. I heard a noise. Kinda low and groaning like—" he gulped and blurted out "—like a ghost."

His friend turned back to his contemplation of the rock. "Ain't no such thing as a ghost."

"How do you know?" Freddy demanded. "Ever see one?"

"No."

"Then that proves it," he announced emphatically.

"Freddy, you're the most muffle-headed—"

"There it is again!" Freddy surreptitiously inched closer to Oliver. "Did you hear it?"

"Hear..." Oliver suddenly froze as a shaky groan echoed through the cave.

"I tell you, it's a ghost," Freddy whimpered. "They always groan."

"Ghosts bedamned!" Oliver hurried over to the wagon and, climbing up on the seat, looked down into the wagon bed.

"Curses!" He slumped down on the seat.

"Is it a ghost?" Freddy asked fearfully.

"Worse," Oliver muttered.

"Ain't nothing worse than a ghost."

"Yes, there is. A witness. It's the driver."

"Driver?" Freddy sidled closer and, standing on tiptoe, peered into the wagon bed. Lying huddled in the small space behind the driver's seat and in front of the bags of gold was the missing driver. There was a purplish bruise on his temple, which was sluggishly oozing blood, and his eyes were still closed.

"Ain't dead, is he?" Freddy asked fearfully.

"Dead men don't groan."

"They do if they're ghosts," Freddy said triumphantly, and then rushed on when Oliver's lips tightened, "what are we going to do with him?"

Oliver sighed. "An excellent question. Would that I had an excellent answer."

"We can't let him go," Freddy said. "He'd tell."

"Undoubtedly," Oliver agreed.

"M'uncle Adolphus will be very upset if he finds out about this," Freddy muttered. "Even more upset than he already is."

"Come to that, my papa will have my head on a platter if he discovers this. Dreadfully stuffy about involving the family name in scandals and all."

"Government'll probably be upset, too," Freddy offered gloomily.

"Count on it. Everyone always gets dead serious about money. Especially a lot of money."

Freddy peered down at the unconscious man. "Maybe he'll die?" he offered hopefully.

Oliver considered it a moment and then said, "Shouldn't think so. Only a bump on the head, when all's said and done. He'll probably just have the deuce of a headache."

Freddy thought about it for a long moment and then took a deep breath. "Perhaps we could help."

Oliver blinked uncomprehendingly. "Help what?"

"Help him die." He gestured toward the driver's prostrate form.

"Hmm." Oliver frowned thoughtfully. "There's no denying it would be convenient if he were dead. It's getting him dead that presents the problem. Mean to say, I'm as game as the next man but . . ." He gestured impotently.

Freddy sighed. "I know. He's such a little man and he's bound to moan a lot, and then there'd be all that blood." He swallowed uneasily. "Never could abide blood."

"Can't say as I can, either." Oliver pulled out his knife and began to cut some of the ropes holding the bags together.

"What are you doin'?"

"Going to tie him up. Here." He tossed Freddy a length of rope. "You bind his legs and I'll get his hands. Can't have him shabbing off when we leave."

"Should say not!" Freddy agreed wholeheartedly, and he made short work of securing the guard. Pulling his mask out of his pocket, he used it to blindfold the man. "Too bad we can't just put him in the dungeons," he mourned.

"You have dungeons at Landsdowne?" Oliver looked up in sudden interest.

"Did, but one of the earls a couple hundred years ago turned them into wine cellars."

"Shame." Oliver shook his head. "No help for it. We'll have to leave him here until we can figure out what to do with him."

Oliver used his own mask to gag the driver and then he cut the horses free from the wagon. He led them to the mouth of the cave and slapped one across the flank. Startled, they all bolted.

"Let's follow the horses a ways to make sure that they don't circle back here," Oliver said.

"Coming." Freddy ran back to the wagon, thrust his hands into one of the bags of gold and shoved coins into his pockets. "Coat's ruined anyway," he offered, when Oliver frowned at him. "And I want to hold some of my money. You want some?"

"No." Oliver handed Freddy his horse's reins and then carefully extinguished the lanterns. "Told you. Have plenty of the ready. Now, come on. We need to make sure the horses are headed away from here and then get back to the house before that guard returns with reinforcements."

Freddy obediently mounted his horse and, falling in beside Oliver's mount, urged the skittish animal out of the cave. Hunching his shoulders against the chill rain, he headed for the main road.

This time, Lady Luck favored them and they made it back to Landsdowne without encountering anyone. Once they had stabled their horses, they slipped silently through a side door and snuck up to Freddy's room, taking great care not to rouse the sleeping household.

Oliver immediately went to the sideboard, where he poured two tumblers of the earl's best brandy. He took a long swallow as Freddy sank into an armchair by the fire, completely oblivious to the way his wet, muddy clothing was staining the pale blue silk upholstery. He handed the second glass to Freddy, who downed it in one strangled gulp.

Handing back the empty glass, Freddy muttered, "More."

Oliver eyed him doubtfully for a minute and then said, "Getting foxed is not going to help the situation."

"Maybe there's some way to wrap up the whole affair in clean linen?" Freddy looked hopefully at his mentor.

"Not unless we first wrap up our witness in burial linen," Oliver replied, dashing his hopes.

"What we need is someone used to killing people. Like a soldier." Freddy brightened. "Like Colonel Standen. Stands to reason," he rushed on. "He's a soldier. Been one for years. Must've been involved in lots of killing and what-have-you. Killing probably don't mean any more to him than us hunting wood pigeons. Ask him to do it."

Oliver thoughtfully sipped his brandy. "But he's still a gentleman. And killing someone already trussed up like a chicken is hardly sporting. Mean to say, not like an affair of honor."

"Don't see why not. He'd be just as dead in the end," Freddy grumbled. "But dare say you're right. It would be just like Standen to refuse to oblige us on such a paltry point.... Maybe we ought to go abroad for a while?" He dug his hand into his coat pocket and pulled out a handful of gold coins. "We've got Napoleon on the run and I got money." He smiled fatuously down at his glittering treasure. As he peered closer, though, a frown marred his features.

"What the matter?" Oliver asked.

Freddy raised a white, stricken face and choked out, "These ain't guineas. They're—they're fakes!" He sagged against his chair in disbelief. The maligned coins slipped from his suddenly nerveless fingers and fell to the floor, where they rolled in all directions.

"What do you mean, fake?" Oliver reached down and picked one up. "Looks like gold to me." He tossed it in his hand. "Heavy enough for gold." He took it over to the brace of candles on the table for a better look.

"Ain't guineas," Freddy repeated faintly.

"I very much fear you're right," Oliver finally said. "You know what we've got?"

"A hornet's nest of trouble and no gold."

"Not exactly. It's gold, all right. These are the new sovereigns I read the government was going to start minting."

"You sure? I ain't never seen 'em before," Freddy said doubtfully.

"That's because they ain't in circulation yet. Don't know exactly when they will be, either." Oliver grimaced. "Trying to spend one would be tantamount to confessing to the robbery."

"Blast!" Freddy shoved his fingers through his sodden locks. "Why didn't Barney warn us?"

Oliver sighed deeply. "If we had confided that we were planning to steal them, he probably would have. You know, there's a lot more to this robbery business than I would have ever suspected."

"Knew it was too good to be true." Freddy drained his glass for the second time and peered blearily at the brandy decanter.

Oliver followed his gaze, and with a sigh, handed it to him. "You might as well get foxed," he said. "Can't think of what else to do at this juncture. Maybe by morning something will have occurred to me," he said hopefully.

Unfortunately, it didn't. Morning came and went without even a glimmer of an idea for extracting them from the bumblebroth. And no idea was strong enough to surface through the massive headache Freddy's overindulgence in the brandy had produced.

By teatime Oliver was showing a very uncharacteristic tendency to fidget, while Freddy meekly accepted a cup of tea from Lucy and then subsided into a chair with a barely muffled groan.

Lucy eyed her cousin with concern. She had no doubt that he was suffering the aftereffects of a heavy night of drinking. What she didn't know was why. He'd shown absolutely no tendency to drink to excess before. Was he worried about having to move out of the London house?

She studied his pale features and bloodshot eyes through the rising steam in her teacup. Maybe she had it wrong. Maybe he was celebrating moving into his own quarters. Maybe he viewed the earl's ultimatum as an excuse to escape from his mother's dominating presence.

Lucy frowned as the sound of angry voices from the entrance hall penetrated the relaxed atmosphere of the salon.

"Well, really!" Amelia sniffed disparagingly. "How dare the servants disturb the family with their petty squabbles?"

"That doesn't sound like a servant to me," Lucy observed, as an imperious voice demanded to see the earl at once.

The earl looked up from the chess game he was losing to Vernon. "What is that infernal racket?" he demanded.

"I'll go see, Grandpapa." Vernon eagerly slipped from his seat and rushed out of the room. He scurried back seconds later, his features pinched and white. He hurried over to Lucy.

"Lucy, we've been invaded!" he whispered.

"Invaded?" Lucy stared blankly at him.

"Don't involve us in your games, young man," Amelia ordered. "Just tell us who is making that unholy racket."

"I told you." Vernon inched closer to Lucy. "Soldiers."

"Soldiers?" Freddy suddenly shot up in his chair, inadvertently spilling his tea all down his pants. To Lucy's surprise, he didn't seem to notice either the scalding liquid or his stained clothing.

"In my house?" the earl asked.

As if to answer the question, a young lieutenant, trailed by three nervous-looking dragoons, marched into the room, with Fulton hovering beside them, looking as close to flustered as Lucy could ever remember seeing him.

"What is the meaning of this outrage, sirrah?" the earl demanded.

The officer seemed slightly taken aback by his reception, but he manfully stood his ground. "Pardon the intrusion, my lord, but we are here on important government business."

Lucy glanced curiously at Freddy when he started at the words. He looked petrified, while Oliver was studying the ceiling's plasterwork with great interest. Lucy felt a momentary flash of unease, followed by a wish that Robert were here. Something was wrong. She wasn't sure what, but she could feel it. Or more accurately, could see it in Freddy's uncharacteristic behavior.

"Only business that concerns me is my own!" the earl snapped.

"Last night a government shipment of gold was robbed not three miles from here," the officer said in stentorian tones. "And the driver disappeared."

Lucy's concern deepened as Freddy seemed to turn even paler.

"Ha!" Amelia looked up from her netting. "Find the driver and you'll find the gold."

"We have reason to believe he was murdered," the lieutenant said importantly.

"No!" Freddy gasped, and sent an agonized glance to Oliver. "Surely not?"

The lieutenant gave Freddy a thin smile. "Your sense of outrage does you credit, sir, but, nonetheless, I fear it's true. We found his bloodstained hat beside the road, and the outrider says that they were attacked by a gang of desperadoes brandishing guns."

"The outrider?" the earl repeated incredulously. "What sapscull sent a shipment of gold out on an open road without a proper escort?"

"I wouldn't know, my lord," the lieutenant said stiffly, "but I believe the plan was to not call attention to it."

"Ha!" The earl gave a bark of laughter. "Damned government never could do anything right. But why tell me about it?"

"As I stated, the deed occurred not three miles from your front gate—"

"Are you accusing me of robbing a gold shipment?" the earl asked, his voice lowered ominously.

The lieutenant swallowed nervously. "Certainly not, my lord. I was simply wondering if perhaps you or one of your guests might not have seen—"

"No!" Freddy blurted out. "Didn't see a thing. Pitch black outside. Raining besides."

"Shut up, you fool!" The earl glared at Freddy. "No call for any of us to deny the imbecile's insinuation. We all know you ain't got the bottom to kick up a spree like that."

"Murder is hardly a spree," the lieutenant muttered.

"Gold is very heavy, Lieutenant." Lucy tried to deflect the man's attention. There was something havey-cavey going on here, and until she found out what it was, she didn't want the lieutenant any more suspicious than he already was. "Have you tried to follow the wagon's tracks?"

"Yes, ma'am, but the road is very rocky and what with the heavy rains last night…" He shrugged. "Fact is, there weren't any tracks to follow."

Lucy frowned inwardly as Oliver's shoulders seemed to relax ever so slightly—even though he didn't waver in his study of the ceiling. Surely Oliver and Freddy couldn't somehow be involved in such a hey-go-mad scheme as robbing a government gold shipment?

"Thank you for your suggestion though, ma'am." The lieutenant smiled at the one friendly face in the room before turning back to the glowering earl.

"My lord, may I have your permission to search for the driver's body on your land?"

"No, you may not! Ain't having no damned pack of buffleheaded soldiers swarming around and frightening the livestock. You stay off Landsdowne."

"Lieutenant, I doubt that a gang of desperadoes would have stopped to bury the driver's body before making good their escape," Lucy said, trying to soften her grandfather's flat refusal.

"True, ma'am, but there are thick hedges on either side of the road that extend for several miles past where we think the robbery occurred. They might have tossed his body into one of them."

"No harm in looking there," Freddy offered, the color suddenly returning to his face.

"Dolt!" the earl snapped. "No one asked your opinion."

"Grandpapa—" Lucy turned to the furious earl "—please give the soldiers permission to search on either side of the road. I, for one, certainly don't want to stumble across a body while I'm out on a ride."

"I should say not!" Amelia shuddered expressively. "This is an absolute outrage. I simply don't know what the world is coming to."

"Oh, all right. Make your damned search," the earl said, capitulating. "But mind you stay near the road."

"Yes, my lord. Thank you for your cooperation." The lieutenant turned stiffly and marched out, trailed by the three nervous soldiers and the disapproving Fulton.

"Really." Amelia dropped her netting. "All this talk of murder has thoroughly unsettled me. Vernon, go find your cousin Kitty and tell her to come up to my room. I feel one of my sick headaches coming on."

"Find her yourself! The boy ain't a servant," the earl said, venting some of his spleen on her.

"I don't mind, Grandpapa," Vernon assured him. "I like to find people. I'd like to find that body." His eyes began to gleam.

"No," Lucy said flatly. "I absolutely draw the line at your dragging home dead bodies."

"Aw, Lucy! You never let me have any fun," Vernon grumbled as he stomped out of the room, followed by his aunt.

"Bah! I might as well go rest, too. Nothing like a robbery and a body to cut up one's peace." The earl stamped out, forcibly reminding Lucy of Vernon.

She waited until she heard her grandfather's footsteps on the marble stairs and then turned to Freddy, studying his greenish complexion and frightened expression. Thoughtfully, her gaze shifted to Oliver, who was nervously drumming his fingertips on the Sheridan table beside him. She turned back to her cousin, recognizing him as the weaker of the two. "Freddy, what about that body the lieutenant's searching for?"

"Ain't no body," Freddy muttered. "'Cause he ain't dead."

"What Freddy means—" Oliver broke in.

"Is exactly what he said," Lucy interrupted. "That he has knowledge that the driver isn't dead. You have no idea how gratifying I find it that my cousin hasn't taken up murder."

"Course I ain't," Freddy said. "Far too messy."

"Quite true," Lucy said bleakly as, for an instant, horrific memories flooded her mind. Determinedly, she pushed them away and focused on the problem at hand. "Tell me, what do the pair of you know about the robbery?"

"Dashed sight more than I wished I did!" Freddy burst out. "Tell you, Lucy, it's all a hum."

She frowned uncertainly. "You mean the robbery?"

"No. How everyone always says that being a highwayman is so exciting and all. Ain't. It's wet and muddy. Ruined my new boots and the stain'll never come out of my jacket," he grumbled.

Lucy stared at him, not knowing whether to laugh or cry. "Freddy," she said slowly, "please tell me that you aren't involved in whatever happened."

"Ain't involved in it," he replied promptly.

"Is that the truth?" she asked.

He gave her an exasperated look. "You said to tell you I wasn't involved in it. You didn't say to tell you the truth."

"My God." Lucy stared at him in horror. "Are you mad?"

"Shouldn't think so," Freddy answered. "Though this business is enough to drive one to Bedlam. Ain't it, Oliver?"

"Dashed well is," Oliver complained. "You've no idea, Lucy."

"Probably not." Lucy eyed them in fascination.

"All we meant to do was to rob the coach, and what happened?" Oliver threw up his hands in disgust. "We accidentally kidnapped the driver, because it was too dark to see anything."

"And not only that, but it wasn't even spending money." Freddy added to their list of complaints. "It's them new sovereigns, and Oliver says we dasn't dare use 'em."

"But why?" Lucy moaned. "Why rob a gold shipment in the first place?"

"It was travelin' through, and I needed the money. Seemed like a good idea at the time," Freddy said simply.

"Freddy—" Lucy pinned him with an accusatory eye "—exactly how much money do you have?"

"There's that wagon...."

"Forget the government's gold."

"Might as well," he muttered. "Can't spend it anyhow."

"What is your personal income?" she persisted.

"Ain't got none," he said baldly.

"Not any?" Lucy repeated incredulously. "Your father—"

"Was a terrible gamester," Oliver said, trying to help his embarrassed-looking friend.

"Even worse, he was an inept gamester," Freddy said. "Never learned that it's fatal to play when you're in your cups."

"But your mother talked about your estate in Kent," Lucy said.

"Had to sell it to pay papa's creditors when he died. Didn't tell anyone, not even Uncle Adolphus, 'cause we didn't want anyone to know we was under the hatches. So we came to live with Uncle Adolphus, and mama had her widow's jointure and I had my allowance as the heir."

"But your mother said—"

"She said you'd marry me if I asked you," Freddy countered. "You didn't."

Lucy grimaced. "True. So, since I wouldn't marry you, you took up robbing gold shipments."

"Didn't mind," Freddy said. "Much rather be a highwayman than get riveted to you."

Lucy swallowed a hysterical urge to laugh and said, "Thank you. That's a relief to my mind. But the point remains that we have to do something."

"What?" Two hopeful pairs of eyes stared at her.

"Where is that guard, by the way?" she asked.

"Tied up in the wagon," Freddy disclosed.

"And where is the wagon?"

"In that cave where m'father said he broke his leg when he was young," Freddy said.

"Yes," Lucy said slowly. "I remember going there once when I was about ten, but it was very damp and cold."

"Still is," Freddy offered.

"That poor driver. He must be starved and frightened," she said worriedly. "We have to do something about him."

"Don't suppose you'd be willing to kill him for us, would you? I mean, it doesn't matter if a female ain't sportin'," Freddy said.

"You suppose correctly! I categorically refuse to kill anyone."

"You have no idea how happy that makes me." Robert spoke from the doorway, and then chuckled as three pairs of startled eyes swung guiltily toward him.

"You don't suppose *he'd* do it, do you?" Freddy whispered to Lucy. "He was our first choice, anyway."

"He's more likely to murder the pair of you," Lucy shot back.

"Really?" Freddy nervously eyed Robert's broad shoulders for a second and then got to his feet. "Must go check on poor mama." He sidled around Robert and scurried out of the room, trailed by the equally cautious Oliver.

Chapter Eighteen

Robert looked questioningly at Lucy. "What was that all about? Something to do with the attacks on Vernon?"

"No!" She snatched the heavy brass poker and relieved some of her feeling of frustration by jabbing the blazing logs in the cavernous fireplace.

Robert watched her as she scattered the glowing coals, frowning slightly as her agitated movements sent a stream of sparks shooting up the chimney. Her face was set in tense lines, her dark gold eyebrows were drawn together, her lips compressed, and two bright spots of color burned in her pale cheeks—color he was relatively certain was caused by inner turmoil and not by the heat of the fire.

His gaze was caught and held by the sight of her breasts as her action pushed them against the thin gauze of her dress. His palms began to tingle when he remembered their warm softness and the pressure of their hardened tips against his hands. He swallowed, feeling a sudden surge of longing to repeat the experience. Soon, he promised himself. Soon she'd be his wife and he would have every right to touch her and kiss her and make love to her whenever and wherever he pleased.

Robert shifted restlessly as his body began to react to the intoxicating prospect. He clenched his hands into fists and tried to concentrate on something else, but he couldn't. Thoughts of loving Lucy filled his mind to the exclusion of every other consideration.

Marriage no longer seemed like an institution to be avoided at all costs. Not only was he finding himself actually counting the minutes until he could make love to Lucy, he realized that she didn't bore him. She never treated him to irrational fits of temperament or expected him to write inane poetry to her. Lucy Danvers had a very clear view of the world and the forces that shaped it. She didn't see herself as the only thing of importance in it. Yes, Robert thought in deep satisfaction, fate had indeed provided him with a perfect wife.

"Let me guess. Oliver has been writing bad poetry for Freddy to spout again?"

"No," Lucy said with asperity. "This time Oliver has been writing criminal scripts for both of them to act out."

"Criminal?" Robert repeated uncomprehendingly.

"Maybe treasonous, too. I'm not sure of the legal ramifications. I can't seem to think beyond the fact that it's a hanging offense."

"Exactly what did they do?" Robert cut to the heart of the matter.

"Robbed the government gold shipment when it passed by on its way north last night," Lucy said baldly.

"Robbed the gold—!" Robert sputtered to a halt.

"Shh!" Lucy whispered, nervously going to the door to peer out into the hallway. To her relief, it was empty. "I don't want this known."

"As a point of interest, how do you intend to keep it unknown?" Robert asked dryly. "The government is not going to view the pilfering of their gold with complacency."

Lucy sighed. "I know. We've already had a visit from some lieutenant during tea. He seemed very determined, and what is worse, reasonably intelligent. If he manages to corner Freddy by himself, he'll have the whole story in five minutes."

"But how did they move all that gold?"

"In the gold wagon. Oliver said they drove it into the cave where my father and his cousins used to play when they were boys. It's only a mile or two from the road."

Robert ran his fingers through his short hair in exasperation. "Tell me, does Oliver have any ideas of how to extricate them from the consequences of what they did? The scandal alone—"

"Promises to make my own blot on the family escutcheon look inconsequential by comparison," Lucy said grimly. "Grandpapa will be mortified, Amelia will be ostracized by society, Kitty will never have a chance to establish herself credibly and I doubt that even the fact that Oliver's father is a duke will save him...."

"Probably not," Robert agreed. "Stealing from the citizenry is one thing, stealing from the government is quite another. If this becomes known, the best we can hope for is to quietly hustle the pair of them out of the country."

"Far out of the country! The remoter regions of India have a certain appeal. Or maybe we could interest Oliver in Chinese civilization," Lucy sighed. "Aunt Amelia is going to be very upset if Freddy has to go abroad."

"She'll be more upset if they hang him," Robert said acerbically. "And from what I've seen of your aunt, if she is upset, she will make sure that everyone around her is upset. So I suppose we had better figure out a way to wrap this whole mess up in clean linen."

"You don't have to help," Lucy forced herself to say, although what she really wanted to do was to throw herself against his chest and beg him to do something—anything. She was so tired of trying to cope with difficult situations on her own.

"Yes, I do." His answer was infinitely comforting. "I would prefer that my future wife's family not be the latest *on dit*. Now then, you say they hid the wagon in a cave?"

Lucy nodded, deciding to ignore his reference to their marriage in the interest of peace.

"How likely is it that someone will accidently stumble across it?"

"At the moment, not very. Grandpapa only gave the military permission to search the ditches on either side of the road, and the cave is a ways from it. And the locals won't go near it. When Grandpapa was just a boy, a party of young men from the village went exploring for a lark and never came out. No trace of them was ever found and local legend has it that their ghosts haunt the cave."

"Hmm." Robert stared out the window at the swaying branches of a wind-driven oak. "Perhaps our wisest course would be to simply wait until this lieutenant you mentioned stumbles across the cave. Someone is bound to mention it to him sooner or later.''

"Not a good idea,'' Lucy told him.

"Why not? I admit I'd prefer to have the gold safely off your grandfather's property, but—''

"The devil take the gold. It's the driver I'm worried about.''

Robert frowned uncomprehendingly. "Is he looking for it, too?''

"He already knows where it is—with him. Freddy and Oliver left him tied up in back of the wagon.''

"Left him tied up?'' Robert stared at her incredulously. "Why would they do an idiotic thing like kidnap the driver?''

"They said it was dark and raining, and in the confusion they simply didn't notice him until they were already in the cave and it was too late.''

"Of all the bungling, inept—''

Lucy unexpectedly chuckled. "How can you say so? They got the gold, didn't they?''

"I hope you still think this is hilarious when the man identifies them. Did he get a good look at them?''

Lucy shrugged. "I don't know. They weren't very specific about details. Once they unburdened themselves, they seemed to feel that they had done their part.''

"Damn!'' Robert exclaimed. "A witness could be a real problem.''

"Mmm,'' Lucy agreed. "Freddy and Oliver have already figured that out. They apparently considered killing him, but in the end couldn't bring themselves to the sticking point.''

Robert grimaced. "So that's what they were referring to when I came in. I suppose we should be grateful. Covering up the robbery is going to be hard enough. A murder would be impossible."

"Does no one in England ever consider the morality of a situation?" Lucy asked tartly.

"What?" Robert stared blankly at her.

"Morality," she repeated. "Surely you've heard of the word? Since I've returned to England, I've had to cope with you trying to blackmail me into marriage, someone trying to kill Vernon with apparently no more thought than they would give to wringing a chicken's neck, Aunt Amelia embezzling thousands of pounds from the housekeeping funds, Freddy and Oliver robbing a government shipment—"

"Why?" Robert suddenly broke into her tirade.

Lucy stared blankly at him. "Why what?"

"Why did they rob the gold shipment? It doesn't seem like them."

"For that most splendid reason of all—money. It would seem that Freddy is in the basket. His mother's tales of his estate in Kent and his income were just that—tales."

"And when your grandfather cut off his allowance and told him to quit the London house..."

"He didn't have anywhere to go," Lucy finished. "From what I can tell, Oliver helped him with the robbery out of friendship and curiosity about whether it could be done."

"But why steal? Why not ask for help?"

"As I understand it, he didn't want to take charity."

"Of course not," Robert said in exasperation. "Highway robbery is certainly preferable to charity. Why didn't I think of that?"

"And to think that for years I believed that if I could just get home to England, everything would be fine. I didn't know when I was well off," she said wryly.

"It will be fine," Robert insisted.

Lucy gave a disbelieving sniff. "How?"

"Well..."

"That's what I thought."

"Let's think of this as a military campaign."

Lucy shuddered. "No, that's the only point I agree with those two sapsculls on. I categorically refuse to murder a defenseless man."

"Death is not a desirable outcome in a military maneuver," Robert informed her. "It's the result of bad planning."

Lucy chuckled. "Or, perhaps, of the enemy not understanding his role in the scheme of things."

Robert ignored her. "Our objective is to extricate those two from the consequences of their actions."

"And to return the gold and free the driver. The lieutenant said something about the government offering a reward for the recovery of the coins," Lucy added thoughtfully. "I wonder how much."

"It's usually a small percentage of the total value. Why? You aren't suggesting we try to get the reward for Freddy and Oliver, are you?"

"Absolutely not! If I had my way, those two would be wearing sackcloth and ashes for their part in this. Besides," she added on a more practical note, "we don't want them anywhere near the driver. He might recognize them."

"True," Robert agreed. "Although, unless he actually heard their names, it's highly unlikely he would know who they were or where to find them. One's mind does not usually jump to the nephew of an earl and the son of a duke when one thinks of possible suspects for a robbery."

"If he knew anything about this family, he would. They are nothing but a bunch of thatch-gallows!" Lucy said tartly.

"I think the best way to handle this is to go to the cave and pretend to stumble across the wagon and the driver."

"Whereupon we utter suitable sounds of horror and free him, hoping he will be so glad to be rescued that he won't ask any awkward questions?" Lucy said skeptically. "Such as why two supposedly intelligent adults would be wandering around the countryside at dusk? Or what an incredible coincidence it is that he first gets kidnapped by two members of the aristocracy, and then gets rescued by two more?"

Robert glanced outside at the deepening twilight and frowned. "You're right about the time, and it's coming on to rain."

"It's been coming on to rain ever since I came back from France," she muttered. "My ancestors should have put in a moat."

Robert smiled at her peevish expression. The poor dear. She really had had to put up with a lot since she'd returned home. But once he had her safely married, he would take her home to his estate in Devon, far away from embezzling aunts, incompetent highwaymen and murderous plots against her brother. The most challenging decision she would have to face was what to wear for dinner, he thought in satisfaction.

"We shall have to postpone our accidental discovery until tomorrow morning," he finally said.

Lucy winced. "That poor driver. He'll be frozen."

"No, he won't. Caves maintain a constant temperature no matter what it's like outside."

"Yes, constantly cold!"

"Any soldier has endured worse." Robert dismissed the man's discomfort. "What we need is an unexceptionable excuse to go there, so that no one asks any awkward questions."

"Vernon," Lucy said suddenly. "My father showed me where the cave was when I was small and warned me about how dangerous it was. And since this is the first time Vernon has been to Landsdowne, what would be more natural than for me to show it to him? We can take Jones along to protect Vernon, and they can go into the village to alert the authorities while we stay with the driver."

"Vernon shouldn't be in danger for much longer." Robert had caught her flash of fear when she'd mentioned the need to bring Jones along.

Lucy sighed. "If I were a foolhardy person, I would ask what else could possibly go wrong, but I won't for fear I might tempt the fates to show me."

"My poor sweetling." Robert brushed his knuckles over her soft cheek and Lucy felt her heart do a flip-flop of longing. "You would have made a great tactician," he said, complimenting her.

"I've certainly had enough practice."

"You wouldn't happen to have any ideas on how we keep the driver from describing his captors, do you?"

"That one's easy. We'll give him the reward that's being offered. It's no more than the poor man's entitled to," Lucy said, with a glance outside at the leaden sky.

"Absolutely brilliant!" Robert exclaimed. "Unless the man's a complete fool, he's not going to do anything to jeopardize a reward. Especially since he wasn't hurt and the government will get its gold back. All that remains to do is to convince those two chuckleheads to play least in sight until it's safe to send them back to London."

Lucy grimaced. "Where Freddy is not going to have a home. I think I shall have Mr. Potter send him a letter saying that Grandpapa has decided to make him a yearly allowance, and then I'll pay it myself."

"Why?" Robert asked.

Lucy shrugged. "Why not? I can afford it, and I consider it a small price to pay not to have to be constantly worrying about what madcap scheme Freddy's gotten himself involved in in an attempt to pay his bills."

"Lucy Danvers, you are a very unusual woman."

"Why? Because I want peace of mind?"

"No, because you're generous."

"It's easy to be generous when you have so much," Lucy said seriously. "Helping Freddy won't cause me the slightest sacrifice."

But few wealthy people were generous, Robert reflected. Her willingness to share what she had was one of the reasons he loved her. The unexpected thought reverberated through his mind with the impact of a pistol shot. He briefly closed his eyes, but the knowledge was still there, imprinted on the backs of his eyelids.

He opened them and stared down into Lucy's puzzled face. Her dear, sweet face with its bright eyes and soft lips. She was so beautiful, he thought achingly. So absolutely beautiful and so determined not to marry him. How could he have fallen in love with her? He certainly hadn't meant to. He had wanted to marry her in the first place only because he had to marry someone, and she'd been convenient and very vulnerable to his demands. But somehow, the better he had come to know her, the more fascinated he had been by her. He wasn't sure exactly when that fascination had slipped into love. Nor did it really matter, he conceded. What mattered was that she was still determined not to marry him.

He felt a painful twist of conscience. If he loved her, shouldn't he respect her wishes not to marry? But she had to marry someone, he argued with himself. There was nothing else for a woman in her position to do. And given that she had to marry, wouldn't it be better for her to marry him than some whey-faced upstart who would neither understand nor appreciate her complex personality?

"Is something wrong?" Lucy finally asked him.

"No." Robert pushed his confused thoughts to the back of his mind and tried to concentrate on the task at hand. "I was just trying to decide how to impress upon our two miscreants the absolute necessity of keeping silent about what they did."

Lucy chuckled. "I think you will find them very impressionable. At least for the moment. They're frightened half out of their wits."

"Good. I intend to complete the job."

"And I'll find Vernon and tell him about tomorrow. He'll be so excited that, even if it rains, he'll beg to go and it'll just seem as if we're indulging him if we go riding in foul weather."

"We'll leave right after breakfast," Robert agreed.

"And I for one intend to spend the evening praying that nothing goes wrong before then. On any front," she added.

To Lucy's unbounded relief, nothing did. Freddy and Oliver ate dinner in their rooms, claiming an endemic cold, and the lieutenant did not return to ask any more embarrassing questions.

As she had anticipated, Vernon was so excited about visiting the cave that he gobbled his breakfast, and then nagged Lucy to finish hers. Not that she minded. As far as she was concerned, they couldn't get there fast enough to rescue that poor driver.

With Vernon urging them along, it took them barely ten minutes riding across the fields to reach the cave. Sending up a silent prayer for success, she dismounted. They left the horses with Jones, who assured Vernon that he had absolutely no desire to venture down into a dank hole now that the sun was finally shining again.

"I'll just stay out here and keep an eye on our flank," Jones muttered to Robert, and Lucy gave the batman a grateful smile.

Robert lit the lantern they had brought and, holding it aloft, headed toward the mouth of the cave.

"Right inside is a huge room with things growing from the roof. It's pretty safe here, but all kinds of passages lead off of it," Lucy warned Vernon, who was hopping with excitement.

"Where do they go?" her brother demanded.

"No one knows. Over the years, quite a few men have died exploring them, and then, when Freddy's father fell and broke his leg, your great-grandfather forbade anyone to go in."

"Seems a shame," Vernon mourned.

"No, it's common sense," Lucy said. "I want your word as a Danvers you will never go inside without me."

"Aw, Lucy!"

"Your word or I shall hire someone to dog your footsteps every time we visit Landsdowne," she threatened.

"I never get to have no fun," Vernon grumbled.

"Any fun," Robert corrected. "And the first thing a gentleman learns is what is reasonable and what is not. Promise your sister, and in exchange, I'll organize a caving expedition later in the summer."

"The first thing a gentleman should learn is common sense," Lucy shot back, appalled at the thought of what might happen to one or both of them down those dark passages.

"I promise," Vernon said, with a wary look at Lucy.

"Don't mind Lucy." Robert gave him a "just us men" smile that made her long to box their ears, but this wasn't the time to fight this battle, she reminded herself as Robert started into the cave. At the moment, she had other, more pressing concerns.

Taking Vernon's hand, she followed the swinging light of the lantern into the darkness.

"It's cold," Vernon said, his voice dropped to a hushed whisper. "And damp."

"There's an underground river that runs through parts of it," Lucy answered absently, her eyes straining through the darkness to see something that resembled a wagon.

Robert pretended to stumble slightly on some of the loose shale and swung the lantern in a wide arc, sending its weak rays into the recess of the cavern.

"What's that over there?" Vernon surreptitiously moved closer to Lucy.

"Where?" she asked, trying to sound casual.

"There." Vernon pointed into the darkness on their left. "It looked like a wagon."

Robert held the lantern up and strode to where Vernon had pointed. "It *is* a wagon," he said, trying to sound surprised. "Do you have smugglers using the cave, Lucy?"

"What would they be smuggling?" Lucy hoped her voice didn't sound as artificially bright as it did to her own ears. "We're much too far from the coast for smuggling to be profitable."

"Wait here." Robert approached the wagon and held the lantern over it.

Peering up at him was the white, terrified face of the driver.

"There's a man in here!" Robert shouted over his shoulder. "He's trussed up like a Christmas goose. There haven't been any escaped felons in the area recently, have there?"

"Not to my knowledge," Lucy said. "I wonder how he came to be here?" She scrambled up on the side of the wagon and looked down at the poor man, feeling guilty that a member of her family could have done this to him.

"A man where?" Vernon scrambled up on the wagon in turn and almost fell on top of him.

The man made a grunting noise through his gag and wriggled.

"The gold robbery!" Vernon shouted gleefully. "Remember, Lucy, that lieutenant that came to the house yesterday? I'll bet this man is one of the robbers."

The driver moaned and shook his head.

"That's right," Lucy agreed. "Vernon, you ride back into the village with Jones and fetch the militia. Hurry," she said, wanting him safely out of the way. There was no telling what he might blurt out if the driver were to say he'd been set upon by two young gentlemen.

"Right away, Lucy." Vernon scrambled off the wagon and skittered across the loose pebbles on the cave's floor.

"Be careful," Lucy called after him.

"I will," Vernon yelled back.

When she heard the sound of Vernon's and Jones's horses heading toward the village, she breathed a sigh of relief. So far, so good. Now to the next part of their plan—convincing the driver that he didn't remember either Freddy or Oliver.

"This could be the missing driver," Lucy tried to sound uncertain. "Perhaps we ought to untie him?"

"Hmm, you might be right," Robert said. "It would make no sense for the robbers to tie up one of their own band and leave him behind."

The driver nodded vigorously.

Robert set the lantern on the wagon seat and, pulling the pocket knife he had purposefully brought out of his jacket, quickly cut the man's bonds.

"Thankee." The driver rubbed his chafed wrists. "That grateful I am to ye, your worship. Don't know which was worse—the cold or the dark, or worryin' 'bout that fool Nat."

"Nat?" Lucy didn't have to fake her confusion.

"The guard. Did he snuff it?"

"Snuff it?" Lucy repeated blankly.

"Get hisself kilt?" The driver rephrased his question.

"No," Robert answered. "I believe he was the one who sounded the alarm."

"Much good it did," the driver said bitterly, slowly getting to his feet. "To think of us bein' so taken in by a couple of nobs. When I get m'hands on 'em..." He scowled furiously and Lucy felt her heart sink. "Hangin's too good for 'em."

"The guard reported that a whole gang of highwaymen attacked you," she replied. "And it must be true. I mean," she said, with a look of wide-eyed innocence that made Robert want to smile, "if there were two of you and only two of them..."

"Well, maybe there was more. A gang, like. But them morts was led by two swells. Talked real refined, they did."

"Two, you say?" Lucy went on slowly. "I don't know who they could be. Other than the members of the earl's house party, there aren't any young men in the area who fit the description."

"I knows what I seen," the driver insisted stubbornly.

"I'm sure you do," Robert said.

"Just please let me know when you plan to tell the earl that two of his guests are highwaymen." Lucy's shudder was genuine. "I don't want to be there to hear what he might have to say to you or to King George."

"He knows the king?" the driver asked uneasily.

"They are old friends," Lucy said, having no idea if it were true or not. More importantly, neither did the driver.

"I tell you, this goes beyond kicking up a lark," the driver muttered.

"That's a nasty bruise on your head. It must have caused you a great deal of pain," Lucy said.

"I ain't dicked in the nob!" the driver insisted, affronted.

"I didn't mean you were," she said soothingly.

"Maybe one of the ruffians had been employed in one of the great houses and talked swell to confuse you," Robert suggested. "And your friend Nat says it was a gang of cutthroat ruffians. The government believes it, too. That's why they sent the army and offered a reward for the return of the gold."

"Reward?" The driver looked up with sudden interest.

"A small percentage of the gold," Lucy said. "Of course, if you are right, and it was just a lark, then..."

"Then what?" the driver asked sharply.

"Nothing. It's just that you and Nat'll look so silly," Lucy explained. "Being taken in by a couple of sprigs, probably in their cups, too. Not only that, but you won't get the reward." She held her breath, waiting to see how he'd react.

"Ain't gonna get it nohow. I didn't find the gold, you did. And even if I had found it, they'd never give it to the likes of me, 'cause they'd say that I shouldn't a' lost it in the first place."

"Oh, we wouldn't dream of keeping it," Lucy said emphatically. "I feel you ought to be the one to get it, since you were the one set upon and beaten by that gang of desperadoes and then left for dead."

"Yes," Robert agreed. "You are the one who should get it. Why, if you hadn't made a noise, I would never have looked inside the wagon. We'd have left, and those ruffians would have come back and probably killed you, and then moved the gold. Besides, we can do what we like with the reward once we get it, and we would certainly insist that it be passed on to you."

The driver scratched his graying head. "They was certainly mean enough t'kill their own mothers," he finally said. "And as many of 'em as there were, I wouldna' stood a chance. Sure is a lucky thing you happened by."

Lucy released her breath in a long sigh as she realized that he was going to go along with the guard's version of what had happened. She didn't know if he was motivated by greed for the reward or by chagrin at having been made a May-game of by a couple of members of the aristocracy. Nor did she care. Her family was safe from the scandal Freddy had almost embroiled them in.

Lucy leaned back against the wagon, suddenly feeling very tired. Somehow, they'd managed to come about. Freddy wouldn't have to flee the country; Kitty would have a chance to credibly establish herself and her Aunt Amelia would not have to suffer the disgrace of having a highwayman for a son.

Now if she could somehow manage to solve the question of who was trying to murder her small brother, then maybe she could find a moment to worry about what to do about her growing fascination for Robert Standen.

Lucy watched as he helped the driver out of the wagon. There had to be a way to convince him that she didn't want to marry him, yet could still remain his friend, she thought with a lost, sinking feeling at the idea of never seeing him again. Surely it wouldn't come to that.

Chapter Nineteen

"I'm sorry to have missed Colonel Standen," the lieutenant said stiffly, keeping a wary eye on the glowering earl.

"I shall tell him that you called," Lucy said. "I'm sure he'll be as disappointed as you were to discover that the driver was unable to shed any light on the identity of that band of ruffians. The poor man."

"Not so poor," the lieutenant said dryly. "Not if you and the colonel are still determined to give him the reward."

"Oh yes, we are," Lucy said. "May I offer you a glass of wine?"

The lieutenant shot an apprehensive glance at the earl and hastily refused. "No, thank you, m'lady, I have several more stops to make this afternoon."

"Some other time, perhaps," Lucy murmured, barely containing a huge sigh of relief as the lieutenant finally left. Maintaining a series of lies was hard work. It took an excellent memory to remember which lie you had told to which person. If only the day would come when she could give up lying and subterfuge altogether, she thought wistfully.

"Young jackanapes," the earl muttered angrily. "I didn't like the way he kept watching me. Almost like he thought I had something to do with the robbery."

"I'm sure he thought nothing of the sort," Lucy said soothingly, knowing full well that the lieutenant had suspicions about all of them. Fortunately, he was far too clever to voice those suspicions without solid proof.

"Young jackanapes," the earl repeated. "He has no respect for his betters. Just like this brother of yours. Beating me at chess." The earl gestured toward Vernon, his pride at the boy's prowess imperfectly concealed.

"I do respect you, Grandpapa. Too much to cheat to let you win," Vernon said with an angelic smile.

Lucy chuckled. "Hoist by your own petard, Grandpapa. What are you doing after the chess game?" she asked Vernon.

"Jones promised to give me another riding lesson."

Lucy breathed an inward sigh of relief. A riding lesson sounded safe enough, and she knew that Jones would protect Vernon.

"Enjoy your game, gentlemen, and I shall see you at tea." She smiled at the earl, who looked up from his frustrated study of the chess board and returned it absently.

Lucy softly closed the library door behind the pair and headed toward the morning room, hoping to find Robert. She wanted to see him. To talk to him. To be near him. It was a desire that bordered on the compulsive. Somehow, she felt better when he was near.

She didn't find Robert, but she did find Fulton. The elderly butler was standing beside a huge collection of boxes and trunks in the main hallway.

Lucy studied the mound for a moment and then asked, "Are they coming or going?"

"Going, Miss Lucy." Fulton frowned at a footman who was struggling down the stairs with two cases and a hatbox.

"Mr. Freddy and Lord Oliver are paying a visit to Lord Oliver's home. I believe an urgent express came for his lordship earlier."

"In the mail?" Lucy asked eagerly, wondering if a message from Potter might not have arrived at the same time.

"No, it is my understanding that a messenger was sent. The colonel drove him into the village a short while ago to board the mail coach."

"I see," Lucy said slowly. So that's where Robert was—in the village. Had the messenger really come from Oliver's father or had Robert simply hired someone to provide an excuse to remove Freddy and Oliver from the scene before they said something that would make the lieutenant more suspicious than he already was? she wondered.

"Miss Danvers!" Oliver hailed her from the top of the stairs.

Lucy turned and watched as the young man hurried down the steps, trailed by the far-more-subdued-looking Freddy.

"We're sorry to leave so suddenly, but my father isn't feeling in such prime twig. I must go support him in his hour of need." Oliver rattled off an obviously rehearsed excuse.

"And I'm going to support Oliver while he's supporting his papa," Freddy offered.

Lucy stifled a grin. If this was a sample of their ability to lie, then Robert was very wise to whisk them away so quickly. She just hoped the poor duke survived all their support.

"I'm sorry you have to leave." Lucy issued the stock social phrase, rather surprised to discover that it was true. Having Oliver as a houseguest added a certain dash to life, and she honestly liked her cousin Freddy. All the more so now that she knew he wasn't the one responsible for Vernon's accidents.

"Sorry to go," Freddy said, fibbing with heavy-handed gallantry. "Suppose I ought to take my leave of the earl?" He glanced furtively up the stairs.

"No, he's resting," Lucy hastily improvised, not wanting her grandfather involved in another confrontation so soon after his meeting with the lieutenant. He'd had enough upsets today.

"I shall give him your regards," she added slowly as she tried to decide whether to say anything to Freddy about the allowance she was going to make him. She had intended to have Potter write to him about it, but she didn't want him left in uncertainty about his future any longer than absolutely necessary.

The last time he had tried to solve his own financial problems, the whole family had almost wound up in the basket. And while she sincerely hoped his brief venture into highway robbery would be his last, she didn't put a great deal of reliance on him. She finally decided that it was probably safer for everyone concerned if she told him now.

"Freddy, I was talking to Grandpapa earlier, and he has a surprise for you that he was going to tell you about tonight."

"Not necessary." Freddy surreptitiously began to inch closer to the front door.

"Not that kind of surprise," Lucy said soothingly. "He realizes he was a trifle hasty about the incident with the waistcoat and he wants to make amends."

"The earl does?" Freddy eyed her incredulously.

"He was feeling a trifle out of sorts that day," Lucy improvised.

"Always is when I'm around," the young man said glumly.

"Got an uncle like that," Oliver said thoughtfully. "Twitches when he sees me. Thing to do is not to let him see me."

"Excellent advice," Lucy said. "Not all unpleasant things in life have to be faced. Some can be avoided. Anyway, what Grandpapa was going to tell you was that he will be making you an allowance so you can have your own establishment. He is also going to pay your tailor bill," she added, wanting her cousin to be able to start with a clean slate.

"He is?" Freddy stared at her in total disbelief. "You sure the earl said that?"

"He feels badly about how he behaved." Lucy attributed to her grandfather the sentiments he should have felt.

"Don't sound like the earl I know," Freddy said dubiously.

"Don't look a gift horse in the mouth," Oliver advised.

"No, no, I don't want a horse." Freddy missed the reference completely. "The allowance is all I want."

"The coach is loaded, Mr. Freddy," Fulton said from the doorway.

"Good!" He cast another nervous glance up the stairs. "No call to linger. Already told Mama where I was going."

"Did you tell her why?" Lucy felt a sudden twinge of apprehension.

"Why?" Freddy eyed her with honest puzzlement, seeming to have already forgotten his role in the robbery. "Oh, you mean to support Oliver's papa? She said it was very proper of Oliver, and even if he wasn't the heir, he still owed him consideration."

"I'm very fond of my father," Oliver said reflectively. "He's a downy one."

"And Mama likes me to visit a ducal seat," Freddy added ingenuously.

"No doubt." Lucy had no trouble believing that. Amelia was very ambitious for her children. If she could just be sure that her aunt's ambitions stopped short of murder...

"Goodbye, Cousin Freddy, Lord Oliver." Lucy saw them out of the house and then watched as the carriage bore them down the long driveway. She felt a tremendous sense of relief.

"Fulton." she said to the silent butler once the carriage was out of sight, "about what I told Mr. Freddy about his allowance..."

"Yes, Miss Lucy?"

"I think it would be best if we didn't bruit the earl's generosity around."

"Certainly. It might come as a shock to him," Fulton said blandly.

"Yes, it certainly might." Lucy grinned at him. "And thank you."

"The staff likes Mr. Freddy," Fulton told her. "There's no vice in him and he's always been very considerate."

The implication that he was unlike his mother hung in the air, but to Lucy's relief, Fulton left it unsaid. She couldn't, in good conscience, defend her overbearing aunt, but Amelia was, after all, a member of the family and as such shouldn't be gossiped about. Even to Fulton.

"Where is Cousin Bevis?" Lucy asked.

"He rode into the village a short while ago with Lord Alridge. His lordship expressed a desire to inspect the local militia and, since the colonel had already left the house with the messenger, Mr. Bevis offered to take him."

"I see," Lucy murmured. That left cousin Kitty and Amelia resting in their rooms and Vernon safely playing chess with his grandfather. It should be all right for her to take a short walk in the gorgeous spring weather. Perhaps the exercise would help to dispel some of the restlessness she felt.

"If anyone should ask for me, I'll be in the gardens," Lucy said.

"Yes, m'lady." Fulton stepped back inside and gently closed the huge double doors behind her.

Lucy skipped down the broad stone steps, breathing deeply of the warm, flower-scented air. Despite all her worries about Vernon, she felt a sense of peace. This was how she remembered Landsdowne in the spring: the air soft and warm, the breezes gentle and the smell of lilacs and other, more elusive flowers perfuming the air.

Her feet slowed as she reached the stable yard. Curious, she looked around, comparing her childhood

memories of bustling activity with the present air of
general decay. There were gaps in the roof where pieces
of slate had fallen off. The weathered boards needed
a coat of whitewash, and to the left of the main doors,
a windowpane was broken.

Lucy sighed. Like Landsdowne, and the house in
London, the stables reflected the earl's complete disinterest in maintaining the properties for Freddy.

She'd have to ask Mr. James, the bailiff, if the earl
had said anything about putting the estate in order.
She would also have to ask him to hire some addi-
tional help for the one elderly groom who had pre-
sided over the stables in lonely splendor for the past
ten years. Lucy carefully skirted a pile of manure. At
his age it was all he could do to take care of feeding the
horses and cleaning out the stalls without trying to
keep the yard neat.

She slipped inside the huge building, blinking to allow her eyes time to adjust to the gloom. The filthy
windows didn't let much sunlight in and, as there was
no one here, no lanterns had been left burning for fear
of fire. She wandered idly down the double row of al-
most-empty stalls. A few horses were peacefully
chomping hay, but other than a barn cat, which disappeared into the last stall, there were no other signs
of life.

Lucy noted with a sense of relief that Bevis's bay
was not there, indicating he hadn't as yet returned
from the village. She wasn't really in the mood to
parry her cousin's elaborate compliments, and she had
the uneasy suspicion that if he were to come across her
in such a deserted spot, he might try to kiss her. It was
an idea that filled her with revulsion.

She frowned, trying to decide why that should be so, when a plaintive squeak from the empty stall at the end of the row caught her attention. Curiously, she followed the sound, wondering if one of the barn cats had hurt itself.

A smile curved her lips as she entered the stall and saw the litter of kittens half hidden beneath the manger.

Lucy climbed over the manger and sat down on the straw-covered floor. She leaned back against the wooden stall and picked up one of the tiny kittens. It purred ecstatically as she gently rubbed a finger under its chin.

The mother cat eyed her anxiously, and not wanting to worry her, Lucy replaced her kitten. Leaning back, she tried to figure out why she found the thought of kissing Bevis totally abhorrent. It made no sense. Bevis was a well-mannered, well-set-up man who had never given her any reason to fear him. So why didn't she want him to kiss her? Especially given the fact that all Robert had to do was glance across the room at her and her insides wobbled and a burning heat scorched her skin.

It wasn't that she didn't like Bevis, because she did, she decided. She simply didn't want him to touch her. She—

Her thoughts were interrupted as she heard the sound of a horse's hooves striking the cobblestone floor of the stables.

"You there, groom, where the hell are you?"

As if she had somehow conjured him from the depths of her imagination, she heard Bevis's voice, and she scrunched a little lower in the stall. With luck, he would simply leave his horse and go without discovering she was there.

"Damn slackard!" Lucy heard Bevis mutter in disgust, and she frowned. She didn't know if the groom were a slackard or not, but she did know he was very old, and very overworked with the house party and their horses here. There was no reason for Bevis to castigate him, especially since her cousin had invited himself along, she thought indignantly. Apparently, he was one of those members of society who saw no reason to waste good manners on the servants.

She waited as he continued to yell for the absent groom.

A few moments later, Lucy heard the sound of a second horse entering the stable, and she considered making her presence known, assuming that the second rider was Lord Alridge, since Fulton had said he had left with Bevis. Her cousin would hardly try to kiss her in front of another person.

She was about to stand up when she heard Robert's voice, and the sheer rush of pleasure that gushed through her momentarily held her motionless.

"I've been looking for you, Bevis," Robert stated, and Lucy frowned uncertainly. Robert's words seemed imbued with anger, almost an accusation. She had never heard him use that tone of voice—not even that night in France at the inn, when he had been so angry at her attempt to proposition him.

This mood was different, very clearly different. He sounded menacing. Dangerous. Lucy felt a frisson of alarm. Not at his tone, but at what had caused it.

Vernon! For a split second, blind panic filled her, before common sense doused its potency. She had left Vernon not fifteen minutes ago playing chess with the earl. There hadn't been time for him to have come to grief. Nor could Robert have known about it, since he'd been in the village.

"Should I be gratified that you want my company?" Bevis sounded unutterably bored.

"No, you should be worried!"

"Of you?" Bevis's laugh grated annoyingly over Lucy's nerves. How dare Bevis disparage Robert! She crouched on her knees and ever so slowly raised her head above the stall, peering around the post, which partially concealed her face. She need not have worried about being seen. Both men were too absorbed in each other to notice her presence.

"If not of me, then certainly of what I know," Robert said.

Lucy watched as he dismounted, carelessly fastened his horse's reins around the post of a vacant stall and then slowly walked toward her cousin.

"And what do you think you know?" Bevis drawled the words, and she felt a distinct prickle of unease. Somehow, Bevis had changed from a bored dilettante to... to what? she wondered.

She squinted through the dim light, trying to see her cousin more clearly. He was partially in the shadows, but what she could see of his face was not reassuring. The pleasant smile that always seemed to hover on his lips was gone. His mouth was now a hard slash across his tense face.

"Enough to convince me that you're the one behind the attempts on Vernon's life."

"I fail to see how I can be blamed if the brat is always tumbling into danger. I could hardly have set those mantraps, as I arrived at Landsdowne at the same time as Vernon. Ask Lucy." Bevis sounded bored. "I caught up with them on the road and gave the young cub a ride up to the house."

"And filled his receptive ears with tales of all the fun you used to have playing soldiers in the home woods," Robert said. "Nor surprisingly, that was the first place he went."

"But, my dear colonel, we did play soldiers in those woods as children. Only in my day we didn't have the mantraps to add a certain spice to the games. And you still haven't told me how I managed to be in two places at once."

"You weren't, of course. But we will get to your man's role in this shortly."

"Oh, by all means." Bevis leaned against the wall, looking the picture of offended innocence. "If you wish to gossip with the servants, that's certainly your privilege. But I'm much more interested in what my motive was."

"Greed." Robert, seeming equally at ease, paused about five feet in front of Bevis.

Was she the only one tied up in knots of anger and disbelief? Lucy wondered incredulously. How could they be so casually discussing something as horrendous as mantraps, with no more emotion than they might show over what was being served for dinner? And what did Bevis's man have to do with this? She tried to recall him, but all she could remember was a small, thin fellow who always seemed to be slipping out of sight.

Bevis shrugged. "You are confused, Colonel. It's cousin Freddy who benefits if the brat snuffs it. Not me. It's cousin Freddy who doesn't have a feather to fly with, not me. I have a sizable estate."

"So heavily mortgaged that the proceeds from the rents won't even meet the interest payments, let alone the principal."

Bevis frowned, his dark eyebrows contracting. "I can see that Potter has been gossiping about his betters, but that still doesn't alter the fact that Freddy inherits."

"The earldom, yes." Robert nodded in agreement. "And that was what bothered me. Freddy had the most to gain, but Freddy was the least likely suspect."

Bevis shrugged. "Appearances can be deceiving."

Robert eyed him narrowly. "So I discovered. After the mantraps, I wrote to Potter and told him everything that had happened, requesting that he check out some items for me. Then I asked his opinion on the matter."

"The opinion of a tradesman about a member of the nobility."

Lucy felt an almost hysterical urge to giggle at Bevis's outraged expression. Apparently, it was all right for him to attempt to murder a child, but no one from a lower class was supposed to comment on it.

"Potter made the inquiries as soon as he could and was sufficiently alarmed by what he discovered that he sent his son to see me. The lad arrived on the stage this morning."

The messenger whom Fulton said Robert had driven to the inn must have been the young Mr. Potter, Lucy suddenly realized. Robert had simply used the young man's arrival to explain Freddy and Oliver's sudden departure. She squinted through the gloom, trying to read Bevis's expression. His face seemed paler and his eyes glittered darkly.

She bit her lip, not wanting to believe that the man who had been courting her, whom she thoroughly liked, could be capable of such appalling duplicity.

"And what maggot does Potter have in his brain?" Bevis asked tightly.

"It seems that my first mistake was in assuming that the earl's wealth went to whomever inherited the earldom. But, according to Potter, only this estate, the London town house and a small one in Kent are entailed. All the rest is the earl's personal property, to dispose of as he pleases."

Lucy closed her eyes in dismay as suddenly, with that one bit of information, everything else made sense. The pieces of the puzzle that hadn't quite fit together before now suddenly assumed sinister proportions. Fulton had given her a clue the very first day, she remembered, but she hadn't realized the significance of his remark that Bevis had been one of the very few people who had continued to come to see her grandfather. Bevis hadn't been motivated by concern for a lonely old man. He'd been motivated by self-interest.

Since all of London knew what her grandfather thought of Freddy, Bevis had to have known that the earl would not be inclined to leave Freddy one shilling more than he was forced to in the entail. Because she and her parents were supposedly dead on the Continent, Bevis had undoubtedly hoped to get all the rest.

Lucy took a shallow breath and tried to still her pounding heart as she continued to listen.

"While it isn't yet common knowledge in polite circles, you ran through your inheritance years ago, according to Potter. He says that you have been living on your expectations from the earl and your prowess as a gambler."

"I don't deny that, but you still haven't explained how killing Vernon is going to help me. That would simply mean that the earl would leave his money to Lucy, not to me. Unless you're accusing me of trying to kill her, too." He managed to invest some of the same scorn Lucy was feeling for him into his voice.

"You don't have to kill her to get control of her funds. All you have to do is marry her. With Vernon dead, you would get her dowry, as well as everything the earl could leave her. And you *have* been courting her." Robert's voice was slightly edged.

"As you have, my dear colonel. As you have. So everything you have said about me holds true for you."

"Ah, but with a major difference, my dear Bevis," Robert mocked him. "My financial situation is impeccable."

"No one ever has enough money," Bevis snapped.

"Or, apparently, common sense," Robert said evenly. "The mantrap was a bad mistake, Bevis. Potter and his son visited every shop in London that sold them, and do you know what they discovered?"

"No." Bevis's smile slipped slightly. "Suppose you enlighten me."

"He discovered a clerk who remembered selling five of them the day before you left London."

Lucy bit her lip. Five. That was exactly the number that had been found in the home woods.

"They were sold to a man who fit the description of your man right down to the crescent-shaped scar on his cheek."

Bevis's shrug was a masterpiece of disinterest. "I can hardly be held responsible for what my servant does."

"Have done with it, Bevis," Robert said harshly. "You are finished."

"On the contrary." Bevis's voice hardened as he suddenly grabbed something from the front of his saddle. Lucy felt the hairs on the back of her neck lift in horror as a fugitive beam of sunlight danced off the grayish barrel of the deadly looking pistol he now held. She closed her eyes and tried to think, but she couldn't form a single coherent thought. Her mind was filled with the horror of having a gun pointed at Robert.

Surely Bevis wouldn't use it, she thought, trying to convince herself without much success. A man who would try to murder a child for financial gain would have no compunction about killing an adult who represented a real threat to his future.

"Don't be ridiculous," Robert said, clenching his jaws. "You can hardly kill me here."

"And who's to see me? Our bucolic groom? No doubt he's sleeping somewhere." Bevis's laugh sent a wave of fear crashing through Lucy, scrambling her thoughts and numbing her body. "Nothing would give me greater pleasure than killing you." His voice hardened. "To have had to watch you sniffing round my cousin's skirts—"

"Do you think she'll marry you even if you do kill me?" Robert asked scathingly.

"She won't have any choice," Bevis said. "I'll make sure that we're caught in such a compromising position that she'll be grateful to marry me. Then, in a few months, it should be easy enough for me to arrange one final accident for the brat.''

"You're forgetting that Potter and his son know what happened. They'll be able to alert the authorities.''

"Not at all,'' Bevis said pleasantly. "I'll dispatch my man to London on the night stage to dispose of both of them. If I know our closed-mouth Potter, he won't have told anyone else.'' Bevis's lips lifted in a caricature of a smile that sent a shiver down Lucy's spine. "But just to be safe, I'll have my man burn his house and office down. There will be nothing left to connect the pair of you.''

"And how do you intend to explain my death?'' Robert asked harshly.

"I don't. I'll be just as surprised and horrified as everyone else when your body is discovered. But I will be sure to suggest that you must have stumbled across the thieves who stole the gold shipment and they put an end to you.''

"In the stable?'' Robert demanded.

"It's virtually deserted and falling to pieces,'' Bevis pointed out. "I doubt anyone has been in the back of it in years. Certainly not that lobcock who pretends he's a groom. Now get moving to the back,'' he ordered.

Lucy pressed her fingers against her forehead and tried to decide what to do. If she did nothing, Bevis would kill Robert. And if he did that, then the only person who knew what she had done in France would be dead. The only person who could destroy her socially would never be a threat to her again. If she just stayed hidden in the stall and did nothing, Bevis would remove her problem. And when he left, she could go

to her grandfather and tell him what she'd seen, and
he would bring charges against her cousin. Bevis
would never be a threat to her or Vernon or anyone
else again.

The sound of Robert's boots striking the stone floor
as he slowly walked toward the rear of the barn conjured up an image of him in her mind. His eyes were
gleaming with laughter and his firm lips were tilted at
the corners. If she did nothing, those eyes would never
laugh at her again, and his lips would never press
against hers. They would never send a burning flush
of desire through her.

If she did nothing, that would be the epithet for the
rest of her life. She finally faced the truth she had been
avoiding for days. She loved Robert Standen. She
loved his laughter, his determination, his loyalty, his
intelligence, his sense of purpose, and she loved the
way he made her feel. With Robert Standen dead, her
life would be over before it had ever properly begun.

For the first time she truly understood why her
mother had slipped out of life so easily after her husband's death. She would feel the same way if she lost
Robert.

She had indeed done what she had feared when
she'd first met him. She had fallen in love with him.
What she hadn't realized at the time was that while the
potential for being hurt was there, the potential for
happiness beyond her wildest dreams was also there.
It was a chance worth any risk. Even death.

"Hurry up, damn you!" Bevis's voice goaded her
into action.

Hastily promising never again to ask for anything
else if God would just get them through this safely, she

stepped out of the stall and said, "Why the hurry, Bevis?"

The effect of her appearance couldn't have been more dramatic if she had fired off one of Whinneygates's rockets.

Bevis swung around, his mouth dropping open in shock.

Lucy glanced disdainfully at the pistol, which was now aimed at her. "Did no one ever tell you it is rude to point a gun at a person?"

"Lucy, get out of here," Robert ordered. "Bevis and I were just—"

"Playing executioner?" she said. "I must say, Robert, I hope you don't plan to teach these reckless games to our children. I can't count on them all having my common sense. One or two might have your flair for adventure."

Robert's lips lifted in a reluctant grin. "How many children are we planning on having?" he asked.

"Shut up!" Bevis swung the gun back toward Robert. "You aren't going to marry her."

Lucy tried to ignore the fear gnawing at the edges of her mind. People could do extremely irrational things when they were about to lose something they wanted very badly, and Bevis was about to lose a fortune as well as his place in English society. He might well decide to take his revenge by killing Robert.

"Really, Cousin Bevis." Lucy affected a drawl. "You are in danger of becoming a dead bore."

"A bore!" Bevis stared at her in shock.

"A dead bore," she repeated, "and a rather silly one at that. What do you propose to do? You can't shoot both of us with one gun. So whichever one you don't shoot is going to lay charges against you. Do

they still have public hangings in London, Robert?"
she asked, watching with satisfaction as Bevis's face
paled alarmingly.

"So I've been told," Robert answered her, narrowly watching Bevis's shaking hand. If he could just
distract the man a little more, he might be able to take
the gun away from him without endangering Lucy. He
tried to catch her eye to warn her, but she was watching Bevis and didn't see him.

"We might have trouble proving you caused Vernon's accidents, but murdering one of us would be
another matter altogether," she continued.

"I didn't arrange all of them," Bevis muttered.
"The brat's fall from his horse onto the cobblestones
in London was all our dear, maladroit cousin Freddy's fault, and as for Vernon's near-fatal tumble from
the third floor, I had nothing to do with it.

"I didn't!" he insisted at Lucy's skeptical expression. "It really was an accident, or, if you must ap-
portion blame, then the earl is to blame. He stopped
doing anything in the way of repairs after your father
disappeared. The whole house was going to rack and
ruin."

"And you didn't mention it to him?" Lucy asked,
unconvinced.

Bevis looked surprised at the question. "No, why
would I? The London house is part of the entail. He
couldn't leave it to me, so why would I care?"

Lucy opened her mouth to tell him what she thought
of him and then closed it. It really didn't matter and
Bevis certainly didn't care. The man seemed positively amoral. It was as if other people only existed as
shadowy beings to be used for his benefit. She shivered. In a way, his attitude was simply an extension of

most of the aristocracy's complete absorption in themselves and their own pleasures.

"Don't move." Bevis caught Robert's slight movement toward him and swung the gun in his direction.

Lucy swallowed against the sudden fear that knotted her stomach. She spoke hurriedly to distract Bevis's attention from Robert. "You may have all afternoon to stand around the stable playing with guns, Bevis, but I for one have better things to do."

"Quite true, sweetlings," Robert murmured, his eyes lingering on the soft lines of her lips. "Therefore," he continued in a brisker voice, "we need to decide what to do about your cousin."

"We could call the constable and lay charges against him for trying to kill Vernon." Lucy watched as Bevis's hand began to shake harder, wondering if his increased nervousness was good or bad. If only he weren't holding that pistol!

"You can't prove it," Bevis insisted.

"Perhaps not," Robert admitted. "However, I think just the fact that the case was brought to trial will blackball you in society. Particularly in the clubs. After all, trying to murder a child to line your pockets is hardly the action of a sportsman, is it?"

Bevis flushed as Robert's hit went home. "But think of the earl's horror of scandal," he countered.

"I still think we ought to lay charges," Lucy said. "I for one won't feel safe with him running loose. What's to stop him from trying again?"

"Oh, come now, Cousin Lucy," Bevis said, showing a flash of his normal sangfroid. "A little less theatricals and a little more common sense. What would be the point of removing the brat now? When you tell Uncle Adolphus, he will immediately cut me out of his will and you'll be wed to Standen, so your dowry is out of my reach. You are both quite safe, you know."

Lucy stared at him in disbelief. How could he so calmly stand there and discuss what he had done as if it were a business deal that had fallen through? Her fingers curled into a fist. She wanted to smash his smiling face, to beat him senseless, to put him through the same fear and horror he'd put her through. Yet there was nothing she could do. Nothing anyone could do. She knew there really wasn't enough evidence to convict him. And what was worse, so did Bevis.

"You will forgive me if I don't take your word for their safety," Robert said. "I would feel infinitely better if you were out of the picture."

"Are you challenging me to a duel?" Bevis asked in disbelief.

"No!" Lucy instinctively protested. She had faced down Bevis to protect Robert. She wasn't going to risk Bevis killing him in a duel.

Unexpectedly, Robert chuckled. "I'm counted a fair shot, Lucy. But you are right, of course. A duel would precipitate us into exactly the kind of scandal the earl would loathe. I suggest that you try travel, Bevis. It's supposed to broaden the mind."

Bevis shrugged. "Unfortunately, I'm none too plump in the pocket at the moment."

"I'll send a note to Potter to pay your passage and instruct my agents in Jamaica to give you another five hundred pounds once you land," Robert stated flatly.

"And if I choose not to go?" Bevis asked with what seemed no more than mild interest.

"Then I shall drop a few quiet words in various ears," Robert said, "in the strictest confidence, you understand."

"In that case, it should take days for the gossip to permeate the ton instead of the usual hours," Lucy said dryly.

Bevis's face tightened in anger, but none of his feelings were evident in his voice. "In that case, what can I say, my dear sir, but that I accept your kind offer. You will understand if I don't take leave of my host?" He gripped his horse's reins and pulled him toward the door, being careful to keep the gun pointed at Robert.

"I shall convey your apologies," Lucy said.

Bevis paused in the door of the stable and studied her for a long moment. "You know, Cousin Lucy, it's a shame you wouldn't have me. We would have been perfectly matched." Lowering his pistol, he swung up into the saddle and rode off.

"If I honestly believed that, Bevis, I would drown myself in the pond," she yelled after him, and then inexplicably burst into tears.

"My poor sweetling." Robert's arms closed around her and he cradled her shaking body against his.

Her cheek was squashed against his crisp neckcloth and she could hear the sound of his heart hammering in her ear. His warm hand was moving back and forth across her back in a rhythmical, soothing motion. She snuggled closer, breathing in the warm, musky scent that was his alone.

"My God, Lucy!" He said the words like a prayer. "I have never been so frightened in my life."

"Me, neither," Lucy muttered, gulping back tears. "Anyone who would try to kill a child is capable of anything."

"Not for myself," he scoffed. "My heart nearly stopped when you popped up from behind that stall. You could have been killed!"

Lucy shook her head. "There was no profit in Bevis's killing me."

"I suppose not," Robert conceded. "Only in marrying you."

She nestled closer still. "At least we managed to find out who was behind all the accidents. I'm so glad it wasn't Aunt Amelia, because I like Kitty and Freddy. Although..." Lucy peered worriedly up into Robert's dear face. "How are we going to tell Grandpapa? I suppose we have to tell him?"

"Definitely," Robert said. "Until the earl knows, Bevis is a threat."

Lucy sighed. "Yes. Grandpapa's going to be very upset. He liked Bevis. Come to that, I liked Bevis. I just didn't want to marry him."

"Because you are going to marry me," Robert said, as if defying her to deny it.

Lucy stared up into his beloved face, her eyes tracing over the creases at the corner of his eyes, down past his sun-browned cheeks and across the dusky pink of his firm lips, which she longed to kiss. She loved him, she thought. Really loved him, and what was it the curé had always said? Love begets love? Robert might want to marry her only because he needed children, but she would love him so much he'd have no choice but to come to love her in return, she assured herself. She loved him enough to tell him so. To expose herself to the pain of rejection.

"Because I *want* to marry you," she corrected him.

"You want to?" he repeated slowly. His large hand cupped her chin and he tilted her tear-blotched face up, peering down at her.

Lucy took a deep breath and blurted out, "Yes, I want to marry you because I love you to distraction."

"You love me?" Robert's eyes blazed with a sudden flare of emotion that left Lucy feeling scorched.

His lips suddenly swooped, capturing hers with a driving hunger that matched her own sense of need. It was as if all the fear and uncertainty that he'd felt were being released in his kiss. A shudder coursed through her body as his tongue pushed roughly against her lips, demanding entry. An entry she joyously gave, welcoming his aggressive masculinity. She felt needed on an elemental level that she'd never experienced before, and she wanted to explore every nuance of the sensation.

Her hand crept up to his face, and she rubbed her palm over his lean cheek. The raspy silken texture of his skin intrigued her and she wanted to explore it with her lips. To rub her own cheek against his. To—

But before she could decide exactly where she wanted to start her exploration, Robert lifted his head and stared down at her. "This is getting out of hand."

"Not yet," she said dreamily, "but I have hopes."

"If I continue to kiss you like this, I'm going to lose what semblance of control I have left, and I refuse to make love to you in a musty stable where anyone could walk in."

"You're right. Bevis did, and the groom should have." Lucy placed what she intended to be a fleeting kiss in the exact center of his chin, but the warmth of his skin caused her lips to cling, and her tongue darted out to touch the small indentation there. The taste of

salt flooded her mouth, stoking the hunger that fed
her.

"Lucy, marry me and let me make love to you tonight."

"I have already said I shall marry you, and you can
make love to me anytime we can escape from the other
guests," she said, chuckling happily. "And once you
have made love to me and I see how one goes about it,
I shall make love to you."

Robert gave her a wolfish grin. "You will find I'm
a very adept teacher."

"We can announce our engagement at dinner," she
murmured.

"I have a better idea. Why don't we get married at
five and announce our *marriage* at dinner." He eyed
her hopefully.

"But the banns—"

"One of the things I asked Potter to get for me was
a special license. When I drove young Potter back to
the inn, I stopped by the rectory and asked the vicar to
come by at five to marry us. Will you wed me this afternoon, if I get the earl's consent, my heart's
delight?" Robert asked.

"With or without his consent, I shall marry you,"
Lucy said seriously. "I love Grandpapa, but you are
the most important thing in my life. I—"

But the rest of her sentence was lost as Robert swept
her into his arms again and pulled her back into an
empty stall.

*   *   *   *   *

Relive the romance....
Harlequin is proud to bring you

A new collection of three complete novels every
month. By the most requested authors, featuring the
most requested themes.

Available in May:

Three handsome, successful, unmarried men are about
to get the surprise of their lives.... Well, better late
than never!

Three complete novels in one special collection:

DESIRE'S CHILD by Candace Schuler
INTO THE LIGHT by Judith Duncan
A SUMMER KIND OF LOVE by Shannon Waverly

Available at your retail outlet from

Where do you find hot Texas nights, smooth Texas charm and dangerously sexy cowboys?

Crystal Creek reverberates with the exciting rhythm of Texas.
Each story features the rugged individuals who live and love in the Lone Star State.

"...Crystal Creek wonderfully evokes the hot days and steamy nights of a small Texas community...impossible to put down until the last page is turned."
—*Romantic Times*

"...a series that should hook any romance reader. Outstanding."
—*Rendezvous*

Praise for Bethany Campbell's *The Thunder Rolls*

"Bethany Campbell takes the reader into the minds of her characters so surely...one of the best Crystal Creek books so far. It will be hard to top...."

Don't miss the next book in this exciting series. Look for
RHINESTONE COWBOY by BETHANY CAMPBELL

Available in May wherever Harlequin books are sold.

Harlequin®
Historical

Looking for more of a good thing?

Why not try a bigger book from Harlequin Historicals?

SUSPICION by Judith McWilliams, April 1994—A story of intrigue and deceit set during the Regency era.

ROYAL HARLOT by Lucy Gordon, May 1994—The adventuresome romance of a prince and the woman spy assigned to protect him.

UNICORN BRIDE by Claire Delacroix, June 1994—The first of a trilogy set in thirteenth-century France.

MARIAH'S PRIZE by Miranda Jarrett, July 1994—Another tale of the seafaring Sparhawks of Rhode Island.

Longer stories by some of your favorite authors.
Watch for them this spring, wherever
Harlequin Historicals are sold.

HARLEQUIN®

Don't miss these Harlequin favorites by some of our most distinguished authors!
And now, you can receive a discount by ordering two or more titles!

HT #25551	THE OTHER WOMAN by Candace Schuler	$2.99	☐
HT #25539	FOOLS RUSH IN by Vicki Lewis Thompson	$2.99	☐
HP #11550	THE GOLDEN GREEK by Sally Wentworth	$2.89	☐
HP #11603	PAST ALL REASON by Kay Thorpe	$2.99	☐
HR #03228	MEANT FOR EACH OTHER by Rebecca Winters	$2.89	☐
HR #03268	THE BAD PENNY by Susan Fox	$2.99	☐
HS #70532	TOUCH THE DAWN by Karen Young	$3.39	☐
HS #70540	FOR THE LOVE OF IVY by Barbara Kaye	$3.39	☐
HI #22177	MINDGAME by Laura Pender	$2.79	☐
HI #22214	TO DIE FOR by M.J. Rodgers	$2.89	☐
HAR #16421	HAPPY NEW YEAR, DARLING by Margaret St. George	$3.29	☐
HAR #16507	THE UNEXPECTED GROOM by Muriel Jensen	$3.50	☐
HH #28774	SPINDRIFT by Miranda Jarrett	$3.99	☐
HH #28782	SWEET SENSATIONS by Julie Tetel	$3.99	☐

Harlequin Promotional Titles

#83259	UNTAMED MAVERICK HEARTS	$4.99	☐

(Short-story collection featuring Heather Graham Pozzessere, Patricia Potter, Joan Johnston)
(limited quantities available on certain titles)

	AMOUNT	$
DEDUCT:	10% DISCOUNT FOR 2+ BOOKS	$
	POSTAGE & HANDLING	$
	($1.00 for one book, 50¢ for each additional)	
	APPLICABLE TAXES*	$ _____
	TOTAL PAYABLE	$ _____
	(check or money order—please do not send cash)	

To order, complete this form and send it, along with a check or money order for the total above, payable to Harlequin Books, to: **In the U.S.:** 3010 Walden Avenue, P.O. Box 9047, Buffalo, NY 14269-9047; **In Canada:** P.O. Box 613, Fort Erie, Ontario, L2A 5X3.

Name: _____

Address: _____ City: _____

State/Prov.: _____ Zip/Postal Code: _____

*New York residents remit applicable sales taxes.
 Canadian residents remit applicable GST and provincial taxes.

HBACK-AJ

INDULGE A LITTLE 6947 SWEEPSTAKES
NO PURCHASE NECESSARY

HERE'S HOW THE SWEEPSTAKES WORKS:
The Harlequin Reader Service shipments for January, February and March 1994 will contain, respectively, coupons for entry into three prize drawings: a trip for two to San Francisco, an Alaskan cruise for two and a trip for two to Hawaii. To be eligible for any drawing using an Entry Coupon, simply complete and mail according to directions.

There is no obligation to continue as a Reader Service subscriber to enter and be eligible for any prize drawing. You may also enter any drawing by hand printing your name and address on a 3" x 5" card and the destination of the prize you wish that entry to be considered for (i.e., San Francisco trip, Alaskan cruise or Hawaiian trip). Send your 3" x 5" entries to: Indulge a Little 6947 Sweepstakes, c/o Prize Destination you wish that entry to be considered for, P.O. Box 1315, Buffalo, NY 14269-1315, U.S.A. or Indulge a Little 6947 Sweepstakes, P.O. Box 610, Fort Erie, Ontario L2A 5X3, Canada.

To be eligible for the San Francisco trip, entries must be received by 4/30/94; for the Alaskan cruise, 5/31/94; and the Hawaiian trip, 6/30/94. No responsibility is assumed for lost, late or misdirected mail. Sweepstakes open to residents of the U.S. (except Puerto Rico) and Canada, 18 years of age or older. All applicable laws and regulations apply. Sweepstakes void wherever prohibited.

For a copy of the Official Rules, send a self-addressed, stamped envelope (WA residents need not affix return postage) to: Indulge a Little 6947 Rules, P.O. Box 4631, Blair, NE 68009, U.S.A.

INDR93

INDULGE A LITTLE 6947 SWEEPSTAKES
NO PURCHASE NECESSARY

HERE'S HOW THE SWEEPSTAKES WORKS:
The Harlequin Reader Service shipments for January, February and March 1994 will contain, respectively, coupons for entry into three prize drawings: a trip for two to San Francisco, an Alaskan cruise for two and a trip for two to Hawaii. To be eligible for any drawing using an Entry Coupon, simply complete and mail according to directions.

There is no obligation to continue as a Reader Service subscriber to enter and be eligible for any prize drawing. You may also enter any drawing by hand printing your name and address on a 3" x 5" card and the destination of the prize you wish that entry to be considered for (i.e., San Francisco trip, Alaskan cruise or Hawaiian trip). Send your 3" x 5" entries to: Indulge a Little 6947 Sweepstakes, c/o Prize Destination you wish that entry to be considered for, P.O. Box 1315, Buffalo, NY 14269-1315, U.S.A. or Indulge a Little 6947 Sweepstakes, P.O. Box 610, Fort Erie, Ontario L2A 5X3, Canada.

To be eligible for the San Francisco trip, entries must be received by 4/30/94; for the Alaskan cruise, 5/31/94; and the Hawaiian trip, 6/30/94. No responsibility is assumed for lost, late or misdirected mail. Sweepstakes open to residents of the U.S. (except Puerto Rico) and Canada, 18 years of age or older. All applicable laws and regulations apply. Sweepstakes void wherever prohibited.

For a copy of the Official Rules, send a self-addressed, stamped envelope (WA residents need not affix return postage) to: Indulge a Little 6947 Rules, P.O. Box 4631, Blair, NE 68009, U.S.A.

INDR93

INDULGE A LITTLE
SWEEPSTAKES

OFFICIAL ENTRY COUPON

This entry must be received by: MAY 31, 1994
This month's winner will be notified by: JUNE 15, 1994
Trip must be taken between: JULY 31, 1994-JULY 31, 1995

YES, I want to win the Alaskan Cruise vacation for two. I understand that the prize includes round-trip airfare, one-week cruise including private cabin, all meals and pocket money as revealed on the "wallet" scratch-off card.

Name_____

Address _____ Apt. _____

City_____

State/Prov._____ Zip/Postal Code_____

Daytime phone number_____
                              (Area Code)

Account #_____

Return entries with invoice in envelope provided. Each book in this shipment has two entry coupons—and the more coupons you enter, the better your chances of winning!
© 1993 HARLEQUIN ENTERPRISES LTD.   MONTH2

INDULGE A LITTLE
SWEEPSTAKES

OFFICIAL ENTRY COUPON

This entry must be received by: MAY 31, 1994
This month's winner will be notified by: JUNE 15, 1994
Trip must be taken between: JULY 31, 1994-JULY 31, 1995

YES, I want to win the Alaskan Cruise vacation for two. I understand that the prize includes round-trip airfare, one-week cruise including private cabin, all meals and pocket money as revealed on the "wallet" scratch-off card.

Name_____

Address _____ Apt. _____

City_____

State/Prov._____ Zip/Postal Code_____

Daytime phone number_____
                              (Area Code)

Account #_____

Return entries with invoice in envelope provided. Each book in this shipment has two entry coupons—and the more coupons you enter, the better your chances of winning!
© 1993 HARLEQUIN ENTERPRISES LTD.   MONTH2